INTENTION

A Political Conspiracy Book 2

By Tom Abrahams

A PITON PRESS book

Intention, copyright © 2016
by Tom Abrahams.
All Rights Reserved.
Edited by Felicia A. Sullivan
Proofread by Pauline Nolet
Cover art by Hristo Kovatliev

PITON PRESS

http://tomabrahamsbooks.com

Go to my website to join my Preferred Readers Club.

WORKS BY TOM ABRAHAMS

POLITICAL CONSPIRACIES

SEDITION
INTENTION

JACKSON QUICK ADVENTURES

ALLEGIANCE
ALLEGIANCE BURNED
HIDDEN ALLEGIANCE

THE TRAVELER POST APOCALYPTIC/DYSTOPIAN SERIES
HOME
CANYON
WALL

PERSEID COLLAPSE WORLD: PILGRIMAGE SERIES NOVELLAS
CROSSING
REFUGE
ADVENT

For the enlightened ones: Courtney, Samantha, and Luke

PROLOGUE

"All the time we are denying with our lips what we are doing with our hands."
—Arnold Toynbee, Historian, June 1931

NEAR THE FLAVIAN AMPHITHEATRE
ROME, ITALY

Feodor Ivanovich's killer walked away and he couldn't do anything about it. He was silently bleeding to death at a corner table in the back of a café.

An unexpected and brutally quick trio of stabs through his serratus anterior muscle underneath his left arm had rendered him minutes from death. He was having trouble breathing. He was slipping into shock.

Though Ivanovich tried gaining the attention of the waiter, the man was engrossed with a pair of giggling women on their third glasses of wine and didn't notice the pasty, thin Slav. It was impossible to find good service in Rome.

Ivanovich searched the café for an ally but found none. People were thumbing through their phones or had their attention focused on those at their table. He reached for his own phone and couldn't find it. It was in his pocket, he thought, though he couldn't be sure. Not with the pain and sweat dripping into his eyes.

The meeting had started unremarkably.

Ivanovich arrived at the prescribed time at the agreed-upon location. He found the tanned, muscled man in the back corner sitting alone, identifiable from behind by the thickness of his neck and a triangular tattoo at the base of his skull. On the table sat an empty water glass to his right and an espresso to his left.

"Have you been to the top of St. Peter's Basilica?" Ivanovich asked as he slid into the seat across from his contact. He immediately saw the black in the man's eyes and what he perceived as a complete lack of fear.

"I have not," the man said, his English barbed with an accent Ivanovich couldn't place. "The climb is too much for me. I have heard the views of the square and city are spectacular."

Ivanovich exhaled and relaxed in the seat, sliding his bag to the floor next to him. He smiled, the wide gaps between his teeth evidence of his poor upbringing. He was new money.

"I am Jon Custos." The man across the table offered his meat hook of a hand and squeezed Ivanovich's fingers into submission. "You are Feodor Ivanovich?"

"I didn't realize we were exchanging—"

"We're not. I'm telling you who I am. I know who you are."

Ivanovich gulped past what had quickly become a dry throat. He looked for a waiter but didn't see one.

"You brought the merchandise?" Custos pulled the cappuccino to his lips. It looked like a dollhouse piece of china in his hand. "And it will perform as you say?"

"Yes," Ivanovich replied. "I have it. It will work. It's undetectable, I assure you."

Custos nodded and set the cup on the table.

"And you have the payment?"

"Pull out your phone and check your accounts." Custos licked his lips, his gaze never leaving Ivanovich.

The Russian did as he was told and pulled his phone from his pocket. He placed it on the table and punched in a security code. Then he accessed a secure banking application.

"It's there, yes?" asked Custos.

Ivanovich looked up from the glow of the screen and nodded. The money was there, all eight figures. He slipped the phone back into his pocket.

"We're finished with our transaction, then," said Custos. "I'll be on my way."

"I'm going to try to find a waiter and have a drink," said Ivanovich. "Business makes me thirsty."

Custos stood to shake his hand.

Ivanovich reached out and accepted the bone-crunching grip, but instead of feeling the pain in his fingers, there was a burning sensation under his arm when Custos pulled him close. At first, he thought the man had sucker punched him. Then twice more a searing jab, thick with heat, and he knew it was worse.

Custos's lips were close to his ear, his breath warm when he said, "*A Deo et Rege. A cuspids corona.*"

Before Ivanovich sank back into his seat, Jon Custos had grabbed what he needed and was gone. He slithered through the crowded café and out the front door. Ivanovich reached for the water glass, forgetting it was empty until he pressed it against his mouth. He blinked his eyes around the room, settling on the entrance where his killer had escaped.

Beyond the glass front of the café were a wide boulevard, the Arch of Constantine, and the walls of the Colosseum, the Flavian Amphitheatre. Trying to focus past the pain and confusion, Ivanovich saw Custos disappear into the throngs of tourists queuing for a tour of the place where, millennia ago, so many gladiators gave their lives for their emperor.

There was something Shakespearean about Ivanovich's death. It was as if Brutus himself had plunged the blade. The Russian died, his head dropping to the table. Only the clang of the flatware alerted the waiter to his customer's condition. One of the inebriated women next to the server screamed when she saw the pool of blood leaching across the floor.

Custos, however, smiled to himself as he dropped the shiv into a trash can and wove his way through the tourists to a waiting car. He disappeared without anyone noticing him, whistling Bartók's "Music for Strings."

He slid into the back of the car, the air-conditioning cold against the sweat on his shaved head, and placed the bag on the seat next to him. He caught the driver's eyes in the rearview mirror and nodded. The car accelerated from the curb and sped toward the airport.

Custos had avoided Rome for so long. He didn't like being there, of running the risk of people recognizing him and reporting him to people who probably wanted him dead. But he did the job because that was what was required of him. His loyalty to the man and to the secret organization, the Brethren, who'd changed his life so many years before, knew no restrictions.

He would do whatever they asked of him, and they paid him handsomely. Custos was nearly unrivaled in his abilities. He'd heard of others who were good. He believed he was better.

That was why they'd tasked him with the job in Rome: acquiring the bag and disposing of the man who brought it. It was step one. He had more tasks to complete.

Custos pulled an unfamiliar phone from his jacket pocket. He entered Ivanovich's security code and dialed a number from memory.

"I have it," he said. "I am on the move. Delete the money from his account."

PART ONE: LIGHTNING BOLT

"The real rulers in Washington are invisible and exercise power from behind the scenes."
—Felix Frankfurter, United States Supreme Court Justice, 1939–1962

CHAPTER 1

THE TOYOTA CENTER
HOUSTON, TEXAS

The needle punctured Horus's left arm, nestling in the basilic vein above the crook of his elbow. He held a tourniquet with his teeth, only letting go of the rubber tube tight around his bicep when a burn followed by comforting warmth filtered through his body.

He smiled at the woman straddling him on the leather sofa in his dressing room. She withdrew the needle, placed it on a glass table littered with spoons, empty folds, lighters, a half-full bottle of Ciroc, and lowered her lips onto his.

"You've done this before," he whispered. "I can tell. You found the vein no problem. It's getting harder to do that." His hands found her hips and squeezed.

"A couple of times, maybe," she said with a throaty giggle. Her long, slow kiss made Horus think of a cat stealing a baby's breath. It was sexy and frightening, like much of his debaucherous life.

"The ride," he said, his eyes rolling back from the drugs racing through his bloodstream. "This is the ride, man." He sucked in a deep breath before she kissed him again, pushing hard against him. She was hungry for him, like so many nameless women with whom he'd shared himself.

Horus was five minutes removed from a sold-out concert in Houston's Toyota Center. The eighteen thousand fans screamed, danced, and sang along with him for the better part of three hours. He fed off their energy, the primal combination of his music and their pulsating, rhythmic sway. He was spent afterward, both from exhaustion and evaporation of the audience's adulation.

This was his reward, his consolation; a woman pulled from the front row and ten milligrams of heroin. His handlers knew how to spot the right groupies, the ones who were ready, willing, and able to do anything with and to the most popular solo act on tour.

The blonde fit the bill. Tight skirt, loose top, inked, and heavy on the eyeliner.

Houston was the last stop on his thirty-five-city trip. Then it was back to Seattle and a few months off before producing another EP. His last effort went platinum, produced three number one sellers on iTunes and a video with forty million views on Vimeo. *Rolling Stone* wrote a glowing profile, putting his ice-blue eyes and five-day stubble on the cover. The issue outsold Britney, Cash, and Morrison combined. Forty million people followed him on Instagram, more than that on Twitter and Snapchat. He streamed a concert live on Periscope, and two million viewed it live on their phones and tablets.

"I'm bigger than John Lennon," he told Oprah. "And we know who he was more popular than." Oprah didn't laugh, but the ratings were insane. Lady GaGa told MTV she could've learned marketing from Horus and his gift for pushing the right buttons at the right time. It was as if he had some secret force, some mind control over his legions of adoring fans.

He'd gone from a no-name wannabe hip-hop pretender to headliner in twenty-four short months. His label pushed him on tour. He was living a dream he'd had as a child.

His iconic hit, "Cleopatra," had him fronting award shows, providing the back track for car commercials, and playing an encore which mostly consisted of Horus holding the microphone toward the crowd such that they could sing the words to the beat of a synthetic 808 drum.

"Am I your Cleopatra?" purred the groupie, her bottle-blonde hair tickling Horus's neck and chest.

Horus enjoyed her hot peppermint-scented breath on his ear before she flicked her tongue and sucked on the black onyx gauge decorating the lobe. The sensation was acute, intense. He couldn't respond. He was already floating above the groupie and looking down on the two of them. He could see himself splayed on the leather, his head back, mouth agape. He could see the surprising but familiar butterfly tattoo on her right shoulder.

A monarch?

Are its wings flapping? Is it escaping its confines, fluttering skyward?

This was a high stronger than he'd ever experienced. He was melting into the leather, disappearing into the room's fabric.

"Mmmm," she moaned into his ear. "Is it good, Horus? Can you feel it? This ain't blanks. I brought you the good H." She bit on his ear and pressed her hands against the back of the sofa, placing one on either side of the musician's head, and pushed herself back. She took his arm in her hand and thumbed the spot where she'd injected him.

It was the freshest of the skin pops, but a few of the others were almost as inflamed. The tracks marked both arms and legs. There were more hidden between the spaces in his toes. Horus had been "riding the horse" for years, and his fame-fueled riches only amplified his search for that first high so long ago.

Drugs and alcohol, especially heroin, were his weakness. They were a salve for wounds so deep they'd never heal. His friends, as they were, enabled him. His family, what was left of it, distanced itself despite his efforts to reconnect. His enemies, and there were many, used it against him.

Unbeknownst to Horus, the smack-filled syringe was laced with Jackpot. At least that was one of many street names for the powerful synthetic opiate fentanyl. Combined with heroin or any other opioid, the fentanyl spiked the dopamine levels in Horus's brain.

His euphoria quickly morphed into confusion.

Who was this woman on top of him?

What did she do to him?

Who was he? Why was he here?

Then the world blurred. Horus crashed.

His heart slowed, and twenty-two seconds after he aspirated on the vomit bubbling in his throat, it stopped.

The groupie watched the life drain from Horus's face. He was gray, his eyes opaque and fixed with the recognition of impending death. She'd seen it before. She'd induced it before.

Wiping her mouth with the back of her hand, she pulled the wig from her head and tossed it on the floor. She pushed herself from the sofa, using Horus's chest for leverage.

The groupie looked in the mirror and ran her hands across her bald head. She'd shaved that morning. The scalp was smooth. She smiled at herself, pulled a lipstick from her cross-body purse and freshened the red sheen.

Smacking her lips, she replaced the gloss, zipped the purse, and slinked back over to Horus. His skin was already slipping from gray to blue. She picked up the wig and carefully placed it back on her head, tugging on it at her crown, and slipped past the guard outside of Horus's room.

The hulk watched her walk away, not at all paying attention to anything above the waist. He couldn't have identified her if she'd been his sister.

However, she wasn't the random groupie anyone in the Toyota Center believed her to be. She was sent there with purpose. A mission.

Silence him.

It was what they'd asked of her.

As always, she delivered.

CHAPTER 2

FEDERAL PRETRIAL CORRECTIONAL COMPLEX
PETERSBURG, VIRGINIA

Prisoner 02681-044 shuffled across the rutted concrete, his eyes on the MAC-10 fully automatic machine pistol ten feet ahead of him. The man holding the pistol gripped it with both hands, the two-stage suppressor aimed at the ground. He was also armed with a standard nine millimeter Glock holstered on one hip, a Taser on the other.

"Keep moving," grunted the prisoner's escort, Deputy United States Marshal Bill Vesper. "We have a schedule to keep. You hear me?"

Prisoner 02681-044 suffered from too much girth and not enough stamina. Despite his time in pretrial custody, he'd not managed to lose much of the weight he'd gained during a life of excess.

"Is that three-piece suit bothering you?" asked Deputy Mario Sanchez, referring to the customary transport restraints at the prisoner's hands, waist, and ankles.

The prisoner didn't answer, keeping his eyes on the MAC-10. He thought it a curious choice for US Marshals. Perhaps, he considered, tighter budgets had prevailed and older machinery was the norm.

He ached to hold the pistol grip in his hands, apply pressure to the trigger and ply the deputies with its forty-five-caliber rounds. He didn't like anyone controlling him, exercising authority over him. He took comfort in knowing it would end soon enough.

Deputy Vesper tugged on the prisoner's left arm, stopping the shuffle as they approached the man with the MAC-10. He, too, was a deputy US Marshal.

"Stop here," ordered Vesper. "Time for a pat down."

This was the third body search in a matter of a few minutes. Procedure dictated each deputy was responsible for his own security when transporting a prisoner. Every deputy who touched a prisoner did his own search.

The deputy, his biceps straining the cotton of his US Marshal Service-issued short sleeved polo, put down the MAC-10 to begin the pat down. He pulled a pair of gloves from one of the thigh pockets of his battle dress uniform pants and slid them on his meat hooks.

"You guys can step back," the deputy said.

Vesper and Sanchez backed away, and Vesper offered a piece of chewing gum to his friend of sixteen years. Vesper took a piece and popped it in his mouth.

Bill Vesper chomped on his Hubba Bubba as he spoke. His hands were on his hips, thumbs tucked into his belt.

"Was he a rapper or a singer?" asked Sanchez. "I never could tell the difference."

"Rapper," Vesper replied. "I think." He shrugged. "Hell, I don't know. All I do know is that he overdosed after a concert in Texas. Dallas, I think."

"Houston," corrected Sanchez. "It was Houston. I heard on the radio it was a mix of heroin and some painkillers."

"Ridiculous," said Vesper, almost inhaling his gum when he sucked in his gut. "I mean, all that money and fame wasted."

"Man, you never know what's really going on with those people," Sanchez remarked. "They've all got demons, it seems like. Every last one of them."

"I never much listened to that rap music," Vesper smacked. "I knew that 'Cleopatra' song."

"How could you not?" Sanchez laughed and then aped the lyrics, *"Too, too good."*

"I'm good here," the muscled deputy called out. "He's clean."

Vesper and Sanchez resumed their positions at the prisoner's side and escorted him the short distance beyond the interior gate of the Federal Correctional Complex in Petersburg, Virginia, and to a three-quarter-ton Ford van. The van, painted white, was reinforced with steel plating around the doors, and all but the driver's side window were protected by heavy steel grates.

"A one-way ticket to Chesapeake Detention Center," Sanchez said to the prisoner. "Your carriage awaits."

The guards helped 02681-044 into the van, positioning him on a bench seat in a secure area toward the middle of the cabin. Vesper took a seat in the front next to the driver. Sanchez rode in the back, behind the secure area.

"We're one on one plus one," Vesper said to the driver, pulling his seatbelt across his lap. He was referring to the USMS policy of one guard for every prisoner plus an additional guard for security.

"That's not saying much when we've only got a single transport," said the driver, also an armed deputy marshal. "Why aren't we waiting until we have more guys going to the same place? It's kind of a waste of Uncle Sam's money to move a single guy, isn't it?"

"It's a priority," explained Vesper, popping a bubble and offering the driver a piece of gum. "He was only here until space opened up at Chesapeake."

"Why not keep him here until trial?" asked the driver.

"This is only medium security." Vesper shrugged. "I guess they want him in a max facility. I don't ask, brother. I do what I'm told." He tipped his USMS ball cap at the driver.

"Why not fly him there?" asked the driver. "It's an hour in the air instead of three and a half on the ground."

"Again—" Vesper chomped "—above my pay grade."

"Gotcha."

"You check in with comms?"

"Yes," said the driver. "We're good with Petersburg Sheriff's Department."

"Secure radio?"

"Yes. We're good."

"Cell phone?"

"Full bars and central dispatch has us on satellite. We're all good."

"Let 'em know we're en route," Vesper commanded.

"10-4," said the driver, picking up a handheld radio transmitter. "PSD, this is USMS JPATS, ready for transport. We have one prisoner aboard. Route is approximately one hundred seventy-seven miles. Over."

"10-19, USMS JPATS transport," a dispatcher responded. "You're 10-1 to Chesapeake. Over."

"Thank you, PSD. Over. Out."

In the middle seat, locked to a bolt, Prisoner 02681-044 closed his eyes. He took a deep breath and exhaled. He listened to the inane banter and considered how clueless his three escorts were. They had no idea what was about to happen. A smile crept across his face.

*

TRIANGLE, VIRGINIA

It was too early in the morning for Doug Salas. He'd only had time for two Red Bulls before he got the call. He'd assembled his team, made the necessary arrangements, and hustled it to an abandoned Ramada Inn in Triangle, Virginia. He lowered the volume on his two-way radio, pressed the earpiece more firmly into place, and joined the others huddled together in the back of the parking lot where they were hidden from view.

"We've got ninety minutes," he told them. "They left FCC Petersburg. They should hit us pretty quickly. What's the traffic?" he asked his logistics chief, a compact but powerful man.

"It's green," the chief said after checking the screen on his computer. He had it perched on the hood of one of four black SUVs. "They'll make good time up I-95."

The team, which looked like a haphazard group of construction workers, consisted of twelve men. Salas was their unquestioned leader. He'd assembled the team, handpicked every one of them for their skill and their discretion. They were the ones of whom the men in the "mythical" black helicopters were afraid.

Salas rubbed his beard with his thick, calloused fingers. His right pinkie was foreign against his skin. The nerves were shot and the finger was permanently numb. Salas barely noticed it anymore. It was only the tension of the pending operation that made him sensitive to it.

"All right," he said, his hands on his hips. "I need Green Team on I-95, diverting northbound traffic onto Joplin Road. I need Blue Team on Joplin, handling the detour back to I-95. Yellow Team takes the block at US1. Red Team is with me. We'll handle communication diversion and extraction. Questions? Let's go piss up a rope."

The eleven men surrounding Salas grumbled their understanding of the operation. In threes, they separated and moved to their assigned SUVs.

Salas was unaccustomed to operating on American soil. Sure, he'd done it once or twice when the circumstances called for it, but it was rare and he didn't like it.

A covert, extraordinary rendition in Ashgabat along the Turkmenistan border with Iran was preferable to operating in Northern Virginia. A fifty-kilometer hike to a black site in Somalia was easier to plan than a diversion and extraction on a freeway interchange.

However, he took the job, as he always did, because this was what he did. He delivered the impossible and would continue to do it as long as it was asked of him.

Thirty-six hours earlier, he'd received a coded message on a prepaid forty-five-hundred-dollar encrypted countersurveillance iPhone. The code contained a time, a drop location, and instructions to alert the sender if the drop was compromised.

Salas would pick up the physical mission instructions by himself. Only after he read through the specifications would he choose his team. Some operations called for light teams; others required a heavier hand. This was the latter.

Every man he contacted agreed instantly to participate. They never said no. They knew better than to turn down a professional like Salas. He wouldn't call them again if they did.

Now they were briefed, armed, and ready to go. Salas rode in the front passenger seat, leaning forward on the leather without a seat belt. He was like Washington crossing the Delaware.

"This is gonna happen rick tic, fellas," Salas told the three men in his vehicle. "We won't have much time to think once they hit us. Every man needs to be squared away and good to go when I give the signal."

The trio acknowledged their leader as the SUV reached its wooded location west of US 1 on Joplin Road. They'd wait there until their target was in range.

"Fisher," Salas said, addressing the communications specialist in the back of the SUV, "you good with the comms? I'll need you intercepting their cells, radios, and jamming satellite when they get within range."

"Not a problem, sir." Fisher nodded. "They'll be talking to us without knowing it. I've already got a fix on the secure channel the local sheriff uses. I can ping the cells when they get closer. Satellite won't be an issue."

"Good." Salas checked his watch. They had more than an hour to wait, hidden among the trees.

"Anybody got a Red Bull?" Salas asked. "I need another one."

*

"There's no detour marked on our map," Bill Vesper said to the driver when traffic slowed near State Highway 619 in Triangle, Virginia. "And I don't recall one being a part of the itinerary. Get the Prince William County SO on the radio."

"Prince William dispatch," the driver said into the handheld transmitter, "this is USMS JPATS requesting information. Over."

There was static.

"Prince William dispatch," he repeated, "this is USMS JPATS. Do you copy? Over." The radio crackled again; then a voice on the other end answered.

"This is Prince William dispatch," said the voice. "We hear you USMS JPATS. Over."

The driver held the transmitter to his mouth. "We're stopped at a detour off I-95 north. We didn't see this on our itinerary. Over."

"There's an integrity issue with the overpass," replied the voice. "You'll need to proceed to the off-ramp with the rest of the traffic. Over."

"We need to get around this backup," said Vesper. "Ask him about alternatives."

"What alternatives do we have?" asked the driver, slowing to a stop a few feet from the exit. Up ahead on the shoulder there were a pair of safety-vest-clad men directing traffic. "We need to get a move on. Over."

"Can't help you there," replied the voice. "There's a deputy there who might be able to help you. He's positioned on Highway 619 past the exit. Over."

"Thank you, Prince William. Over." The driver hung up the transmitter on the dash and edged toward the exit ramp.

"I can't get the GPS to work," said Vesper. "My cell phone isn't working."

"Bad signal," said the driver. "We're in the middle of nowhere Virginia."

The driver inched the van down the ramp, following a half dozen other cars and trucks past the men with the safety vests. A few yards ahead was a man in a deputy's uniform. He was helping guide the traffic across Joplin Road and onto a cut through that ran north, parallel to the interstate. The van stopped at his side and the driver rolled down the window.

"Deputy," the driver called, "we're transporting a prisoner, and we're on a tight schedule. Is there a way around this mess?"

The deputy, with a thick beard likely not Prince William County regulation and a pair of reflective sunglasses straight out of *Smokey And The Bandit*, pressed his hands against the open window frame. He leaned in and looked back at the prisoner in the middle compartment.

"It is a mess, ain't it?" He grinned, his teeth almost visible beneath the scraggle of his mustache. "Who you got there in the back?"

"High-value prisoner," said Vesper, leaning toward the open window. "Gotta get him up north. Any ideas?"

The bearded man in uniform rapped his fingers on the sill before taking a step back and pointing across the roof of the van. "You can take a right here onto 619. It connects with US 1. They've got it blocked down there to stop traffic from coming up this way and making the congestion worse. Tell them I said it was okay."

"Your name?" Vesper narrowed his eyes, straining to read the brass nameplate on the deputy's chest.

"Smith." He rapped on the hood with his fist. "Deputy Smith."

The driver pressed on the accelerator and the van lurched forward. While the rest of the traffic continued north, the deputy marshals and prisoner 02681-044 headed east on Joplin Road/SH 619. The road was narrow and shrouded by trees on either side, and the morning sun cast shadows that hindered the driver's vision, so he slowed his speed to compensate for the relatively poor visibility. They'd traveled about a half mile when they saw a roadblock up ahead. In the distance, maybe one hundred yards past the roadblock, was the intersection with US 1.

"My GPS still isn't working," said Deputy Vesper. He was holding his phone up above his head and out in front of him, searching for a signal. "I can't get a signal."

"The guys up here will know where to head," said the driver. "Plus you do have a map."

"As a last resort." Vesper chuckled.

One of the three uniformed men at the roadblock walked toward the driver's side of the van. The window was still down.

Wearing a uniform and glasses identical to the one they'd met a moment ago, the deputy was approaching with purpose. He was waving his left hand, indicating he didn't want the van approaching any further.

"Go ahead and stop," said Vesper. "He may not see the markings on the van."

The deputy strode alongside the van, trailing his hand along the hood as he approached the window.

"Hey, I—"

Thump!

The driver never finished his sentence.

The deputy raised a nine millimeter handgun, reached through the open window, and pressed it against his forehead. He never felt the bullet shot into the side of his forehead.

Bill Vesper tried to scramble for his service weapon, but only managed to unsnap the strap across his Taser when a second bullet tore through his neck and a third into his temple.

Thump! Thump!

A black SUV pulled up behind the van and stopped perpendicular to the rear door, its tires squealing against the sudden pressure from the brakes.

Inside the back compartment of the van, Deputy US Marshal Mario Sanchez was trying not to panic. His heart was thumping against his chest, making the bulletproof vest feel even more constrictive than usual. He tried to remember his training, the countless drills and scenarios he'd experienced. The adrenaline and fear were clouding his memory.

Think! he told himself. *Think!*

He checked his cell phone. He had no signal. Still, he dialed 9-1-1 and pushed the speakerphone button. He left the phone on as it searched for a signal and set it on the floor.

Deputy Sanchez pulled a MAC-10 mounted to the interior wall of the van and checked it. It was loaded and its thirty-round detachable box-magazine was primed to unload heavy fire at eleven hundred rounds per minute. He ran his sweaty hand across the threaded barrel and checked the suppressor. Sanchez turned to face the rear doors of the van, bracing his legs and leveling the MAC-10 at the thin joint between the two doors.

From the floor, he heard a faint voice through the speaker on his phone.

"9-1-1. What is your emergency? Do you need police, ambulance or fire?"

"All three!" he yelled as loud as he could. "I'm a federal agent and I'm under attack."

*

Doug Salas unbuttoned the top button of his Prince William County uniform. The shirt was irritating his neck. He stood on the passenger side of the van, the van's keys in his hand. He was waiting to slide open the door until the dude in the back was handled.

"Let's go," Salas said to the five men standing at the rear of the van. "We don't have but another three minutes and we need to be on our way."

"Less than that," Fisher emerged from the rear of the van. "The cell jammer failed. They've probably signaled for help."

"Do I have to do everything myself?" Salas huffed and marched to the rear of the van.

"We're ready with the SLAM, sir," said the operator in charge of explosives. "I think we're good."

"Set it then," Salas rolled his eyes. He'd lost his patience. They should have already been in their SUVs and on the road with the target in custody.

"Everybody clear," said the operator. "We need some space. Detonation in thirty."

Five men ran to the southern edge of the road and found safety in the dry draining culvert. It was a perfect bunker. The sixth man got behind the wheel of the SUV and drove it west toward I-95 and stopped about fifty yards from the van.

Attached to the back of the van was an M2 Selectable Lightweight Attack Munition, a SLAM, which could deliver an effective explosion needed to enter or destroy an armored vehicle.

"You know this is probably overkill," Salas said to the explosives operator.

"Probably, sir. It's all I had with me on short notice."

"It better not frag the target."

"It shouldn't. It's at the rear of the vehicle. The lethality is only a couple of feet at the set charge. I'm at 20mm."

Salas braced himself for the explosion, lowering his head to the ground. Instead of the concussive force of the SLAM, he heard the repeated crack of an automatic rifle.

"What the—?"

The cracking MAC-10 was buried under the explosion of the SLAM against the back door of the armored van.

Inside the device, the explosive material lodged inside of it rapidly decomposed the instant the timer hit zero, releasing nitrogen and carbon oxides that expanded at more than twenty-six thousand feet per second. After the initial blast, those gasses rushed back to the center of the explosion, causing a second wave of energy.

That second wave pushed the blasted doors inward, and incalculable amounts of shrapnel ended Deputy Sanchez. He'd unloaded the entirety of the thirty-shot magazine to no effect.

He never knew what hit him.

Somehow, the van stayed upright. The explosives operator did his job well, having measured the right amount of RDX and polyisobutylene to accomplish exactly the right amount of destruction.

The van was smoldering when Salas unlocked the center passenger-side door and slid it open. Inside was the target, prisoner 02681-044, somewhat stunned but apparently unhurt.

The prisoner was quiet as Salas worked on unlocking the chains around his wrists and ankles. He stood, wobbling before catching himself on the bar in front of him, and Salas unlatched the waist restraint.

The two climbed out of the van and back to the street where five other team members were standing. Salas could see their eyes passing judgment on their target; a fat, old man with more girth than worth. He also figured they knew who he was. He was too recognizable not to identify immediately.

"You're that dude who blew up the Capitol," said Fisher, turning his glare to Salas. "Why are we acquiring this piece of—"

"Enough!" Salas raised his hand. "We do what we do. Period. We don't ask questions about why. You know that. We need to go." Salas grabbed the prisoner by the arm and led him to the SUV pulling up beside them.

"Thank you," said Sir Spencer Thomas. "Your timing was impeccable."

CHAPTER 3

THE NATIONAL MALL
WASHINGTON, DC

Matti Harrold stood on the National Mall, her back to the White House. Though she was winded after a long run, she felt good. The endorphins were coursing through her body, and the cool fall air made sweating all the more an accomplishment.

She looked to her left and started walking in the direction of the Capitol building. Checking her watch, she knew she had a good fifteen minutes before she needed to be back at the White House. That would give her thirty minutes to shower and change before her appointment with the president in the chief of staff's office.

She forced herself to look at Capitol Hill, or what was left of it. Nine months removed from the terrorist attack that leveled the symbol of her nation's power, the dome was as yet unconstructed. There was a shell there. Metal latticework surrounded what would be a renewed Capitol building.

Matti shuddered, remembering the day.

"I failed," she told herself every time she glanced at the reconstruction. "I didn't stop it."

She didn't allow herself the satisfaction of knowing she'd saved lives, including that of the current president, Felicia Jackson.

Instead, she focused on what she hadn't done. She hadn't stopped the attack despite knowing who the conspirators were. They'd succeeded in replanting the seed of insecurity so prevalent in those days after 9/11.

There were conspiracy theorists who believed she'd failed on purpose, that she was part of some grand government takeover. "It was an inside job," they'd said. "The NSA and FBI could have worked together. They knew who these people were. They could have stopped it if they'd wanted to."

Matti testified to her part in the debacle. Some members of congress dubbed her a hero while others castigated her for her inability to prevent the bombing.

There were six conspirators. Five of them were in prison awaiting trial. One was dead, killed by his compatriots for his misgivings about their plot.

Along with a struggling economy discussed in every morning White House staff meeting, the incomplete Capitol was a daily reminder of it all—for Matti, for the NSA, the White House, and virtually every American. Her current boss, President Jackson, was working hard to move the country past the pain and into emotional and economic recovery.

Matti smiled at the man jogging past her toward the Washington Monument. He was a regular, like her, using lunchtime to burn off steam. He nodded at her and strode past her at a quick clip, and there was a buzz against Matti's hip.

She pulled her phone from a clip on her waistband and checked the screen.

CALL ASAP. BL

"All caps," Matti mumbled and dialed the number to the White House chief of staff, Brandon Goodman, "it must be important."

It rang once before he answered, "Goodman."

"Hello, sir," Matti said. "It's Matti Harrold returning your text."

"Hi, Matti," he said, his cadence faster than usual. That was saying something too. Goodman was known for the speed with which he could deliver vast amounts of information. "I need you back here now."

"Yes, sir." Matti started walking toward the White House, foregoing the rest of her cooldown. "Is everything okay, sir?"

"No. We have a security situation, and the president wants your input immediately."

Security situation? Matti unconsciously picked up her pace. "On my way now, sir."

"You jogging?" he asked, aware of her daily routine.

"Yes, sir."

"Don't bother changing," he instructed. "Forego the protocol. Understood?"

"Yes, sir." Matti knew the conversation was over, but waited to end the call on her end until she heard Goodman hang up.

This must be serious.

President Jackson was adamant about her dress code. She wanted her staff to respect the office, the positions they held. Nobody was allowed in the West Wing, outside of the residence, without a jacket unless in uniform. The media protested. Jackson didn't care.

Unlike President Obama, who relaxed the code, or President Carter, who allowed cardigan sweaters, Jackson wanted to follow the footsteps of Presidents Reagan, George H. W. Bush, and George W. Bush.

"It speaks to who we are," Jackson told her staff on her first day in office. "We are both the head of government and the head of state. That's a unique responsibility."

Much of her staff, in the first few weeks, was a holdover from her predecessor Dexter Foreman, who'd died in office. They were still in mourning from his death and the subsequent terrorist bombing. They didn't argue.

But Jackson later fired two well-liked staffers for their passive-aggressive refusal to adhere to the dress code. The president was that serious about it.

To forego that requirement, Matti knew something urgent was afoot. Had the fragile economy collapsed further? Was North Korea attacking sensitive computer systems again? Were the Barcelona meetings in peril?

She'd hit a full sprint by the time she reached the security entrance.

*

"Houston?" Dillinger Holt said through a clenched jaw. "Are you kidding me?"

"No," said his online content editor at PlausibleDeniability.info, a Washington, DC-based website. It was a politically-themed news site with TMZ sensibilities. "I need you there tonight."

"I cover politics," Holt argued, leaning against the glass doorway to his editor's corner office. "I don't do entertainment. You've got people for that. Besides, I'm still prepping for the trip to Barcelona and the G12 meetings. This SECURITY Act thing is huge."

The editor scratched her head, her face glued to her desktop monitor even while she spoke with Holt. "I know, but I've got one reporter on maternity leave, another out sick, and a third in rehab."

"That's my problem because…?"

"Plus, I may have to send someone to a developing story in Virginia. Some ambush on a highway. Not sure yet. What I do know is that I trust you. I value you," She looked up from the screen and clasped her hands in prayer. "I'm asking you to do this as a favor."

"It's a drug overdose," Holt countered, not wanting to budge.

"He was the biggest thing in music," she answered. "Go down there, dig a little, eat some barbecue, file a couple of stories, and fly back."

"You're not really asking, are you?"

"Not really." The editor winked at him. "Thank you, Dillinger. You're the best."

"Fine." Holt spun on his boot heel and left the editor to her computer. He wove his way through the maze of cubicles to the opposite end of the expansive newsroom and his small, windowless office.

He plopped himself down at his desk, the door still open, and picked up his desk phone.

"Travel," he said, "this is Dillinger Holt. I need an open-ended ticket to Houston, Texas, a hotel room, and a rental car." He cradled the phone in his neck and opened his laptop. "Downtown, please. A midsize car is fine."

He opened his browser to a search engine and typed "Horus music death drugs Houston." He knew that keyword search would populate the most recent news about the singer. He'd start with that and work backwards.

"Four o'clock?" he asked, checking his watch. "From Reagan? I can make it. Thanks." He hung up the phone and looked at the search results on his screen.

There were offers for concert tickets, a Wikipedia article already updated with the performer's death date, and Horus's official website.

Holt scrolled past all of that to the most recent news accounts of his death. He found one that piqued his interest and clicked on it: *"Dead Singer Foretold of Death, Warned He Was Target"*

Houston—Popular hip-hop artist Horus may have known his days were numbered. The twenty-three-year-old superstar, who skyrocketed up the charts with hits such as "Cleopatra" and "1776", told friends he feared for his life.

"He was, like, always looking over his shoulder," said a close associate who agreed to speak with us on the condition we do not reveal his/her identity. "He was talking about buying a piece, for protection, you know. And he was always recording conversations with people. He called it 'insurance'."

Houston Police, who call Billboard's Artist of The Year the victim of a possible overdose, say they have no reason to suspect foul play. The toxicology results are not expected for weeks, but investigators say they did find drug paraphernalia in the singer's backstage dressing room. They also found what they believe are packages that contain what they believe is heroin residue.

His body was discovered by a security guard after a sold-out concert in Houston, Texas. That guard says Horus was in the room with a female companion. She left after a half hour, and when the singer didn't respond to a knock on the door, the guard entered the room. He found the singer unresponsive and called 9-1-1.

Police say they have not been able to identify the woman seen leaving the room, but they are convinced the death was accidental. Horus's friends knew him to have an addiction problem.

"He was hooked on smack," said one acquaintance. "He was always high. This isn't a surprise."

"He was so talented," said another. "But he was haunted by demons."

Was it the "demons" that had Horus afraid for his life?

"Maybe there is more to this," Holt considered, mumbling to himself. He pulled out his phone and scrolled through his contacts to see who he knew in Houston. Finding nothing, he thumbed to the search bar and typed in "Houston." Two names popped up. One was a political science researcher for the Baker Institute at Rice University. The other…

"Bingo!"

Holt slapped shut the laptop, slipped it into a messenger bag next to his desk, and slung it across his shoulder. He'd make his flight, but he'd have to hustle.

*

Ronald Reagan walked into James Baker's office in the early days of his first term as president and said to his chief of staff, "James, this is a mighty big office."

"Yes, it is," replied the lawyer from Houston, smiling back at the affable commander-in-chief.

"It's not oval," Reagan said, chuckling.

Matti thought about the retelling of that story as she sat in Chief of Staff Goodman's corner office. She'd heard Baker himself relay the exchange to a gathering of politicos six months earlier while they worked to stabilize the reeling nation.

President Jackson worked hard to mine the experience of diplomats on both sides of the aisle. She publicly proclaimed a true post-partisan Washington, not the false compromise so many before her promised but failed to deliver. Baker had become a close ally, along with Madeleine Albright, Condoleezza Rice, and former presidents Clinton, Bush, and Carter.

"Matti," Goodman prompted, "are you with us?"

"Yes, sir." Matti blinked back to attention. She flexed her hand to control an imperceptible tremor. "I'm sorry. I was thinking."

Goodman leaned against his desk, loosened his tie, and turned his attention back to the president. She was seated between her chief National Security Advisor and the Homeland Security secretary. "As I was saying, Sir Spencer Thomas is no longer in custody. We have no idea where he might be or who is responsible for the attack that freed him."

"No idea?" President Jackson turned her head to look across the room to CIA director, Will Dixon. "Is it Tea Party folks, Will? Is it ISIS? The Russians?"

Her national security team suggested a meeting in the situation room, a fifty-five-hundred-foot complex in the West Wing's basement. The president insisted on a group of advisors in the less formal setting of the COS office.

"The Tea Party has never shown a propensity for violence," answered Director Dixon. "Thomas's group was radicalized. They weren't really part of the Tea Party."

"And the others?"

"ISIS would have claimed responsibility." Dixon shook his head. "There would already be a viral video on YouTube from some cleric damning us to Hell. The Russians? Maybe. We have analysts listening to the communications and trying to isolate any satellite transmissions."

"Did we have any eyes flying over the area at the time?" Goodman asked.

"We're checking that right now," answered the National Security Advisor. "Given its proximity to Washington, there's a really good possibility we'll be able to isolate something."

"How quickly?" The president stood from her seat and walked to Goodman's desk.

"A few hours at most."

Goodman was thumbing his Blackberry, talking as he read updates. "The media is on it. It's on Twitter, and the *Post* is reporting a major incident involving a prison transport. They don't have much information, but it's only a matter of time."

"Any video or photographs from the scene?" asked President Jackson.

"No," Goodman replied, "not yet. And there shouldn't be. There's a wide perimeter around the scene and the airspace is capped."

"Then the bigger question here," President Jackson said, leaning against Goodman's desk, her hip bumping his, "is how we handle this publicly."

"Agreed," said Goodman.

"It's a matter of minutes before the media goes with this ad nauseam," said Dixon. "Damn vultures."

"Do we hold a briefing and get ahead of it?" Goodman half-asked, half-suggested.

"I don't know that we should—" the National Security Advisor said before the president held up her finger.

"We should get ahead of this." She nodded. "I like Brandon's thought. Though I think we stay away from some of the particulars."

"What particulars?" asked Matti. Everyone in the room spun to look at her. It was the first thing she'd uttered since arriving sweaty and out of breath.

"I want the director of the Marshal's Service standing next to me," the president said. "Get her butt to cross the Potomac ASAP. She'll handle most of the questions."

"Who briefs her?" asked the National Security Advisor. "Since she was not included in this meeting?"

"Do I detect sarcasm?" President Jackson.

"No, Madam President."

"Then you can brief her."

"Yes, Madam President."

"I'll handle the overview," said the president, her eyes moving from person to person. "I'll talk about the incident, thank our brave men and women in uniform, blah, blah, blah."

"What about the threat?" asked Goodman. He'd grabbed a pad from his desk and was jotting down the president's instructions.

"I want Homeland Security to talk about our efforts to determine the perpetrators," she answered. "Everyone good?"

When everyone nodded, President Jackson ushered her guests to the door.

"What particulars will you avoid?" Matti repeated her unanswered question, resuming the meeting before everyone could adjourn.

President Jackson looked at Matti and licked her lips, then conceded her intentions. "We're telling everyone Spencer Thomas is dead."

"Why?" Matti questioned.

"Because we are."

"Madam President, I—"

"Matti," the president said, invoking a motherly tone as best she could, not ever having been a mother, "we'll talk about this in the Oval in a minute. Go wait for me. I've got some calls to make first. I need to talk with some folks about the SECURITY Act.

Everyone else is excused. We'll have the briefing in an hour. Brandon, tell the press office."

The chief of staff rounded his desk to get on the phone. The president strode from the office and down the hall, through her private dining room, and into her private study adjacent to the Oval Office.

The rest of the staff filed out of the room, leaving Matti alone with Goodman. He was holding the phone in the crook of his neck, his fingers poised above the number pad.

"I don't get it," Matti said to Goodman.

"What's that?" he asked, waiting to dial.

"Lying to the American people about this," she said. "I don't get it."

"It would be stranger if we told the whole truth, Matti. You should know that by now."

Matti nodded and flexed her hand. The tremor was getting worse.

CHAPTER 4

NORTHERN VIRGINIA

Sir Spencer Thomas was the man everyone needed but nobody wanted. He'd always been the man in the background, the out-of-focus character at the edge of a scene. However, he had more power by proximity than almost anyone in the Western world.

He'd counseled Secretary of State John Kerry during the Iranian nuclear arms talks in early 2015 while at the same time he was on the phone with Israeli prime minister Benjamin Netanyahu, suggesting the appropriate level of public outrage.

From K Street to Wall Street, from the Hague to the Kremlin, he knew people. And so, when he manipulated a group of misfits into plotting against their own country, it was not without the permission of people in the highest levels of government.

Riding in the back of an armored black Suburban with false plates, Sir Spencer rubbed his wrists, bruised from the cuffs he'd worn for the better part of the day. He was tired and hungry and irritated.

"Where exactly is it we're headed?" he asked Doug Salas, measuring the barrel-chested, bearded hulk in the seat next to him. Sir Spencer assumed he was CIA, special operations, or a contracted thug. The man looked like every operator or Spec Ops superhero with whom he'd worked in Afghanistan or Pakistan as he dealt information and arms to the Taliban on behalf of the United States.

Salas chewed on his gum, but he didn't acknowledge Sir Spencer. He pulled a cell phone from the thigh pocket of his cargo pants and checked the screen. He pressed two buttons and handed the phone to Sir Spencer without looking at him.

Spencer looked at the phone. It was dialing an unidentifiable number. "Is the line secure?"

Salas nodded. He leaned his head back and closed his eyes.

Sir Spencer pulled the phone to his ear in time to hear someone answer on the other end. It was a familiar voice.

"That was a bit more violent than I was anticipating," Sir Spencer began. "I assumed you'd have everything a bit more staged to minimize the collateral damage.

"Since when are you concerned about collateral damage?" the voice replied. "I don't recall any worries when you blew up the Capitol Rotunda."

"Different circumstances." Sir Spencer chuckled.

"They're all the same circumstances."

"I heard about our good friend Horus," Sir Spencer said, cradling the phone in his neck to rub the soreness from his wrist. "Pity."

"He was a threat. Just like Bill Davidson."

Bill Davidson, a former US attorney general and one of Sir Spencer's flunky conspirators, was cracking in the days leading up to the execution of the plot, so he'd been executed. Or at least he would have been, had he not committed suicide first.

"I liked Horus's music," Sir Spencer offered. "He was such a clever lyricist."

"A little too clever," said the voice. "I wasn't a fan."

"So what's next?" Sir Spencer asked. "I imagine the world knows, or soon will, I am a free man."

"Not exactly."

"How so?" Sir Spencer leaned forward in his seat, stretching the seat belt's shoulder strap. The conversation was, for the first time, interesting.

"You were collateral damage during the escape attempt."

"I see." Sir Spencer considered the freedom his supposed death afforded him. "Brilliant."

"It's for the cause," the voice explained. "You're a more effective asset if you can work your black magic undetected."

"Agreed." Sir Spencer adjusted his girth, shimmying into a more comfortable position in the seat. "However, I would counsel my visage is as well-known as the president's. Fox News, CNN, MSNBC, the History Channel, all of them are fans. That insufferable Vickie Lupo character, the woman on the program *Constitution Avenue*, can't stop talking about me."

"I gather you had access to television while incarcerated?"

"There's access to everything if you know who to ask." Sir Spencer laughed, his deep voice resonating in the back of the SUV and forcing open the operator's eyes. The bearded spook scratched his neck, glowered at Sir Spencer, and shook his head.

"You'll be working from a secure location," the voice said. "That's where you're headed now."

"When will I see you?"

"I have a trip planned to the location. It'll be soon."

"Soon it is, then." Sir Spencer lowered the phone and disconnected. "Here you are." He offered the device to Salas.

Salas took the phone and slipped it back into his thigh pocket. "I agree with Fisher." He looked straight at Sir Spencer without a hint of expression on his face. "You're a piece of trash."

Sir Spencer studied the operator's face for a moment, noting the deep ray of sun-induced crow's-feet spreading outward from his eyes. His beard was closely cropped, thick enough to make his face indistinguishable from all of the other operators with whom he worked. Spencer looked at the man's hands, thickly calloused and muscular. His left pinkie rested askew, as did his middle finger.

"That's interesting," said Sir Spencer. "You put bullets into the heads of men who swore to defend the same constitution to which you are loyal, and you judge *me*."

"I killed them to set you free," said Salas. "I did my job. Nothing more. Their deaths, while tragic, serve a purpose."

"And yet you can't see why the deaths of those inside the Capitol, while tragic, also serve a higher purpose?"

"Whatever," Salas grunted and closed his eyes, lying back against the headrest.

"Well then," said Sir Spencer, a smile snaking across his cheeks, "I'll thank you for your service and sacrifice to this nation. But I daresay, your myopia could be your downfall. There is always a bigger picture, always a grander scheme. You, like the marshals, are pawns. Unwitting or otherwise."

CHAPTER 5

THE WHITE HOUSE
WASHINGTON, DC

Matti Harrold sat down on the sofa, sitting on the edge with her back straight. She was never quite comfortable in the Oval Office. She wasn't certain if her unease was because of what the office represented or because of what she knew had happened there.

To her left was the famed Resolute Desk. It was where laws were signed and important addresses televised. John Kennedy played hide and seek underneath it, Monica Lewinsky played something else aside it, and President Dexter Foreman died behind it.

None of it made her comfortable. She squeezed her left hand into a tight fist and then flexed it, trying to fight off an involuntary tremor. She didn't want her boss to see it. She didn't want questions.

"So, Matti"—President Jackson strode back into the room from her private office and gracefully took her place on the sofa opposite Matti—"how are you?" She crossed one leg over the other, the bright red leather on the bottom of her sole conspicuous.

"Ma'am?"

"You were privy to some information I imagine was quite personal for you." President Jackson leaned forward, her hands clasped on her lap. "I know you've struggled with what happened, your role in it…"

"Yes, Madam President," Matti said, "I have struggled. But the guilt is a little less overwhelming every day. The work you provide for me here is a privilege and a salve."

"Don't be so damned formal with me, Matti," President Jackson scolded. "Who the hell says salve? C'mon, girl. Tell me what you're thinking."

Matti shifted on the edge of the cushion, considering her response. "I don't know that we should be lying to the American people. If Sir Spencer Thomas is alive and on the run, don't you think we should tell them?"

The president slapped her leg and sprang from her seat. She walked around the coffee table separating the two sofas and sat next to Matti. "I knew you didn't like the idea. I could see it on your face,

Matti. You're still coping with the whole white hat, black hat sense of things, aren't you?"

"Not really. I—"

"Look, Matti"—the president lowered her voice, softened her tone—"I know you're more of a Dudley Do Right than James Bond, but consider the consequences of telling the world Sir Spencer escaped our custody."

Matti's eyebrows furrowed. "What do you mean?"

"Our economy is teetering. Confidence in this administration is shallow at best. We're about to head to Barcelona for a key meeting with the European Union. I can't go there from a perceived position of weakness."

"I understand the optics of it," countered Matti. "I fully comprehend that relative ignorance is relative bliss, but lying to the country is—"

"Is what presidents do," Jackson interrupted. "We are parents who've yet to reveal the truth about Santa Claus and the Easter Bunny. We don't lie for the sake of it. We lie to keep alive the illusion of magic and unfettered benevolence."

"Who in the hell uses the word unfettered?" Matti mumbled through a self-conscious smile.

"Ha!" The president nudged Matti with her sharp elbow. "Good one."

"I don't agree with your metaphor, however," Matti said, the smile evaporating as quickly as it appeared. "The people should know."

"They'll know eventually. Because eventually, and not too long from now, we'll catch him and kill him. The reality will meet the truth."

"Understood." Matti nodded. "And I wouldn't say anything, except that you asked."

"I know that. You're loyal, Matti. And that's not easily found inside the Beltway."

Matti nodded again and stood to leave. She offered the president her hand.

"I do want to know how you are." President Jackson took her aide's hand and stood as she gripped it. "Are you okay?"

"As good as ever, Madam President." Matti forced a grin. "When are you addressing the media? I'd like to be there if that's okay."

"Of course." President Jackson let go of Matti's hand and folded her arms across her chest. "Should be in an hour or so. I think the press is in the media room already and they're being briefed ahead of time. By the way, how are things moving along with the SECURITY Act?"

President Jackson had tasked Matti with backchannel work on pending legislation called the SECURITY Act. SECURITY was an acronym for Surveillance of Electronic Correspondence Under Regulated Intelligence and Telecommunication. It was a successor to the PATRIOT Act, whose teeth were pulled in the final days of the Obama administration. The NSA's broad powers to eavesdrop on Americans without warrants was also technically nonexistent.

Now, in the wake of the Capitol Hill attack, the president was trying to push through a far more invasive form of surveillance and counterterrorism tactics that would essentially dilute the Fourth Amendment. The idea of homegrown, mostly white, non-Muslim terrorists had weakened the resolve of those opposed to the lessening of personal freedom for the sake of security.

The president knew Matti was the perfect person for the job, despite her issues. She was former NSA, she was a hero, and she had the soft touch needed to massage the brokers on Capitol Hill.

"Good, I think," Matti said. "We've got a majority on board in the House. The key will be a handful of senators who could go either way on it. They never liked the PATRIOT Act."

"Of course," said the president, shaking her head. "I could have Edward Snowden on my team, and some of those ideologues would oppose anything that keeps our country safe."

"I think they'll come around," said Matti. "I've developed a decent rapport with their chiefs of staff in a short period of time. If you reached out directly…"

"Not a problem." President Jackson snapped her fingers and pointed at Matti. "A little private luncheon here after the Barcelona trip should do it."

"Thank you." Matti turned to leave the office and she glanced over at the desk. Her eyes were drawn to the blotter covering much of the wood. It was there to hide the indelible stain from Dexter Foreman's blood.

CHAPTER 6

BUSH INTERCONTINENTAL AIRPORT
HOUSTON, TEXAS

Dillinger Holt connected his phone to the rental car's Bluetooth and dialed the number pulled up in his contacts. It rang once.

"What do you want?" The greeting was as cold as a corpse.

"Really, Karen?" Holt laughed nervously. "That's the greeting I get?"

"What. Do. You. Want?"

"I need your help." Holt was sitting in the parking space in the rental garage, the engine idling.

"Of course you do."

"Can we meet?"

"Why?"

"C'mon, Karen," Holt pleaded. "I've apologized."

"On the back of a napkin. On the nightstand. Of a hotel room for which I paid."

"Pleeease?"

"You're infuriating, Dillinger," she huffed. The ice was thawing.

"It's my eyes, isn't it?" Holt chuckled and adjusted the side-view mirrors.

"Something like that," she mused. "This is about the rapper, isn't it?"

"Yep." Holt dropped the phone from his ear and tapped the speakerphone option.

"You know everybody and their brother wants a copy of that report." Karen sighed. "I'm not going to be able to give you a copy. Plus, the toxicology won't be back for a while."

"What about dinner, then?" Holt suggested. He thumbed through a dining app on his phone, looking for the name of a familiar restaurant. "I know you like Goode Company Seafood. It's what, fifteen minutes from your office?"

"I can't bring the report with me either, Dillinger," she explained. "I'd lose my job."

"I thought you were in charge," Holt countered.

"Everybody has a boss. But I can meet you in a half hour. We can talk about it. But nothing on paper."

"Got it," Holt said, tapping off the speakerphone and drawing the device back to his ear. "See you at seven thirty."

Holt backed out of the spot and eased through the garage and the spaghetti maze of perpetual airport construction on his way into Houston. He punched on the radio and thumped his fingers against the steering wheel to the rhythmic beat, wholly unaware he was listening to a previously unreleased song from Horus.

In the darkness I fly, paper it hides
The need for real life.
Changing, I'm gaming and slaying not staying the same.
From alleys to galleys, I'm cooking the words.
Absurd.
They know I'll keep spitting,
The rhythm it's gettin' too hard to control.
From spinning the lies, the secrets unbridled,
I gallop.
Choking on scallops and Dom,
I'm long gone.
Without power, the shower it dries
In the darkness I fly.

Holt turned up the volume, his head unconsciously swaying to the concussive bass, the monotone depth of Horus's voice. He merged to the right and accelerated south along the Hardy Toll Road toward the 610 Loop surrounding the city's urban core.

They'll clip my wings,
Cut the cord when I sing.
I'm high but I'm grounded.
Trying not to flounder.
But they got me.
They'll hook me.
In the darkness.
In the darkness.

No light.
No flight.
All gone.
In the darkness.

Holt passed a large eighteen-wheeler and directed the rental back into the center lane. To his left was a train barreling down a set of tracks separating the north and southbound lanes of the toll road. He didn't like being that close to a locomotive.

In God We Trust, climb the bricks we must,
To the top of the peak, one eye open, collapsed.
Take a nap, take the rap, fill the gap in the wall
On the street, we will meet, so discreet.
Avengers unite, for the fight, in the night.
No light.
In the darkness.
No flight.
All gone.
In the darkness.
In the darkness.

He didn't notice the song was over and a deejay was talking until the name "Horus" broke through his fog.

"Hard to believe he's gone, people," said the deejay. *"That new track, 'Darkness,' wasn't supposed to drop until next month. It leaked on the 'Net and now it's on iTunes. It's haunting, right? Completely haunting. Rest in peace, Horus. Your talent will be missed, brother. We'll be right back with more of today's top hip-hop. I'm your deejay GUNK. You know!!"*

Holt picked up his phone and tapped the iTunes icon on his phone. It opened on the screen as his eyes danced back and forth between the road and the screen. The application opened and proclaimed the new, exclusive release of Horus's posthumous track.

He thumbed a purchase and downloaded the song onto his phone, narrowly avoiding a motorcyclist when he kept his eyes off the road for a beat too long. He dropped the phone into the passenger seat and refocused on his driving, speeding toward his dinner date.

CHAPTER 7

THE MAYFLOWER HOTEL
WASHINGTON, DC

Horus's assassin stood nude at the bathroom mirror of her suite at the Mayflower Renaissance Hotel. The spacious room was on the club level of the architecturally masterful building. Her palms were pressed flat against the Carrara marble vanity, the water running cold from the stainless faucet. To her right was a frameless glass shower encased on three sides by white subway tile. The floor was black and white, the pattern designed to mimic a basket weave.

She stared at herself in the mirror, examining the imperfections on her scalp, the faint tan line that marked what should have been her hairline. Her eyes moved along her body, across her broad but feminine shoulders, to her décolletage and waist. She stood back from the vanity and traced a hand along her flat stomach, a finger flicking the tiny stud piercing her navel.

She inhaled, savoring the fruit of the long hours of work it took to maintain a body worthy of the tasks given her. The assassin bit her lower lip and looked down at the vanity.

Next to a folded white washcloth, a brown bottle of peroxide, a tube of Neosporin, and a wide bandage was a surgical-grade scalpel.

The assassin bit harder into her lower lip, drawing blood, and picked up the scalpel with her right hand. Holding its handle as she would a pencil, she pressed the carbon steel blade against her wrist and dragged it upward toward her forearm. Blood leached to the surface, coloring the two-inch cut, which ran parallel to a trio of scars.

The scars were similar in length, the thin bands of fibrous tissue resembling a violent cat scratch. Each one, however, was a deliberate exorcism. Together they symbolized a ritualistic rite of passage, a masochistic joyride she'd long employed to cope with her enviable existence.

The assassin wasn't in the Mayflower Hotel by choice. She hadn't straddled and executed Horus because she wanted to do it.

The tattoo on her shoulder wasn't the dark design she would have picked among the options in the tattoo artist's répertoire.

The assassin was a puppet whose strings were always taut. In the five years, three months, sixteen days, twelve hours, thirteen minutes, and eight seconds since she was pulled from a pool of her own vomit in an underground New York City nightclub, her life had not been her own. Unlike those who controlled her, the assassin had no manifest destiny.

She was a slave with invisible binds she could not break, mostly because she was unaware they existed. Instead, she soldiered from one assignment to the next without question.

Plant a listening device in a congressman's Georgetown brownstone? Done. Seduce an intelligence analyst at the FBI for access to his encrypted data files? No problem. Dress as a man and knock on the hotel room door of a former presidential cabinet member to put a bullet in his prostitute girlfriend? Check.

She was among a kaleidoscope of assets netted for the kind of black-ops, off-the-books work her country often employed under the guise of patriotism and freedom. Each of them had their own unique skills. She was the best among them.

For every asset admired for her beauty, she eclipsed her. For those feared for their lethality, she was more poisonous. For the ones admired for their intelligence, she outsmarted them. Her handlers secretly called her "Bourne", after the popular Robert Ludlum spy.

She would have snapped Bourne's neck before he could remember his name.

And despite the briefings, which spoke of national security and protecting liberty, she knew the missions were more about power, money, and the control of information than anything else.

She knew Horus talked too much. He'd stumbled, through arrogance or stupidity, out of the cage marked "asset" and into the one labeled "liability". It was a mistake, or a call for help, she'd witnessed so many others attempt to make.

Some waved umbrellas at the paparazzi. Others shaved their heads. Still more claimed they were clinically bipolar or suffered from exhaustion as they entered "rehab".

The assassin laughed every time she read a news account about another emotionally wayward young star or starlet. It was their weaknesses, the shallow vulnerability of artists, that forced her handlers to rethink their recruitment techniques.

That was how they found her. She had no aspirations beyond the next empty bottle of vodka. She was a nobody, a fundamentally brilliant, beautiful, pathologically soulless nobody.

They put her in a cocoon and nourished her. They broke her free of her addiction to pain-numbing and helped her embrace its sting. Pain, they taught her, was proof of life. It was validation that her heart, as it were, was beating and pumping blood.

They did other things too while she was in the cocoon; things she couldn't remember exactly but which triggered her impulses and put her to work. When she was ready, when the metamorphosis, in its Kafka-esque glory, was complete, she emerged anew.

She was a butterfly. Mesmerizing, delicate at first glance, but lethal to her predators.

The assassin was immaculately conceived and judiciously deployed. While she awaited her next assignment, she took the bottle of peroxide and squeezed it over the wound. Wincing, she licked her lips, relishing the metallic taste of her blood as she dabbed the bubbling wound with the washcloth.

She applied a dollop of Neosporin to her wrist and then, one handed, managed to apply the bandage. The assassin looked up at herself in the mirror, her bottom lip swollen and red, the faintest gloss of moisture in her eyes.

It was time for room service.

*

Matti sank into the ergonomic chair at her cramped desk in the West Wing. It was one of a series of offices sandwiched between the president's dining room and the chief of staff's expansive space.

She looked over her shoulder and, certain nobody was around, unlocked one of her desk drawers. Her hand trembling, she rummaged through the mess of notepads and briefing guides to find an unmarked bottle hidden at the bottom of the drawer.

Matti gripped the bottle with one hand and palmed the top of it with the other to force open the container. She shook two blue oval tablets onto the desk and then shoved the bottle deep into the drawer. She locked the drawer and then slid a half-empty bottle of water toward the edge of the desk.

She considered the consequences of taking the pills longer than she weighed those of not taking them. She popped both of them in her mouth and followed them with a swig of room-temperature water.

She sat there watching her hand, her finger spread wide. Slowly, as if magically, the trembling subsided. With her steady hand came a feeling of calm. She inhaled deeply and smiled. Matti suddenly imagined she was in a warm bath, the water relaxing every tension or ache.

Taking two pills was new. It was double the dose her doctor prescribed in the days after the Capitol exploded. He told her it was a temporary fix for her anxiety. After a couple of months, he stopped prescribing, fearing she was becoming addicted and using the medication as a permanent crutch.

He was right.

Now she paid a ridiculous amount to a guy named C-Dunk on Seventh Street Northwest. She had little guarantee the "bennies" C-Dunk supplied were Xanax at all or whether they were a mix of valium and sawdust compressed into a pill with blue dye number two. She didn't care. As long as C-Dunk's junk calmed her nerves and eased the shakes, she was good with it.

They helped her sleep without dreams, without the retelling of the day her world changed. Even though she didn't see the Capitol explode and collapse as it happened and never watched it replay on television, her nightmares provided a moment-by-moment account.

She could see, as if floating above it, the violent blast and its aftermath. Atop the rotunda, two hundred sixty-nine feet above the Capitol's east front plaza, the Statue of Freedom dropped to the rotunda floor, rupturing it. The cast-iron globe upon which she had long rested snapped. The encircling words *E* and *Pluribus* were separated from *Unum*.

All thirty-six windows surrounding the dome were shattered. The sandstone walls extending upward forty-eight feet from the rotunda floor and the separating Doric pilasters were crumbled such that the fireproof cast-iron upper half of the walls collapsed upon them. Each of the eight niches, containing large scenes depicting the Revolutionary War and early exploration, were unrecognizable, fragments of the canvasses smoldering amidst the rubble.

The statues and busts lining the walls were reduced to large chunks of marble. Vinnie Ream's Lincoln and Houdon's Washington were indistinguishable from those of Garfield, Grant, or Hamilton. The gold replica of the original Magna Carta, a gift from the British government in 1976, melted from the explosive flash of heat.

There was a thirty-foot-wide hole in the floor where President Foreman's casket was perched upon the catafalque. He would have no burial at Arlington. In her dream, he called to her. He blamed her. He told her the nation's pain was her doing. She was a failure and a disappointment.

More importantly, and more grounded in reality, Matti blamed herself. She couldn't reconcile the loss of life, the stain on her agency, her inability to stop the threat. Matti was a wreck. A sleepless, dysfunctional mess who barely coped from minute to minute.

President Jackson knew about Matti's anxiety. She gave Matti the number to her physician. She arranged for the consultation and the months of therapy.

Matti told her boss she was improving, she no longer needed the counseling or the drugs. She was coping and President Jackson told her how proud she was of her honesty and her recovery.

But Matti wasn't coping without the drugs. She wasn't recovering. She needed them.

So she calculated carefully, the good outweighed the bad. It was black and white. And despite knowing her mother's addictions were her own undoing, Matti took the risk.

Sitting alone at her desk, all was good with the world. For the moment.

CHAPTER 8

LEONARDO DA VINCI INTERNATIONAL AIRPORT
FIUMICINO, ITALY

The dead Russian was right. So far, the contents of the bag were undetectable. Neither the agents nor the dogs sensed anything as Jon Custos worked his way through the security checkpoint. It was a gamble, taking it as a carry-on bag through a major international airport. Custos thought it better to test the promise now than later, when it really mattered.

With the bag still slung over his massive shoulder, he handed the gate agent a Mexican passport. Its green cover was worn from use, the pages stamped full of international destinations: Istanbul; Washington, DC; New York; Moscow; Cairo; and others. The photograph and the vital description matched Custos. Everything else was fabricated, but it was done to such a degree that even the most skilled at detecting fraud would never have known. It was a real passport in every sense of the word.

"*Gratzi*, Mr. Vasconselos." The agent smiled, her cheeks bubbling. Custos took the passport from her and moved to an empty seat near the boarding entrance. He had some time before his flight, but he couldn't get away from Rome fast enough. He secretly hoped sitting near the gate might facilitate the flight's departure.

Jon Custos was a ghost. Whether he was traveling as Jose Vasconselos or Giuseppe Garibaldi, Custos was a man who lived in the shadows and worked for those who ruled from them. He was ethnically ambiguous, born of Roma stock. His parents were nomads who traveled from place to place, eking out an existence off the backs of others.

From an early age he had a gift for subterfuge, for ignoring whatever moral line might exist in others. Custos was always stronger than the others his age. He was the first volunteered for the worst of his clan's jobs: pickpocketing near police stations, thieving on tourist-heavy trains, fencing counterfeit goods to new customers.

The adults in his tribe knew he was fearless. They could see the black in his eyes, his pathological stock, every time he opened his mouth and lied about the truth. His father was proud and, because of his son's skills, became a part of the chieftain's inner circle. Custos was an asset.

He was smart and innately gifted at language. He picked up English and Portuguese from listening to tourists. By age thirteen, he was fluent in five languages, including his native Rromanës.

When he and the lesser-skilled children would swarm an unsuspecting target, he could gauge their nationality and speak their language. That engagement gave the others the extra seconds they needed to rifle through pockets and bags without notice.

Custos was a prize for any woman in his kumpania, what his people called a caravan or group. He was the favorite of the Phuri Dai, the senior woman in their band, and she chose for him a beautiful girl to marry. They were young, but arranged marriages for teenagers was customary. A large, ornate wedding was planned southwest of Rome on Isola Sacra.

Sixteen-year-old Custos was not interested. He wanted a life beyond the confines of his tribe and his extended family. Before sunrise on the morning of the wedding, he took a pocket full of euros from his father's bedroom and left. He never saw his family again.

He wandered around southern Europe for close to two years, beating paths from Florence and Milan to Zagreb and Dubrovnik. Custos was always a meal away from hunger and a pick away from jail. He was happy. At least he thought he was.

It was when a wealthy man caught him pickpocketing atop the Acropolis in Athens that Custos's new path was forged.

The target was an Englishman, a cane in his left hand, an expensive Savile Row suit draping his large frame. He seemed distracted by the ruins, reading the informational placards outside the Parthenon's roped exterior, but he caught Custos by the wrist with his hand still inside a satin-lined pocket.

Custos tugged against the mark and tried to run, but the Englishman was strong. He said nothing to Custos, looking into the boy's eyes. His lips, pressed together, spread into a smile.

"Let go," Custos said, twisting wildly, trying to free himself. "Let go!"

"Calm down," the man said softly, as if trying to calm a wild horse. "I'm not going to call the police. Calm yourself and I'll let go."

Custos's eyes searched the man's face. He didn't seem angry or upset like most of the tourists who nearly caught him. There was something fatherly about him. Though Custos didn't know what to make of it, he stopped tugging and stood still with the man's hand still gripped around his wrist. The sun, blazing between the columns of Pentelic marble, was as unrelenting as the man's grasp.

"That's better," the man said. "Now, I promised I'd let you go, but first, I have a couple of questions for you. Clearly, you speak English?"

Custos nodded. He looked around at a family of Americans staring at him. They stood at the edge of the path between the placards and a waist-high wall. He thought they looked ridiculous with their sunblock-streaked cheeks and their baseball caps. He cursed himself for not having picked the high-sock, Bermuda shorts-wearing patriarch of that family. Custos figured if he had, he'd be halfway down the granite peak and on his way to the camouflage of the National Gardens near the city's center.

Athens was a city of ruins, both historic and modern, but the gardens were beautiful. He could escape both his pursuers and the Mediterranean sun within its expansive canopy. Only the hum and rumble of buses, taxis, and motorbikes on the ridiculously crowded streets nearby would interrupt the solitude he could find there.

"What other languages do you speak?"

"Spanish, Italian, Portuguese, and Rromanës."

"Rromanës? So you're a Gypsy?"

Custos bristled at the term and tried to yank his wrist free from the bigot's grip. By now, if he'd picked the right mark, he'd be grabbing a coffee in Monastiraki, hiding in plain sight amongst the throngs who rushed between the shops and restaurants lining the narrow alleyways.

"I'm sorry." The man tightened his grasp and loosened the condescending sarcasm. "Did I offend? Perhaps I should call your people Roma or Romani? Traveler maybe? Regardless, I now know your stock."

"What do you want?" Custos spat. "If you don't call police, what are you doing?"

"What do you call yourself?"

Custos hesitated before answering. "Jon."

"Jon what?"

"Custos."

"Perfect." The Englishman laughed. "So perfect."

"What?" Custos was confused. Nobody had laughed at his name before. "Why you laugh?"

"Your last name is Latin for the word *guard.*" The Englishman chuckled. "And given the job offer I have for you, it fits."

"You have a job? Good money?"

"Yes," the man said. "Can I let go of your wrist without you scurrying off like a gutter rat?"

Custos nodded and the man freed his wrist. He pulled it to his chest and rubbed the bruise.

"Good, then." The Englishman leaned on his cane. "Let's walk to somewhere shaded where it's not so hot. We can talk about my offer. Past the entrance gate there is a nice frozen lemonade stand. I'll even buy you two. You like?"

Custos was fascinated by the man, by the possibility of a job and its good pay. There was something about the Englishman that gave Custos hope. It was an unfamiliar feeling for a boy who'd lived his life off the achievements of others.

The man walked alongside him and they started their descent down the steps and through the Propyla. He put his free arm around Custos and introduced himself as they passed the Athena Nike Temple to their left.

"I am Sir Spencer Thomas," he said. "And I have a feeling we'll become fast friends."

The man was right.

Now, years later he sat in an airport, enlightened and on the verge of completing the biggest job yet on behalf of his mentor. He closed his eyes and sucked in the airport's recirculated air, thinking about the work he still had to do. There wasn't much time and there were so many moving parts. He trusted everything would fall into place as it always had.

"Volo trentatre vincolao per Barcelona," the gate agent announced into the loudspeaker, *"salirà a bordo in cinque minuti."*

Custos stood from his seat, anxious to leave. His flight to Barcelona was boarding in five minutes.

CHAPTER 9

GOODE COMPANY SEAFOOD
HOUSTON, TEXAS

Holt spotted Karen the instant she stepped into the restaurant. She was without a hint of makeup, and Holt wondered why he'd left her without saying goodbye or why he'd not called her sooner.

"Hello, you!" He leaned in to kiss her cheek. She smelled sweet, a hint of something floral at her neck. "You look amazing."

"Uh-huh." She turned her cheek to the kiss. "You say that to all of the girls."

"I mean it this time." He knew it sounded crass, but he didn't care. Holt was there for one thing. Maybe two. But that second depended on whether or not she forgave him his trespasses.

"Do we have a table?" Karen asked. "I'm hungry."

Holt raised a finger to the hostess, telling her his guest was here and they were ready to be seated. He turned back and flashed a smile at Karen. Her arms were folded across her chest, purse draped over one shoulder. Her subtly highlighted hair was pulled back tight into a ponytail.

Holt admired how a woman as smart as Karen cared about her appearance too. He knew too many people in the web business, men and women, who flippantly overlooked their clothing or hygiene.

"You really do look good," he purred as she stepped past him, following the hostess to their table.

After helping her into her seat, Holt slid in across from her and leaned on the table with his elbows.

"How long has it been?" he mused. "Was it the untimely death of that Houston congressman? What was his name?" Holt snapped his fingers.

"Gruber."

"Yes! Gruber. Wow! Good memory."

The dim candlelight flickered a flattering glow across Karen's face. Holt lost his train of thought.

"Let's forego the foreplay, shall we?" Karen reached into her purse and pulled out an iPad mini.

Holt looked past her and caught the attention of a waiter. "Could we please get some water and a bottle of your Ferrari-Carano Sauvignon Blanc?"

"I'm not drinking." Karen looked at Holt over the top of her glasses. "So the bottle is yours."

"Fair enough." The reporter shrugged and asked the waiter for two glasses.

"I have some information on my iPad here." Karen tapped on the screen and then pushed her glasses against her nose with her index finger. "I'll need to explain some of this to you, and I can't let you take this information with you. So either you'll need a notepad or a good memory."

Holt pulled a digital recorder from his jacket pocket and slid it onto the table. He pressed a button and a red light illuminated. Karen pursed her lips, looking at the recorder, then initiated her tutorial.

"Let me begin with the basics. At every death there are at least two scenes we consider. One is the location of the death. The other is the body itself. We're responsible for the analysis related to the second scene. Any questions you have about the first scene won't be answered by anything I have to tell you."

"Got it."

"Our work consists of a gross external examination, a gross internal examination, toxicology, and a microscopic examination. Together, those four elements help us determine how the subject died." Karen paused as the waiter returned with a bottle of wine.

He presented it to Holt and uncorked it, pouring a taste into Holt's glass. The reporter swirled the wine around in the glass, as he'd seen real oenophiles do, and then sipped from his glass.

"It's good." He tipped the glass toward Karen.

Karen rolled her eyes and nodded. The waiter filled both glasses and offered to return with a description of the evening's specials.

"As I was saying—" she took a sip of the wine, her tongue gliding across her upper lip "—the internal investigation is what most people consider the autopsy. That's where we take an in situ inventory of the organs before we remove them, weigh them, and then examine them thoroughly. We are looking for signs of disease, trauma, or anything abnormal. Once we examine the organs, we then collect samples from each for microscopic examinations."

"And that's it, aside from the toxicology?"

"No. When we finish with our report, we have to take into account what the death investigation finds. That's typically handled by a police agency that is in charge of that other 'scene', the location of death. Once we get that report, we incorporate it into our findings and issue a final autopsy report. That's when we release the cause and manner of death."

"Like homicide?"

"Like homicide, suicide, accidental, or undetermined. And we'll typically accompany that with the contributing or causal factors. Those could be a cardiac arrest, asphyxia, blunt force traum—"

"Drug overdose."

"Yes." Karen nodded. "Drug overdose." She looked down at her iPad and tapped it twice before running a finger along the center of the screen.

"So now that I've completed Autopsy 101," Holt said, "what's on that iPad?"

"We haven't completed the autopsy. It's still in the preliminary phase."

"What are you waiting on?" Holt took another swig of his wine.

"Toxicology isn't back. And neither is the death investigator's report."

"So what's the preliminary cause?"

"Overdose."

"Even without the toxicology?"

"There are signs."

"Like track marks?"

"Among other things."

"C'mon, Karen," Holt smirked. "Quit being coy."

"I thought you liked that," she zinged as the waiter returned and offered the night's specials. They both ordered from the menu.

"So you were talking about the signs of a drug addict," Holt said, refilling Karen's glass after the waiter walked away. She didn't protest.

"There are so many." She picked up the glass, waving it like a wand. "In this instance, the subject's liver was inflamed. That's a symptom of hepatitis, a common infectious disease contracted by intravenous drug users. Additionally, and more importantly, were the vascular issues."

"How so?"

"Repeated heroin use clogs the blood vessels supplying the lungs, liver, kidneys, and brain," she explained. "That's because whatever is in the heroin, the stuff that's not naturally part of the opiate, doesn't dissolve properly."

"And Horus—"

"The *subject*," she interrupted, her eyes looking down to the glowing red light on the digital recorder, "presented with all of these issues. Put that together with the track marks on his arms and feet, and it's a safe deduction he was a heroin addict."

"That leads you to conclude overdose?"

"There was also a remarkable arthritis in his elbows and ankles."

"Remarkable?"

"For someone his age, he shouldn't have suffered from that degree of inflammation in those joints. It's another side effect of the heroin use."

"Just because he was an addict," Holt countered, "it doesn't mean he overdosed. I could be a smoker and not die from lung cancer."

"True."

"So why the overdose determination?"

"We have some basic information from the death investigation, despite not having the report." Karen took her napkin and dabbed the cloth on either side of her mouth.

"And?"

"There was a large amount of heroin at the location," she answered. "He had a needle in his arm. There was drug paraphernalia strewn about the location. I could go on…"

"You're not telling me anything the police haven't already said publicly." Holt poured the remainder of the wine into his glass. "Aside from the clogged arteries and the arthritis."

Karen's eyes narrowed behind her frames. She pushed them up the bridge of her nose without taking her eyes off Holt's. Her expression was unchanged, but Holt sensed she was telling him to keep asking questions.

"What about the female companion?" he pressed.

"What about her?"

"Did she leave any evidence?"

"Finally." Karen pulled the glass to her lips and smiled. "You're asking the right questions." She took a sip from the glass. "Order another bottle."

CHAPTER 10

THE WHITE HOUSE
WASHINGTON, DC

Felicia Jackson stood in front of the mirror, fixing her hair. She glanced at her husband's reflection over her shoulder. "I don't have much time. I have a press conference."

"I don't know why tonight should be any different," he bemoaned, stepping to within a few inches of her. He put his hands on her hips and she flinched.

"Really?" Her blue eyes were icier with every passing moment; she rolled them and returned her attention to styling her jet black, shoulder-length hair. "Passive aggression doesn't suit you."

"We need to talk about this," he pressed, pulling his hands from her hips and moving them to her shoulders. He squeezed gently. "You're going to Camp David and then straight to Barcelona."

"I'm glad you at least pay attention to my daily schedule advisories." She shrugged herself free of his hands.

"I spoke to Chapa," he said, lowering his voice.

"What?" Jackson whipped around to face her husband. She was a good six inches shorter than the First Husband, but she was glaring down at him nonetheless. "Why? You were supposed to cease all communication with him after the inauguration. That was the deal. You know all the communication in the White House is logged. It's all public record."

"We met at Crystal Thai," he said, "near our loft on Clarendon."

"Seriously? In person? At a place where you're well known? What were you *thinking*? For a neurosurgeon, you're an idiot sometimes."

His shoulders shrank and he stepped back from her, shoving his hands into his pants pockets. "I don't like your choice of words," he countered flatly. "I picked a place where my presence would appear normal, where nobody would care, and where there wouldn't be any cameras."

"You didn't need to pick any place. You were supposed to cease contact. We cannot be connected to Chapa anymore. Not at all."

"He wanted to be certain his name would never be attached to anything."

"Attached to anything?"

"I assured him there wouldn't be any questions. That he is, for all intents and purposes, invisible."

"On whose authority?" The president folded her arms and stepped into her husband's space.

"I assumed I had the latitude to make that promise given the previous arrangement."

"Chapa was paid. You were paid. I made certain…concessions. That was years ago, and that was where the previous arrangement started and stopped."

"Understood, Felicia," he said, shaking his head. "I get his concern. All of these threads, regardless of how tangential they might be, tie together."

"How naïve *are* you?" she sneered, turning her back on him to face the mirror again. "If there weren't questions then, or questions after the bombing, why would there be questions now? Have you thought of that?"

"I—"

"Has Chapa thought of that?"

"He—"

"Good lord. There's a joke that brain surgery ain't rocket science. It's more on the nose than I'd have thought."

"What's happened to you?"

Felicia Jackson looked at her husband's reflection and the nauseated frown on his face.

"Less than a year ago we were good, Felicia. We spent time together. We liked each other's company. I…."

"You what?"

"I loved you."

The president started to turn around to face her husband, but she stopped herself. She plucked at the part in her hair.

"Don't kid yourself," she said, staring into her own eyes. "This marriage hasn't been the same since we left South Carolina. You and your buddy Chapa saw to that."

He laughed incredulously. "Chapa and me? That's rich. Because *your* need for power had nothing to do with any of this, right?"

"Tell yourself whatever helps you sleep at night," she hissed.

"Sure thing, Madam President." He snapped a mocking salute, spun on his heel, and marched out of the room. Felicia could hear his steps bounding down the hall of the residence.

"I hope you enjoyed the curried chicken," she called after him, instantly regretting the tone of the longest conversation they'd had in weeks.

She bit the inside of her lip until the pressure hurt. It wasn't much of a mea culpa.

They were both right; they were both wrong. The relationship had soured after her inauguration, after their move from the loft to the White House. But the slow decay of the marriage had begun long before that. When she ran for office, he was a proud advocate.

He beamed the night she won her congressional seat all those years ago and, without her asking, he gave up his practice to follow her to DC. They kept a condo in their home district and bought another inside the Beltway.

As she collected favors and made enemies, they drifted farther and farther apart. He was there to counsel her and have dinner warm when she ate at home. He tried. She knew he'd tried.

But his distaste for her style of governance was evident. He stopped attending banquets and parties. He avoided Capitol Hill. He retreated into his own world, playing golf and reading political thrillers.

"If somebody wrote a book about what you've done," he told her, looking over his reading glasses on their second night in the West Wing, "nobody would believe it. The way you've ascended to power is diabolical. Frankly, Felicia, it's too ridiculous to be plausible."

That was the last night they shared a bed. Though he later apologized and made efforts to repair the damage, it was too late for her.

The apple, as it were, was rotten.

Felicia Jackson took a deep breath, pinched her cheeks, and forced a smile. The press was waiting.

*

"It's a little late for a press conference, isn't it?" the slender, chain-smoking White House reporter for *The Huffington Post* asked Brandon Goodman as the corps gathered in the press room at the edge of the West Wing.

Goodman smiled without saying anything, his dimples digging into his cheeks for effect.

"We're hearing that a traffic accident in Virginia includes a national security component," the reporter said. "US Marshals are involved. The scene is secured. The airspace over it is closed. Kinda strange, huh?"

"It's a little late for background, isn't it?" Goodman replied. "Why don't you take your seat. The president's about to come out."

The reporter cleared her throat of phlegm, rolled her eyes, and slinked back to her seat in the third row. That seat indicated her perceived cachet among the White House press corps. It was better than some, not as good as others.

Goodman looked across the room, noticed all of the regular seats among the seven permanent rows of seats were filled, and the cameras along the back row were manned, as were those along the left side of the room. He gave a thumbs-up to the assembled media and then turned to wave the president into the briefing.

A cacophony of camera shutter clicks filled the space as Felicia Jackson took to the blue lectern at the front of the room. She tugged at the bottom of her smart black suit jacket, straightening it. She smiled and acknowledged a couple of the network correspondents seated in the front row.

"Good evening, everyone," she began. "Thank you for joining us on short notice and late in the day. This is an urgent matter I thought was best to handle immediately and with candor.

"Earlier today"—she worked her eyes around the room, paying attention to the intensity of the reporters' faces—"a US Marshal Service vehicle transporting a high-value prisoner was attacked en route from one federal pretrial facility to another."

President Jackson paused to accommodate the murmurs in the room. Younger reporters were tweeting on their phones, the older ones scribbling notes on pads.

"The US Marshal Service, as many of you know, is responsible for the transportation of more than one thousand prisoner movements each day under the Justice Prisoner and Alien Transportation System, otherwise known as JPATS," the president said from memory, her voice low and measured. "They do an outstanding job of working hand in hand with the Department of Justice, and I'd personally like to thank all of our deputy marshals and their families for the dedicated service to our nation.

"The ambush-style attack was well coordinated and our early intelligence suggests professionally managed. I have tasked the directors of our various national security agencies to determine the group or groups responsible. And I can tell you, without equivocation, these cowards will be brought to justice." The president took a deep breath, inhaling the last of the calm before the storm.

"In the course of the attack, the entirety of the escort team, which consisted of three deputy marshals, and the lone prisoner were killed. The prisoner was Sir Spencer Thomas, who was awaiting trial for the bombing of the US Capitol building some nine months ago."

The room exploded, the reporters restless and uncontrollable in their seats as they strained to gain the attention of the president. Phones vibrated, laptop keyboards clacked, and murmurs rumbled throughout the room.

President Jackson raised her hand to silence the mob aching to light her on fire with its argumentative, inflammatory statements disguised as questions. "Before I take any questions, I'll finish telling you what my aides have told me; then I will turn it over to the director of the US Marshal Service, who will provide background about the three deputies involved."

The rumble subsided. The president looked over to Goodman, who managed a reassuring nod.

"The attack was brutal," President Jackson said, referencing her notes for the first time, being careful to stick to the precise language upon which she, Goodman, and two speechwriters had agreed minutes earlier. "The attackers were in four vehicles. We understand they essentially 'boxed in' the transport vehicle so that it could not move. Armed men emerged from the vehicles and opened fire on the transport vehicle. At some point, an explosive device or devices were used to gain access to the interior of the transport vehicle. Everyone inside the vehicle was executed. They were dead when emergency responders arrived at the scene. Now I will take questions." She pointed at her favorite network correspondent. "Jake, go ahead."

"Madam President, why do you think Sir Spencer Thomas was targeted, and who do you think is responsible?"

"As I indicated," she said, "we don't yet know who is responsible. No group or organization has claimed responsibility. We hope to have a good handle on who was involved within the coming days."

"Why was he targeted?"

"I didn't say he was targeted, Jake." President Jackson glared at him for a moment and then turned to point to another reporter. "Anne, from the *Times*."

"If he was the only prisoner," Anne pressed, "then isn't it a safe assumption he was targeted? Given his high value and the proximity of his trial, shouldn't there have been more security around him? Is this a lapse in judgment akin to that of the Secret Service during the Obama administration?"

"That's three questions, Anne," President Jackson bristled. "I'll take them one at a time. No. No. No," she replied, counting off on her fingers. "Next question. Bob?"

"How can you suggest this is not a lapse in either judgment or security given what happened?" asked Bob, a longtime White House correspondent. His seat was front row and center, and the president respected him.

President Jackson gripped either side of the lectern tightly. "Bob, we don't know what happened. We don't yet have enough information to call this…" She paused to choose the right word.

"A terrorist attack, Madam President?" Bob said helpfully. "I mean, can't we be frank about this? That's what it was."

"Bob, I was unaware of your security clearance or your expertise in the subject matter," President Jackson responded. "A Pulitzer does not an intelligence analyst make."

"In all fairness," Bob said, "you told us you'd speak with candor. That's not what this is."

"This is also not a debate, Bob," the president snapped. "I am giving you information. I'm not going to speculate. I'm not offering supposition. I will repeat, we are working diligently to ferret out the facts and use them to lead to whoever is responsible for the violence. I do think this attack"—the president raised a finger and waved it at the cameras in the back of the room"—regardless of the motive or group responsible, underscores the necessity of the SECURITY Act currently under discussion in Congress. Electronic intelligence is more critical than ever in our effort to prevent violence against our citizens. Valuable tools were stripped from our arsenal when key elements of the PATRIOT act expired and the NSA lost its ability to conduct wide-net surveillance."

"Isn't it true," Bob asked without an invitation, "that parts of the SECURITY Act essentially nullify the Fourth Amendment?"

"Nullify is an overstatement," President Jackson said, shaking her head. "The Bill of Rights is unaffected by this. There are four other Western nations, all part of the G12, who are considering nearly identical legislation. This is a global effort at peace.

"What we are hoping to achieve with these new capabilities, should my colleagues in the House and Senate see the light and pass the legislation, is an opportunity to better protect our people. What greater responsibility does a government have than to keep its citizenry safe? Had the PATRIOT Act not been castrated years ago, had Edward Snowden not devastated our electronic surveillance, maybe we could have prevented the attack on the Capitol. Maybe our economy wouldn't be teetering. Maybe the global marketplace would be more stable. Maybe unemployment would be at manageable levels."

"That's a—" Bob started before the president cut him off.

"*Huffington Post*, your turn."

"We have information that the scene was quickly secured," said the slender chain-smoker, the rasp in her voice distracting. "And that the airspace within a five-mile radius was closed below five thousand feet. Can you confirm that? And if it is true, why?"

President Jackson looked over at her National Security Advisor, who offered a subtle nod. Goodman followed.

"Yes," she answered, speaking slowly and minding the adrenaline, "the alert activated by the deputy marshals triggered a rapid response. We were able to locate and address the scene quickly. A secure perimeter was established. I am told, as you can imagine, containing the scene and preserving any evidence is paramount. That is also the reason for the restricted airspace."

"It wasn't to prevent cameras?" asked the *HuffPost* puffer.

"No. I'm a firm believer in the Constitution and the First Amendment. All right—" President Jackson forced a smile "—last question. Gary at the *Post*. Go ahead."

"How might this affect your Barcelona trip?" he asked. "Any additional security concerns?"

"There's no impact, Gary," she said. "We already have an advance team on the ground there, planning ahead. As for specific security changes, that's above my pay grade."

The reporters laughed.

"I'm still headed there for what I know will be critical meetings as it relates to the world economy and our relationship with the European Union," she added. "I've got a quick trip to Camp David, of which I'm sure you're aware, where we'll prep for the G12 meetings. But again, no alterations as far as I'm concerned. We have the people's business to do. That's it for the questions. I'll turn it over now to the director of the US Marshal Service. Thank you all for coming."

The president turned to her right and swiftly strode past her team and into the recesses of the West Wing. She ignored the volley of questions tossed at her as she left.

*

NEAR THURMONT, MARYLAND

Despite the darkness of the night, Sir Spencer recognized the secure location as soon as the armored Suburban rolled up to the gatehouse at the only entrance to the wooded and fenced facility in Catoctin Mountain Park, Maryland.

"Ah," he said, elbowing the bearded operator. "I know where we are. Shangri-La, as it were."

"You've been here?" The operator's left eyebrow arced higher than the right.

"A few times," said Sir Spencer, rubbing his hands together. "None of them official visits, you know."

"Of course not." The operator rolled his eyes. He handed Sir Spencer a pair of dark glasses and a Washington Nationals baseball cap.

"How ridiculous."

"You said yourself how recognizable you are," replied the operator. "Let's mitigate that as much as possible."

The facility was under the joint operation of the United States Navy and the Central Intelligence Agency. Its official name was Naval Support Facility Thurmont, and it was as secure a location as was possible at the moment.

A Marine stepped from the gatehouse and the driver rolled down his window, offering his identification and clearance information. The Marine, in his blue dress uniform, peeked his head inside, shining a flashlight at each of the faces in the vehicle.

"Just the three of you, sir?" The Marine stood straight, examining the paperwork as he spoke.

"Yes," the driver responded.

"Thank you, sir." The Marine returned the documents. "I'll need you to drive directly to the barracks at the rear of the property. You'll drive straight ahead, continuing straight at a four-way intersection. You'll pass the lighted tennis courts on the left, a parking lot on your right, and the barracks will appear on the left. You'll find an escort waiting for you. He will direct you to the proper location."

The driver rolled up the window and accelerated slowly along the narrow road. Occasional streetlights provided the only glimpse of the century-old trees lining the asphalt on either side.

"When were you here last?" the operator asked Sir Spencer without looking at him.

Sir Spencer rubbed his chin, considering his most recent visit. "It's hard to remember. It may have been after Osama Bin Laden was killed. Your agency needed a new villain. We worked hard to create one."

"Create one?"

"Really?" Sir Spencer chuckled. "You know how these things work. Well, I certainly hope you do. I always assumed you operators were as much a part of the charade as the rest of us."

"I don't—"

"Today's friend is tomorrow's enemy," Sir Spencer counseled. "Today's enemy might be tomorrow's friend. It's a game played by every nation in the world. Do you really think Vladimir Putin went from threat, to ally, to legitimate threat again in a matter of a decade?"

"I—"

"Of course not. He was always a threat. We just made the world believe until we couldn't anymore that he was our ally. It had to be that way post-9/11."

The operator scratched his beard, both eyebrows knitted together. Even in the dark, Sir Spencer could see the wheels grinding.

"Chris Osman ring a bell?" Sir Spencer asked, adjusting the sunglasses.

"Bin Laden's agency handle?"

"Yes." Sir Spencer nodded. "Did he go from CIA asset to American enemy? Or did we make everyone believe he did? Was Saddam Hussein really a threat to our security? Of course not. It was about the oil. It was about the perception that we were doing something about terrorism."

"What's your point?"

"My point is"—Sir Spencer rubbed his wrist, wincing against the bruise—"I was here last to help create the next persona non grata. Good cannot exist without evil. We provide the balance. The yin and the yang. Bin Laden existed as an enemy because we made him one. North Korea is a threat to democracy because we act like it is. Iran is the flavor of the month. It's amazing to me the American people don't see it. Nobody in the Western world sees it, for that matter. They just choose to believe the pablum we feed them."

"You're a lunatic," the operator mumbled, turning away from his charge to look out the window at the darkness whirring past them.

"Without the crazy," Sir Spencer replied, "the sane are irrelevant. I'm disappointed someone of your skill was so blind to the way things work. Maybe I've said too much."

"I do my job," said the operator. "I protect my nation. I don't ask why. I just do it."

"And therein lies the beauty of it all," chided Spencer, content to let the operator squirm and scratch his beard.

The Suburban slowed near the glow of a parking lot to its right. In the middle of the two-lane road stood a Marine waving a flashlight. He was directing the driver to the lot, pointing and waving until the SUV swung to the right and into an empty spot.

A third Marine stepped to the side of the SUV as the men opened the doors and stepped out into the damp cool of the

Maryland night. Sir Spencer took note of the man's youth. He could have been no more than twenty years old.

"We have space for you in Linden," the Marine said, his back ramrod straight as he stood at attention. "I'll be escorting you there. It's a short walk from here."

"Lead the way," said the operator. He gestured for Sir Spencer to follow their liaison.

The path was narrow but short. It led directly from the northeastern edge of the parking lot to a grouping of cabins, each lit with the soft yellow glow of their door lights. They passed two of the cabins on the right before finding Linden on the left, a wooden plaque engraved with its name in white paint.

"This is Linden," announced the Marine, his flashlight pointing at the vented front door. "You'll find what you need inside, sir."

Sir Spencer thanked the Marine, climbed the two concrete steps to the door, pulled it open, and walked into the dark confines of the cabin. He reached to his right, his hands wiping the roughhewn wall until he found a light switch. He flipped on the light and took stock of his surroundings. They were better than a federal penitentiary, but paled in comparison to the Hay-Adams.

The operator stood in the doorway, leaning against the jamb. "I'll be outside if you need anything."

"I'll be fine," said Sir Spencer without turning around. "No need for a child minder."

"You don't have a choice," said the operator. "Neither do I." He stepped back onto the concrete step and closed the door, its springs creaking resistance as it slammed shut.

"*A Deo et Rege*," Sir Spencer whispered to himself. "From God and the King."

*

WASHINGTON, DC

Matti was asleep at her desk, her forehead on the edge of the laminate wood, when a knock at her door woke her from her nap. It wasn't until the second set of raps that she responded.

"Yes?" she called, clearing her throat. "It's unlocked. Come in."

Matti rubbed her eyes and tried to squeeze the sleep from them as the door opened. It was Brandon Goodman. He leaned into the doorway without stepping into the room.

"You okay?" he asked, his eyes narrow with concern. "You don't look good."

"I was just sleeping. Trouble sleeping lately. Just dozed off for a minute."

"Uh-huh." His tone told Matti he didn't buy it, but he didn't probe. "I need to know if you're still headed to Camp David. We're leaving first thing in the morning."

"Of course," she answered through a yawn. "Why wouldn't I be going?"

"You weren't the most engaged person in the meeting," he answered. "And the president seems to think you're a bit off."

"I'm fine," Matti insisted. "I'll be ready to go in the morning."

"Okay then. We're taking Marine One at oh-seven-hundred. Are you staying here tonight or going home to Baltimore?"

"I'll stay here," Matti said. She'd kept her place in Charm City despite moving to the White House from the NSA. The president insisted she move inside the Beltway, but Matti wanted to hold on to some sense of normalcy. "I've got a change of clothes. I'm good."

"Might want to get some coffee too," Goodman suggested. "And a shot of adrenaline. Your input, especially as it relates to problem solving, is critical as we get ready for Barcelona. Got it?"

"Yes, sir."

Goodman said goodnight and closed the door as he left. Matti got up from her desk and stretched, turning her head toward a bookshelf on the wall opposite her desk. Her eyes caught a familiar slim blue book nestled between books written by Robert Gates and Michael H. Hart.

She inhaled deeply and stepped over to the shelf, pulling the book by its narrow spine. It was a journal with no markings on the outside. Matti pulled it to her chest, cradling it with her arms folded across it, and sat back down at her desk. She carefully placed the journal in front of her and dusted off the cover before cracking it open.

She ran a finger down the outer margin, feeling the indention of the hurried script, noting the fervor with which the barely legible words were written.

"Spencer Thomas," wrote the author, *"is a megalomaniac. He has conceived this violent plot to overthrow a government he believes is ill-equipped to serve its people. I know that our path as a nation has strayed from one that is truly righteous and abiding of the constitution. He is misguided.*

"For years," the author scribbled, *"I have gone along with the idea that we could effect change at the highest levels of government. Never did I envision violence. The greasing of palms and the quid pro quo of political favor was murky enough for me. I did not sign up for murder."*

The author was Bill Davidson, the former attorney general of the United States, a conspirator in the Capitol bomb attack, and the man who'd given her a stack of journals as a parting gift before he killed himself.

Matti saw it as an act of contrition; a realization he'd strayed from his core beliefs into a dark work clouded by angry rhetoric and violent deeds. He'd entrusted her with the journals in an effort to prevent the attacks. They detailed years of thoughts, activities, meetings, phone numbers, bank account tracking information, and more. Despite its value, it hadn't worked.

Matti offered the entirety of them to her boss at the NSA. He'd taken them in the days after the attack. They were part of the record during the congressional hearings at which Matti testified. There were twelve of them submitted as evidence.

Matti kept the thirteenth for herself on the shelf in her White House office. It was so conspicuous, nobody ever noticed it. Matti couldn't be sure anyone even suspected it was missing.

She licked her finger and carefully flipped backward in the book, skimming pages. She'd read most of these notes and missives before. This was a ritual of sorts: Matti replaying her failure in her mind, searching for clues, patterns, codes hidden in Davidson's diatribes.

"Sir Spencer tells us the endgame is regime change," Davidson had written. *"He tells us that the founding fathers were heroes to us and terrorists to the British. The man convicted of blowing up Pan Am Flight 103 was a terrorist to us. But when the Scottish released him from prison, the Libyans rejoiced in the*

streets. He contends that the line between patriotism and terrorism is all in the eye of the beholder."

Matti flipped back some more. There were addresses, a note about his prostitute girlfriend, a mention about a meeting at the Cato Street Pub. There was also a passage about a journalist named Dillinger Holt.

According to Davidson's notes, Holt appeared on the television news program *Constitution Avenue* with host Vickie Lupo minutes before she interviewed Davidson on the day President Dexter Foreman died at his desk.

"Dillinger Holt," he wrote, *"reporter at a website called PlausibleDeniability.info, sounds smart. He's not the typical bombastic self-promoter Lupo likes to have on the program. Get his number. He might be of use, should higher levels be interested."*

Matti read the passage again.

Matti, an eideteker who could memorize vast amounts of information, was a speed reader. She closed the journal and opened it at the first page. She placed her index finger at the top of the page and, as she ran it down the center of the text, scanned for the phrase "higher level".

Even in the fog of her prescriptively altered mind, she knew something was odd about that characterization. Bill Davidson was an attorney by trade, a lawyer who chose his words carefully. He wouldn't have chosen those particular words without intending them.

There was something there. Something she'd missed. Something that could redeem her now. Matti scanned page after page, reading each page more quickly. And then she found it.

How could she not have seen it?

*

The assassin sat on the edge of her bed, the room service table pulled close. The plate was empty, except for the red liquid pooled in the center. She took a doughy roll from the basket on the table and tore it in half, dipping one end into the juice and sopping up as much as the bread could hold.

She pressed the bread to her lips and sucked. She closed her eyes, tasting the salty residue on her tongue. It was satiating.

The assassin had long thought the red liquid that leaked from an undercooked steak was blood. She enjoyed the sight of it spilling onto her plate as she cut into the meat. There was something sacrificial about it.

But even after she learned the liquid was a mixture of water and a protein called myoglobin, and not blood, she held onto the belief that somehow she was freeing the beef of its soul in a ritualistic, serrated slaughter. It was an exsanguination.

Having sopped the remainder of the juice into the bread, and having sucked it dry, she poured herself a glass of water and bowed her head in prayer. Her eyes pressed together, her hands raised above her head, she spoke.

"Blessed are the eyes that see what you see," she hummed. "For I tell you that many prophets and kings wanted to see what you see but did not see it, and to hear what you hear but did not hear it. You, brothers and sisters, are not in darkness so that this day should surprise you like a thief. You are all children of the light and children of the day. We do not belong to the night or to the darkness. So then, let us not be like others, who are asleep, but let us be awake and sober. For those who sleep, sleep at night, and those who get drunk, get drunk at night."

The assassin licked her lips, interlocked her thumbs, and flapped her hands as though they were wings. She inhaled until her lungs were full and then she slowly exhaled. This was a ritual the assassin repeated after every meal.

She pushed away from the table and reached for the television remote, pushing the power button as she slid back onto the unmade bed. She looked at the clock on her bedside table. It was after midnight. The day's cable news programs were repeating their earlier broadcasts. She skipped past them to a music channel.

One music video was ending and another beginning, the rhythmic beats of the two songs mixed as the screen dissolved from one artist to the next. The assassin was half paying attention, her thumb on the remote, until she heard a familiar tempo stylized by most East Coast hip-hop artists.

The screen was black, except for a pyramid of bright blue light that pulsed with the thump of the artificial 808 drumbeat. Slowly, from the light, emerged a shadow of a man. He was cloaked and hooded in cerulean blue. In his left hand was a large cane.

The light transitioned from blue to red, the man's robe taking on a purple hue as the thick strum of a bass guitar joined the drum. The assassin knew the song. She'd seen the video before. She was nonetheless transfixed.

The man on the screen held up his right hand, his fingers spread wide and his palm facing the camera as he lifted his head. In the center of his palm was an eye. Its iris was red, the pupil dilating with the beat of the music.

The camera zoomed in slowly to the man and he started to rap. The hood was still on his head, but his left eye was visible through the shadow it cast on his face. The assassin turned up the volume.

> *From the darkness it comes,*
> *the snake in a dream, unseen*
> *so real, revealed,*
> *to me in the gutter*
> *don't clutter your thoughts*
> *'cause it will consume you*
> *and ruin you*
> *The all-knowing slither*
> *come hither*
> *don't ask questions just go*
> *give your soul for the gold*
> *and the fame it's the same*
> *as taking a bite from the apple*
> *in the garden of Eden*
> *I'm pleadin' to release me from this*
> *I need peace from this not a piece of this.*
> *not a taste, not a bite,*
> *venom.*

The assassin sat unblinkingly as the pyramid of light turned white and unglued the screen when the chorus began. The rapper's voice was replaced with what sounded like a Gregorian chant.

> *The venom, the venom, seeps through the vellum.*
> *It facilitates bedlam and tremendous momentum.*
> *From order comes chaos,*

From chaos comes the lesson.
The poison will save you.
Succumb to the venom.

The bright light dissolved, revealing the cloaked man in the middle of a windswept desert. He was standing on the middle of a dune, alone, but there were two sets of footprints leading to him. He was still holding the cane in his left hand, his head cloaked in the hood, as he recited the second verse. He raised his hands and the cane above his head as the refrain began again. He slowly dissolved into the sand, melting into the dune.

The assassin laughed at the absurdity of it, the overdone transparency of the symbology. She wondered, for an instant, why the masses failed to see it. Then, just as quickly, she remembered they were blind. They were unenlightened. Despite the ubiquitous pyramids, eyes, and colors all around them, the people could not conceive of the bigger picture. They were numb to it.

Horus took it a step too far. His music was too "on the nose". He tried to lift the veil, to warn the blind of the dangers ahead. That was unacceptable.

He wasn't the first to try. He wouldn't be the last. That was why she was who she was. That was why they relied on her, why they allowed her the power to silence those who challenged the order of things and threatened the greater good.

The assassin shook her head at the television and turned it off. She needed sleep and she had a sense that her next mission would begin soon.

CHAPTER 11

THE GALLERIA
HOUSTON, TEXAS

Dillinger Holt was sitting at the desk in his hotel room. It was close to two o'clock in the morning.

"I don't know how reporters did their jobs without the Internet," he mumbled to himself, awash in the blue glow of his computer screen. His fingers typed another set of search words and he waited for the results to populate. It took an instant.

FBI Analyst Kills Self After Internal Investigation Found Wrongdoing

Holt copied the link to the two-year-old article and emailed it to himself. Then he read the highlights. He couldn't believe what he was reading. Despite the headline, there was more to the story than a guilt-ridden suicide.

> *Erik Majors, thirty-eight, of Alexandria, was found dead from an apparent drug overdose in his one-bedroom apartment. Majors, a systems analyst with the Federal Bureau of Investigation, was on unpaid leave during an internal audit of his work. Court documents filed the morning of his death charged him with violating the 1917 law prohibiting the sharing of classified information.*
>
> *Majors was found in his bed surrounded by drug paraphernalia, according to an unnamed source close to the investigation. The initial findings indicate he intentionally overdosed on an illicit drug believed to be heroin.*
>
> *However, the lead investigator said at a press conference late Monday, he could not rule out the possibility of foul play.*
>
> *"There are indications that despite Mr. Majors' state of mind," said Sergeant Kevin Boxell,*

"someone else may have played a role in his death. I'm not one hundred percent convinced he killed himself."

The FBI has declined comment on the case against Majors or his death. Court documents, however, reveal concern regarding the information Majors may have leaked, given his access to sensitive documents and operations.

Holt took a pair of earbuds connected to his voice recorder and put one of them in his right ear. He pressed play on the recorder and typed notes into his computer as he listened.

"There was the smallest trace of lipstick on Horus's ear," Karen's voice said. The sounds of the restaurant made it somewhat difficult for Holt to hear. "It wasn't much, but we swabbed it and tested for DNA."

Holt put the other earbud into his left ear and turned up the volume on the recorder.

"As a matter of procedure, we swabbed it and submitted it to CODIS," she said.

"That's the DNA database?" Holt heard himself ask. He didn't like the sound of his voice. It was higher pitched and not as masculine as it sounded in his head.

"Yes," Karen answered. "The Combined DNA Index System. The FBI runs it out of Virginia."

"You found something?"

"Yes. I think so."

"That quickly? The guy's been dead, like, three days. I thought DNA tests took weeks or months."

"With backlogs it can take that long. The testing itself takes anywhere from a couple of hours to four or five days. I know some people there at the lab, and they rushed it for me."

"What did they find?"

"They got a hit with a sample from a three-year-old case," Karen answered.

"Who was it?"

"There's no name attached with the hit," Karen said. "All CODIS has is the DNA profile, the name of the agency that worked the case, the specimen identification number, and the person who ran the original profile."

"No," said Holt. "I meant, what case."

"Oh. It was a drug overdose. Heroin. At first they thought it was a suicide, but they later ruled it a homicide. There was a fair amount of evidence at the scene that indicated someone forced the drugs into the victim's bloodstream."

"Just like Horus."

"Yes."

"So what does that mean?"

"You're the reporter," said Karen. "That's up to you to figure out."

"Who else knows there could be a killer out there?"

"Just my contact at the FBI lab and me, I assume. There was never an arrest in the case. Despite the match, there's no way of knowing whose DNA it is."

"So there's no investigation?"

"Well—" Karen sighed "—I would guess the original investigative agency, the Alexandria, Virginia, police department, would probably get a notification. Houston police will get a notification. So there could be one."

"How soon before HPD and Alexandria police get notified of the connection?"

"I don't know," she said. "HPD won't know anything until we turn over the official death report. I can't speak for Alexandria."

"You okay with me putting together a piece on this?"

"As long as you don't quote me," said Karen. "Just cite unnamed sources."

"Give me a second source."

"I just did. The FBI."

"They won't talk to me," Holt said. "Maybe Alexandria will."

"Maybe. And there's one more thing."

"What?"

"The information comes with a price."

Holt pulled the earbuds from his ears and stopped the digital recorder. He looked at his notes.

"I've got to call that sergeant with Alexandria in the morning," he murmured to himself until a voice from behind him startled him.

"Will you be here when I wake up?" Karen tugged the sheet up toward her neck. She was lying on her back, propped up by all four pillows on the bed.

"You scared me." He laughed, turning to face her.

"Sorry."

"You're awake," Holt said. "I'm here."

"You know what I mean," she purred.

"It's my room. I suspect I'll be here." His smile was genuine but laced with a hint of the devil that tempted Karen from her car, into the lobby, and up the elevator into his room. "I thought you were asleep."

"I was for a second. I can't believe I did this again." She pulled her hands to her face, covering it as she groaned. "I have no self-respect."

"I respect you," Holt said, having already turned back to his computer.

"Right."

"I do." He laughed, spinning in the chair to face her. "I respect that…that thing you did with your—"

"Shut. Up." Karen reached behind her head and lobbed one of the pillows at Holt. It hit him in the chest. "I should go."

"No." Holt stood from his chair and tossed the pillow back onto the bed as he climbed onto it with his knees. "Stay with me. I'll be here in the morning. I promise." He slid up next to her, resting his head next to hers.

"It's actually already morning," she said. "It's two o'clock. And I have to work. I should go."

"Sleep here. I'll lie here with you until you pass out."

"How thoughtful."

"No," he backtracked, "I mean, I've got some work I have to finish. I won't leave. I was a jerk for doing that last time."

"Yeah. You were."

"You like me anyway."

"Yeah. I do."

"Maybe you shouldn't go back to sleep just yet."

"Maybe I shouldn't."

CHAPTER 12

SOMEWHERE OVER SOUTHERN EUROPE

The first-class flight attendant couldn't keep her eyes off the man in 2D. He was incredibly attractive, strong, with perfect olive-colored skin. She imagined the definition of his muscles through his sheer linen shirt. His eyes, though. They were what gave her pause. There was something sinister in their darkness. It made her heart flutter against her chest, her pulse quicken as he scrolled through his iPad.

"Is he not ridiculously hot?" she asked her coworker.

"In a Vin Diesel kind of way," the friend answered.

She'd passed by him once after the plane reached altitude. His head was turned toward the window and she'd noticed a triangular tattoo at the top of his neck.

Could he be any sexier?

She stood at the front of the cabin, leaning against the edge of the galley. She lowered her chin and willed him to stare back at her. He was only one of three people in first class. The other was a couple in row four. They were asleep.

He looked up and she averted her eyes quickly. She knew, though, he'd caught her staring.

"May I refill your drink, Mr. Vasconselos?" she asked, bending at the waist to offer him more than a drink. "I thought you might be thirsty."

He looked up from the tablet and into her eyes. He was searching her soul, she was certain. Her cheeks flushed.

"*Por favor*," he said. "I would like another water. With gas."

"My pleasure, Mr. Vasconselos," she purred, leaning across his body to take his empty glass and wet napkin, purposely brushing her blouse against his arm.

"Anything else I could get you with your drink?" She pulled away, hoping her freshly applied citrus scent would appeal to him.

"You're American?" he asked without any inflection.

"Canadian." She smiled, her red lips drawn on wider than their natural boundaries. "Toronto."

The hunk nodded, his mouth turned down at the corners. He looked down at his tablet, perhaps signaling his lack of interest. The flight attendant took what she perceived as a hint and returned to the galley to refill his drink.

After dropping in some fresh ice and topping the glass with Pellegrino, she adjusted herself, hoping she'd be more likely to quench his thirst than the refill. Checking her reflection in her iPhone, she smacked her lips and pinched her cheeks before returning to 2D.

"Here you go, Mr. Vasconselos." She smiled as she set down the glass on his armrest. "Is it too forward for me to ask you if you're traveling for pleasure or business?"

"What's the difference?" he asked without looking up from the iPad. He was scrolling through a news website, using the airplane's Wi-Fi service to connect to the Internet.

"Uh," she gulped her awkward response, "I guess it depends on what you consider pleasure and what you consider business." She shrugged, a hint of double entendre in her smile.

"*Es verdad*," he said. "You speak the truth."

"You should stop by and see me." Enough game playing. He was either uninterested or oblivious, she figured. "I'm right on the water. Really nice hotel."

"Really?" His eyes shot up from the iPad. "Which hotel?"

"The Eurostars Marina. It's right on the pier next to the World Trade Cen—"

"I'm familiar with it," he said. "It looks like a cruise ship?"

"Yes!" Her eyes lit up. "That's the one. I have two days before I have to fly to—"

"I'll stop by tomorrow," he cut in. "We could have breakfast."

"You could stop by tonight," she said, leaning in, making sure his eyes saw her assets pressed together beneath her strategically unbuttoned uniform blouse. "We could still have breakfast tomorrow."

"I could do that." He looked up from her assets and into her eyes. She lost her breath in the darkness of them. There was something wild or reckless hidden beneath the surface.

"Give me your hand," she said and pulled his left hand toward her, gently unfolding his fingers. His hands were enormous, his fingers smooth, his manicure perfect. She pulled a pen clipped to her blouse and wrote on his hand. "I really don't do this. Ever," she lied as she scribbled her name and cell phone number onto his palm. "I just find you so incredibly attractive. I'd love to get to know more about you."

"That's very kind of you," he said, his eyes flitting between his palm and her eyes. "I find you attractive and I'd like to get to know more about you too." There was something odd in the way he said it. It was as if he was parroting her without understanding the meaning of the words. She ignored it, choosing to anticipate his hands on her body.

She giggled, feeling the warmth return to her cheeks.

"*Señorita?*" 4B called out. "*Café, por favor?*"

The flight attendant smiled and nodded at 4B. "*Sí, señor, un momento.*"

"I'll see you tonight, Mr. Vasconselos." Her hand trailed along his arm and she returned to the galley to brew fresh coffee for 4B.

She had no idea what she'd done.

CHAPTER 13

NEAR THURMONT, MARYLAND

There was nothing to occupy Sir Spencer other than his imagination. He was freed from federal prison, but the cabin in the woods was every bit a cell. He lay on the bed, more plush than he'd felt in months, and stared at the roughhewn ceiling before closing his eyes to think.

His mind drifted from what was to come to what had been. He thought of his attorney, Braxton P. Mayhew, and the conversation they'd had shortly after he was imprisoned.

Mayhew was all business then. "Do not talk to other inmates," he'd warned as they sat across from each other in a visitation room.

"I'm in solitary." Sir Spencer laughed.

"Do not talk to family members or anyone who visits you. The conversations in the visitation room are frequently recorded and used as evidence," advised the attorney.

"I've no family nor expected visitors."

"So let's talk about your alleged co-conspirators." Mayhew nodded, his eyes fixed on his client. "Jimmy Ings isn't talking. He's too loyal to you, despite whatever happened at Arlington. And much of the physical evidence points to him. The explosives, the meeting place, pretty much everything has his hands on it."

Sir Spencer ran his tongue across his teeth. "As it was intended to be."

"Secretary Blackmon has also retained counsel and isn't speaking," said Mayhew. "He's in a federal facility in Miami. I don't expect him to be an issue."

"Nor do I," said Sir Spencer. "He's the only one who blew up the Capitol."

"Bill Davidson—"

"Is dead," Sir Spencer cut in.

"Art Thistlewood is squealing like a pig," Mayhew continued. "He's spilling everything he knows. We have people who can neutralize the threat."

"Ha!" The knight laughed. "I assumed we did. If you'd told me we didn't, I'd have neutralized you and we'd have found someone else."

"So that leaves young George Edwards," said the lawyer, unamused by Sir Spencer's threat. "He could be tricky."

"How so?"

"My contacts within the bureau tell me there may be credible surveillance linking you to Edwards—photographs, phone recordings.

"Not an issue." Sir Spencer shook his head. "It's circumstantial and, given that Edwards is a United States citizen, the eavesdropping might be illegal. There's so much NSA backlash, I'm confident you'll get it tossed."

"There's another problem with Edwards."

"Which is?"

"We don't know where he is at the moment." Mayhew shifted in his plastic seat.

"Come again?" Sir Spencer's eyes narrowed.

"Well—" Mayhew cleared his throat again "—you're each being held in separate locations."

"So?"

"Ings is in the Arlington County Jail," Mayhew answered. "They've sent Thistlewood to the Big Sandy facility in Kentucky. You're here at Lee. They'll transfer you to another facility shortly. Probably Chesapeake."

"I'm not concerned with myself. Where is Edwards? Any fool with an iPhone and a wireless connection can find federal prisoners."

"Sir Spencer"—the lawyer's tone was sharper and frustrated—"I am aware of that. I know how the system works and how it doesn't work."

"Not well enough," Sir Spencer chided before licking a bleeding crack on his lower lip.

"They're using a pseudonym," said Mayhew. "They've disguised his identity."

"Why would they do that with him and not with the others?"

"There could be a host of reasons." The lawyer shrugged. "Other than Davidson, who's dead, he was the most well-known among you. His art sells for ridiculous sums of money and is likely to sell for even more now. It could be that. Or…"

"Or what, Mayhew?!" Sir Spencer slammed his fists onto the table. The lawyer jumped back in surprise.

"Or, since he knew everything you knew, they're protecting him from you."

"I find that fascinating."

"Why?"

"Because George Edwards certainly did not know everything I knew. He does not know everything I know. And because you think they can protect him from me. From us?"

"I'm just saying that—"

"We led a self-loathing band of misfits to murder hundreds of people when one assassination would have accomplished the same result. We manipulated cabinet members and the former head of the Department of Justice to betray their instincts and destroy a powerful symbol of democracy. We put a bullet into a perfectly beautiful courtesan. Do you really think anyone can protect George Edwards from us?"

"Us?" the attorney asked, his eyes dancing with confusion. "Who's us?"

"Oh, Mayhew." Sir Spencer laughed. "Really now. I thought you knew. I really did. Open your eyes. Just open your eyes."

Now Sir Spencer opened his eyes. Studying the wooden beam stretching across the vaulted ceiling, he decided what needed to happen next. He would tell his host upon arrival. It was urgent. If they were to continue with their plan, with the next steps in the grand scheme so many decades in the making, Art Thistlewood and George Edwards needed to die.

*

WASHINGTON, DC

Matti checked her watch. She had a couple of hours before Marine One was wheels up from the South Lawn. She pulled a laptop from her messenger bag and plugged in the air card that allowed her Internet access without going through the White House router. She didn't need anyone knowing what she was doing.

She was a YouTube addict, having spent countless hours with a mouse in one hand and an ice-cream-laden spoon in the other.

From the ridiculously mind-numbing to the educational and thought-provoking, she couldn't get enough of the endless offerings.

One video would lead to another and to another. Eventually, she'd find herself watching uploads on the most random subjects. Getting lost in YouTube was like a stream of video consciousness. She wondered how the site calculated its algorithms to offer its related recommendations.

Matti went to the site and typed "Bohemian Grove" into the search bar. A list of eighty-two thousand videos populated the list underneath the video box. She scrolled down until she found a video she'd previously seen. It was highlighted in purple.

She clicked on the link. The video described the twenty-seven-hundred-acre retreat north of San Francisco. It was a summer camp of sorts for rich and powerful men. It was invitation only and carried with it rumors of Gnosticism and simulated human sacrifice.

The Grove was the summer getaway of the Bohemian Club's estimated twenty-five hundred members. For two weeks each July, they would descend upon the private encampment hidden in the redwood forest.

There were countless references to the Bohemian Grove and the club that ran it as Satanic or anti-Christian. There was a secretly recorded video shot in 2000 that purportedly showed what was called a "Cremation of Care" ritual, in which a "sacrifice" was offered at the base of a forty-five-foot-tall stone owl. Some contended that much of what occurred in the Grove was sexual in nature.

Matti even came across a broadcast network news report produced in 1981, in which the correspondent talked about the exclusivity of the retreat, the rituals and stage performances, the inaccessibility to the press. There were anecdotal accounts of nuclear development taking shape during meetings at the Grove, of other global policies gaining international support during alcohol-fueled campfire chats. It seemed to her that Bohemian Grove was about the worst-kept secret in the world of secrets. But there was something there.

Matti discounted most of the bizarre, salacious aspects of the Bohemian Grove legend and focused on one key element: its elitist, global membership. She clicked on a second video and started taking notes.

The second video detailed the list of members past and present. It spoke of the rumored twenty-five-thousand-dollar initiation and the requirements for invitation. Occasionally, she learned, artists or movie stars were included as members or guests, but most were powerful cabinet members, industrial tycoons, and foreign heads of state. There was a mention of former President Richard Nixon, who said in 1972, "Anybody can be president of the United States, but few can ever have any hope of becoming president of the Bohemian Club."

Former President Dexter Foreman was a member, as was Secretary John Blackmon. So was Bill Davidson. It was his journal that tipped her off. There was a scribbled mention of "Bohemia" next to a set of dates in July along with the word *Zaca*. Matti missed the reference so many times before. But somehow, that night, she made the connection between the obscure reference and a video she'd seen years earlier. Zaca was one of the Grove's one hundred plus "camps". Each member belonged to a camp.

Seeing his name among the members only confirmed her suspicion. She opened a new page on her browser and started looking for a more comprehensive list. Matti was searching for a couple of names in particular. It only took her a few minutes to find it.

Buried in a list of attendees from 2003 was a program of the nightly activities and the featured entertainment. On one night, Saturday, July 19, the topic was "One World, One People: The New Order of Meritocracy", and the speaker was Sir Spencer Thomas.

Matti pounded her fist against the desk. She knew it.

There was something bigger. Sir Spencer, Bill Davidson, Blackmon, and the others couldn't have acted alone. They had to have help and there was a bigger play at hand.

Seeing Sir Spencer's name on the screen of her laptop wasn't proof. She couldn't do anything with a couple of YouTube videos, some scribble in a stolen journal, and the list of members of some Skull & Bones-esque secret society.

Matti started processing what she thought she knew and what others would say if she shared it. She kept circling back to the same conclusion.

If she went to anyone with her burgeoning, unsubstantiated theory, she'd be lumped in with the birthers and the fringe thinkers who still espoused that 9/11 was an inside job. Matti had seen the videos about WTC building seven, and she found their evidence compelling; she didn't want to be associated with them.

Her mind was spinning. She didn't know if it was the drugs or the adrenaline.

Her bosses at NSA hadn't acted on her suspicions the first time, before the Capitol attack. They certainly wouldn't listen to her now without real proof. And even then, she considered, if they were a part of the conspiracy and allowed the Capitol to explode, she had nowhere to turn regardless. Though there was one man, still at NSA, she could trust. Maybe she'd reach out to him. Maybe he could poke around.

Matti disconnected the air card and closed her laptop. She needed more evidence. She needed to know the endgame.

Maybe then she'd redeem herself. She'd be the hero and not the goat. She was deep in thought when a knock at her office door snapped her from a trance.

"Yes?" she called, slipping her laptop back into the messenger bag.

"It's Brandon," said the chief of staff. "We need to go. Marine One is on the lawn and waiting."

"Okay, sir," she said. "I'm coming. I know we've got work to do."

CHAPTER 14

THE GALLERIA
HOUSTON, TEXAS

The phone rang for the third time and Holt was about to hang up.

"This is Boxell," a hoarse voice answered.

"Detective Boxell?" Holt sat up straight in his chair.

"Sergeant Boxell. Who is this?"

"Sergeant"—Holt cradled the phone in his neck, his fingers poised above his keyboard—"my name is Dillinger Holt. I'm a reporter with Plausible Deniability dot info. I was—"

"I don't talk to reporters about pending cases."

"This isn't about a pending case," explained Holt. "This is about Erik Majors. He's the former F—"

"I know who he was," Boxell said. He sounded like he needed to suck on a lozenge for a month. "What about him?"

"You didn't think he killed himself, right?"

"Right."

"Why not?"

"A bunch of reasons. Where is this going? What's your point?"

"I don't think he killed himself either," answered Holt. "And I think whoever killed him had a role in the death of Horus."

"Who?"

"Horus. The hip-hop rapper who died recently."

"Yeah," Boxell conceded, "I've heard of him. I heard he died in Texas."

"Yes." Holt looked back at the hotel bed behind him. It was empty; Karen had left a couple of hours earlier. He missed her. It was an alien feeling.

"So where is the connection?"

"DNA."

"What?"

"DNA," Holt repeated. "There's a match from both scenes."

"Whose is it?"

"I don't know that," said Holt. "What I do know is that both men died from heroin overdoses made to look like intentional or accidental suicides. And in both cases DNA from the same person was recovered."

"You get this from the FBI?" asked Boxell. "It's their system. So they found the match? They should have alerted us."

"This is, as we'd say in the news business, breaking information," answered Holt. "I'm not giving you my source, but I can tell you this is a new development."

"So why are you telling me?" Boxell asked. "What do you want?"

"I just need confirmation that there are those within your department who still believe Erik Majors didn't kill himself." Holt readied his fingers for the response.

"On background?"

"Yes."

"Yeah," Boxell hedged, "I don't know if I can do that. I don't know you. I don't trust you. Once we get confirmation from the—"

"It will be too late then," pleaded Holt. "I need something now. I'm not using your name. If I betrayed you now, you wouldn't help me down the road as this develops. I'm not in the business of burning people. Google me. I spent three days behind bars for contempt after refusing to identify a source in a story about a congressman's death."

"Hang on…" Boxell put down the phone, and Holt could hear him typing away on his computer.

While he waited, Holt Googled the sergeant and looked for images. He wanted to put a face with the voice. An album populated quickly. Boxell was tall and thin. He had a full head of hair and looked to be in his mid-forties. Several of the photographs showed him at crime scenes, talking to the DC media. A couple of them featured the police sergeant behind a set of drums, playing music with a band. Another, from Facebook, was on a tropical beach with who Holt assumed was his family.

"Okay." Boxell was back. "I looked you up. You seem legit. I can go on background. But no names, no details about what I do."

"Got it."

"I'll say this, on background," Boxell said. "There are several people within the department who've long thought former FBI special agent Erik Majors did not kill himself. We're certainly interested in evaluating any evidence that pushes forward that theory."

"I can quote that?"

"Yes," Boxell said. "I want you to keep me updated as you learn things. We've started a quid pro quo here."

"You sound like Hannibal Lecter."

"I'm worse." Boxell laughed. "I have a badge and a gun."

"That's not endearing," said Holt.

"It wasn't meant to be. Don't burn me."

"Got it."

Holt hung up the phone and opened a new page in his browser. He went to Amazon and found a decent pair of drumsticks. He looked up the address for the Alexandria Police Department and sent the sticks to Boxell, including a gift message:

To a cop on the beat.
Quid Pro Quo.

*

Horus wasn't his real name. He was born Harold Richard Singleton to a bartending mother and a software-selling dad and spent his early days in a two-bedroom apartment in Shreveport, Louisiana.

Harry, as his parents called him, showed an early aptitude for music. His parents indulged him, buying an acoustic six-string guitar at a pawnshop for thirty-five dollars. They paid for piano lessons at an after-school program and exposed him to Stevie Wonder, The Commodores, Ray Charles, and Run DMC.

He could read music before he could read English and would rather have spent time penning a new song than writing a book report for school. Harry was destined for a life filled with music.

By the time he was in middle school, his parents had split up. Both of them were drinkers. His dad quit. His mom didn't, but she got to keep him. She moved to Vegas. Harry's soundtrack turned sour.

He found solace in his music. He would stay locked in his desert bedroom, headphones wrapped around his sweaty ears, pumping ideas and thumping therapy. He could escape with the help of Carl Carlton or Kool Moe Dee, Al B. Sure and Eminem. They spoke to him about work ethic and real passion. They taught him about relentless pursuit and blind ambition. He would sneak into the dank, off-the-Strip clubs at which his mother poured shots and mixed watered-down screwdrivers and listen to the deejays spin. Sitting in a corner booth, he'd take notes on the back of a cocktail napkin and measure beats. He'd memorize the transitional rhythms and lyrical irony of mixing particular songs together.

By the time they moved to Atlantic City when he was seventeen, he'd found a voice and developed a sound. His mother was dying of cirrhosis and she was even less of a caretaker than she'd been in Vegas.

His father moved to nearby Strathmere, New Jersey, so he could reconnect with his teenage son. However, the damage was done. Harry was a child of hip-hop and rap and rhythm and blues.

When he gained the confidence and saved enough money from shining shoes to pay for a cheap camera and a nice laptop, he uploaded his first effort to YouTube. He used Garage Band to mix the music and record his voice. He then lip-synced it into the camera and edited it using iMovie.

It was a crude effort, but his talent was evident. Horus was born.

Harry used his initials, HRS, to come up with his stage name. He loved it. It was the name of a falcon-headed Greek god to whom kings prayed. From the reaction to his first upload, Horus's teenage hip-hop incarnation was worthy of worship.

In the first forty-eight hours after the upload, he had fifty thousand views. In a week it was two hundred thousand. Horus started uploading new music every week and gained a cult following. He started earning money on a dedicated YouTube channel. Apparel companies gave him logo-embossed clothing to wear in the videos, and advertisers paid to embed their messages before and after his uploads. He dropped out of high school with six months to go so that he could concentrate on his growing business.

Then his mother died, and his father fell off the wagon. Both of them had debt. To keep a roof over his head, Horus was forced to confront the reality of the world. He needed more than free clothes and a few hundred dollars a month. He needed a real job. The uploads stopped.

He kept writing songs, jotting down lyrics, humming melodies as he worked two jobs: ten hours changing oil at a one-hour oil-change business followed by eight as an overnight stock boy at a grocery store. He was making almost enough to pay his bills, and on the odd weekend, he'd catch a deejaying shift at a local club. He was subsisting for three years. It was chance, or maybe misfortune, that changed his path and alit the fast-burning flame that consumed him.

He was twenty-one years old and was unloading cartons of Borden milk during a late shift. He was wearing headphones and rapping one of his own creations as he worked.

> *I'm too busy, hair too frizzy*
> *face too greasy, life not easy in the slow lane*
> *working past the pain to earn a check*
> *chick check mic check on the deck*
> *rising up again to fight the man*
> *work for the man bow down again*
> *he ain't no friend, but I've got plan*
> *to amp up the sound, jump from the ground*
> *into the sky and atmosphere far from here*
> *I'm almost there, so hard to bear*
> *'Cause I'm too busy, hair too frizzy.*

He was about to hit the second verse when there was a tap on his shoulder. It startled him and he dropped a half gallon of two-percent, splattering it against the case and on the floor.

"Dude." A man laughed, stepping back from the expanding pool of milk so as not to ruin his pristine white Nike Air Jordans. "You need to chill."

Horus pulled the headphones down around his neck, a pained look on his face until he recognized the man in the expensive shoes. His jaw dropped.

"You a rapper?" the man asked, offering Horus a fist bump. "'Cause you can spit. Seriously, brother, you got flow."

"Thanks," was the best Horus could conjure. He reciprocated with a bump and then reached for his walkie-talkie. "I need a mop by dairy, please."

"Sorry about the mess, brother. I just heard you and thought I recognized you."

"You. Recognized. Me?" It was laughable. "You're Vav Six, the producer, right?"

"Yeah, yeah, that's me," said the music mogul. "But we're talking about you. You deejay up at Club 33, right?"

"Sometimes."

"I've seen you. You're good."

"Thanks. That means a lot."

"Those words, what you were just doing, they're yours?" Vav Six looked down at his iPhone while he talked. He typed out a text with his thumb.

"Yeah."

"Got any more?" The producer looked up from his phone, his eyebrows arched.

"I've got a notebook full of them."

"Cool. Write this down." He gave Horus his number. "Give me a call tomorrow. We'll set something up. See if you're for real."

Horus saved the number in his contacts. "I'm Horus, by the way."

"I know." Vav Six left Horus to clean up his mess and then signed him to a record deal three days later.

Within eight weeks, they'd released his first single. In twelve months he was touring with three platinum singles and an addiction to smack. Add another year, he was dead.

CHAPTER 15

CAMP DAVID
CATOCTIN MOUNTAIN PARK, MARYLAND

"I'm not much for this place," President Jackson mumbled as Marine One landed at Camp David just sixty-eight miles from the White House. "I think President Obama was onto something."

"He didn't like it here?" Matti asked.

"No," said Jackson. "At least not as much as Bush before him and the others after him."

"I didn't know that." Matti shook her head, waiting for the rotors to slow before their escort notified them it was okay to disembark.

"Something the great Matti Harrold didn't know?" joked Chief of Staff Goodman. "We should write this down, Madam President."

"Oh, I'm certain Matti has already committed this moment to her photographic memory. Haven't you?" President Jackson smiled at her aide.

"Maybe," Matti smirked. "I do know that President Obama spent his fifty-second birthday here. So I guess I just assumed—"

"And there's your mistake." The president held up a finger as she stood. "You assumed."

"Yes, Madam President." Matti took the lead and stood, following the president through the cabin of the fourteen-person Sikorsky helicopter. "I'll make a mental note of that advice." She winked at Goodman as she stepped past him toward the exit.

The air was surprisingly cool, given how much warmer it was on the South Lawn. Matti stepped from the helicopter, thanked the Marine standing at attention to her left, and followed the president toward the field house on the northern edge of the landing pad.

"Why don't you enjoy it here?" Matti asked above the din of the slowing engines. "It's so serene here."

"Maybe that's why." The president shrugged, slowing her pace to keep even with Matti. "I like the hustle and bustle of the city. I enjoy the frenetic pace of it. This is too…it's too…peaceful."

"Not enough chaos?" Matti asked, reminding herself of what she'd read in Bill Davidson's journal.

"Perfect word." The president stepped into the field house, a Marine saluting her as she entered. Matti followed.

Brandon Goodman was a step behind. "I've got some calls to make before we meet later this morning," he said. "We'll meet in the Aspen Lodge at three. Good?"

"Good with me," said the president. "I've got a couple of things to do myself before the briefing." She found a spot on a worn, saddle-leather sofa and crossed her legs.

"So you don't need me, then?" Matti asked. "I'll see you at three?"

"That's fine, Matti." The president looked up from her Blackberry. "I'll see you then. I'll have Secret Service escort me to the lodge when it's time. Do you know where you're housed?"

"I'm at Aspen with you, Madam President. I'm in bedroom four."

"See you later, then."

Matti backed out of the field house and out onto the helicopter pad. She thought it odd the president would spend any time in the field house. She'd never done that before. Matti suspected that she wanted some privacy.

Matti looked to the southwest at the little-used skeet range and then walked to the parking lot at the edge of the helicopter pad. Unlike Felicia Jackson, Matti enjoyed the relative tranquility of Camp David. There was so little downtime when working in the White House, especially as a close presidential aide whose responsibilities ran the gamut from gofer to confidante, it was nice to get away for a couple of days.

She followed the narrow road to the northeast and the heart of the camp. Matti's messenger bag was slung across her back, the strap running diagonally across her chest. She carried an overnight bag on one shoulder and her purse on the other. She gripped her purse strap and then flexed her hand against a tremor.

Fighting the urge to rip open her bag, find the prescription bottle, and pop a pill all the way, she looked up at the trees and tried to clear her mind. She was fine seconds earlier, but the tremor reminded her of how much she needed her meds.

The path opened to a four-way stop. She continued straight, toward the camp commander's quarters. Passing the intersection, a pine-needle-strewn nature trail extended to the east. She liked the trail. She'd jogged it during previous trips here. It curved around the golf course, north to the Laurel Lodge, where it reconnected with the paved road. Its tributaries branched throughout the central part of the camp.

She was focused on getting to the Aspen Lodge and locking herself in her bedroom. She needed to fight past the urge and work through her anxiety without artificial help. This was as good a place as any to do it.

She'd reached the commander's quarters when she heard a voice behind her.

"Matti?" It was Brandon.

"Hi!" she said, stopping for him to catch up with her. "What are you doing? I thought you had stuff to do."

"I was at the gatehouse," he said. "I wanted to make sure the guards had the information for our guests. They'll be here in a couple of hours."

"Policy people, right?" Matti asked. "With ideas for talking points in Barcelona?"

"Yep." Brandon touched her shoulder. "Matti, are you okay?"

"Why?" She unconsciously flexed her hand.

"You look clammy," he said. "You're sweating and it can't be more than sixty-five degrees here."

"I'm fine," she said. "Maybe a little cold or something."

"Okay," he said. "Just checking. Are you headed to the lodge?"

"Yes," she said. "Gonna freshen up and review notes before the meeting. Maybe I'll take a jog."

"Sounds good. I'll walk with you, if that's okay. The fresh air is invigorating."

"Of course," she said. "The more the merrier."

*

Sir Spencer took a sip from the steaming cup of coffee he'd brewed. It singed the end of his tongue, which he ran along the back of his teeth. The battery-operated clock on the table next to his chair told him it was eight thirty in the morning when someone knocked on his door.

"Come in," he called without getting up from his seat. He took another, more careful sip of coffee. "It's open."

The door swung open and Doug Salas walked through, his hulking frame backlit by the sunlight filtering through the trees outside. He stepped to Sir Spencer and motioned for him to stand.

Sir Spencer stood, still holding the cup of coffee, and rolled his eyes. "What?"

"I need to frisk you," Salas said. "Assume the position."

Sir Spencer set down the coffee cup and raised his arms above his head.

Salas used the backs of his hands to check Sir Spencer's arms, legs, groin, and waist. He asked him to open his mouth and stick out his tongue. Sir Spencer complied.

"Okay," Salas offered. "You're good." He walked out of the cabin, leaving the door open. A moment later, an old friend walked up the stoop and into the room.

"Sir Spencer, welcome to Camp David. I hope the Linden meets your standards."

"Madam President, thank you for the hospitality. It's not the Lincoln bedroom, but it will do. How is Dr. Chapa?" The veiled reference to their past was intended to draw a smile from the leader of the free world. Instead she grunted.

"Ask my husband," she said. "I try not to tip the boat in muddy water."

"He was at the inauguration, no?"

"Yes. Enough of the past. Let's talk about the future."

The two exchanged a brief hug, and Sir Spencer offered Felicia Jackson his seat. She obliged and set her Blackberry on the table next to his coffee. She glanced at the steam wafting from the cup.

"That makes me think of our good friend Dexter Foreman," she said. "The hot cup of coffee every morning before his day began."

"Ahhh…so you'd like to linger on the past a bit longer, then." Sir Spencer smiled. "Yes, it is reminiscent of our dearly departed friend's nasty caffeine habit, except that mine isn't laced with amphetamines as his was."

"For months?"

"For months." Sir Spencer walked over to his bed and sat on the edge, facing the president. "He never knew. And then, one day, boom!" He made a gesture with his hands mimicking an explosion. "An aneurysm. Nobody was the wiser."

"It didn't hurt his family had a predisposition for cerebral whatever-it-was," she said.

"Cerebral arteritis."

"We never really had a chance to talk about everything, did we?"

"We were otherwise engaged." Sir Spencer chuckled.

"I'm still not thrilled about the near-death experience at the Capitol." The president's eyes narrowed. "What would you have done had I died?"

"There were contingencies," he acknowledged. "There always are. You know we work like the mythical hydra, wherein one head is lost and another two take its place."

"I'm well aware—"

"Then you'd best not question the order of things," Sir Spencer said, his tone sharpening. "Do not confuse your position with my authority."

"Whatever." She waved him off. "It worked."

"Everything has worked thus far," said Sir Spencer, edging toward the president in her seat. He looked down at her as a teacher would a pupil. "Though we have some issues if we are to continue with this phase of the plan."

"What's that?" she asked, crossing her legs and adjusting her knee-length skirt.

"George and Art may be a tad loose-lipped," he said. "They seem to lack the discretion needed. They may not understand the order of th—"

"It's already taken care of."

"It is?" Sir Spencer stood upright, his eyebrows arched and eyes wide.

"Yes," she said. "Horrible prison accidents. Both men are silent."

"Really?" Sir Spencer recoiled further. He hadn't authorized the killings. "When did you—"

"Oh, come on," she said, mocking his accent. "You aren't the only one capable of violence. One doesn't rise within the ranks of our club without the willingness to do whatever it takes to advance the agenda."

"Touché."

"Now"—she shifted in her seat—"I don't have much time. So let's get down to business."

"Let's." He nodded.

"I'll need you in Barcelona ahead of me," President Jackson said. "It's critical you lay the groundwork with our friends before my arrival."

"Understood."

"You'll find all of the necessary documentation and talking points in a locker at the Rising Sun Aviation FBO at Dulles. There will be a private jet waiting for you. Our friends have arranged for some clothing, toiletries, and an encrypted phone. They'll be on board when you arrive."

"How efficient." The hint of sarcasm was fueled by Sir Spencer's dislike for how long he'd been out of the loop.

"We'll meet somewhere privately once I'm in Spain. I don't know the details yet, but somebody will let you know."

"Goodman?"

"Brandon?" She laughed. "No. He's blind. He has no idea what's happening. Just know, someone with mutual interests will keep you in the loop."

"And the SECURITY Act?"

"We're moving it along," said the president. "We've got the House on board. The Senate is a bit trickier."

"One more domino and they'll be begging for it." Sir Spencer licked his upper lip, feeling the sting of the coffee burn.

"That's what we're hoping for." President Jackson looked at her watch.

"Anything else?"

"Yes." The president picked up her Blackberry. She thumbed the screen and handed it to Sir Spencer. "This."

Sir Spencer took the device and held it far enough away from his eyes so that he could read the small print. It was a news article from the website PlausibleDeniability.info.

*Authorities Investigating Link Between Death of
Rapper and FBI Agent
By Dillinger Holt, Senior Correspondent*

*What is the connection between the hottest music act
on the planet and a disgraced FBI agent? That's the
burning question now that we know DNA found at the
scenes of their deaths is a match.*

*Houston, TX
—EXCLUSIVE—*

*In a development straight out of a conspiracy
novel, we've learned EXCLUSIVELY that DNA found
at the scene of rapper/hip-hop star Horus matches a
sample found at the death of an FBI agent three years
ago.*

*Horus, whose real name is Harold Richard
Singleton, was found dead from a drug overdose
earlier this week after a concert in Houston's Toyota
Center. Autopsy results are pending, but heroin is the
likely culprit.*

*There was also DNA pulled from his body that
pinged a hit on the national DNA database known as
CODIS. That hit, surprisingly, matches a sample
taken from the scene of the suspected suicide of a
disgraced FBI special agent in northern Virginia.*

*That agent, Erik Majors, also died from a
drug overdose. The agency investigating his death
never concluded definitively that he killed himself.*

*Speaking on the condition of anonymity,
someone with knowledge of the Majors case told us,
"There are several people within the department
who've long thought former FBI special agent Erik
Majors did not kill himself. We're certainly interested
in evaluating any evidence that pushes forward that
theory."*

*So does that mean neither man killed himself
but, instead, both men were targeted? It's certainly a
possibility investigators will consider as they work to*

identify the owner of the DNA. Despite the match, we've learned there is no identity attached to it.
We know the next step is communication amongst the agencies involved as they try to piece together how these two men were connected.
Developing...

"Hmmm." Sir Spencer handed back the phone, surprised at what he'd read.

"Who's the leak?" asked the president.

"We'll find out," said Sir Spencer. "Just send our little butterfly to figure it out."

"She's the one who left the evidence in the first place," argued President Jackson.

"So let her clean it up."

*

WASHINGTON, DC

The message was simple. Find the leak and silence it.

It was coded and encrypted, but the assassin knew what it meant. She had work to do.

She popped open her laptop and connected remotely to a secure server that would mask her location and keep her online activity hidden. Once logged onto the network, she searched for all references to Horus and found the most recent article, written by Dillinger Holt.

She searched the server's archival feature for Holt and found several references. He was on a watch list her employers maintained. There were more than two million names in the database, which was larger than the FBI's one-point-five-million-strong terror watch list.

Her employers had reach.

The assassin studied Holt's background and read a few of the articles deemed "of interest". Most of the reports focused on the economy, world currency, state-sponsored terror, NSA data mining, and the PATRIOT Act. He was a political reporter based in Washington who'd covered the White House and Capitol Hill. He'd been the beat reporter at the State Department for a year and even filled in at the United Nations desk.

"No wonder he's on the list," the assassin murmured as she scrolled through report after report. "He's a threat."

Satisfied she'd absorbed enough cursory information about Holt, she searched the surveillance history. Her employer, the people who had taken her from caterpillar to chrysalis, had files on Holt dating back to 2005.

His report about the DNA connection dealt with two locations; Houston, Texas and Alexandria, Virginia. She cross-referenced his known acquaintances in both cities. Alexandria was daunting. He lived in DC. His connections in northern Virginia ran into the hundreds. Finding a leak there could take days or weeks.

However, in Houston, he had only three connections. One was a deputy constable in Harris County. One was a ticket broker. Neither of them piqued her interest. The third did.

Karen Corvus was a coroner at the medical examiner's office.

The assassin checked cellular records and researched every phone call Holt had initiated within the last seventy-two hours. She isolated the numbers with Houston area codes and then used a backward directory to identify the owner of each number.

She learned Holt contacted Corvus within the last twenty-four hours. They had spoken for several minutes. She found a receipt for dinner at a seafood restaurant Holt had charged to his company account. There were two meals.

Karen Corvus was the leak.

After taking a deep breath, the assassin found her way into the website for the Harris County Institute of Forensic Science. She clicked on the Missing Persons tab and then searched for a listing of Unidentified Decedents.

Underneath a bold red warning at the top of the page, she scrolled to a list of unidentified dead people organized by date, sex, and presumed age. Some of the listings included macabre photographs of corpses or less inflammatory pictures of identifying marks or belongings.

The listing went as far back as 1957, though most of them were from the last thirty years or so. One of them, from 2016, was a middle-aged Caucasian or Hispanic woman. The assassin clicked on the flyer associated with her case to learn more about her.

The woman was found at a Metro bus stop and was wearing a pair of blue jeans, a white shirt with black checkered trim, white socks with no shoes, and a pink and green rubber bracelet on her left wrist.

She was sixty-four inches tall and weighed one hundred and thirty pounds. She had a tattoo of a cross on the nape of her neck.

There were case numbers for both the police agency investigating the death and one for the medical examiner's office. At the bottom of the flier was a phone number for the Identification Unit.

The assassin cleared her throat and dialed the number from her encrypted phone. It flashed a false, randomized number on the receiving end of every call she placed. It rang twice before a woman answered.

"Harris County Medical Examiner."

"Is this Karen Corvus?" the assassin asked, using a hint of a Spanish accent.

"No," the woman answered. "I can get her for you." There was a click as the woman put the call on hold. A minute later, another woman answered.

"This is Dr. Corvus."

"Hello, Doctor. I need your help."

"Who is this, please?"

"This is Hilda Mentiroso."

"Do I know you?"

"No," said the assassin, "and I don't know you. I do need your help."

"You said that."

"My mother's been missing for some time now," the assassin slowed her cadence, her voice warbling. "I—I—I think I found her on your website."

"You found her?" Karen's tone softened. "Do you mean you located her description in our Unidentified Decedent section?"

"Yes." The assassin exploded into a sobbing blather about how she missed her mother, had feared the worst but didn't want to accept it. Now she was certain the woman on the website was her mother.

"We can't confirm anything over the phone, I'm afraid," Karen explained. "You'd need to come here to identify her."

"I could do that," the assassin whimpered. "I could come there."

"Our hours are posted on the website," said Karen. "Just come when you're able. We'll help you."

"I could be there later today."

"Okay," Karen acknowledged. "I'll be here. So will the rest of our staff. Someone will be able to assist you with what we know is a difficult process."

"It is difficult. Thank you for your kindness." The assassin hung up the phone and returned to her computer.

She logged into a secure travel site at her disposal and logged into her account. There was a nonstop flight from Reagan National to Houston Hobby airport leaving in two hours. She could fly commercial without compromising the mission, she concluded. She ordered the first-class one-way ticket and began packing. There wasn't time to waste.

*

Sitting on her bed, briefing notes fanned across the thin floral duvet, the ringing phone startled Mattie.

"Matti? How are you?"

"Hi, Dad." She sighed. "I'm good. You?"

"I'm okay," he said. "I haven't heard from you in a couple of weeks. I thought I'd call."

"Sorry, Dad. I've been busy." She'd been avoiding him.

"I know, but I worry about you. With the whole Spencer Thomas thing, I was concerned you were, I don't know, emotional."

"Me? Emotional?" She laughed.

"You don't have to pretend with me, Mattie. I know you. None of this is easy. If you run yourself into the ground, you're no good to anyone. You have to take time for yourself. Are you still seeing the counselor?"

She rolled her eyes and huffed. There it was. And that was why she'd avoided talking with him. Every time he called, it was the same thing.

"I'm fine. I don't need to keep seeing the shrink. I've dealt with it. I'm over it."

Matti and her father had only recently talked about things that mattered. For much of her childhood, he'd been the emotionally unavailable one.

In the wake of her mother's death, he'd sleepwalked through life. He cooked her breakfast, went to teach at the high school, came home and made dinner, watched some television, and went to bed.

He never talked about his wife, Matti's mother, except in his dreams. He'd call out to her in the middle of the night while Matti lay awake in the next room, powerless to help him.

"Matti," he said pleadingly, "your mother never dealt with her issues. They controlled her. They—"

"They killed her?" Matti snapped.

"No." Her father's voice softened. "A hit-and-run driver killed her."

"The drugs killed her, Dad. It was the cocaine and whatever else she used. I know that. You know that."

"Yes," he agreed. "That too. She never sought help for her demons. You have demons, Matti, whether you want to admit it or not."

"I can't do this now," she said. "I've got too much happening at the moment. I'm at Camp David. I'm heading to Spain in a couple of—"

"I can hear it in your voice."

"What?"

"You're in pain," he said. "You can't get over the guilt you imposed on yourself in a few months. It can't be done. You need help. You need to forgive yourself."

Matti pulled her hand to her head and gripped her hair, squeezing her eyes shut, gritting her teeth. She wanted to throw the phone across the room.

"Do you remember McPherson Square?" he asked. "Do you remember what I told you there about your mother?"

Matti remained silent, tears welling in her eyes.

"I told you, 'I'm to blame.' And you corrected me, Matti. You said, 'No, you're not, I am.'"

"I remember," Matti said against the knot in her throat. "I told you I could have saved her. I told you if I'd put the pieces together, I could have saved her. And I told you that if I'd figured out sooner how she died, I could have saved you."

"What did I tell you then," he whispered into the phone, "that applies every bit as much to what you're going through right now?"

"You told me…" Matti whimpered and wiped the tears from her cheeks with the back of her hand. "You told me it wasn't my job to save anyone."

Matti's father let the echo of what she said reverberate in her mind before he spoke again.

"I love you, Matti. And you have to move on from this. You have to reconcile that you did everything you could do. You, alone, cannot save the world."

Matti understood what he was saying, and she knew he was right; however, it didn't change her beliefs. It didn't change that she'd failed. It didn't change the idea in her mind that there was more to the attack on the Capitol than what it appeared to be. She couldn't tell him any of that, so she appeased him.

"I know, Dad." She sniffed back the remnants of her emotional outburst. "You're right."

"I know I'm right." He laughed. "I wasted half of my life doing what you're doing now. Stop living in the past. Cope with it, shove past it and—"

"Enough," she interrupted. "I get it. Okay?"

"Okay."

"I love you."

"I love you too."

"I really have to go, okay?" she said, looking at the notes she had yet to review. "I've got a meeting with the president this morning. I have to be prepared."

"Understood," he said. "We'll talk soon."

Matti ended the call and tossed the phone onto the pillow. She took a deep breath, exhaled, and started fishing through the stacks of papers on her bed.

Buried underneath was Bill Davidson's journal. She found a dog-eared page and thumbed open the blue book, cracking its worn spine. Amongst all of the seemingly innocuous political rantings of an aging statesman-turned-would-be-terrorist were salient observations and countless clues to a hidden current of power flowing underneath the noses of everyone in Washington.

Bohemian Grove was just one of those clues. There were more. The word "chaos" appeared dozens of times.

"From chaos order is born," he wrote. *"It is irrefutable that people are most willing to accept order after enduring the terror of chaos. The greater the anarchy, the stronger the desire was for an*

enforced peace. Without chaos, however, the need for order is difficult to understand."

She ran her finger down the middle of pages, scanning for more references.

"Even Churchill, the great statesman," he'd scribbled, *"believed in the social chaos theory. How can I refute it? Ordo ab chao."*

Matti fished her phone from the pillow and opened the browser. She typed in "Order and Chaos". The first three items on the list were about Horus. He'd had a hit called "From Chaos Order". His death had reignited the popularity of all of his music.

She thumbed past the Horus references to find mentions of Churchill, found several links, and opened the most interesting.

"From the days of Spartacus," Churchill wrote in an oft-quoted letter, *"this world-wide conspiracy for the overthrow of civilization and for the reconstitution of society on the basis of arrested development, of envious malevolence, and impossible equality, has been steadily growing. It has been the mainspring of every subversive movement during the Nineteenth Century."*

In the same link featuring the Churchill letter, Matti found a reference to Georg Wilhelm Friedrich Hegel. She knew him as the man whose work had inspired Karl Marx. He wrote that the state has *"Supreme right against the individual, whose supreme duty is to be a member of the state."*

Hegel, she read, believed that the ruling body must enact a crisis to cause its citizens to demand a solution. The rulers then offered a predetermined, extreme solution to the crisis they created. The people became divided. The rulers created a villain. Hatred of the villain united the divided people. The rulers enacted the solution. It was the ultimate sleight of hand.

Her wheels were spinning. There was something to this.

Order from chaos. *Ordo ab chao.*

Matti stood from the bed and stretched. There was time for a quick run before the meeting, and she needed to clear her head, fighting against the urge to take another pill.

She slipped on a pair of Lycra leggings, a Georgetown T-shirt, and a pair of running shoes. It would feel good to sweat. Maybe the run would help the ideas coalesce in her head.

Who were the rulers? What was the crisis? What was the solution?

The air outside the cabin was still thick with Southern Maryland humidity and the late morning sun found its way through the towering trees. Matti strode north along the road until she found the nature trail at the Sycamore Lodge.

She leaned against a tall pine and grabbed her foot, pulling her calves against the back of her thighs, feeling the strain in her quads one at a time. She twisted at her waist, stretching her core.

Were the conspirators who blew up the Capitol the rulers, or were they pawns? Was the Capitol bombing the crisis? Or was there more? If there was a bigger crisis at play, did the conspirators know the endgame?

Matti took a deep breath and released it from her cheeks as she started her run. She headed south, running parallel to Camp David's eastern perimeter fence. Her legs felt good, the breathing easy and in rhythm.

Matti's mind, clouded by the need for pills, was clearing infinitesimally while she plodded against the pine needle floor of the nature trail.

The conspirators were pawns. Otherwise they wouldn't have been caught. There was a higher authority at work.

Matti blinked against the first of the stinging drops of sweat in her eyes. She rounded the southeastern corner of the path, turning west toward the main entrance, her pulse thumping against her neck.

Bill Davidson knew there was more at hand, which was why he'd given her the journals. If the conspiracy began and ended with one act of defiance, of radical violence, why turn them over?

Matti reached the spot where the trail merged with the main road and turned right, picking up her pace as she passed the camp commander's quarters. To her right was a building called Rosebud.

She smiled at the name, as she always did. It reminded her of the classic film *Citizen Kane*.

"Rosebud," she whispered, licking the sweat from her upper lip. She moved toward the camp office in the center of the property.

"Rosebud" was the deathbed confession of Orson Welles's title character. The smile disappeared from Matti's face as she imagined the close-up of Kane's mouth uttering the word.

Confession…

To whom else had Davidson confessed his sins?

Matti recalled from his securities dossier he wasn't close to many people. His parents were dead, he wasn't married, and his most trusted friend was a high-priced call girl, a hooker who shared Davidson's secrets with the NSA.

What else did Davidson confess to his prostitute girlfriend? What did she know that she never got to tell Matti as an NSA asset? She'd provided so much valuable information, given Matti so many clues before she was killed. What did she know that she didn't have time to reveal?

Matti strode past the bowling alley, rejoining the nature trail where it split the northern collection of cabins. Her calves were arguing with her about the upward slope, but she kept the rhythm. Her breathing was even, her heart rate steady.

It didn't matter what the call girl knew. She was dead. Davidson was dead. It was a dead end. The answer was somewhere...

Even against the doubts scratching at the back of her mind, telling her she was irrational and delusional, Matti believed she could figure it out. She could stop it. She could fix what she broke. She worked in the White House. She had crazy clearance and friends in the intelligence community. If anyone could do it, she could.

As she pressed uphill, straining to finish the first of three laps, all of her doubts evaporated. She knew she wasn't crazy, though she could have sworn she was looking at a ghost.

Standing in the open doorway of a cabin nestled amongst a cluster of tall pines, Matti saw Felicia Jackson, president of the United States, talking to a man who looked exactly like Sir Spencer Thomas.

PART TWO: ALL-SEEING EYE

"Very soon, every American will be required to register their biological property in a national system designed to keep track of people."
—Colonel Edward Mandell House, 1921

CHAPTER 16

CARRER DE BERGARA
BARCELONA, SPAIN

The white sunlight of the early evening forced Jon Custos to slip on a pair of shades as he stepped from his hotel on to Bergara Street. He looked both ways and then started northeast, parallel to the coastline, crossing the Plaça de Catayluna, an open plaza in the heart of the central city.

He considered a taxi or a train, but decided to walk the city, one of his favorites. The wide "carrers", lined with tall birch trees and dotted with tapas bars, were among the most fantastic in Europe. The smells of fresh bread and the bustle of the Catalan people seemed surreal at times. Perhaps he'd have time after his date with the flight attendant to enjoy a sirloin with pepper, some breaded calamari, and a good beer.

A trio of motorcycles buzzed past him, and the men in business suits and helmets accelerated amongst the congestion of buses and smart cars. He found a narrow alleyway, three stories high with balcony-adorned flats, and slipped his hands into his pockets. Custos knew this part of the city as the Gothic Quarter. It was teeming with tourists oblivious to their surroundings. He pressed forward along the cobbled streets, whistling a familiar tune from Edvard Grieg, and ignored a man trying to sell him a two-euro selfie-stick for ten, and waved off another offering bottled water.

He checked his phone for the proper address of his destination against the marble etched street marker on the corner building. He was looking for a high-rise apartment building in Bac de Roda. It was an older building, as were most of those around it, but it was awash in a bright coral and Mediterranean blue that made it inviting. He found it next to a pharmacy and slipped his phone back into his pocket.

Custos walked up the short set of concrete steps to the front glass door and tugged. It was locked. Within seconds, an elderly woman appeared in the lobby and backed her way out of the entrance, escorting a small dog on a leash.

Custos held the door for her. She thanked him and the dog yapped, but neither noticed him slip inside the building.

Inside the un-air-conditioned lobby, Custos removed his sunglasses and pulled a piece of paper from his front pocket. He checked the information on the scrap and then grabbed the stair rail to begin his climb. His heavy steps echoed in the narrow stairwell as he trudged upward.

The echo of children playing beyond the doors of their apartment homes and the smell of what he assumed was chicken or maybe rabbit cooking consumed the space. Sweat dripped from Custos's bald head when he bent over to catch his breath on the third floor.

Wiping his brow with the back of his long-sleeved khaki linen shirt, Custos looked down the long hallway lined with doors. He took a deep breath of the stale air and stepped along the terrazzo floor, checking the numbers on the doors: 304, 306, 308 on his right. 305, 307, 309 on his left.

At the end of the hall he reached flat 310. He pressed his ear to the wood door, its paint peeling in clusters. Somebody was home. The television was on. Custos put his left index finger over the fish-eye peephole at the door's center and pressed a button next to the door with his right.

The buzzer rang until he released his finger. He pressed again and again in short bursts.

"*Un moment*," a gruff voice called from inside the apartment, telling the visitor to wait. He was on his way. *"Espereu si us plau! Estic arribant. Estic arribant."*

Custos set his feet shoulder-width apart. The man's footsteps were getting louder.

"Qui és?" the man asked. *"No puc veure. Qui és?"*

Custos said nothing, but pushed the buzzer and held it for several seconds. He clenched his jaw.

"*Déu meu,*" the man said through the door. He opened it, not releasing the chain, preventing it from opening fully.

When he pulled back on the handle, Custos pulled up his leg and, with all of his force, thrust his foot at the center right edge of the door. The door exploded inward, snapping the security chain and slamming into the old man.

Custos checked the hall in both directions and then stepped into the apartment, shutting the door behind him. The man lay on the floor, dazed and babbling incoherently. Custos locked the door and found a chair to place underneath the handle, bracing it against the only interior entrance to the apartment.

Custos stalked the home, marching through the two bedrooms and single bathroom, making certain they were alone and that all of the windows were closed and locked. He drew the sheer blue curtains closed in the master bedroom and closed the blinds in the spare one. He checked the floor-to-ceiling glass sliding doors at the back of the unit. They opened to a patio overlooking Paseo de Taulat. Custos found a broom handle in the kitchen, broke it off at the top of the handle, and used the wooden shard to brace the glass doors. Nobody could get in or out of the apartment without his permission. And that wouldn't be happening.

The man was slowly gaining his wits, and he tried sitting up on the floor, but Custos pushed him on his back with a boot to the chest. The Romani then squatted, straddling his much-smaller prey as the confused man squirmed in pathetic futility.

"*Silencio!*" Custos pulled a finger to his lips. "*Sierra la boca, por favor. Entiende?*"

The man, grimacing, nodded that he understood. Though Custos didn't speak Catalan, most everyone in Barcelona spoke Spanish too.

The man whimpered his compliance and complained that he couldn't breathe with a giant sitting on his chest. The man pressed his eyes closed, the wrinkles at his temples and in his forehead deepening as he whispered a prayer.

"*Jesús no esta aquí,*" Custos mocked, telling the man Jesus wasn't there to help him. "*Y ello no te ayuda.*"

The man continued his prayer, ignoring the giant. Custos bound his quarry's wrists with plastic zip ties he'd carried in his pocket alongside his phone. He warned the man not to move, then grabbed the man's jaw and forced open his mouth, stuffing it with a cloth napkin he'd found on the kitchen counter.

"Habla ingles?" he asked. The man nodded and Custos stood, relieving the pressure on the man's chest.

"I have some questions for you, then." Custos could have continued speaking in Spanish. He was recording the audio on his phone and wanted to make it easier for those who'd later listen to the forthcoming interrogation.

The man's eyes, wide with the fear that came only from knowing pain was in the offing, darted around the room from his position on the floor. He couldn't see much: a chair against the front door, the patio door closed and locked, a giant looking down on him.

"Let's begin with who you are." Custos moved out of the man's line of sight and found a comfortable seat on a worn brown leather sofa. He propped his feet on the wooden coffee table in front of him. "I will ask you questions, and you will nod your head for yes and shake your head for no. I want you to stay flat on your back on the floor. *Entiende?"*

The man nodded.

"You are Fernando Barçes?"

Fernando Barçes nodded, trying to crane his neck to see the giant.

"You live here in this flat?"

Another nod.

"You work at the hotel on the water, the one next to the trade center, yes?"

Barçes lay still.

"I asked if you work at the hotel by the port. The one next to the trade center. It looks like a big ship."

This time, Barçes slowly nodded, as if he was afraid revealing that information alone would kill him.

"You are a maintenance man there? You clean and fix." Custos knew the answers without having to ask them. Still, he enjoyed the game.

Barçes didn't answer immediately. Custos grunted. He dropped his heavy feet to the floor and marched loudly to the kitchen. He returned with a stainless steel cheese grater. Barçes was flushed and sweating. His pupils shrank to pinpricks.

Custos squatted next to Barçes. He pressed the grater to the side of the old man's face. From his training, Custos knew the fear of pain was more effective at eliciting a response than pain itself. He didn't have time for sleep deprivation, nor the privacy for noise-induced exhaustion or water-boarding. Pain, if it came to that, could be counterproductive. He was secretly hopeful the threat of a cheese grater was enough.

Barçes gagged against the napkin shoved into his mouth. Tears welled in the outer corners of his eyes. They spilled down the sides of his face. He was shaking.

Custos grazed Barçes's cheek with the grater. He pushed it up toward the old man's eyes and lowered his lips to whisper, *"Su trabajo por favor."*

Barçes squeezed his eyes closed and nodded.

"Bueno." Custos pushed himself to his feet, using the grater pressed to Barçes's face as leverage. "Now I need your keys."

He looked down at the broken man and admired his quick work. Barçes's chest heaved with each sob, snot bubbling from his nose, and he choked against the gag. He was shaking his head back and forth.

"The answer is yes, *Abuelo*." Custos nodded. "You'll give the keys."

CHAPTER 17

STARBUCKS
HOUSTON, TEXAS

The tweet was cryptic but crystal clear.

`I got something you want. It'll cost $5k.`

Dillinger Holt rubbed his chin, staring at the direct message on his Twitter account. He didn't know the account holder. The profile was intentionally vague, with a single tweet. The account had no followers and only followed Holt.

Holt followed back and sent his own message.

`I'll bite. Whatchu got?`

He adjusted his laptop on his table at a Starbucks on the corner of Buffalo Speedway and the Southwest Freeway. He needed coffee and he needed to work. His editor wanted a follow-up to his hit-generating piece on the connection between the deaths of Horus and an FBI agent. Barely two hundred words into a five-hundred-word piece, and he was on his third Americano, completely wired. His knee bounced up and down while he awaited a reply. Instead, his phone rang.

"Dillinger Holt."

"Mr. Holt, I'm with the Houston office of the Federal Bureau of Investigation. You called?"

"Yes." Holt opened a new screen on his laptop to take notes. "I am looking for reaction to my article. I'll guess you've read it."

"I have."

"Can you comment? What role is your office now playing in the investigation into Horus's death?"

"I can't comment," the pleasant-sounding woman answered. "I'm sure you know anything like that has to go through DC. I can give you the number to the Public Affairs officer there if you need it."

"No, thanks. I've got it. Can you tell me if there's been any discussion at the SAC level? Any talk about it at all? Is he aware of the article?"

"I really can't comment." She paused. "I can confirm, on background, the special agent in charge, Rick West, is aware of the report. That's it. Okay?"

"Got it."

Holt hung up and then hit the speed dial for the PAO's office for FBI headquarters.

"FBI Public Affairs."

"Hi, Freddie. This is Dillinger."

"Dillinger!" Freddie's voice jumped an octave. "How's it going, bud? You haven't been to the gym in a couple of weeks. Everything okay?"

"Yeah," Holt answered, "just busy with work. I'm traveling a lot. How are you?"

"I'm good. Trying to stay in shape and get back to the ripped abs I never had."

"Funny. Hey, I've got a question for you."

"On the record?"

"That depends on you."

"Go ahead. Shoot."

"You know about my article, right?"

"Everybody does."

"What kind of effort is there to flesh out the connection between the two deaths?"

"I can't speak to that," Freddie answered. "I can tell you on the record that the agency is aware of the report and is coordinating a response. If there is, in fact, an evidentiary connection between the deaths of Mr. Singleton and Special Agent Majors, we will pursue it in coordination with the local agencies involved."

"Got it." Holt was thumping away at the keyboard. "What can you tell me on background? I'm greedy."

"Nothing." Freddie laughed. "I think this line is bad. Let me call you back in a minute."

Holt knew Freddie wouldn't give him anything valuable on a recorded government line. He'd await a call from him from his cell.

Holt opened his Twitter page and saw a new direct message waiting for him. He clicked on the envelope icon.

Check your email. A little taste. I don't trust police. Don't call them.

Holt rubbed his chin and took a sip of his coffee. He opened his email. There were three new messages. One was from his editor. A second was spam. The third, the newest, was from a Gmail account with a series of random letters and numbers. Holt opened it.

Mr. Holt: Attached to this email is a still frame from a cell phone video I shot. I will let you see the whole video if we can agree to financial terms. The video shows the aftermath of the shoot-out in which the president says Spencer Thomas was killed. I was nearby, at the Marine museum, when the shooting happened and was able to get close to the scene.

There are only three body bags. There were three US Marshals killed. Where is the fourth body bag? I saw the bodies put into the bags. They were all marshals. Somebody is hiding something. I am not a conspiracy nut, but I think something weird is going on.

I like your reporting. I think you are fair. I get your reports sent to my inbox. Reply here with an answer. I think 5k is a good price.

Holt thumbed up to the paperclip attachment and clicked it. His screen filled with a blurry image of three body bags next to each other on a road. In the background was what looked like a US Marshals' transport vehicle. There were at least a dozen federal investigators in the frame: FBI, USMS, ATF. It looked legitimate. Holt drew another sip of coffee, considering what to do with the email, when his phone rang.

"Hi, Freddie."

"Hey. On background, and not attributable to me or anyone at the agency, I can give you a couple of nuggets. That work?"

"How do you want me to sell it?"

"Just attribute to a law enforcement source with indirect knowledge of the investigation. Say the source is not authorized to speak publicly on the issue. That always sounds good."

"Got it. What's the info."

"They're freaking out about this. They're already knee deep in the US Marshal debacle. They're blindsided."

"Who is they?"

"The intelligence community. I was in a briefing this morning. It was low-level stuff, but the tone in the room was not good. I'm not privy to what the top brass is saying, but I do know they're scrambling to put together a team to look into this."

"What can you tell me about Agent Majors?"

"I wasn't here then," Freddie said. "I was in the Army. I was a PAO at Landstuhl. I've just heard the anecdotal, rumor stuff."

"Which is…?"

"I don't want to go there, man. I mean, I trust you, but I can't talk about it today. Maybe over a beer in a few weeks."

"A few weeks doesn't help me, Freddie."

"I hear you. I can't give you any more today. I hope that's cool."

"It's cool. Thanks for everything. I owe you."

Holt looked at the image on his screen. He opened up Twitter and typed a response.

`checking with boss. will reply to email.`

Holt clicked on the browser icon on his computer and went to PlausibleDeniability.info. His article's link was top corner, left and in bold. That was the above-the-fold spot on the site.

Next to his article was a large photograph of President Felicia Jackson at her press conference, with the quote *"The attack was brutal"* in red underneath the picture. There were three or four articles about the attack. Holt scanned through all of them, better familiarizing himself with the details. Then he called his editor.

"You got the update for me?" she asked without a greeting. "I need to get it up quickly. Your piece, incredibly, is getting more unique views than the marshal ambush stuff combined. Unreal, right?"

"Yeah," Holt said, unamused that his sideshow of a story was outperforming the reporting on an issue of national security. "And yes. I'll have your update in ten minutes. I've got sources telling me the FBI is reacting to our report. That's enough for now, right?"

"Perfect."

"There's something else."

"What? You want off the Horus story? Not gonna happen. I'm probably gonna send someone else to Barcelona. You're too valuable on this."

Holt gritted his teeth. "I'm being punished for doing my job?"

"I don't see it as punishment."

"Whatever," he dismissed, working hard to not raise his voice. "My perception is my reality. It's punishment. Regardless, I've got a tip I need to discuss."

"What about?"

"An anonymous person reached out to me on Twitter and then sent me an email. I forwarded it to you. Read it. Tell me what you think."

"I see it," she said. "Hang on a moment."

Holt started writing his update. He clicked between his notes and his draft, drawing from his notes as he wrote. He'd gotten three sentences finished when the editor interrupted.

"Is this for real?" she asked. "Seriously?"

"It looks legit," Holt said, adjusting his Bluetooth earpiece. "I can't really know without seeing the video."

"Is it going to cost us five grand to take a look?"

"I think so."

"Do it."

"So you want me working both stories? Or you want me to switch to the tip? I mean it's national security. It's more up my alley, and I—"

"Work both. Or give the tip to someone else. Up to you. Get me the Horus update in ten minutes. I need it up by the top of the hour. If you can, shoot a forty-five-second teaser with your laptop camera. We'll upload it with the piece. It'll do huge numbers."

Holt hung up and cursed his editor. He was stuck in Houston on schlock. True, he was doing everything he could to make it newsworthy. It was still gossip-mongering page six crap. He wanted to be on his way to Barcelona. He wanted to be ogling bikini-clad women playing beach volleyball near Port Olympic as he sipped beer and prepped for the G12 SECURITY summit.

He slugged back the rest of his third Americano, wincing at the bitterness of the cold remnants at the bottom of the cup. He typed an email to the anonymous tipster, agreeing to the price, and suggested a delivery method. Holt went back to his update and within ten minutes had it finished. He recorded a brief video introducing the piece and sent that.

He looked around the coffee shop. There were some moms in yoga pants commiserating about nannies at one table and a couple of businessmen talking oil prices at another. This was not where he wanted to be. However, he was a pro; he would make the best of it. And maybe he'd meet up again with Karen.

*

The assassin thanked her Uber driver and hopped out of his Prius a block away from what served as the Harris County morgue. She was dressed in a cheap black pantsuit, an expensive, shoulder-length mousy brown wig, and dark sunglasses. She was lugging a large, floral-printed canvas handbag.

The assassin had never been to Houston and underestimated the thick, ubiquitous humidity. She was sweating by the time she'd reached an aging convenience store across the street from her intended destination.

She asked the clerk for the bathroom key and agreed to purchase something in exchange for use of the facilities. Inside the cramped space, which doubled as a custodian's storage room, she slipped out of the pantsuit and into a pair of acid-washed blue jeans and a T-shirt bedazzled with plastic emeralds. She replaced the brown wig with a shorter black one and slipped on some uncomfortable twenty-dollar high heels. The assassin unzipped a compartment inside the bag, which was resting on a mop bucket, and pulled out a vial of saline solution. She squeezed several drops into each eye and held her eyes shut. After a look in the warped, barely reflective mirror, she was ready.

She zipped up her bag and returned the key to the counter with a pack of gum and a bottle of water. The clerk, who seemed oblivious to the change in appearance, took her money and waved her out of the store. The security cameras behind the counter weren't working. The associated monitors were awash with static.

The humidity hit her like a steam bath when she stepped out into the store's parking lot. The wig, new and scratchy, irritated her scalp in the heat. She willed herself to ignore the discomfort as she had with so many other things and walked quickly across the wide street to the Forensic Science building in the Texas Medical Center.

Inside the lobby, behind a booth encased in thick glass, was a security guard.

"May I help you?" asked the thin, balding man from behind his Coke-bottle glasses. He wasn't a threat.

"Yes," the assassin answered, lowering her sunglasses. Her eyes were bloodshot, her voice salted with a pinch of the Rio Grande Valley. "Please. I am looking for my mother. I think maybe you have her body here."

"And you are?"

"Hilda Mentiroso. I spoke with your Dr. Corvus. She said she could help me."

"Let me check." The man made a brief phone call and hung up. "She'll be right out. In the meantime, I need you to sign in. And I'll need an ID, please."

The assassin stepped closer to the glass booth and pulled a clipboard through an opening. She signed a name and her time of arrival. She noted that all other guests had signed out already. She was the only visitor inside the building. That was a bonus. It would lessen collateral damage.

"I'll need the ID." The guard looked over his glasses at her scoldingly. "I can't let you in without it."

"I'm sorry." She smiled. "Here you go." She fished an identification from her purse that matched the name she'd given them. It was one of her dozens of identities. She cycled through them as needed.

The guard took the driver's license and compared its photograph to the woman standing in front of him. They looked similar enough. He wrote down the driver's license number and then slid it back through the pass-through.

"Here's a visitor's badge. Please keep it visible at all times."

The assassin smiled and took the badge. She pinched the clip on its back and attached it to her T-shirt, right between her breasts, noticing the guard pay attention.

"My eyes are up here, sir," she scolded coyly, giggling.

He cleared his throat and quickly looked down at the clipboard, his lips pursed with embarrassment.

A moment later, a slender, pretty woman emerged through a locked door that led into the lobby. She was wearing a long white lab coat, her hair twisted into a bun with a sharpened pencil at its center.

"Ms. Mentiroso?" the woman said, offering her hand. "I'm Dr. Corvus. I'm so sorry you had to come here to Houston."

"It is okay." The assassin shook Karen's hand with both of hers. "It was a quick flight. And this, I pray, will put to an end so much suffering for my family." The assassin crossed herself and kissed her thumb before raising it to God.

"You flew here?"

"Yes."

"Wow. You did get here quickly, then. Where did you travel from?" Karen punched a passcode into the door, nodded at the man at the desk, and invited the assassin into the secure area of the building.

"I came from El Paso," she lied. "We are from El Paso. My mother, me, my sisters."

"Tell me more about your mother. What makes you think you found her here?" Karen led the assassin through a maze of narrow hallways. The assassin marked her steps, dropping mental breadcrumbs with each turn.

"Your website said the woman was my mother's height. She had a tattoo of a cross on her neck. My mother had that tattoo. And she was wearing a pink and green bracelet. That bracelet was a gift from my sister."

Karen stopped at a wide doorway at the end of a hallway near the rear of the building. She punched in a number to crack open the door and then paused.

"This could be very emotional," she said to the woman posing as Hilda Mentiroso. "I want to prepare you for that. Your mother will look different from how you remember her. Despite the cold temperatures, organic changes do happen. You may not recognize her, even if the woman is your mother."

"I understand." The assassin looked over her shoulder, noting the lack of security cameras at this end of the hall, and followed Karen into the room.

CHAPTER 18

CAMP DAVID
CATOCTIN MOUNTAIN PARK, MARYLAND

"So the British and the French are on board?" President
Felicia Jackson stood at the head of a table in the Aspen Lodge.
"We've got to work on the Spanish and the Italians."

"To clarify," explained Brandon Goodman, "we got
Downing Street and Elysee Palace on board. I can't speak to how
amenable the British and French people will be to the proposals."

"The British won't be a problem," said a young analyst with
expertise in Western European policy. "They've already accepted
security cameras on every street corner. They won't balk. The
French are another story."

"How so?" The President put her hands on her hips and
glanced at Matti, who hadn't looked her in the eyes the entire
meeting.

"They're still upset about our government spying on their
government for much of the last two decades."

"WikiLeaks," the president bemoaned. "I hate those jerks as
much as I hate lawyers."

"The prime minister isn't bothered by it," the analyst told
her. "He knows the game. However, his people haven't forgotten
about it all of these years later. And they don't like the idea of the
United States bullying its leadership into some sort of surveillance
legislation drafted by Americans."

"We didn't draft it," the president corrected. "We just made
strong suggestions with recommended language."

"Either way"—the analyst shrugged—"it could be a tough
sell. The French feel somewhat insulated from terror. Nothing has
happened there since Charlie Hebdo in 2015. They have short
memories."

"Joie de vivre?" the president joked.

"As for the Spanish and Italian delegations"—Goodman
pushed forward without laughing at his boss's joke—"it's more of an
uphill fight."

"Go on…" The president walked around the table as she
listened. Her focus, however, was on Matti. Something was off, even
more than usual.

"It's good news that the talks are in Barcelona," said Goodman. "That means the Spanish are amenable to the idea of the shared legislation. We do know they have reservations about some of the finer points."

"As in?" The president stopped behind Matti's chair and put her hands on her aide's shoulders. Matti tensed at her touch.

"The shared data pool," said the analyst. "They're not convinced of the need. They contend they already share relevant intelligence with the CIA. They don't necessarily believe unfettered access is a good idea."

"It goes both ways," argued the president, squeezing Matti's shoulders. "There's a trust there. We give, we take. They give, they take. This is a global fight. What happens to one of us affects all of us."

"That's where the Italians have a problem," Goodman said. "They think this falls under the auspices of NATO, the United Nations, the World Court, and the IMF. All of them are affected by this. We're talking about security, law enforcement, international justice, and banking."

"The secretary general is publicly opposed to SECURITY or any of its duplicate programs. He says it violates human rights to monitor, gather, and store the data that's included in the act."

The president let go of Matti's shoulders and moved around the table to her seat. "Where is he privately?"

"He doesn't care," said Goodman. "Our ambassador tells us he thinks it makes his job easier if we've got absolute access to everything. He was never a fan of the Magna Carta."

"He's Russian—" President Jackson laughed "—so that's not surprising."

"He thinks it would give him leverage in negotiations. It gives him power."

"How so?"

"There's a provision in the act that allows for the sharing of collected data with any multilateral organization of which the United States is a member."

"Did I know that?" asked the president, taking her seat.

"Yes," Matti said. "We discussed it four weeks ago at a meeting in the Old Executive Office Building."

"She speaks!" exclaimed President Jackson. "Matti, it's good to know you're with us."

Matti smiled thinly.

"Remember, Matti—" the president stared into her aide's eyes, waiting for Matti to look away "—you're with us or you're against us."

*

Sir Spencer Thomas felt blessed to be in a fresh change of clothes. Granted, it wasn't the kind of apparel to which he was accustomed, but it was better than the overstarched, cheap cotton-blend prison uniforms he'd worn for nine months.

Reclining aboard a private Gulfstream 650 aircraft thousands of feet above the Atlantic, he admitted to himself there were times he wasn't sure he'd be free again. He occasionally lost faith and feared he'd forever remain prisoner 02681-044. It was a calculated risk he'd taken, getting caught with the others as he had.

It was sad, really. The others were either dead or imprisoned. They'd played their parts so perfectly. He reached over and picked up a leaded snifter full of brandy. Sir Spencer dipped his pinkie into the glass and sucked the liquid. He closed his eyes and relished the sweet taste of the distilled wine.

He'd missed this.

He wondered, as his plane screamed toward the next phase of the grand design, if they could pull it off.

Could they succeed, or would they fail as they had before? Would the few men more powerful than he sacrifice him as they had when the Capitol exploded?

For millennia, the Brethren had secretly pulled strings, toppled governments, influenced policy, and redistributed wealth with impunity. In the last half of the twentieth century, their veil was lifted and their power threatened.

A young, brash politician stood before the American Newspaper Publishers Association in April 1961. He told those assembled, "There is a grave danger that an announced need for increased security will be seized upon by those anxious to expand its meaning to the very limits of censorship and concealment. We are opposed around the world by a monolithic and ruthless conspiracy that relies on covert means for expanding its sphere of influence—on infiltration rather than invasion, on subversion instead of elections. It is a system which has conscripted vast human and material resources into the building of a tightly knit, highly efficient machine."

That politician was John F. Kennedy. He was assassinated thirty-one months later. Instead of working hard to again bury their highly efficient machine, a newly empowered group of leaders suggested the acknowledged myth of the Brethren could become more powerful than its denial.

Unlike his father, and his father before him, Sir Spencer was among those contrarians; those who believed they could effect more change by lurking in the shadows than by hiding in the dark.

One summer, at their annual California retreat, a much younger Sir Spencer proposed the grandest of all ideas. He opened with a biblical reference, which surprised his brothers, but had them nodding their heads in agreement.

"The greatest trick the Devil ever played was convincing the world he didn't exist," Sir Spencer told them. "Perhaps, had he hinted all along at how powerful he could be, without ever denying the reality of his influence, we'd live in different times than those in which we find ourselves. Maybe we would have already realized the new order."

Over the next several summers, he and some other powerful Brothers formulated a decades-long plan to reshape their membership. They would stop denying their existence and would use commercialism to reinforce it. Their symbology would be everywhere. It would be so evident it would become invisible, like the mountains to those who lived amongst them. The messaging would be embedded in their minds. They would see it yet be blind to it. It was brilliant.

The Queen knighted him for his loyalty. The Sultan of Brunei rewarded him with immeasurable wealth. His influence and power grew. By the end of the first Gulf War, he was near the top of the Brethren's hierarchy.

Sir Spencer's job was to recruit those who could contribute to the establishment of the new world order in a variety of ways. Those recruits would make the new order palatable to the uninitiated. They would welcome it without knowing what it really meant for their lives, for their liberty.

His unofficial title was Brother In Charge of Diversification. He was toasted and regaled whenever news reports subtly hinted at machinations of his doing. From the energy industry, to fast-food chains, food products, and even Hollywood, Sir Spencer found ways to impart his influence.

He'd made mistakes along the way, however. Some of the young recruits in the entertainment industry couldn't handle their programming. Their minds weren't strong enough. Despite the fame and riches afforded them by their loyalty to the Brethren, they flaked. Sir Spencer would read about them or see their meltdowns on television and regret his decision to choose them. Many of them died of overdoses or previously undiagnosed heart conditions.

There was the occasional intelligence operative who failed or who suddenly succumbed to a misguided conscience. One FBI analyst named Majors came to mind. He'd stopped providing valuable back-channel correspondence about domestic threats and counterintelligence methodology. He was warned. He didn't listen.

Others, politicians most notably, strayed from the herd as they absorbed their own power. They thought they were above what got them to their lofty perch. They, too, found the gravity of the Brethren inescapable. Dexter Foreman was the biggest of those disappointments.

Horus was also one of Sir Spencer's regrets. His disintegration was more subtle. It wasn't a publicly self-destructive dénouement, despite his heroin addiction. Instead, he'd chosen to write lyrics and publish music that increasingly hinted at the nature of the Brethren's plans. The viral symbology morphed into references of abuse and social repression. That was not part of the deal. If he'd just named an album Magna Carta, there'd have been no problem, Sir Spencer laughed to himself.

Sir Spencer shifted in the leather captain's chair. He was the only passenger among the eight seats, and he sighed aloud at the loss of the musical protégé, considering what had gone wrong with Horus.

What was it that had spooked Horus? Why had he turned? Did he know something he shouldn't have known?

Sir Spencer took another sip of the brandy and swished it across his tongue. His thoughts turned from Horus to another protégé, one with so much more promise and whose skills had proven so much more useful.

He was eager to land and reacquaint himself with Jon Custos. It would be good to visit with him again, especially since it would likely be the last time they'd see each other.

CHAPTER 19

AVENUE DE LES DRASSANES
BARCELONA, SPAIN

Custos strolled east along the Avenue de les Drassanes, whistling "Danse Macabre," a haunting piece from Camille Saint-Saëns. His hands were in his pockets, his eyes on the smartly dressed people who lived and worked in an area that had become as elite as the Zona Alta in the hills. At the end of the avenue was a large statue of Christopher Columbus, called the Mirador de Colom. Custos's eyes climbed to the top of the sixty-meter-high monument and he laughed to himself. The explorer's likeness was facing into the distance, toward the New World. It was magnificent, except for the fact that the statue pointed in the wrong direction.

He passed the monument and crossed the circular square to the Rambla del Mar, the seaside promenade adjacent to a beautiful marina. Custos looked north, his eyes dancing along the forest of sailboat masts dotting the Reial Club de Barcelona.

Without taking his eyes from the swaying masts, he pulled his phone from his pocket and dialed. The flight attendant answered on the first ring, and after he apologized for ringing her earlier than planned, she offered to meet him at one of the restaurants lining the beach. He'd suggested room service instead. His treat. She devoured the invitation and gave him her room number. He'd be there in ten minutes, he told her.

"Back to work," he mumbled to himself and turned his back on the masts. In one pocket he held onto his phone. In the other, he played with a set of keys.

Ahead of him, to the south of the Rambla del Mar, Custos noticed flashing police lights and heard the overmodulated, unintelligible instructions of an officer on a bullhorn. Beyond the lights, as he walked closer, he could see a group of demonstrators corralled in an area at the edge of the man-made peninsula on which the World Trade Center and its adjacent hotel were perched.

The demonstrators, who numbered no more than fifty, were protesting the upcoming G12 summit. They were chanting and thrusting posters up into the air. The police, in full riot gear, were surrounding them.

Custos overheard a pair of officers talking about the demonstrators. The day before there were just a dozen of them. Now there were four times as many. They anticipated thousands by the time the summit started in two days.

As he approached the western entry to the peninsula, an officer held up his hand, asking Custos to stop. After a few questions, he let Custos walk past a single row of wooden barricades toward the World Trade Center and the Eurostars Grand Marina Hotel.

Custos ignored the chants and the occasional wail of a siren as he neared the hotel entrance. The large building was designed to embody the spirit of an ocean liner, its lines curved and sloped like that of a ship in port.

At the entrance to the hotel, protected by a series of two-foot-high cornet pillars, he found the doors protected by armed guards. He was stopped from entering the hotel, despite insisting he was there to visit a guest.

"I am sorry, sir," said a black-suited man with a deep tan, which made his teeth appear impossibly white. "You must have a key. Or you must have an escort who has a key. It is a safety measure. I am hopeful you understand."

Custos called up to the flight attendant. She apologized and assured her guest she'd be downstairs immediately. He'd barely replaced the phone in his pocket when she fluttered through the front door and instructed the tan man to allow her guest inside the hotel.

"I'm so glad you called me," she said breathlessly, skipping through the polished travertine lobby toward a spiral staircase. "I wasn't sure you really would." She reached back to grab his hand and pulled him up the stairs, gliding to the second level and to a bank of elevators.

"We didn't need to take the stairs." She giggled, pressing an elevator call button. "I just love the romance of it. A spiral staircase? It's so magnificent. It makes me feel like Scarlett O'Hara. You know? *Gone With The Wind.*"

Custos smiled at her, his fingers still entwined with hers. He'd play the suitor for now. There was no harm in allowing her the fantasy for a while longer.

The elevator door opened and she pulled him inside. She keyed her floor, the doors shut, and she turned to face him. Keeping his head down to avoid the security camera mounted in the ceiling, he took her shoulders and spun her around so his back was to the fish-eye lens.

"So, Mr. Vasconselos," she purred. "What's for dinner?" She took his other hand and pulled it around to the small of her back.

He looked down at her and the counterintuitive innocence of her face. Her cheeks were round, her almond eyes framed by long lashes. Her lips were thin but nicely shaped around a warm smile. She was a pretty woman, and more so without the requisite makeup of her job.

He leaned over and kissed her. She closed her eyes as he pressed his lips onto hers. She let go of his hands and drew hers to the back of his head. Had he not pulled away, they'd have missed their floor.

Giggling and walking on her toes, she led him down the hall. She opened the door to room 3669 and tossed the key onto a sleek wooden table near the entry. Custos took note of the room as she made her way to the large bed. The furnishings had a Scandinavian flair; they were modern and artful but utilitarian. The large picture windows opposite the entry overlooked the concrete peninsula. She didn't have an ocean view, but that was good.

"You are anxious," he said to the flight attendant, who sat on the edge of the bed. "You need patience."

"Why is that?" She bit her lower lip and loosened the top button of her blouse.

"Because the anticipation is often more powerful than the act itself," he said, knowing his intention was lost on her. "I enjoy the anticipation." He walked to the window and drew the curtains. Even at this elevation, it was better to be careful.

"Then I will too." She worked free another button.

"Perhaps," he said, removing his jacket to drape it across a corner chair, his eye catching a glimpse of the room key on the wooden table nearby. "Perhaps."

An hour later, she'd long stopped enjoying anything. Her room key was stuffed into Custos's pants pocket. On his head was a pink and white Toronto Blue Jays baseball cap he found when emptying her baggage.

He locked her door behind him, placing a "Do Not Disturb" tag on the handle, and worked his way through the hotel's labyrinth and to the World Trade Center with its enormous conference rooms and banquet halls.

Custos would flash the room key when challenged by the occasional security guard, and they'd let him pass with little more than a suspicious look. He found a service elevator and, after fumbling to find the right key, activated the call button and descended to the basement.

Custos knew from having viewed schematics of the building where he would find soft spots and access points. He needed to familiarize himself with more than two-dimensional drawings. He needed to feel the space, gain a poacher's familiarity with it.

He was alone in the basement, walking with purpose from one end of the building to the other. He pulled the ball cap low over his eyes. Though he imagined his hulking frame would give him away if he became a target, at least his face and bald head wouldn't be instantly recognizable to the growing security force.

Stopping at one end of the building near a storage supply closet, he checked his keys. Guessing, he found the right one to access the closet and entered the room filled floor to ceiling with cleaning supplies, lightbulbs, batteries, and spare parts.

Large metal storage racks framed the room on all four sides. Custos picked the one on the right, tested its strength, and climbed up the half dozen shelves to reach the ceiling. He wrapped his left arm around one of the vertical support beams on the metal rack and used his right to poke a two-by-two composite ceiling tile. It came loose without much effort, so Custos climbed higher. He shoved aside some cans of paint thinner on the top shelf and positioned his body such that he could use both hands to access the space above the ceiling.

Poking his head inside and using his phone flashlight to see, he surveyed the cavernous space above the ceiling. There were electrical conduits, plumbing pipes and joints, and other mechanical features that were all labeled. Arrows pointed flow and direction. Numbers corresponded to rooms and halls he knew were listed on the schematics he'd studied.

This would be so much easier than he'd anticipated.

It was as if he was destined to facilitate the new world order.

"*A Deo et Rege*," he mumbled.

CHAPTER 20

TEXAS MEDICAL CENTER
HOUSTON, TEXAS

The assassin closed the stainless steel door, sliding it shut with a final heave. The freezer cabinets weren't designed to hold two bodies.

Karen was a tall woman. Despite her slender, enviable figure, the assassin struggled to accommodate her in the narrow drawer atop the nameless woman she'd pretended was her mother. The assassin rubbed the goose bumps on her forearms before pulling out her phone to send a text message:

> done with first. on to second.

She slipped the phone back into her bag along with her visitor's badge, Karen's phone, eyeglasses, car keys, and the red-stained pencil she'd acquired from Karen's bun. Then she punched in the passcode to exit the room and welcomed the relative warmth of the hallway, casually striding through the maze of hallways, her heels clicking on the linoleum.

At the front of the building, before she reached the coded door leading to the lobby, she encountered the guard. He tilted his head. His eyes narrowed.

"Weren't you escorted by Dr. Corvus?" He stood from his bar-height seat and planted his hands on his hips.

"I was." The assassin smiled. "She had to stop to use the ladies' room. She told me to go ahead and sign out."

"I'm going to need you to stay here until she catches up." The guard rubbed his forehead with one hand and took a step toward the assassin. "And where is your visitor's badge? I'll need that back. You should have been wearing it. All of this is highly irregular."

She patted her chest as if looking for the missing badge. "I'm so sorry. I think I slipped it into my bag." She unzipped the bag and stuffed her hand inside. As she fished through the contents of the bag, she subtly stepped closer to the guard.

"You said she went to the bathroom?" He looked past her, down the hall, craning his neck toward the water fountain flanked by bathroom doors. "And she told you to leave on your own?"

"Yes." She nodded, her eyes smiling from her cheeks. "She was such a sweet lady." The assassin slid another step toward the guard. Her eyes darted from his glare to his neck and then to his hands. She kept digging around in her bag, blindly searching its contents.

"Did you determine the woman you were here to see was your mother?" He bit his lower lip, knitted his brow.

"Yes." The assassin nodded, calling on tears, which welled immediately.

"Oh." The guard's stance softened. "I'm sorry."

"It's fine." She shook off the faux melancholy and looked into her bag. "Here it is."

"Wait a second." The guard held up his hand.

"What?" The assassin looked up, her eyes wide and her hand still in the bag.

"You said Dr. Corvus was a sweet lady?" The guard put his hand on his hip above his Taser. "That's an odd—"

Before he could finish his thought, the assassin pulled her hand from the bag. In her fist was Karen's pencil. With one single, artful movement, she drove the sharp end of the pencil into the guard's throat, removed it from the puncture and plunged it deep into his right ear.

The wounds, she knew from experience, were not fatal. But they were effective.

His hearing was likely ruined in the one ear. The pencil tip passed through the tympanic membrane and cochlea before tearing part of the audiovestibular nerve. It was so painful the guard likely wasn't even aware of the thick ache from the initial wound. That puncture to the throat was expertly placed between the guard's Adam's apple and the cricoid cartilage. It was essentially an unnecessary tracheotomy. Air oozed from the hole, blood leaking in tiny bubbles that oozed and popped against his neck.

As he writhed on the floor, grabbing his throat with one hand and his ear with the other, she bent down onto one knee. The goose bumps returned to her arms.

"You'll be fine," she advised. "You really should have let me leave without the hassle."

His eyes were wild, pupils smaller than the holes in his throat and ear. She knew he wasn't registering what she was saying, but she was compelled to speak with him nonetheless. She smiled at him and stood over him for moment before punching the exit button to the lobby.

She started to leave, then turned and walked back to the welcome desk. She pulled the clipboard through the opening in the thick glass and signed out.

"Wouldn't want to break the rules," she mumbled. "That would be highly irregular."

By the time a custodian found the guard passed out and wheezing through the hole in his neck, the assassin was downtown in Karen's Saab, looking for a free parking spot along the curb in front of Treebeard's restaurant. She was craving something spicy.

Over a bowl of beans, rice, and andouille sausage, she scrolled through Karen's phone. She found photographs from trips to the beach, nights out with girlfriends, and a happy-looking mutt with a purple tongue.

The contact list was relatively short, and several of the entries were listed by what the assassin assumed were nicknames. There was no listing for Dillinger or Holt. On a second scroll, she noticed an entry for "Dolt" with a 703 area code. The number matched a couple of incoming calls.

The assassin put the phone on the table and looked across the busy dining room. Businessmen and women were going about their lives blindly. They sucked down their drinks and shoveled plates full of food into their mouths.

Oblivious.

She rolled her eyes at one man in particular. He was wearing an expensive-looking suit, the jacket draped over the back of his chair. He kept fiddling with his onyx and silver cufflinks, chatting up the young woman sitting across from him. He'd occasionally rattle his wrist, revealing what the assassin imagined was a pricey Swiss watch. The man thought he was a player, his arrogance seeping from his laser-cleaned pores.

He was clueless with no idea of the forces that secretly controlled his existence.

A puppet.

She raked her fork across the bottom of her bowl and plucked the last piece of andouille with its tines. She pulled the piece of meat into her mouth and chewed it, mashing it into smaller and smaller pieces before swallowing.

The assassin wiped the corners of her mouth with a paper napkin and took a final swallow of ice water. She picked up Karen's phone and sent a text message to Dolt.

> Would love to see you again. Tonight?

A minute later, Dillinger Holt responded.

> Of course. I'm stuck here for a couple of days. You'll make it worth it. Where?

The assassin smirked and considered her response. She remembered from the dinner receipt she'd found that they'd had drinks.

> Your hotel. Remind me though. I was a bit tipsy. What hotel and room #?

Holt responded with the information. The assassin used Karen's phone to input the hotel into the GPS application. She was close.

So was the end of the mission.

CHAPTER 21

CAMP DAVID
CATOCTIN MOUNTAIN PARK, MARYLAND

Matti sat across from the president in the Aspen Lodge meeting room. They were alone. It was late in the day. Matti was hungry and tired and fighting against the urge to pill pop.

"What's going on with you, Matti?" President Jackson sounded like the frustrated mother of a teenager. At least that was how Matti imagined a mother would sound.

"I don't understand."

"I'm getting tired of having these conversations. You're clearly distracted. You're not the heroine I hired. Out with it."

Matti threw caution to the wind before she had a chance to think about it. As soon as the words jumped from her lips, she regretted having said them.

"Saw who?" The president leaned on her elbows and pressed against the table toward Matti.

"Sir Spencer Thomas."

"Where?" The president's eyes narrowed. "On television?"

"No. I saw him here. With you."

President Jackson's eyes widened and she threw back her head in laughter.

"It's not funny." Matti wasn't amused by the charade. "Why is he here?"

The president shook her head and planted her palms flat against the table. "Oh, it's not funny. I'm laughing at the ridiculousness of it."

"Why is he here?" Matti studied her boss. The president was either telling the truth or was pathological. She wasn't giving anything away.

"He's not, Matti."

"I saw him. You were with him in one of the cabins on the northern end of the property. I was jogging by. I saw you both."

"Are you sure?"

"Yes."

"Really?" The president lowered her voice. "Are you *really* sure? What you're suggesting…"

Matti considered the president's conviction, her measured but firm response. She paused, flexed her hand, and nodded.

"First of all—" President Jackson sighed "—I'm going to forgive the treachery of your allegation and talk this through with you as someone who cares deeply about your well-being."

Matti slunk back against her chair, folding her arms across her chest. She didn't want a lecture, but she'd quickly lost control of the conversation.

"I know you're an addict, Matti. I've known it for a while. I've overlooked it, and maybe I've enabled you. That's my fault."

"I'm not—"

"Let me finish." The president held up her hand, stopping Matti mid-defense. "I've seen your hands shake. I've noticed the mood swings, the dark circles under your eyes from insomnia. You're struggling, I get that. Whatever it is you think you saw was a figment of your drug-addled imagination."

Matti tried looking the president in the eyes, but couldn't. Instead, she focused on the table in front of her. Her head was down.

"You're searching for something, Matti," the president suggested. "You can't accept you did everything you could to stop the terrorists. Now you're on some ridiculous mission to redeem yourself. I hear it in the way you talk; I see it in the things you do. And I know about Bill Davidson's journal."

Matti snapped to attention, her mouth agape.

"It's my White House, Matti." The president pushed back from the table. "I know everything that happens there. And I know you need help. After Barcelona, you're getting treatment. That is, if you think you can make the trip to Spain?"

Matti nodded.

"Good." President Jackson's hand trailed along the table as she walked. "Now enough of these conspiracy theories, Matti, or your promising career could come to a swift, ignominious end. Far worse than those hearings you endured. Understood?"

Matti nodded again.

"Now"—the president rapped her knuckles on the table "—I'm going to get a late dinner and a power nap before we leave. I think we're out of here around three. A nice red-eye to Barcelona." She winked, turned her back, and slunk out of the room.

Matti knew better than to say anything to dispute the president's assertions. Much of what her boss had said was true. She *was* an addict. She *was* looking for redemption.

However, the president's quick dismissal of her without any plausible explanation for what Matti knew she saw was a de facto admission as far as Matti was concerned. That, followed by the threat of career destruction and public embarrassment from a woman who claimed to care deeply for her, was enough to affirm what Matti had seen.

There was something bigger at play, something more sinister than the attack on the Capitol. Matti wondered into what rabbit hole she'd fallen and if she'd be able to find her way out of it before it collapsed around her.

CHAPTER 22

WASHINGTON, DC

Horus didn't trust many people in the course of his abbreviated life. Aside from an accountant and a business manager he knew would ensure his financial security, he didn't invest in people. It was easier to enter any relationship with a healthy amount of distrust.

One of those relationships was with a Washington, DC, call girl. She was recommended to him by a mutual friend who promised discretion.

He enjoyed her company so much he would fly her to meet with him in various cities. He knew she had other clients, some of whom were powerful men with agendas more critical than penning angst and screaming into microphones at disaffected crowds. He didn't care.

He loved her intoxicating smell: cinnamon, chocolate, and fruit. He'd bury his face in her neck and inhale. She was as good as any drug. Her pale, almost translucent skin was like porcelain, adorned with an Aquarian tattoo on the inside of her arm and a diamond navel piercing. The diamond was a gift from another client, she'd told him when he'd asked about it.

"Who's the client?" Horus asked as they lay in bed together for the last time. "I might have to buy you a bigger diamond."

"That's not necessary," she purred. "And I can't tell you who he is, you know that." Her finger dragged along his chest, the long red nail tracing the cut of his muscles.

"What's he do?" Horus pressed. "Is he an athlete?"

"No." She giggled. "He's a...politician."

"That narrows it." Horus laughed. "You live in DC. It could be anybody."

"Exactly," she hummed. She patted him on the stomach and then slid away from him. "I have to use the little girls' room."

Horus watched her glide away from him, his eyes transfixed on her immaculate figure. She was magical. He closed his eyes and replayed the previous thirty minutes in his mind. He was mid-highlight when she called from the bathroom.

"Hey, can you do me a favor?"

"Sure. What do you need?"

"Can you slide my cell phone under the door? I meant to grab it. I need to check messages before I get in the shower."

Horus slid out of the comfort of the bed and moved to the chair where she'd disrobed. Her dress was there. Her high heels were unstrapped and on the floor next to her bag. He didn't see her phone.

He dug into her purse, feeling around for the phone. He didn't find it. So he opened up the bag with both hands and looked inside.

There was a makeup bag, some loose change, a box of condoms, a roll of cash bound with a red rubber band, some pepper spray, and a large headset.

He picked up the headset and rolled it over in his hands. It looked like something a telephone operator would wear. He set it aside and then stuffed his hand inside the bag again. He found the phone and a blue journal.

Horus placed the phone next to the headset and thumbed through the notebook. In it, he saw the names of people he knew. They were part of the organization that had funded his rise. Vav Six, the music producer, had introduced many of them at the Brethren's late night gatherings.

What was she doing with this information? And what were these people planning?

Semtex? Assassination? Plot? Funeral? Government course-correction?

"Did you find my phone?" she called from the bathroom. The shower was running. Horus looked up and saw steam misting into the room from the space between the bottom of the bathroom door and the floor.

"Yeah," he called. "I found it." He walked the few steps to the bathroom and slid the phone to her. "Here you go."

Horus backed away from the door and dropped to the edge of the bed. He stared at the journal, understanding he was in over his head.

His fame, his popularity, was a product of some secret cabal bent on more than subliminal advertising or a cultural revolution, as he'd been told. He now understood he was a pawn in some dark, far-reaching conspiracy of violence.

He stood from the bed and put the journal and the headset back in her bag, considering his options.

He could confront the hooker: What was she doing with the journal? How did she know the people he knew?

He could ask Vav Six about what he'd seen: Who were these people, really? What were they planning?

He could go to the authorities. Like they'd ever believe him. Or if they did, who was to say they weren't part of the plan too?

Or he could forget about it and pretend it didn't exist.

It was just a bunch of names and places on paper. It wasn't real.

He ran his hands through his hair with a heavy sigh. The decision was easy.

Horus rolled over to the nightstand and shook out a line of cocaine, which he immediately inhaled. He pinched the end of his nose, wiping away the excess powder, and walked back to the bathroom door.

He found it unlocked and opened it a crack. "Mind if I join you?"

"Of course not," she called. "I'm just getting in."

That was the beginning of the end.

Within days, she was dead and the Capitol was rubble. While Horus watched the drama unfolding on television, he called Vav Six and told him what he'd seen in the journal.

The music producer told him to forget about it, to keep quiet. He told Horus their lives depended upon it.

Horus couldn't forget. His music began to reflect his growing disillusionment. It was a problem, and despite Vav Six's warning, Horus couldn't contain himself.

His growing popularity only compounded what the more powerful of the Brethren believed was a burgeoning threat. If they allowed him to continue much longer, he'd cast his own shadow and they'd be unable to control him.

So they stopped him.

CHAPTER 23

HOUSTON, TEXAS

The video was convincing. Dillinger Holt watched it for a fourth time and was certain Sir Spencer Thomas was alive. Or if he was killed, it hadn't happened during the ambush. It was worth the five thousand dollars.

Holt started the video again on his laptop. The audio was captured with an ambient microphone and was muddled at best.

"We transporting all three to the same location?" Holt could hear one of the voices say. He couldn't hear the response; then the first voice spoke again.

"Three bodies and four ME vans? What's that about?"

"Above my pay grade," said the second voice. *"I just do what I'm told."*

"I won't ask, then."

Gusts of wind made the rest of the conversation inaudible. But the remaining video clearly showed bodies being loaded into three different vans. The fourth van was empty and left without a body in the back.

In all, the video ran just three minutes, but it was more than long enough to cast doubt on the official story. Holt pulled the headphones from his ears and looked around the Starbucks. Another wave of customers had come and gone. He checked his watch; it was getting late and he'd spent way too much time in the coffee shop.

He'd intended to visit the Toyota Center and try to talk with the security guard who'd seen a woman leaving Horus's room before he died, but the video had taken precedence. He'd spent much of his day negotiating, acquiring, and reviewing it. He'd even written a rough three-hundred-word post and sent it to his boss. He was waiting for the attorneys to finesse it and okay it for publication.

Holt checked his phone, swiped it open to his messages, and sent a text to Karen's phone. He was anxious to see her.

you available early?

He immediately saw the little dots on the left side of the screen. She was responding. Holt smiled to himself. Maybe there was a real connection with her. His phone buzzed.

of course. thirty minutes?

He replied with a devil emoji and a smiley face. Then Holt opened up his email program on his laptop and checked his inbox. There was a new email from his boss.

This is fantastic, Holt. Lawyers like it. As long as we couch the language, we're good. We're posting with a question as the headline. Here's the dead link before it goes live. Let me know your thoughts with the tweaks we've made. Once you're good, we'll post. Nice work!! But you're still not going to Barcelona...

Holt opened the attachment and read his reworked piece. It would be his third big post in as many days. He deserved a raise.

Is Capitol Conspirator Really Dead?
EXCLUSIVE VIDEO Casts Doubt On White House
Claims
FBI Now Involved
By Dillinger Holt, Senior Correspondent

A new video, obtained exclusively by PlausibleDeniability.info, clearly shows three bodies at scene of ambush shoot-out. White House claims four people died. So where is the additional body? You decide.

—EXCLUSIVE—
    In the minutes after a deadly, well-executed ambush of a United States Marshal transport, a bystander captured three minutes of video with a cell-phone camera. Though shaky, at times out of focus, and shot from a distance, what it reveals could

counter the claims that four people were killed in a brazen daytime assault in rural Virginia.

In the video, there are three bodies covered with cloth and laid upon gurneys. Each of the bodies is placed into a separate van for transportation from the scene in Triangle, Virginia.

A fourth van is present, but no body is ever placed in the vehicle.

At a White House press conference, President Felicia Jackson told reporters there were four fatalities: three deputy marshals and the man they were transporting from one detention facility to another, Sir Spencer Thomas.

Thomas was awaiting trial for the bombing of the US Capitol building last year. The president would not speculate as to whether or not Thomas was the target of the Special Operations-style attack.

Could it be the attack's mission was to free Thomas and not kill him?

"I definitely saw three bodies," said the person who shot the video, and whose identity we are keeping hidden as a safety precaution. "All of them were law enforcement. They were wearing uniforms. I didn't see their faces. But they were wearing uniforms."

Further casting doubt on the president's version of events is a conversation recorded on the short video. In it, two members of the recovery team are discussing the presence of three bodies and four vans.

As of the posting of this article, neither the White House nor the USMS has responded to our request for comment. The FBI, however, has asked for a copy of the video. We are complying with that request.

DEVELOPING...

Holt was good with the minor changes and was glad they'd reached out for comment and even happier there wasn't a response yet. He replied to his boss. In a few minutes, the post would go live.

He closed his laptop and sat back in his seat. He looked across the room to a frowning barista at the cash register. The barista rolled his eyes.

Clearly, Holt had outstayed his welcome. He slid his laptop into a backpack and pocketed his phone. In a few minutes, he'd be back at the hotel, awaiting his date for the night.

It could be worse, he thought to himself as he trudged to his rental car, not realizing how right he was.

*

The assassin's eyes moved from the rearview mirror to the phone in her hand and back again. She was trying to make herself look as much like Karen Corvus as possible. It would give her the added seconds she needed. While her mark stood confused, trying to rationalize who she was, she'd have his heart in her hand, so to speak.

She mimicked Karen's eyeliner, penciling the color just beyond the outer edge of her lid. Above the liner, some muted shadow.

The lips were easy, a burnt red hue applied sparingly. She was nearly finished with the look, pleased with herself, when she had second thoughts. The assassin thumbed through more photos. In most of them, Karen wasn't wearing any makeup.

The assassin thought back to the morgue. Karen wasn't wearing any makeup there either, she recalled. It was just the glasses and the effortless pencil-twisted bun.

Frustrated with herself for having wasted her time, the assassin found some napkins in the glove box and wiped clean the makeup from her eyes and lips.

She was in the parking lot of the reporter's hotel. He'd not arrived yet, and she was parked such that she'd notice when he did.

Though it was raining and the windshield was fogged, she could see through it. If nothing else, the rain might provide the additional cover she'd need until she was up against her mark.

She pulled on a wig that most closely matched Karen's hair color and then worked it into the messy bun she'd seen Karen wear.

She found a pair of brown-tinted contact lenses in her survival kit and fingered them onto her eyes. Once she'd blinked them into place, she eased on the tortoiseshell glasses.

Close enough, she thought to herself. It was nearly dark. That would help.

She'd wait in the car until he arrived and then honk the horn. He'd recognize Karen's car and assume the woman emerging from it was his date.

How would she kill him?

It would be fast. With car keys. Or one of her high heels.

The rain intensified, thumping against the roof of the car. She turned on the engine and activated the windshield wipers, clearing her field of vision. A car pulled into the lot, splashing a puddle from the rutted asphalt, and parked in front of the hotel.

The driver's door opened and a man emerged, covering his bald head with a briefcase. It wasn't the mark.

She'd recognize the reporter from photographs she'd found of him on the web. He was younger, good-looking, with a full head of hair.

The fog reappeared on the windshield, with the wipers doing little to alleviate it. The assassin cranked the defrost and checked her phone. He should arrive any minute now.

To be certain she hadn't missed him, she picked up Karen's phone and pecked a text message.

    i'm here. u?

Within ten seconds he responded.

    stuck in traffic. rain. be there in five.

She acknowledged his text and eased her seat back, reclining it with the manual lever between the cushion and the driver's side door. The waiting was always the most difficult part of the job for her.

She was a woman of action. That was what they'd told her when they gave her this new life. She'd fly, they promised. Untethered by convention or the rules of morality, she could soar.

They were right, of course. The freedom with each pull of the trigger, swipe of the blade, or push of the needle was intoxicatingly powerful and indescribably liberating.

What they didn't tell her was that those were the only moments in which she'd feel alive and above the clouds. The rest of the time, those hours and days or weeks and months between assignments, was gray and suffocating. With each successive kill, the dark periods, as she privately called them, grew more unpalatable.

She bit down on her lower lip, relishing the sting. The rain obscured her view again. She flipped the wipers on again.

The sound of the rain mixed with the squeak of the blades was hypnotic in its rhythm. She closed her eyes and listened. She was nearly lost in the musicality of it when Karen's phone chimed.

The assassin sat up and checked the display.

`I'm here.`

She looked across the parking lot. There he was, standing underneath the lit portico outside the hotel entrance and waving at her.

It was pouring now, and the rain beating against the roof was deafening.

The assassin flashed her headlights against the curtain of water and turned off the car. She pulled the key from the ignition and slipped the sharp end between her middle and forefinger.

This would be quick.

The assassin covered her head with a folded map she pulled from the center console and walked purposefully across the parking lot. She would approach him, embrace him, and end his life.

Before he hit the ground, she'd turn around and walk back to the car. The deluge would give her ample cover to drive away without notice.

He was standing, his hands on his hips, with a backpack slung over his shoulder. He started toward her, a move she knew would hasten his death and make her return to the car even faster.

Halfway across the lot, however, her phone buzzed in her hip pocket. It was her phone, not Karen's. She'd left Karen's in the car.

She pulled the phone to read the display. She thumbed rain from the glowing, rain-distorted screen and squinted through the contacts.

`Abort.`

She slipped the phone back into her pocket and kept walking toward the hotel entrance. As the reporter approached, his arms open, she sidestepped him.

"Excuse me," she said, affecting a Southern lilt, "do I know you?"

"Uh—oh..." The reporter wiped the rain from his eyes and stared at the assassin. "I'm sorry. I thought you were someone else." He looked past her, toward the car, and then back at her again. He was studying her face, her body, her hair.

"I get that a lot." The assassin smiled and kept moving. "Have a nice evening. Try to stay dry."

The reporter stood there in the rain for another moment, looked back at the car once more, then turned back to the relative protection of the portico.

Standing inside the lobby, the assassin saw him check his phone. He pulled it to his ear and paced back and forth, fingering the rain from his mop of hair.

Finding a dark corner near the elevators, she pulled her phone from her pocket. She activated the encrypted feature and dialed a secure phone number.

"I've aborted," she whispered into the phone.

"You have a new target," said the voice on the other end of the line. "I'm uploading the particulars now."

The assassin looked at the phone and opened a proprietary application hidden on the home screen. She entered a key code and her screen filled with a list of mobile documents. She opened the first and looked at the photograph of a familiar face. She recognized the person, but wondered if there was a mistake.

"Is this information correct?" she asked. "You've sent me the new target?"

"Yes," President Jackson said without hesitation. "I want you to kill Matti Harrold. She's become a liability."

"What about the reporter?" asked the assassin. "I can still finish the job. It won't take but a minute."

"No," said the president. "He's untouchable at the moment. Get on the next flight to Barcelona."

CHAPTER 24

PARK GÜELL
BARCELONA, SPAIN

Park Güell was a mosaic jewel perched above the city on Muntanya Pelada. It was a steep climb to the park's grand entrance along Carrer de Larrard. Sir Spencer was there early, ahead of the daily tourist rush, to avoid the relentless heat of the high desert clime. He took each step slowly, leaning on his cane, as he navigated the narrow sidewalks.

He stopped short of the main entrance to catch his breath and admired the ornate, graphic entrance. Along the high walls that surrounded the park were tiled designs. Inset in those designs was symbology representative of the Brethren.

The architect of the park, Antoni Gaudí, and his patrons, the Güell family, were devout members whose loyalty and financial contributions were immeasurable by today's standards. Gaudí had meticulously woven marks of the organization into many of the iconic pieces that defined Barcelona as a city of modernism. Even his signature Temple of the Sagrada Familia, a Catholic church, bore the marks of the Brethren in the luminescent lighting and garish ceiling elements.

Sir Spencer's gaze lingered on a six-pointed star embedded within the park's logo. A smile snaked across his lips. This was a good place for the meeting. There were few, if any, security cameras, and they would easily blend with nature lovers and the curious.

"You are here," a voice called from behind Sir Spencer. "And you're early."

Sir Spencer turned around to see his protégé approaching him with open arms. Jon Custos looked older than Sir Spencer remembered. He was more muscular too. His thick neck was planted squarely into his brickwork shoulders.

"I'm trying to avoid the wretched heat." Sir Spencer raised his arms to meet Custos's embrace, which was a bit strong for the old man's liking.

"There's a lemonade stand just inside the entrance." Custos pulled back and held his mentor at arm's length, his hands gripping Sir Spencer's shoulders. "My treat."

"I accept the offer." Sir Spencer winked and leaned forward on his cane, hinting they should move.

Custos led Sir Spencer past the gated entrance, turning left to find the drink stand. As he walked ahead, another man approached Sir Spencer with a fistful of dripping water bottles.

"One euro each," said the vendor, shoving a pair of bottles toward Sir Spencer, who declined and wove his way to a nearby bench. The man followed for a beat and then gave up, peddling to the next person entering the park.

Once seated, he pulled a linen handkerchief from his blazer pocket and dabbed the beading sweat from his forehead. It was just seven thirty in the morning and he was melting.

A family of four walked past him: a mother, father, and two young boys. The boys held their mother's hands and argued about which of the many paths to take. They were speaking German. Sir Spencer understood some of the discussion, but wasn't interested enough to home in on the conversation as they walked farther from him.

He looked up at the canopies of olive and carob trees. They were native to the arid slope, growing tall and stretching their branches outward, as if protecting the visitors from the dry heat.

Gaudí had enhanced the native vegetation when he designed the park, using it to ease the erosion of the dry soil. He chose trees and shrubs that relied on little water. Oleander was a favorite that bloomed throughout the acreage. Explosions of chartreuse and pink dotted the greenery, accenting the stonework and crushed granite paths at points of interest.

Sir Spencer leaned the cane against his lap, regretting not having slept more on the transatlantic flight and having chosen a dark suit from among the clothing options provided him on board. He welcomed the cold, sugary drink when Custos returned with a pair of cups.

"You spent some time in prison," said Custos. "How was it?"

"It was as you imagine it." Sir Spencer took a sip of the lemonade, smacking his lips together against the tartness. "It wasn't enjoyable."

"It was worth it, no?"

"We shall see. That part of the story is, as of yet, unwritten."

"We are moving forward. I have made good progress here."

"Tell me about it."

"I've achieved access to the site. I'll be able to make the required arrangements."

"How did you gain access? The security along the shore, particularly around the World Trade Center, will tighten significantly as the meetings draw closer."

"I have a room key."

"I hope you didn't let a room there."

"No. I have someone else's key."

"Good."

"I also have keys to the prescribed soft points in the building."

"And the most important piece of all?"

"It is secure."

"You have it?" Sir Spencer lowered his voice to just above a whisper.

"Yes."

"It is as advertised?"

"Yes. It flew with me on a commercial flight. No issues."

"Very good." Sir Spencer raised his cup in a toast and Custos reciprocated. "Very good."

"So why are we meeting?" Custos lowered his cup and set it on the bench. "Why are you here?"

Sir Spencer smirked, his fleeting smile deflating into a sympathetic frown. He'd trained Custos too well. The boy was suspicious by nature, but the Brethren programming he'd undergone years before had narrowed his focus and sharpened his radar.

"Jon, your mission is a bit different from what was originally explained." Sir Spencer paused, and Custos's black eyes searched his own until they widened in epiphany.

"This is my final mission," Custos said, swallowing hard against the final word.

Sir Spencer nodded and moved his hand to Custos's tree-trunk thigh. He squeezed gently as a father would in reassuring a frightened child.

Custos inhaled slowly and closed his eyes. His jaw tightened.

Sir Spencer slid over on the bench, folding his hands in his lap. He caught the eye of a water vendor and waved him over.

"*Dos aguas, por favor*," he said and handed the man two euro in exchange for a pair of sweating, partially frozen sixteen-ounce water bottles. Sir Spencer handed one of them to Custos.

Custos held the bottle to his forehead before unscrewing the cap and squeezing out a swig of water. He looked over at his mentor and nodded.

"I wish there were another way," Sir Spencer said gently.

Custos recapped the bottle and used it to point along the path ahead of him. "You know, Gaudí originally designed this park as a housing development for wealthy families. There were to be sixty triangular lots connected by an intricate network of paths, stone steps, and even viaducts. He wanted to restrict the building on those lots, allowing construction on just one-sixth of each parcel. The buildings could not block any other's view of the sea below us or the sunlight above us."

"As above, so below." Sir Spencer chuckled.

"Only two of the houses were ever built." Custos pointed to one of them just to his left and up the hill. "It was too complicated a venture, so it became a large private park until the 1960s. Then it became public."

"And here we sit." Sir Spencer cracked open his water and sipped from the bottle.

"*The best laid schemes o' mice an' men*," said Custos, "*Gang aft a-gley.*"

"Robert Burns?"

Custos nodded.

"You learned well."

"You taught me." Custos laughed. "You recall the rest of it, right?"

"*An' lae'e us nought but grief an' pain*," Sir Spencer said. "*For promised joy.*"

*

The tag on the door suggested the guest in room 3669 wanted privacy. She hadn't answered her prearranged wake-up call, and a coworker insisted she check on her friend's well-being.

"She has three hours until checkout," the desk clerk had said, urging patience. But the brash French-Canadian flight attendant in a neatly pressed uniform would not be dissuaded.

"She's not answering her cell phone," the friend explained. "She's not returning texts. She hasn't even read them. And I tried snapping her. She didn't respond."

"Snapping?"

"Snapchat," said the flight attendant. "She always snaps me back."

The clerk relented and called for a shift manager to assess the urgency of the request. After hearing the French-Canadian's red-faced plea, he conceded it wasn't against policy to check on the guest's well-being. He insisted, however, that she wait in the lobby or her own guest room for the status of her "missing friend".

The manager, escorted by security, took the service elevator and thumped his way along the hallway to room 3669. As he approached the room, his pace slowed. The hairs on the back of his neck tingled. He looked over his shoulders in both directions. His stomach tightened, and he fought against the subconscious voice telling him to turn around and return to the comfort of his first-floor office. His pulse quickened another beat as the guard opened the door to blackness, and a blast of cool air hit them like a high-tide wind.

The manager slid the master key into a slot on the wall that powered the lights throughout the room. He flipped the adjacent switches and spun the thermostat ten degrees warmer. The air-conditioning was set to an uncomfortable fifteen degrees Celsius.

The room slowly alit in a soft yellow glow, and the manager walked into the open space of the room. The security guard trailed a step behind.

"Something is not right here," he said to the guard in impeccable Catalan. He crossed to the large picture windows and pulled open the drawn curtains. From the window, he turned back to the room, hands on hips, and surveyed the modernist space.

Everything was in its place, but a chill ran through the manager's core. He looked to the bathroom and gave a subtle nod to the security guard.

The guard stepped to the bathroom, reaching around the door to flip on the light. He disappeared for a moment and reemerged, shaking his head.

"Nothing is touched," said the guard. "The soaps are in their boxes. The shampoo bottles are full. Both towels are hanging."

"Both?" The manager cocked his head to the left, his eyes narrowed. "There are three towels in every room. Check again."

The guard checked. "Just two."

"Somebody cleaned this room," the manager said. "Somebody cleaned up."

"Ha!" The security guard chuckled through a sneer. "Who are you? Pepe Carvalho?"

The manager frowned. He didn't like being compared to a fictional detective, even if he was Spain's most beloved.

"No. I have an eye for detail. That is why I am good at my job. Details are important."

The security guard pursed his lips and shrugged. He pulled a tin of mints from his pocket and popped a couple in his mouth.

"Plus," added the manager, as a point of clarification, "I don't mingle with prostitutes as Carvalho did."

"What's wrong with prostitutes?" asked the guard, sucking on the mints.

The manager put his hands on his hips and scanned the room again. His eyes stopped at the accordion closet opposite the windows. One side wasn't pushed flush with the track.

"There!" He pointed at the closet.

The guard lumbered the short distance to the closet and pulled open the doors, revealing the safe, an ironing board and iron, an extra pair of goose-down pillows, and a green suitcase.

The guard saw the case and immediately stepped back, nearly tripping over his own feet. He looked back at the manager, his face ashen.

The manager took a step forward, trying to rationalize the reveal with an internal explanation less macabre than what he saw in the closet. He couldn't. There was only one conclusion as to what had happened in the room.

The suitcase, though zipped closed, was distended. It stood upright. And toward the bottom of the case, its bright green color took a darker hue as if stained with an intentional ombré effect. A dark red puddle on the closet floor, oozing outward from beneath the case, indicated the color-blend was not original to the suitcase.

The guard bent over at his waist, resting his hands on his knees. He pressed his eyes closed and breathed heavily through his mouth. In and out. In and out.

The manager felt a sense of calm wash over him. The room wasn't as cold. He walked to within a foot of the case and squatted down for a closer look.

It was blood on the floor. No doubt. And there was a body, or parts of one, inside the suitcase.

"Call the police," he said without taking his eyes from the wheeled, makeshift sarcophagus in front of him. "We need to leave."

CHAPTER 25

CAMP DAVID
CATOCTIN MOUNTAIN PARK, MARYLAND

It was nearly two o'clock in the morning and Mattie had a half hour until Marine One lifted off, carried the White House team to Andrews Air Force Base, and they boarded Air Force One for Barcelona.

It was more than enough time.

Sitting on her bed in the Aspen Lodge, she worked the subtle tremor from her right hand, the sleep from her eyes, and logged into a secure connection on her laptop.

She opened an installed program that masked her keystrokes before activating a plug-in that changed her traceable IP address every thirty seconds. She couldn't risk anyone knowing what she was about to do.

She went to an email drop box she kept for private communication. Using an online email server, she opened up the message option, typed a brief note, and then saved it without sending it.

She closed that program and then linked to a public message board. She found the right chat room and logged in under a default username. Matti ran her fingers through her hair as she waited for the room to authenticate her account. She checked her phone. Still plenty of time.

Once in the room, she typed a short message telling her contact to go open the saved email message online. That email, once opened, would tell the contact everything he needed to know. She just hoped he was still active in the chat room. Otherwise, he'd never see the message.

Matti closed the browser, deleted her history and the associated cookies, and then reopened the browser again. She then logged onto PlausibleDeniability.info. The home page was populated with articles by Dillinger Holt. Matti had read all of them in the last hour. The most recent, the one about Sir Spencer, was dangerous.

Her eyes raced across Holt's report, her lips mouthing the words as she read them. Could it be the attack's mission was to free Thomas and not kill him?

Matti made a mental note of additional questions she needed to answer. If the mission was to free Sir Spencer, as she now believed, why did the president want him alive? What purpose could he serve? And had the president been involved in the destruction of the Capitol?

Matti remembered Felicia Jackson repeatedly telling the story of her near-death at the Capitol, of running across the mall and face-planting into the grass when the explosion thrust her forward into the air.

Still, on the heels of her recent discussion with the president, Matti knew she wasn't crazy. The president knew it too. It wasn't good.

Matti was surprised, in fact, the president hadn't confronted her yet. It had been several hours since the ultimatum meeting, and she hadn't seen Jackson since.

Maybe the talk would occur on board Marine One or Air Force One. Maybe President Jackson was planning to kick Matti off the team. Or maybe worse.

If this conspiracy, whatever it was, involved blowing up the United States Capitol as a precursor to something bigger, it would be nothing for them to silence her one way or another.

Regardless, Matti needed to reach the right people and reach them quickly. She clicked on Dillinger Holt's byline and it linked to an email address. Matti copied the address without sending a message from her embedded laptop account. That was too risky. Instead, she went to an online email provider, created a new account, and sent Holt a message from there. It was the safest way to do it, even if it involved way too many steps. Strangely, Matti missed employing her tradecraft.

She'd joined the National Security Agency out of college because it fit her. She liked solving puzzles. And nowhere could one effect more positive change and solve puzzles than as a signal intelligence analyst. She was a code breaker. Codes were black and white. The job was easy, emotionless. Nobody got hurt.

And then her supervisor, out of the blue, had called her into his office and given her an assignment involving human intelligence.

Humans weren't black and white. They were colored with shades of gray, unpredictable Gordian knots whose actions defied natural law.

Matti had been neither an officer nor an agent before that assignment. She was just a YouTube-loving, emotionally detached, eidetic analyst who got thrown into the deep end of a shark-filled pool without much more than floaties. She'd figured it out and survived. For the first time in months, the pangs of guilt gave way to sparks of hope. Where a therapist failed, and pills only dulled the edge, returning to her roots would save her. She would employ all of the skills the clandestine agency had given her. She'd redeem herself. Matti felt a tingle of adrenaline as she typed her email to Holt.

> Mr. Holt: I've read your recent reports with great interest. I've seen Sir Spencer alive. There is something big at play here. I'm in a position to help you, if you can help me. Please respond to this email address with a good phone number. When I tell you who I am, you'll trust everything I tell you. The key will be getting me to trust you. Thanks.

Matti's finger hovered a moment before she clicked send. She exhaled and checked her phone. She had a few minutes left.

She closed out her browser, deleted her history and the cookies, and then returned to the original online email server. Her pulse thumped against her neck as she checked the unsent message, hoping to find a response despite the late hour.

Matti flexed her hands and moved her fingers to open the message. It was longer than when she had left it, and she quietly pumped her fist at the three additional words added to the bottom of her request.

> I will dig.

That was enough of a response from her contact. By the time she landed in Barcelona, assuming she was allowed to travel, she'd have a much better handle on what it was she faced.

She logged off the computer, powered it down, and removed the battery. She slipped the computer into her messenger bag and then checked her carry-on. Everything was packed.

Her phone buzzed, as if on cue. It was Goodman.

wheels up in ten. need u on M1.

The tension in her shoulders eased.

on my way. see you in a sec.

She slipped the phone back into her pocket and gathered her bags. She stepped from the Aspen Lodge into the choking humidity and looked up toward the sky. The moon glow illuminated the thick cover of clouds, which gave the sky a milky appearance. She inhaled the smell of pine and marched south toward the helipad. Amid the chorus of crickets and tree frogs, her feet crunched against the path. Matti considered the work ahead, that these might be her final moments of peace for the foreseeable future. An unconscious smile slipped from her face and she wondered if her momentary sense of relief was warranted.

CHAPTER 26

THE GALLERIA
HOUSTON, TEXAS

"I'm not sure what happened," Dillinger Holt said. "I'm sorry if I did something wrong."

He was sitting on the edge of his hotel room bed, his fingers tracing the thin stitch of the polyester duvet.

"I really did have a great time last night. I was hoping we could stay in touch after I left town. I really like you. And it was my mistake last time. I was a jerk. I…"

Holt ran his hand through his wet hair and felt the water drip onto his neck. A chill ran down his back.

"It's pretty late. I waited for a few hours. Sorry to leave another message. This is…I don't know. I'm just…call me back if you get a chance."

Holt tossed the phone onto the bed, slid over to the desk, and opened his laptop. Half the night was over; he hadn't slept. *What's another few minutes online?* he reasoned through the fog of disappointment-induced insomnia.

He opened his email and clicked through a litany of press releases. One email in particular piqued his interest. At first he thought the random combination of letters and numbers in the address was indicative of spam. But the subject line, MR HOLT—HELP ME HELP YOU, got him to click it open.

The writer claimed to have seen Sir Spencer alive and insisted that he, or she, was well-known.

Reporters like Dillinger Holt got dozens of tips a week. Every subsequent call, text, or email promised bigger implications and more earthshaking revelations than the one before. Holt estimated one out of fifty of the tips turned out to be remotely close to what was promised. One of fifty of those had reportable evidence or information. And of those, maybe one or two had sources willing to go on the record.

His initial thought was to hit delete and move along. Instead, he wrote back.

Thanks for your email. If what you're telling me is true, then your information is valuable and I would love to work with you. You can understand, however, my skepticism. You contact me from some random email account that appears as though it's spam. You don't give me a name or any other way in which to contact you. Give me another piece of information I can validate or something that tells me you're not a flake. Then I'll be happy to send you my personal phone number for further communication. Whatever you choose to tell me will stay between you and me unless you grant me permission to report it. I grant all sources that level of protection. I've gone to jail before to protect a source. I'd do it again. And clearly, you already trust me to some degree or you wouldn't have emailed me in the first place. I'm looking forward to hearing from you ASAP.

—DH

Holt sent the email and then spun in the swivel chair to check his phone. No messages. He resisted the strong urge to call Karen again, for the fourth time, and plead his case. He feared he'd already come across as Jon Favreau's character Mike from the movie *Swingers*.

He swung back to the desk and planted his elbows on it. His head in his hands, he gritted his teeth. In his mind, he saw Karen's car in the parking lot. He'd been certain the woman walking through the rain, directly to him, was her. It turned out not to be.

It didn't make sense. She'd texted him while he was in traffic, said she was already at the hotel and waiting for him. Five minutes later he was there. She wasn't.

Holt slapped his hands on the desk and pushed himself to his feet. He paced back and forth in the tight space between the bed and the rest of the furniture. Something wasn't right. He was growing more certain of it by the hour.

However, Holt, perpetually in a narcissistic coma, couldn't admit to himself whether he was worried for her safety or whether his discomfort was with a woman ditching him. Either of those possibilities sent a thin trail of bile worming up his throat.

Treading the short distance from wall to wall, his socks dragging along the beige Berber carpet, he replayed, over and again, the last two days in his head. They'd moved quickly. Maybe he missed something. Maybe she'd played him.

She was cold at first, but she thawed. Then she warmed to him and, by the end of the night, shared her body heat. They'd laughed. They'd had fun. He'd told her how foolish he'd been not to keep in touch with her.

Karen forgave him, he thought, at least four times, and she seemed eager to see him again.

Holt glanced at his computer; the home page of his employer refreshed automatically.

On PlausibleDeniability.info, across the top of the home page was a new banner:

DILLINGER HOLT: FINDING THE TRUTH, GETTING RESULTS
FBI PROBING TWO EXCLUSIVES:
DEATHS OF RAP STAR, FBI AGENT, AND CAPITOL
CONSPIRATOR

The headline, while flattering, was misleading. There was no connection, as far as he knew, between Horus, Special Agent Majors, and Sir Spencer Thomas.

Was there?

Holt threw himself back into the chair and pinched the bridge of his nose, squeezing his eyes shut for clarity. He blinked them open and looked at the clock on the laptop. He should be asleep.

He opened three windows and started a search engine in each of them. In the first he searched for "Horus conspiracy". In the second he chose the search terms "Erik Majors conspiracy FBI". In the third, "Sir Spencer Thomas Capitol conspiracy".

Each open window populated with thousands of results. Holt bit his lower lip and started scrolling through the links.

The Erik Majors search didn't provide much help at first. The only credible element at all was his appearance at a political fundraiser for some Virginia state representative who was later convicted in a bribery scandal. Holt dismissed it as irrelevant and moved to Horus.

The rapper's death was a conspiracy theorist's dream. Countless sites argued his overdose was an offering or a sacrifice of some sort. They connected it to the deaths of other young, famous musicians and actors who'd overdosed. One site claimed Horus was a blood sacrifice for a group called the Brethren, some shadowy puppet master of an organization that funded coups and facilitated revolutions through mind control and devil worship.

The Brethren sounded vaguely familiar to Holt. He'd read about them on 9/11 conspiracy sites, but he'd always dismissed them as some Illuminati-esque rumor. After he clicked on a few of the embedded links referring to Horus and the Brethren, a pattern emerged. Holt slid a hotel notepad next to his computer and grabbed a pen to jot down common words.

In multiple posts he found references to new world order, one world government, ritualistic behavior, global influence, powerful families, and paganism.

He opened a new window and searched Horus's lyrics. Repeatedly, Holt read references that could easily apply to the Brethren. It was so obvious, in fact, Holt was flush with embarrassment for not having seen it before. Still, despite the conspiratorial intrigue of what he'd found, there was no obvious link amongst the three. He rubbed his eyes and looked at the clock again. He'd been online for more than an hour and he hadn't gotten to Sir Spencer Thomas yet. Then he clicked on a low-budget YouTube video with only thirty-three views. It made a case that the Brethren were employing a subconscious infiltration into mainstream society through music, entertainment, and Wall Street. Its goal was to ripen the populous, get them accustomed to the idea of the so-called "New World Order", which was effectively a police state disguised as a socialist democratic-republic.

"Blah, blah, blah..." Holt was about to close out of the video and move on to his Sir Spencer keyword search when a photograph caught his attention.

Holt sat up, clicked pause, and rubbed his eyes. He slowly moved the cursor back a couple of clicks to get a better look. At exactly eleven minutes and six seconds into the video, there was a black-and-white photograph. Though it was grainy and suffered from being copied too many times, Holt was sure of what it showed, despite the lack of a caption or narrated explanation.

The photograph was taken in a bar. Behind the counter, on the wall, was a large sign that read Cato Street Pub. Leaning on the bar, from behind the counter, was a rail of a man Holt recognized as Capitol conspirator Jimmy Ings. Sitting on the stools in the foreground were Horus and music mogul Vav Six. In the corner of the photo, shadowed from view, was a tall, heavy man leaning on a cane. He was watching from across the room. "It's just a photograph, right?" Holt mumbled. "So they were in the same place. What does that mean?" He puffed his cheeks and sighed. He could feel the weight of insomnia in his eyes. They burned.

Holt shook off the exhaustion and changed his Sir Spencer query. He added the words "new world order" and "Brethren" to the search. It yielded nothing. He tried "Sir Spencer" and "Horus". Nothing again. Five similar searches got him nowhere. Ready to call it a night, he decided on one final search. "Sir Spencer" and "Erik Majors". It produced a single result; an article from Erik Majors's high school newspaper. It had featured him in an alumni section three years before his death.

Years before he signed up to be a special agent at the Federal Bureau of Investigation, Erik Majors was a standout student at Memorial High School and was a National Merit Scholar. He played varsity soccer and was voted Most Likely To Run A Country by his classmates. After graduation, he attended Yale and was the recipient of the prestigious Grove Scholarship.

In the middle of the article was a series of three photographs. One was Majors's official FBI portrait, another was his yearbook photograph from his senior year in high school, and the third was a photograph taken at the Grove Scholarship awards ceremony. It featured, as the caption below it indicated, "a young Erik Majors with Grove Committee Member Sir Spencer Thomas."

"Holy—" Adrenaline jolted Holt awake. He copied the link to the article and emailed it to himself. Then he put pen to paper:

THE BRETHREN—NEW WORLD ORDER
SIR SPENCER—THE BRETHREN
SIR SPENCER—ERIK MAJORS
SIR SPENCER—HORUS
HORUS'S DEATH—ERIK MAJORS'S DEATH
HORUS—THE BRETHREN
ALL CONNECTED??

THE TIMING??
WHAT'S THE GOAL??

Looking at it on paper made it seem plausible. Holt rubbed his temples. If this were true, and there was even the most tenuous connection among Majors's death, Horus's death, and Sir Spencer's escape, the repercussions were incalculable. At least they were in the throes of Holt's sleep deprivation.

Sir Spencer. New World Order. Horus. Murder. FBI. Karen. Conspiracy. The Brethren...

His mind swirling, he considered calling his editor immediately. He thought about calling Karen. He wondered if he should call the FBI. He needed time to think. He needed to rationally connect the dots.

He closed the laptop and leaned back in the swivel chair, wondering if something as simple as a Google search had pieced together something nobody knew was coming.

*

The assassin sat alone in economy class. She'd purchased three adjacent seats to ensure privacy on the transatlantic flight from Houston to Amsterdam. She'd just managed to catch the last Europe-bound flight of the night. Amsterdam wasn't ideal, but it was a short layover and she'd be in Barcelona by the end of the day. Plus, there was a contact in the Dutch capital who could provide her with some much-needed supplies.

While most on the flight watched movies or slept, the assassin went to work. Using the aircraft's Wi-Fi, she accessed a secure site and uploaded the newly added dossier to her account.

"Would you like a drink?" a flight attendant asked, pulling alongside the assassin with a large aisle-wide service cart.

"A cup of ice, please," said the assassin. "No drink."

"Certainly," said the flight attendant, a big lipstick smile plastered on her face. "And I love your hair. It's such a pretty color."

"Oh." The assassin touched her head, recalling which wig she'd chosen for the trip. "Thank you." She smiled back before whispering with a wink, "It's not my natural color."

"Oh, girl," the flight attendant said, shoveling ice into a cup, "mine would be eight shades of gray if it wasn't for Nice 'n Easy."

"Me too." The assassin played along and took the cup from the attendant. "Me too."

The attendant unlocked the cart and moved it along. "If you need anything, just let me know."

"Thank you."

The assassin shook the cup and pulled a cube of ice into her mouth. She sucked on it for a moment before grinding it with her teeth.

She slipped on a pair of headphones, plugged them into her computer, and opened her music files. Scrolling down to "H", she picked Horus and clicked on his latest, and last, album.

The music started softly, a thick beat accompanied by an alto saxophone. A couple of bars in, Horus began rapping, and the assassin inhaled through her nose. For a moment, she could smell him. She closed her eyes and she could taste his sweat. His voice was hypnotic. She allowed herself the first minute of the song, her head bobbing with the rhythm. Then she opened her eyes and popped another ice cube in her mouth.

Pity. He had talent.

With the music playing in the background, she clicked on the dossier. It opened and revealed a photograph of the mark. She was a beautiful young woman. To the assassin, she looked like the girl in *Rebel Without A Cause*, the one who drowned in the 1980s. The assassin couldn't remember her name. It didn't matter. What mattered was the information in front of her. The assassin would need to devour the information and formulate a workable solution before the plane began its descent. She forged ahead, scrolling to the executive summary.

Subject:	Matilda Harrold (Matti)
Age:	30
Current:	White House Special Assistant To The President.
Former:	NSA SIGINT Analyst
Education:	BA Linguistics, BS Mathematics Georgetown University
Skills:	Eideteker. Photographic memory. Remarkable problem solver. 162 IQ.
Family:	Father (living), Mother (deceased)
Associates:	None
Allergies:	N/A

Surgeries:	Wisdom teeth removed.
Medical:	Addiction to anxiety medication.
Hobbies:	YouTube, Sudoku, Jogging
Clearance:	SECRET (formerly TOP SECRET)

The assassin skimmed the rest of the summary. She resolved Harrold was smart, resourceful, and troubled. Her mother's death had left an indelible mark on her psyche. It plagued her professionally and personally. She'd have made a good asset for the Brethren.

Ice broke between her teeth, and the assassin scrolled through documents and diagrams, maps and schematics. According to the official schedule, she knew where Matti Harrold would be in Barcelona, and she knew when she'd be there. This would be easy.

The assassin pushed the recline button on the side of her seat and leaned back. She closed her eyes and sucked on the chips of ice melting into her throat.

It was a long flight. She could afford to sleep for a couple of hours to recharge, to dream of the fun that lay ahead.

She'd been struggling with the last-second abortion of her previous mark. It was as if someone stopped her short of a climax, frustrating her with the loss of something she could feel building within her before a primal, satisfying release.

With an image of Matti Harrold floating behind her eyes, the assassin's frustration gave way to anticipation. She was eager to get on the ground. She was eager to hunt.

CHAPTER 27

WORLD TRADE CENTER
BARCELONA, SPAIN

The French-Canadian flight attendant was inconsolable. Sitting in the shift manager's office behind the reception desk, she couldn't catch her breath.

"Try this." The manager handed her a brown paper bag. "Breathe into it. Maybe it will help you."

She took the bag, thanked the manager, pulled the bag to her face, and vomited into it. The color leached from her face, aside from the black mascara staining her cheeks.

A tall man in a brown suit walked into the office. His collar was turned up on one side, and there was a yellow stain on one lapel. His shirt was loose around his neck, as was the mustard-colored necktie. His gut hung over his waistband, stretching the pants beyond their comfort and hiding the cracked brown leather belt he'd hand punched with an extra hole for the buckle.

The flight attendant gagged and then whimpered as the man found a chair in the corner and spun it around backwards. He straddled the seat and offered a weak smile as he sat.

"I'm here to talk to you about your friend," he said, his English accented with Spanish. "She was your friend, yes?"

The flight attendant nodded and crumpled the top of the bag. She held it in her lap, not sure where to put it.

"I'm involved with finding out what happened to your friend." He scratched the top of his balding head. What few strands he had left were combed from front to back. "I'm hopeful that you help me. Is it best I ask you in English?"

"Or French," she mumbled.

"We'll speak in English," he conceded with a smile that revealed poor dental habits. He was missing three teeth on the bottom and two on the top.

"C'est bien."

"Tell me about your friend," he said, pressing his chest against the back of the chair. "Did you know her outside of your jobs?"

"A little. If we crewed a flight together, we'd eat together or maybe go to a nightclub."

"Did you meet men at these discos?"

"Sometimes."

"Did you take the men to your hotels?"

"I'm not..." She hesitated. "I don't—"

"I know the question is...indelicate," the man said. "I think it's important."

"Yes."

"Yes, what?"

"Yes, sometimes we would bring men back to our rooms."

"Was it ever a problem?"

She shook her head.

"How about last night?"

"I didn't see her last night," she said. "She told me she'd call me this morning."

"She had other plans?"

Her eyes searched the room for the answer until they widened with recognition.

"There was a man on the flight," she said. "She thought he was attractive. I told her I thought he looked like Vin Diesel."

"Vin Diesel?"

"The movie star. You know. He was in *Fast & Furious*."

"I know the movie. Yes. The bald one?"

"Yes."

"What else can you tell me about this man?"

"I think she gave him her number," she offered. "I'm not sure."

"Can you give me a better description of him?"

"He was tan and muscular. His shoulders were huge. He looked like he worked out a lot."

"Tanned, muscular, and bald."

"And his eyes were black."

"Dark brown, you mean to say?"

"No. They were black."

"Would you recognize him if you saw him again?"

"Yes. I think so."

The inquisitor pushed himself from the chair and left the room. Less than a minute later, he returned with a laptop computer under his arm. He plopped back down into his seat and balanced the laptop on the back of the chair. He opened it and spun it around so the flight attendant could see the screen. A looped video was repeating itself on the display.

The video showed the hallway outside of room 3669. It was at a distance, but the flight attendant could clearly see two people emerge from one side of the hallway and walk toward the camera. The pair was talking to each other and holding hands as they walked. The man was much taller than the woman.

The flight attendant watched the video until she couldn't. She covered her face with her hands and sobbed. Once she'd composed herself, she looked up at the investigator with red, swollen eyes and nodded. Her lower lip quivered, threatening another emotional outburst.

"That's him."

CHAPTER 28

ABOARD AIR FORCE ONE

President Felicia Jackson stood with her arms folded across her chest. She was in the press cabin, her least favorite section of the Boeing 747 VC-25A. It was at the rear of the aircraft, and although it was configured like a commercial aircraft's first-class cabins, she found it cramped.

It didn't help it was occupied by journalists, who were, in her opinion, less respectable than lawyers.

She glanced at the dozen reporters as they readied their recorders and notepads, and then glared at the television photographer operating the pool camera. He would later share his video with all of the television networks.

"Are we ready?" she huffed. "I'd like to get this gaggle over with pretty quickly."

The reporters looked at each other and nodded their heads. The president imagined they'd like to finish this and get some sleep before landing in Spain.

"I'll start by saying I'm excited about the possibility of what we can achieve during these meetings. If we can, as a coalition, come to agreement regarding surveillance and security, it will usher in a new era of cooperation and intelligence gathering. It will make the world a safer place."

The president gauged the reporters as they scribbled and reflexively nodded. She knew they weren't really listening. They were too anxious to pepper her with questions.

"If our partner nations can agree with us, and if they can ratify similar language in their own legislatures, we'll be in a fantastic position to root out evil before it strikes. This is critical to the economic and cultural well-being of all civilized nations. With that, I'll take some questions."

"Madam President," said Bob, the dean of the correspondents, "I'd like to ask about the likelihood that Congress approves the Surveillance of Electronic Correspondence Under

Regulated Intelligence and Telecommunication Act as it's currently written. Even if these other Western nations agree to submit similar legislation, enter into an agreement to share data and intelligence, and they pass it in their own parliaments, isn't it a moot point if you can't cobble together the votes in the House and the Senate?"

"I'm not sure I agree with the word *cobble*, Bob," the president said with pursed lips. "I think what we're trying to do here is difficult. We're presenting legislation to the people's elected representatives at home while trying to facilitate similar legislation overseas. And in the middle of that, reach a multilateral agreement that provides for an unprecedented sharing of critical, life-saving information. All the pieces will fall into place. I'm confident of that."

"You don't have the votes right now," countered Bob. "And there is a buzz in the intelligence community that you'd be emasculating the FBI, the CIA, and the NSA. Your Director of National Intelligence has publicly questioned the sanity of this approach."

"Is there a question there, Bob, or just a sweeping judgment?"

"The question, Madam President"—Bob shifted uncomfortably in his seat, but the skepticism remained in his tone— "is whether you're in over your head."

The cabin fell silent aside from the muted roar of the aircraft's four General Electric turbofan engines. Every eye in the cabin was on Bob.

President Jackson inhaled and smiled, flashing the grin she usually saved for her attorney general. She swallowed and waited a beat, letting the discomfort of the moment swell for effect.

"Bob," she said softly enough that the reporters had to lean forward to hear her, "I'll excuse the tone but not the sexist implication—"

"Madam Pre—" Bob started to defend himself, but stopped at the direction of the president's finger pressed against her lips.

"It's my turn, Bob."

He nodded and shrank a little in his seat. Bob swallowed hard enough the president could see his Adam's apple quiver.

"Your sexist implications, as they were, included the word *emasculate* and questioned if I, a woman president, was in over her head. I don't see you asking the same question of Dexter Foreman,

Barack Obama, or George Bush. I don't even think Hillary Clinton would be so attacked."

The president unfolded her arms and stepped forward, dragging her hand along the seat backs as she moved closer to Bob. She was keenly aware of the camera following her, and she knew this would make for good television.

"My DNI is fully supportive of our efforts. He is my DNI, after all. If he weren't on board with the plan, he wouldn't be on board, so to speak. Congress will be a challenge. We have some convincing to do, as do our partner nations when they return home from the summit. However, the timing is such that, if we have to put the horse before the proverbial cart, it's worth doing. The SECURITY Act, in all its forms, and the associated agreements will save lives."

Bob nodded. He looked away from the president, backing down as would a dog not able to win a staring contest with its master.

"Any other questions, Bob?" President Jackson asked. "As a woman, I'm more than happy to explain the finer points of things to any man."

Bob shook his head. His face reddened.

"*Huffington Post?*" asked the president. "You have a question?"

"Yes, Madam President," the reporter replied, glancing at Bob. "Why not insure passage in Congress first? Especially since there are reports the other countries are hesitant to back you without the SECURITY Act having become law here."

"This is how the calendar fell," explained the President. "Of course I would have loved for the Speaker and the Majority Leader to have already voted and passed the SECURITY Act. Yes, that would have been preferable. To me, the sooner we move on this, the better. Every day without the latitude afforded us by the Act is another day we, as Americans, are vulnerable."

"What kind of indication are you getting from the other heads of state?" asked Anne from the *Times*.

"Thanks for that question, Anne. The president put her hands on her hips. "We're still in the middle of a dialogue with the teams from all of the partner nations. They have their concerns, as they should in any deliberative debate, about the implementation of certain aspects of the plan. We'll do what we can to help alleviate any of those concerns. That's what this summit is about, ultimately. So we have time to tweak what needs tweaking and strengthen what needs strengthening. Ultimately I am confident all four of our partners will ratify the agreement and present their legislation to their respective elected bodies."

The president considered ending the gaggle there, but there were three hands still raised. She pointed at the young woman from *The Washington Post*.

"Madam President, could you please comment on the reports that Sir Spencer Thomas is still alive?"

Felicia Jackson pursed her lips again and folded her arms. She rocked back and forth on her heels. "I'm not going to comment on tabloid speculation."

"But—"

"But nothing. I'm going to rely on the credible information I receive in briefings, not on wild stories about missing bodies. It's ludicrous. And quite frankly, I'm disappointed you would bring it up. I'm finished here. Enjoy the rest of the flight." She spun on her heels and ignored the peppering questions behind her. She nodded at her press secretary as she passed him, and he handled the remainder of the "no comment" session.

*

President Jackson marched from the press cabin and into a hallway that ran along the left side of the aircraft. She passed a pair of Secret Service agents, nodded, and turned right into a large conference room. Previously a situation room, it had long ago been converted into a staff meeting area.

The president exploded into the room and scanned the faces at the table and those along the long white sofa occupying an interior wall of the room. In the corner, next to a lamp, she caught Matti Harrold's eyes. She glared at her aide and then motioned to her. Matti popped up and followed the president out of the conference room and into her private quarters at the front of the main deck.

President Jackson sat on the long sofa bed on the left side of the cabin and offered Matti a seat on the matching sofa opposite her. She crossed her legs and adjusted the drape of her twenty-five-thousand-dollar black Chanel skirt.

Matti sat with her legs pressed together, her hand in her lap. She ran her right hand through her hair.

"You really should dress better," the president said, her eyes trailing from Matti's flats, up her legs, and from shoulder to shoulder. "You work in the White House, for Lord's sake."

"I'm dressed for comfort, Madam President," Matti explained, looking down at her tan chinos. "I have nicer clothes in my suitcase."

"Dressed for comfort," the president sneered. "You know, I'm not sure right now why I put you on my staff. I don't know why I've put so much trust in you after so little time. Most of my aides, who I trust half as much, have been with me ten times as long."

"I appreciate your trust," Matti said. "I know that—"

"You know what, Matti? You know what it's like for a woman in politics? You know what it took for me to get here? You know how I'm castigated regardless of my actions? Too harsh, I'm any host of misogynistic pejoratives. Too weak and it's the same."

The president's jaw tensed and she again gave Matti the once-over. She leaned forward at her waist.

"What is your game?"

"Excuse me?"

"What is your game, Matti? I can't figure you out."

"Madam President, I'm not sure I—"

"You work for the NSA, which is such a trustworthy organization, right? You're a code breaker who suddenly graduates to field agent. You almost, but don't quite, stop a terrorist attack. You come to work for me. I give you important work. You become a self-loathing drug addict. Now you're doubting the veracity of what I tell you?"

"I don't doubt—"

"Sure you do. I saw it in your eyes at Camp David. Now there's some tabloid making up some farcical nonsense about him, and I've got reporters asking me about it on board my plane."

"I didn't say anything to any reporter." Matti's eyes narrowed as she spoke. The president couldn't tell if it was from confusion or fear.

"I'm not suggesting you did," President Jackson said, though she was. "I need to know you're on my side. I need to know you're focused. I need to believe you when you tell me you're ready for the summit. Otherwise, you might as well not get off the plane when we land."

Matti sank back into the sofa. The look on her face hadn't changed.

"There's a lot at stake here. We don't need distractions. And I don't need to be worried about whether or not you're on board."

"I'm on board," Matti said as someone knocked on the cabin door.

"What?" the president said without taking her glare off Matti.

"It's Goodman," said the chief of staff.

"Come in, Brandon," the president huffed.

Goodman opened the door and walked into the suite, taking a step before realizing he'd entered what looked like a cross between an intervention and the principal's office.

The president turned to look at Goodman.

"We've had a security situation."

"Be more specific."

Goodman took another step into the room but didn't sit. He glanced at Matti before looking again at the commander-in-chief.

"It's fine," the president assured him. "Right, Matti? We can trust you?"

Matti nodded. "Yes, Madam President."

"Go on then."

"Our advance team is reporting a homicide investigation at the hotel where you're scheduled to stay and at which we'll be holding the summit. A woman, a flight attendant, was murdered in her room."

"Who is handling it?"

"Local police and private security hired to handle G12 logistics. Secret Service is assisting."

"What happened?" Matti asked, leaning forward in her seat.

"Not certain," said Goodman. "We know the killer tried to make the room appear empty, except that he left a body in a suitcase in the closet."

"Big suitcase," the president surmised.

"No." Goodman shook his head. "It was a small suitcase. Gruesome."

"So what's the threat assessment?" asked the president. "I would guess, from the suspect description, they have someone in custody."

"Not yet. The folks on the ground don't seem to think it bears concern. There is, however, a media blackout on the death. It's being kept quiet."

"Part of the protest?" Matti asked.

"They're not sure. They have video of the suspect on their CCTV. Our folks are helping with facial recognition software of the suspect against the surveillance video of the protestors outside the trade center."

"So the other delegations know?"

"I can't be sure," said Goodman. "Again, they don't think there's a threat. The initial guess is a domestic between a flight attendant and somebody she met."

"Thank you, Brandon."

"Yes, Madam President." Goodman stopped short of genuflecting as he backed up a step and left the room.

"Matti—" the president stood and extended her arms "— come here."

Matti rocked forward and stood, taking two steps toward her boss. Her arms hung at her sides.

"Give me a hug." The president motioned with her fingers. "I want to hug this out. I want to press the reset button."

Matti stepped into the president's embrace and wrapped one arm around her back. President Jackson pulled Matti closer and squeezed.

"I'm sorry for my tone," she said. "I just need to know we're on the same team. I worry about you." She clenched Matti's shoulders and pulled away as she held her.

"I am," Matti said. "On your side, that is. And I understand. I've given you reason to worry. It's under control."

"Good to hear. Now go get some rest. We'll be in Barcelona before we know it."

*

Matti couldn't help but wonder about the president's schizophrenia. She was alone in one of the staff quarters toward the front of the aircraft. The door was closed and she opened her laptop. Her fingers poised above the keys, she considered Jackson's Jekyll and Hyde performance.

"She's not a very good actor," Matti mumbled and logged onto the Internet through the plane's satellite connection.

The onboard server would recognize she was online, but using the masking software she'd installed, there'd be no record of what sites she visited or what she typed.

She went to her email drop site and logged in. There was an attachment saved to her original, unsent email.

She clicked the attachment, dragged it to her desktop, and disconnected from the server. She deleted her history and cookies and then opened the attachment on her desktop.

The beginning of the document included a note from Matti's contact at the NSA, her former supervisor. He was the man who ultimately believed her Capitol conspiracy theory and was the one who'd held her in the moments after the explosion. They'd kept in touch, as much for the friendship as for the information they could swap.

> Here's what we've got on SST. It's more than what you had nine months ago. Hope it helps. If you need more, I'm here. Travel safe.

The remainder of the attachment was, on its face, gibberish. It was a seemingly random collection of numbers and letters. Matti selected the entirety of the lengthy document and copied it to the computer's clipboard. Then she deleted the attachment and removed it from the computer's hard drive.

She clicked to the computer's list of programs and opened a game called Solitaire. The traditional card game filled the screen with a prompt.

Would you like to continue your existing game?

Matti declined and the screen went black for a moment before a flashing red cursor appeared in the center of the screen. Matti typed in a password and waited while the screen changed from black to gray to white.

Another prompt appeared, and Matti entered an encryption code, telling the phantom program which of the code keys to apply to the text she was about to enter. The screen flashed and a cursor appeared at the top left, awaiting her input.

She pasted the text of the supervisor's attachment, and the program began deciphering the encoded message. Line by line, the gibberish morphed into legible Arabic text. In the upper right of the screen a timer indicated the process would take six minutes. It was a large file.

While the program uncorked the message, Matti read the government's "unofficial" file about Sir Spencer Thomas. She knew, hidden somewhere in the file, she'd find a clue about what was coming, his role, and his connection to the president.

She scrolled through the biographical information she already knew and scanned the peripheral intelligence about the advisory roles he'd played for various administrations and regimes.

Matti smirked at the references to Bohemian Grove and the suggestions that he was part of a subversive, secretive, but unnamed organization. She scrolled through the translation without much focus until she came upon a section detailing his known associations.

There were names she expected; all of the Capitol conspirators who identified themselves as Daturans, some defense industry magnates, a Ukrainian mobster named Liho Blogis, the deceased and disgraced former governor of Texas, a couple of energy executives, and some missing political aide named Jackson Quick.

Those were all known names, people who'd been in the news for one reason or another. But there were a couple of people Matti didn't recognize, and there was little information about them.

One was unnamed. There were three photographs of a tall, bald man with broad shoulders and a thick neck. In one photograph, a tattoo was visible on the back of his neck. His connection to Sir Spencer was based on a single, unencrypted phone call in 2008 to a payphone in Rome and a bank transfer within minutes of the call. The man's photograph was captured on a bank surveillance camera.

The account was in the name of one of Sir Spencer's holding companies. There was little money in it. Surveillance beyond the photograph had never turned up anything remarkable about the man or the money.

Matti wondered, however, why Sir Spencer would have been under electronic surveillance in 2007 and 2008?

The second name was Dr. Miguel Chapa, a neuro-ophthalmologist from Charleston, South Carolina. There were photographs of Chapa and Sir Spencer strolling along the Battery Promenade. There was a list of phone calls, which Matti noted were dated 2007, and a series of financial transactions that revealed an influx and immediate withdrawal of six-figure cash deposits to a series of accounts with Chapa's name attached.

Matti more closely read Chapa's associated biography, and suddenly, the connection between Sir Spencer and the president became clear. Chapa was a partner in Felicia Jackson's husband's medical practice.

When Jackson first won her congressional seat, her neurosurgeon husband had sold the practice to Chapa. Somehow, at some point, Chapa and Sir Spencer connected.

There was no direct link to the president, except a notation that he'd attended her inauguration. It was close enough. It was smoke. No need for fire just yet.

The file finished its conversion, and Matti looked for more about Chapa. She reconnected to the satellite and reopened the dummy email account.

Matti looked at her hand. It was trembling. She reached into her bag and pulled out a bottle. Gripping it in her hand, she stared at it, considering the consequences of opening it. She closed her eyes. An image of her mother flashed in her mind, and she stuffed the bottle back into her bag.

She considered the most efficient use of words and typed additional notes in the unsent message. She had three questions.

Who is Miguel Chapa? Why were eyes on SST in 2007–8? Am I safe?

She exited the mail program and, without spending time on her security protocol, moved straight to her new email account, opening it up to find a reply message from Dillinger Holt. It was about what she expected. Coy, arrogant, skeptical. She played along.

She aimed the laptop's camera at a blue and gold coaster embossed with the presidential seal and snapped a photograph. She attached the photograph to a new message and typed her reply.

I'm sending this email from Air Force One. And I'm
not in the media cabin.

She sent the message, closed the account and the browser,
deleted her history and the cookies. She erased the photograph and
was logging out of the satellite connection when, without warning,
the door to the cabin swung open.

"Matti, I was just—" Brandon Goodman stopped short when
Matti slammed shut her laptop. "Sorry. Was I interrupting
something?" He was carrying a plate of food: a sandwich and a bag
of chips. A bottled water was tucked under his arm.

"Uh, no," Matti said, "you just startled me."

"Sorry." Goodman held up the plate. "You hungry? You left
the staff room before the galley staff brought in our gourmet meal."
He pulled the bottle of water from under his arm and shook the
sweat from it.

"I'm good, thanks," she said. "You're welcome to have a
seat."

Goodman flashed a grin and shut the door with his elbow. He
dropped into the seat opposite Matti, balancing the plate and the
bottle. "At least take the water."

"Thanks." She took the bottle and set it in the seat's cup
holder. "Can I ask you a seemingly off-the-wall question?"

"Shoot." Goodman adjusted the seat and set the plate off to
the side.

"You were part of President Foreman's staff, right?" she
asked, knowing the answer.

"Yes. I worked on his campaign policy team. He liked that I
was a West Point graduate with a background in international
relations. I'd served overseas. That was a plus. After the election, I
worked transition. I was at the State Department as an
undersecretary for a year before moving back to the White House. I
worked as a special assistant, like you do for President Jackson."

"I'd forgotten you were a veteran."

"I don't talk about it much."

"Special Forces?"

He winked. "I don't talk about it much."

"So why did the president make you chief?"

Goodman chuckled. "I don't know." He reached for the bag
of potato chips and pulled it open. "I guess I was a link to the past,

but young enough to have forward vision. I made her transition easier. I don't know, really."

"People were as critical of her hiring you as they were of her hiring me," Matti said. "They said you didn't have the experience."

"That they did." He popped a chip in his mouth. "Thanks for reminding me."

"It's been nine months," Matti replied. "How's it going?"

"It's going. Sometimes I do feel overwhelmed."

"Overwhelmed?"

"More than that. I'm out of the loop. For a chief, there are a lot of conversations that don't include me. I take comfort in the big office."

"I knew that."

"Knew what?"

"That you were an outsider," Matti said. "Like me. We're kept at arm's length."

"So why do you think she hired us?" Goodman sat up in his seat. "Between you and me?"

"I don't know. I haven't figured that one out yet. I was just excited to be at the inauguration. Then to be offered a job? Crazy."

"I remember you at the inauguration," he said. "You stood out against the others."

"You're funny." Matti's face reddened. "I don't remember you."

"Ha!" Goodman crumpled the empty chip bag and tossed it at her. "You don't play games, do you?"

"I didn't know a lot of people there," she said. "It was all government people."

"And some family friends," Goodman added. "People from South Carolina."

"I do remember that. I got introduced to a doctor from there. I don't remember his name."

"Couldn't help you there, Matti," he said. "Like I said, I'm not part of the inner loop. But those chips made me thirsty. Can I have the water?"

"Of course." She tossed him the bottle. "I think I know why."

"Why what?" He uncapped the bottle. "That was conversation whiplash."

"Sorry. My mind is going a thousand miles a second."

"As always."

"I think I know why the president hired us," she explained. "She thinks she's smarter than us. She needed people in seemingly key positions who were so happy to be part of the party that we wouldn't ask too many questions. We wouldn't push for information or influence."

Goodman took a swig of water and recapped the bottle. As he lowered it to his lap, Matti noticed his demeanor morph. He slipped from jovial and playful to wounded and withdrawn. He licked a drop of water from his lower lip and looked down at his lap.

"I didn't mean you're not good at what you do," Matti backpedaled. "I'm not implying that. I didn't mean that."

"I didn't take it that way." Goodman shrugged. "I think you're right. I believe the president wants a small circle of trust, as it were. And we're not a part of it. She needs chumps, and she needs somebody to blame when things don't go her way."

"So you agree?"

"Yes," he said. "Otherwise, why would she keep you on the payroll? I like you, Matti. You're a smart woman with a good heart. You're a PTSD-suffering drug addict with no policy experience. Two plus two doesn't equal four in your case."

"You don't play games, do you?" Matti forced a smile and flexed her hands.

"Nope." He stood from his seat. "I'm the chief of staff." He winked and moved to the door. "I'll leave the sandwich. You might get hungry."

"Thanks."

"And whatever you were doing on that laptop"—he glanced at the computer and then back up at Matti—"be careful."

CHAPTER 29

WORLD TRADE CENTER
BARCELONA, SPAIN

Jon Custos was at home amidst the ballooning crowd of demonstrators protesting the arrival of G12 summit participants. They were a motley mix of hemp enthusiasts and anticapitalists. Some of them wore the overplayed Guy Fawkes masks. Others held signs or bullhorns to proclaim their disaffection.

Despite his size, he moved among them without issue, occasionally raising his fist and shouting with them. They were held in an area between the Ronda Litoral and Plaça de les Drassanes, two circular drives that formed a figure eight of sorts at the entrance to the man-made peninsula on which the World Trade Center and the Hotel Eurostars were built.

Police blocked them from moving in any direction other than directly away from the peninsula and west along the Avenue del Parallel. Custos joined the group from the west, paying close attention to the numbers of police and their weaponry. He counted vehicles and estimated distances. The level of security was significantly more impressive than the day before.

A red double-decker tourist bus chugged northeast, toward Port Olimpic. The tourists' necks craned in unison as they passed, seemingly more interested in the protest than the history of the port. Custos's eyes followed the bus until a collective roar from the protestors drew his eyes back to the peninsula.

A pair of black Lanca Thesis armored limousines led a caravan of five cars turning from Ronda Literal onto the peninsula. They carried Italian flags on one front quarter panel and a banner with an inset Emblem of Italy on the other.

"Are they the first to arrive?" Custos asked an unwashed, screaming Englishman next to him.

"Why would I know?" the man spat at Custos and then turned back to shaking his fists at the oblivious motorcade.

Custos cursed the man under his breath and slid a step to the left. He stood directly behind the Englishman and lifted the demonstrator's wallet from the frayed back pocket of his jeans. He slipped the wallet into his own pocket and then moved to another section of the crowd.

He found himself next to a tall, thin woman in a loose tank top who wore no makeup. Her face was flushed from the heat, her long hair matted against the back of her neck. She was shouting in Spanish. He wondered what circumstances had put her there. What had happened in her life that compelled her to fight what she thought was unjust?

She had to know that nothing would come from her civil disobedience. She couldn't be naive enough to think any real change could happen without incivility.

Sir Spencer had taught him about the need for violence, about its role throughout history. From Mesopotamia to Egypt and dynastic China, bloodshed was the only real means by which leaders of men could effect true change.

"Peace," Sir Spencer told him, "is the space in time between wars. It is the time during which we plot."

Whether it was the French, American, or Russian revolutionaries freeing themselves from oppressive rule, or nineteen suicidal al-Qaeda militants seeking to spark a new caliphate, a big stick was far more likely to accomplish the job than speaking softly.

Protests did not matter. Action mattered. And Custos was acting.

He was prepared to give his life, and take countless others, to create the kind of change the world needed. He looked at the people surrounding him, feeling the bile rise in his throat. The protestors, with their masks and clever posters, were false prophets. They had to know they were ineffective.

What change had they ever brought? Even the peaceful American Civil Rights Movement of the 1960s required violence and death before the laws changed.

That was the way of the world.

Custos saw another motorcade turn on the peninsula. It was a much larger motorcade than the Italians'. Two motorcycle officers led a pair of Range Rovers that were, in turn, leading a trio of Jaguar XJ Sentinels. They were unmarked, but Custos recognized them as the official vehicles of the United Kingdom and the British prime minister. It wouldn't be long before all of the member nations arrived.

He backed out of the crowd and started across the Plaça de les Drassanes. He hailed a cab and asked the driver to take him to Parc de Sant Marti. The ten-kilometer trip took twenty minutes in the heavy traffic running northeast along the coast.

The driver pulled up next to the park. Custos paid in cash and waited for the cab to merge back into the lunchtime traffic. Satisfied the driver was gone, he walked three blocks from the park to Bac de Roda.

He found the bright coral and Mediterranean building next to the pharmacy and walked up to the glass front door. He pulled a keyring from his pocket and, after attempting three keys, found the right one. He opened the door and coughed against the blast of heat from the lobby.

He begrudgingly climbed the stairs, cursing the old man, Fernando Barçes, for not having lived in a more modern building.

He reached the third floor and trudged along the terrazzo to flat 310, found the right key, and shouldered himself into Barçes's apartment. Custos locked the door behind him and made a straight line to the refrigerator. He found a red-labeled bottle of Estrella beer and popped it open, swigging it on his way back to the living area, grabbing a bag from the kitchen table when he passed.

The television was on, the volume low, and BBC World was reporting about the summit. On the screen was an aerial shot of the World Trade Center. Custos didn't bother turning up the volume as he sat on the floor and crossed his legs. He set the beer on the floor and centered the bag in front of him.

He'd only opened it once since taking it from the pasty Russian, Feodor Ivanovich, in a Roman café. That check had been to ensure he'd retrieved the right goods. Now they needed closer inspection.

He took another sip of the beer, puckered his lips at the sour taste, and unzipped the bag. Custos pulled open the sides of the bag and reached inside to remove its contents.

He held a pair of devices in his hands. They were small, lightweight, and devoid of metal, just as the Russian promised they would be.

For months, Custos had negotiated with black market proxies. One meeting led to another. At one point, after paying a large sum of money to an operative representing AQAP, Al-Qaeda Arabian Peninsula, Custos was ready to give up. Nobody could produce the magic beast he sought. The operative never had a chance to spend the money. Instead, he'd wound up at the bottom of the Euphrates.

Out of the blue, Custos had gotten an email from a man claiming to have what he sought: an undetectable explosive. Custos was told there were only two groups in the world who'd mastered it. AQAP and an off-the-books section of Russia's 12th Chief Directorate, the military agency in charge of nuclear security. AQAP's version of the explosion was essentially an IED made in back-alley kitchens. They were cheap but likely effective. Russia's version was more sophisticated, more versatile, but nearly cost prohibitive.

Since AQAP was out of the question, Custos, with the help of Sir Spencer's Ukrainian connections, worked to gain the confidence of the Russian source. That source, Feodor Ivanovich, negotiated a fair price on behalf of his employers and agreed to sell two units to Custos.

Custos recalled the hassle, the meetings, the money, and the murder it took to hold the devices in his hands. These were world-changers, he thought, balancing their weight in his palms.

They were better than an underwear or shoe bomb, more clever than a liquid-explosive-filled Gatorade bottle.

They were a unique mix of ingredients meant to catch fire, explode, and emit. Both incendiary and dirty, they were the cutting edge of what was possible: a catastrophic mixture of thermite and nuclear material in an untraceable nonmetal casing.

What made these devices better than the junk AQAP had promised but not delivered was that they were surgically implantable. The carrier, or anyone with the correct information, could detonate the device from a cell phone or a laptop.

Custos turned over the devices in his hands, looking at the genius of them. He should have known from the beginning that one of the devices was meant for him.

He replaced the twin devices in the bag, zipped it up, and carried it back to the kitchen. He went to the bathroom, flipped the toilet lid, and relieved himself.

He stood there, one hand on his hip, and turned to the cast-iron tub on the opposite wall. He smiled as he urinated.

"I've got plans for you, old man," he said to Barçes, who was hog-tied, barely conscious, and lying on his side in the tub. *"Tengo planes para ti. Planes muy grande."*

*

Sir Spencer limped along the cobblestone street in the city's Gothic quarter. He drifted amongst the tourists shopping in the high-walled streets and alleys, occasionally stumbling from a misplacement of his cane on the stones.

It was less hot than he'd found Park Güell, but still not temperate enough. Sweat collected in the small of his back and under his arms, drenching the linen shirt he'd purchased from a shop just an hour earlier.

This was freedom he'd not tasted in months, and despite the heat, he relished it. The bustle, the energy, the optimism of the people shuttling in and out of storefronts and cafés invigorated him.

He found a gelato and coffee stand and stopped for a rest and a cone. He'd taken his first taste when his phone rang. He pressed the encryption key and answered.

"Is your man in trouble?" President Jackson snarled.

"Why are you calling me?"

"It's a secure line."

"No government line is secure."

"I'm in the air. It's secure."

"Not sure how that makes a diff—"

"Answer my question."

"I don't know if he's in trouble. Why would you suggest that?" He took a napkin from the tabletop dispenser and wiped the edge of the cone before taking another lick.

"There was a murder in the hotel at the World Trade Center."

"And you immediately assume our boy had something to do with it?"

"It complicates everything."

"Not necessarily."

"It better not," she growled.

"Before I disconnect the call, might I remind you I don't typically respond well to threats."

"It's not a threat."

"Don't confuse your power with my authority." Sir Spencer ended the call and slid the phone onto the table. His gelato was a mess, having succumbed to the heat far too quickly.

He didn't like that Felicia Jackson had called him from a government line. That was about as stupid as anything she'd ever done.

She was never his first choice for the Oval Office; Secretary Blackmon was. She'd survived the Capitol explosion. Blackmon, the idiot, got caught. The Brethren were stuck with her.

Jackson, he'd long believed, with her devil black hair and demonic blue eyes, was too quick to light a fuse. She was impulsive. She was dangerous.

He pushed himself to his feet and tossed what was left of the cone in a nearby trashcan, slid his phone into his pocket, and merged back into the flow of pedestrians. He looked up to the wrought-iron balcony of an apartment some thirty feet above. A woman leaned on the railing, her arms crossed in front of her as she gazed out from her landing. Tendrils of cigarette smoke escaped her nose as she exhaled.

Sir Spencer passed underneath the woman and considered Felicia Jackson's concerns. Despite her impudence, she had a point.

If Custos had erred, it was a serious complication. Custos, as good as he was at what he did, shared the same impulsivity as Felicia Jackson. He was quick to act and less contemplative than Sir Spencer would have liked.

While they were sitting on the bench at Park Güell, Custos had told him he'd procured a hotel room key. Killing someone for the key was unnecessary.

Sir Spencer turned a corner into a narrow alley. The sun was blocked by the tall buildings on either side, and it was considerably cooler in the alley. He stopped and stood in the middle of the cobblestone pathway. He closed his eyes. In the apartments above him, a couple argued about an unpaid bill, a baby cried, someone was cooking curry. To his left, a young man mumbled to himself as he passed. On his right a woman hummed sweetly.

All of them are blind.

He opened his eyes and pulled his phone from his pocket, turned on the encryption, and called Custos.

"Where are you?" he asked when Custos answered.

"I'm in an apartment."

"What are you doing?"

"Preparing."

"Is your line secure?"

"Yes."

"Did you kill someone in the hotel?"

"Yes."

"I see." Sir Spencer tapped his cane on the uneven stone. "Why?"

"I needed the key."

"And you couldn't have procured the key without violence?" Sir Spencer asked. "You couldn't have just let a room at the hotel yourself?"

"I didn't think about that," Custos admitted. "I did what was easiest."

Sir Spencer smiled but said nothing.

"Is there a problem?" Custos's voice elevated an octave.

"Possibly. You left a body."

"It's not a problem." Custos cleared his throat. "It won't affect the plan."

"You can't say that with certainty." Sir Spencer started walking toward the end of the alley. "It's likely they have video of you. They'll know what you look like."

"I'll work around it."

"I trust you will."

Sir Spencer hung up and stepped gingerly toward the alley's intersection with a wider, busier street. He was on the edge of the Gothic Quarter, making his way to his flat.

It was smaller than he'd have liked, and without much of a view, but it was better than a cell. He paused at the intersection to let a pair of nuns pass him. They smiled at him and he nodded before rounding the corner to merge into the bustle.

*

Jon Custos looked at the phone, his eyes lingering after Sir Spencer hung up. He clenched his jaw.

"I trust you will?" he mocked. "You left a body."

Custos gripped the phone, as if to crush it, before tossing it onto the kitchen table. He bit into his lip until his tongue was dipped in a warm, salty mixture of saliva and blood. He yanked open kitchen drawers until he found a lighter and a steak knife.

"I've never failed him," he muttered and moved to the cabinet under the sink. He crouched and yanked open the cabinet doors. "Never. And he doubts me. He doubts *me*, a martyr for the greater good. I'm a hand of the Brethren."

He sucked against the wound in his mouth and searched the space under the sink, finding a large bottle of hydrogen peroxide and a bottle of vodka. Custos moved three steps to the pantry, where he grabbed a half-full bag of granulated sugar. He took the bag and the bottles with him to the bathroom.

From a mirrored medicine cabinet, Custos plucked a box of bandages and some cotton balls. He slapped shut the toilet lid and placed his findings atop the bone-colored porcelain.

"Viejo," he called to Barçes, barely drawing a reaction from the weakened, semiconscious janitor, *"donde esta aguja y hilo?"* He needed a needle and thread.

Barçes mumbled something unintelligible that was more groan than Catalan. He smacked his lips and tried licking them.

Custos grunted and thumped to the bedroom to rifle through dresser drawers. He found a travel sewing kit and dropped it into his pocket. It would do.

Returning to the bathroom, he grabbed the vodka bottle and uncapped it. He took a swig and winced against the burn then bent down onto his knees, sitting on his heels, and gripped Barçes's face at his jaw. He held open the old man's mouth just enough to funnel in a couple of shots' worth of vodka.

Barçes gulped the drink at first, perhaps thinking it was water, before coughing it up. Custos held onto his jaw and poured in another double. He wanted the man inebriated and feeling no pain.

While he waited for the vodka to take effect, Custos returned to the kitchen. He unzipped the bag containing the Russian devices and removed one of them. He checked to make sure it was properly sealed and marched back to the bathroom.

The old man had slipped from semiconsciousness to virtual delirium and was on his back in the tub, drooling and breathing heavily from his mouth. His legs were splayed and one of them hung over the edge of the tub.

Custos watched Barçes's chest heave up and down for a minute before he returned to the bedroom. He stripped the sheets from the bed and laid them on the floor, then took a pair of towels and spread them on top of the sheets.

It took him five minutes to move Barçes from the tub to the sheets. He arranged the old man on his back with his arms extended and his legs spread. He looked like an unconscious Vitruvian Man, with his wrists and ankles bound to the heavy furniture in the room. Custos knew if Barçes struggled from the pain, he'd need restraints.

His last preoperative step was music. A clock radio was perched on a bedside table, and Custos switched it on, spinning the tuner to a classical music station. He thumbed up the volume and sat on the edge of the bed, listening for a moment.

To his surprise, Custos recognized the piece. Sir Spencer had long tried to educate him about the virtue of the classics. Most of it had fallen on deaf ears. But a few of the more aggressive composers spoke to Custos. Among them was Dmitri Shostakovich, a Russian composer and pianist who rose to fame during the early days of the Cold War.

He was an obsessive man who often sent letters to himself to test the effectiveness of the postal service. He synchronized all of the clocks in his apartment. He suffered tics. He was a genius.

Custos thought about the man as the clock radio blared the dark, measured angst and anger of Shostakovich's Fifth Symphony. The strings cried and wailed in the early minutes of the piece, and Custos's mind flashed to Feodor Ivanovich. Did the Russian gangster share the same appreciation for Shostakovoch? It was fitting, Custos thought, that he should work with one Russian creation as he listened to another.

He pushed himself from the bed and found his place on the floor at his patient's side. He plucked the knife from the floor and sterilized it with the lighter before pressing the hot stainless steel to Barçes abdomen, above the navel.

Forty minutes later, the work nearly complete and Barçes on the edge of consciousness, Custos poured sugar into the wound and stitched closed the five-inch incision. He stuck the needle downward through the subdermal layer of skin. He didn't want the stitches tearing. They needed to hold. He passed the needle through the wound and then up through the skin to the other side of the cut. He worked quickly but with precision.

The music was at its crescendo, the woodwinds and brass singing for attention as the percussion quickened its rhythm, thundering to the melancholy conclusion. Custos admired his handiwork. He'd only tried this once before, and septicemia had killed the patient within hours of the surgery.

He knew this time, as he cut the thread and knotted the end of the final suture, he'd succeeded. He doused the edges of the wound with hydrogen peroxide and wiped it dry with cotton. The patient stirred, tugging against the binds with his arms.

"Què va passar?" Barçes gargled in Catalan, his eyes flickering as he questioned what happened to him through the haze of dehydration, alcohol, and pain. *"Què vas fer?"*

"What did I do?" Custos asked reflexively in Spanish. "I did only what needed to be done."

He went to the kitchen to get ice from the freezer. He brought a cup back to his patient and told him to suck on the cubes.

"You'll need your strength now," Custos said. "We don't have much time left and I need you to be strong, *viejo*."

CHAPTER 30

THE GALLERIA
HOUSTON, TEXAS

Holt rubbed his jaw, staring at the words on his laptop screen.

I'm sending this email from Air Force One. And I'm not in the media cabin.

The implications were ridiculous. He'd had high-level sources before: on Congressional committees, Homeland Security, at the Pentagon, and in the State Department. But a potential West-Winger? Someone close enough to the president that he or she was riding on Air Force One for an overseas trip? He uncapped a Gatorade and gulped it.

He responded to the email with his cell phone number, his personal email address, and a note expressing how anxious he was to connect. He hit send and looked at the note he'd scribbled and added a line at the bottom.

THE BRETHREN—NEW WORLD ORDER
SIR SPENCER—THE BRETHREN
SIR SPENCER—ERIK MAJORS
SIR SPENCER—HORUS
HORUS'S DEATH—ERIK MAJORS'S DEATH
HORUS—THE BRETHREN
ALL CONNECTED??
TIMING??
WHAT'S THE GOAL??
IS THE WHITE HOUSE INVOLVED?

Holt checked his phone. Still no messages or texts from Karen. He looked around the hotel room at the unmade bed, the pizza box, his suitcase. He needed to leave. There was nothing more he could accomplish by sitting in his hotel room.

He'd go to the forensics center and check on Karen. If nothing else, he could make sure she was okay. Holt packed up his belongings and within twenty minutes was on his way to the Harris County morgue.

He'd driven a couple of miles when his phone rang. He pressed the Bluetooth button on the car's steering wheel and answered.

"Dillinger Holt."

"What have you got?" his editor asked. "I need you to feed the beast."

"Your entire homepage is my stuff," he answered. "I'd say the beast is fed."

"Not hardly," she replied hollowly, clearly on speakerphone. "The traffic on the site is insane. We're setting records for unique visitors and time per page. I need more to keep the momentum going."

Holt knew the beast was always hungry. The more he gave, the more was expected. The news cycle had evolved. Instead of twenty-four hours, it was more like twenty-four minutes. Everything was *Breaking!* or *Developing!* or *Exclusive!* and it was constant. The top story in the morning was below the proverbial fold by noon. By dinnertime, there might not even be a link on the home page.

Much of it wasn't even news anymore. It was photo galleries and click-bait, teases designed to get unique users to stay on the site and click through as many pages as possible.

Holt lived with the reality because it *was the* reality. He'd never been anything other than a journalist. He'd take the business in whatever form it existed.

"I've got something," he admitted to the web editor. "A second source on the Sir Spencer angle." He pressed the accelerator and sped up to keep pace with the vehicles traveling around him.

"What's the source say?" There was a click and the editor's voice was suddenly louder and clearer. She'd picked up the receiver. "Is he alive?"

"Yes. According to the source, Sir Spencer is alive."

"Get me five hundred words ASAP," she said breathlessly. "This is huge. Who is the source?"

"I don't know yet." Holt slowed at a yellow traffic light.

"What does that mean?"

"I'm working on it." He pressed the brake and stopped.

"What does that mean?"

"I'm still working to identify the source," Holt explained. He looked up ahead and to the left. There were red and blue lights flashing behind a thicket of oleanders guarding the forensics center. He craned his neck but couldn't see much through the greenery.

"Can we go with it?" the editor pressed. "Do we need to identify the source?"

"Give me an hour or two."

The light turned green and Holt pushed the accelerator. The tires squealed as they lost their grip on the pavement.

"I don't have an—"

Holt pressed the END button on the steering wheel and urged the rental car faster. As he approached the oleanders, his stomach sank. They were wrapped in yellow crime scene tape, blocking his entrance to the parking lot.

He slowed, rubbernecking past the lot. There were uniformed officers and deputies dotting the property, a half dozen marked cars pulled along the building, and a couple of television crews straining to get a view from beyond the yellow tape.

Holt swallowed hard, took a deep breath, and yanked the wheel to the left to jump the curb. He punched the hazard lights on the rental and jumped out, jogging back to the lot at a near run.

The doors to the forensic center were propped open. Uniformed deputies and plainclothed investigators walked in and out of the building, shaking their heads. One of them, a young-looking deputy with a crew cut and pelican neck, bent over at his knees and vomited onto the grass near the building's entrance. Another deputy, with less hair and a bigger gut, put his hand on the younger one's back.

Holt waved at one of the sergeants and called for him to come over, but the man shook his head and turned his back. Holt checked his phone and sent another text to Karen.

Are you okay? There's a crime scene at your office.

He marched over to the pair of television crews and flashed his press identification.

"Hey," he said to a blonde woman he assumed was a reporter. She was holding a wireless microphone under her arm as she typed away on her phone. "I'm a reporter from DC. I just drove by this. I'm wondering what happened."

"Multiple homicides," the woman said without looking up from her phone. "We're hearing one man and one woman."

"When did you get here?" Holt asked, turning to look at the open doorway. "You been here long?"

"Ten minutes, maybe," she said. "The PIO hasn't given us anything yet."

"No names yet?"

Instinctively, Holt knew Karen was one of the victims; the acidic ache in his gut told him as much.

The blonde shook her head.

"They're both county employees," offered the photographer. The blonde shot him a look and he shrugged. "He's not the competition."

"Thanks." Holt checked his phone again. No response from Karen.

He looked at the organized chaos unfolding in front of him. He'd been to crime scenes before, watched the choreography of it too many times to count. He'd never seen it unfold with a weakness in his knees.

Somehow his sixth sense, his reporter's intuition, told him he was responsible. Karen was dead, and it was his fault. All of it was too coincidental not to be his fault.

She'd given him information he wasn't supposed to have, he'd published it, and she'd paid for it.

Sir Spencer. New World Order. Horus. Murder. FBI. Karen. Conspiracy. The Brethren...

They were connected.

If Karen died because of it, he had to be on the list too. He scrolled through his text messages again, stopping at the ones he'd exchanged with Karen before he arrived at his hotel the night before.

i'm here. u?

That was her last message. She was at the hotel. He'd responded immediately.

stuck in traffic. rain. be there in five.

He'd arrived in four minutes. He saw her car and thought he saw her...

Her car...

Holt walked the perimeter of the yellow tape toward the employee parking lot. There were three cars, none of them Karen's. He wasn't sure what to make of it.

He turned back toward the growing gaggle of television crews, figuring that location was his best bet for information. His phone buzzed against his hip. He looked at the screen and rolled his eyes before answering.

"You hung up on me, Dillinger," the editor whined.

"I told you to give me an hour."

"I don't have an hour," she harped. "I need something now."

"Just put up a 'developing' banner across the top of the page," Dillinger suggested. "Tell readers we'll have new information about a critical story in an hour."

"Why would—"

"Get one of your web guys to add a countdown clock to the homepage. It'll get buzz. I promise. Blast an alert through the app. That'll add to the excitement. I'll have something to you shortly."

He didn't wait for an answer before hanging up. A plainclothed deputy was walking toward the ballooning group of television cameras. Holt counted six as he walked to the impromptu staging area on the edge of the yellow tape facing the door.

The deputy tugged on his belt as he approached. He stood about five feet from the cameras, just beyond the handheld microphones reporters pointed at him. "All right, we've only been here about a half hour. Call came in two hours ago when the morning shift showed up for work. All we can tell you right now is that we have two bodies. One male, one female, both deceased. I can't give you cause of death or identities yet."

"Motive?" chirped the blonde reporter.

"Don't know." The deputy sighed. "We're in the early stages. I just figured I'd come out and give you something before your noon newscasts. I really don't have anything else."

"Where were they found?" asked Holt, catching the deputy as he turned to walk away.

The deputy pursed his lips and adjusted his belt. He looked at Holt and nodded. "They were not together. One of them was near the front of the building. The other was…" He caught himself and his eyes narrowed. "The other was in the back of the building."

"In the morgue?" asked the blonde.

"I'm not going to answer anything else." The deputy waved off the reporters and started his walk back to the building.

Holt moved in the same direction as the deputy. He called to him and waved him over, away from the cameras and other reporters. The deputy rolled his eyes but met Holt at the crime scene tape near the cluster of oleanders.

"I don't have anything else to add."

"I'm Dillinger Holt." Holt offered his hand and flashed his press badge. "I'm a reporter with PlausibleDeniability.info, the website."

The deputy shook Holt's hand. "I know the site, but I'm not saying anything else."

"This isn't on the record," Holt said. "It's not even on background. It's potentially evidence."

"How so?"

"Quid pro quo here," Holt offered. "I need the name of the woman killed. If it's who I think it is, I have information that could help."

"It doesn't work that way, son," he said. "If you have information and you withhold it, that's a problem."

"It's not relevant unless I know who died."

The deputy tugged on his belt. His jaw tightened.

Holt gripped the yellow tape in his hands. "I need to know if my friend is in there. This isn't for reporting."

"Give me a name," the deputy relented.

"Karen Corvus."

The deputy didn't answer Holt. He didn't have to say anything. His eyes gave it away with a twitch, his jaw relaxed, and his shoulders drooped. All of it was subtle, nearly imperceptible had Holt not been looking for it.

"It's her, isn't it?" Dillinger's eyes welled. He swallowed against a thickening knot in his throat.

The deputy nodded, his eyes looking at his feet.

"Okay." Holt sucked in a deep, ragged breath. "I owe you then. Take a look at this." He pulled out his phone and slid open his text messages with Karen. He handed the phone to the deputy.

"This is with Miss Corvus?" The deputy scrolled through the messages.

"Yes."

"This was last night?"

"Yes."

"I don't get it." The deputy looked up from the screen. "You were on your way to meet with her, but she stood you up?"

"Not exactly," Holt explained. "Look at her last text, not the thousand I sent her afterward. She told me she was at my hotel waiting for me."

"You never saw her?"

"No."

"She wasn't at your hotel?"

"No. I thought she was. It was raining and I thought I saw her car. A woman got out of the car and walked toward me. I thought it was Karen until she got closer. It wasn't her. But the more I think about it, I'm pretty sure the woman wanted me to *think* it was Karen. I don't know."

"Then you kept trying to get ahold of her?"

"Yes. She never replied."

"What was your relationship with her?"

"We were friends." Holt shrugged. "Maybe a little more than friends. She was a source on a couple of stories. I think maybe one of those stories might have something to do with this."

"You know I'm going to need you to come to the office with me," the deputy advised. "I'm going to need an official statement. If you need an attorney—"

"I don't need an attorney," Holt bristled. "I didn't do anything. I'm trying to help."

"Whoa!" The deputy took a step back and raised his hands in mock surrender. "I'm not insinuating anything. I'm just giving you the option."

"I don't really have time right now," Holt said. "I've got a story to file. I've got some calls to make. Can we do this later? My cell phone is on the card."

"I don't think so." The deputy slipped his hand under the yellow tape and raised it above his head. "You need to come with me. Now."

CHAPTER 31

EL PRAT INTERNATIONAL AIRPORT
BARCELONA, SPAIN

President Jackson stood at the doorway of Air Force One, waving at the gathering of television and still cameras corralled one hundred yards away. She smiled and then began a measured descent down the steps to the tarmac.

At the bottom of the steps was a contingent of Spanish legislators, the US Consul General assigned to Barcelona, and a few local dignitaries. The president shook each of their hands and then found her place in the backseat of the presidential limousine, a Cadillac affectionately called "The Beast".

She rubbed her hand on the presidential seal embroidered between the two blue leather seats and then rested it on the burl wood inlay that served as an armrest. She tapped her fingernails for a moment and then picked up the inset black telephone.

"Brandon," she said to her chief of staff, "are you in the Suburban?"

"No, I'm in the decoy Beast."

"Who's with you?" The president slipped on her seat belt as the car jerked forward.

"Matti Harrold, the press secretary, a couple of Secret Service agents."

"All right," she said. "When we get to the hotel, I want a quick meeting with the policy folks, our intelligence liaison, you, and me."

"And Matti?"

"No."

"She's your congressional liaison, Madam President," argued Goodman. "She's best suited to sell some of the finer points of the package. It's what she's been doing for weeks in the House and Senate."

"She doesn't need to be in the meeting." President Jackson cradled the phone in her neck and looked at her fingernails. She needed a manicure. "You can handle that part of the discussion."

"The talks start tomorrow. I think—"

"I didn't ask what you think, Brandon. Tell Matti she's welcome to tour the city or go for a jog or do whatever she wants until the dinner tonight."

"You're certain?"

"Yes, I'm certain. Just have her keep you posted on what she's doing and where she's going."

"Yes, Madam President."

President Jackson hung up and reached for a bottle of water. She looked out the window at the clear skies. A motorcycle zoomed past her window and joined the rest of the local police at the front of the motorcade. Their sirens wailed as they merged onto the C-31 highway and headed northeast toward the World Trade Center.

She took another sip of the water and laid her head back against the blue leather and stared blankly out the window. This was the perfect place to carry out the plan.

For so many years, the Brethren had shunned the inclusion of women in the highest levels of their club. They'd made an exception with her. And here, in the city of Gaüdi and Miró, she would prove her worth. She would facilitate the single largest advancement of their cause since the formation of the World Bank in 1944 and the creation of the United Nations a year later.

Not since 1918 and Woodrow Wilson's Fourteen Points for a New World Order had they been so close. And when Wilson let the world know of his plan, he'd had more resistance from France, the United Kingdom, and Italy than she anticipated during the G12 summit.

Wilson had blindsided the allies with his desire for a borderless, barrier-free economy among nations and a military softening. She'd given her counterparts plenty of advance warning. She told them of the stakes and what was expected of them.

This would be a true shift in the order of things. It wouldn't be the glasnost "New World Order" promised by George H. W. Bush and Mikhail Gorbachev.

Instead, it would be what David Rockefeller foretold when he said, *"We are on the verge of a global transformation. All we need is the right major crisis and the nations will accept the New World Order."*

She laughed to herself. It would begin with the sharing of intelligence: intelligence gathered electronically on every single citizen. The SECURITY nations would track, record, share, and act on the information they obtained.

Next would be the borderless economy and a borderless military. Eventually, everyone would be subject to the same one world government.

This was what Sir Spencer had promised her during her first weeks in Washington all those years ago. It was his money that had funded Miguel Chapa's purchase of her husband's practice. He'd approached Chapa. Chapa went to her husband. Her husband went to her.

"Meet with the man," her husband implored. "There's nothing lost in a simple meeting."

She'd agreed, and Sir Spencer had cut to the chase.

"Chapa doesn't have the cash. I do," he'd said, sipping hot tea in her cramped basement office in the Cannon House Office Building. "I'll give him the money. I want just a little in return."

She was rightfully wary. "What?" she asked.

She was to keep him in the fold, allow him to dictate measures of policy, and he would reward her. She would rise quickly through the ranks, become a member of leadership. Sunday talk shows would clamor for her, and she'd be unbeatable at the polls.

The thought of so much power was too much for her to turn down. She'd agreed to the Faustian arrangement. Nearly everything had happened exactly as Sir Spencer promised it would.

Now they had everything in place. The hardest parts, killing an American president and then blowing up the United States Capitol, were accomplished.

What had seemed impossible a year earlier was well in motion now. Within a decade, the world would revolve within the new order of things.

All it would take to gather an irreversible momentum was blowing up Barcelona's World Trade Center. That would happen in a short twenty-four hours.

PART THREE: ETERNAL FLAME

"They know that there is a power somewhere so organized, so subtle, so watchful, so interlocked, so complete, so pervasive, that they better not speak above their breath when they speak in condemnation of it."
—Woodrow Wilson, 28th President of the United States of America

CHAPTER 32

ATATÜRK INTERNATIONAL AIRPORT
ISTANBUL, TURKEY

The assassin sat alone inside the terminal of the Istanbul Atatürk Airport. The molded gray metal seats were uncomfortable. She was running out of time.

She'd need to board her flight to Barcelona soon, and her friend was late. He was mere feet from her, but he couldn't leave his post inside the Türkiye Bankasi, and he told her making the exchange at the bank teller window was too risky.

"Wait," he told her. "I have a break in a few minutes. We'll make the exchange over there." That was a half hour ago.

Obtaining what she needed would have been easier had she been able to leave the airport. Her layover was too short. So she'd messaged ahead to her friend, telling him what she needed and when she needed it.

He'd promised to deliver it to her at the airport. His shift at the bank, doling out cash and exchanging Turkish lira for euros and US dollars was perfectly timed with her flights.

She was concerned that the delay was because he couldn't obtain what she'd asked for. It was not an easy find. She'd given him only a few hours, emailing him from her laptop on board the flight.

He'd always been reliable, which was why she'd asked him to perform the near impossible. If anyone could do it, it was him. He was one of the few men on Earth with whom she'd spent any time in bed and hadn't killed.

Finally, when she was about to give up, he approached her. His hands were in his pockets, his head down.

"Aydin," she said, standing to greet him. "You needn't look guilty." She looked into his eyes, her stare telling him to relax. She kissed him on both cheeks, lingering a moment longer than customary.

"Mariposa," he said, addressing her by a name few knew. "Let's walk," he said after returning her kisses. "There are some places hidden from cameras." He took her hand and gently led her along the concourse.

"My gate is in the other direction, Aydin," she said. "I'm about to miss my flight. You kept me waiting."

"My coworker was late, and I could not close the exchange. Many apologies. We must walk this way." He quickened his pace, tugging her along.

"You have what I need?" she asked, adjusting her fingers to his grip.

"Yes," he said, his eyes forward, darting from side to side as he hurried. "I have it. I found it near Taksim Square. Not difficult."

"And you altered it to match my specifications?"

"Yes," he said. "You were very specific, Mariposa."

Aydin stopped at a magazine stand and pulled the assassin in with him. He took her to the far corner of the shop and turned to face her.

"This is good here," he said. "No cameras."

"I'm not sure why we needed the cloak-and-dagger game, Aydin." She looked over her shoulder at the store clerk, who was preoccupied with a paying customer.

"There are eyes everywhere," he said. "Everywhere."

"Fine." She sighed. "Let me see it."

Aydin reached into his jacket pocket and pulled out a manila envelope. He opened the flap and slid the contents into the assassin's hand. She looked at her hand and smiled.

"Perfect, Aydin."

"I'm pleased it is okay." He exhaled. "I am happy to please you."

"The color is perfect," she said. "The size and shape look good. Even the imprint is exact. I'm impressed you did this so quickly."

Aydin smiled. He handed the assassin the envelope and she returned the contents to it.

"You have a plane to catch," he said. "Let's go."

"Yes," she said and took his hand, leading him out of the store. "I cannot miss my flight."

They walked hurriedly through the concourse until they reached her gate, where the attendant was announcing the final boarding call.

"*Teşekkür ederim*," said the assassin. She placed her hand on the back of Aydin's head and gently tugged on the thick black curls, pulling his face to hers. She kissed him firmly on the lips and then dragged her hand across his cheek. She remembered the taste of him and she licked her lips.

"You are welcome, Mariposa." he said, dazed by the unexpected affection. "Very welcome."

"You'll find your payment in the usual place," she said and left him to board the plane.

Aydin waited until she handed her ticket and passport to the agent before disappearing into the jet bridge. He slipped his hands into his pockets and walked back to the bank.

CHAPTER 33

WORLD TRADE CENTER
BARCELONA, SPAIN

"I don't get it either," said Goodman. He led Matti to the lobby of the Eurostars Grand Marina Hotel. "I wouldn't worry about it though. She suggested you take a run or go swimming. Whatever it is you want to do. Just be back for the dinner."

"It's okay." She shrugged, following Goodman into the hotel's large lobby and flashing her White House badge to the security guard manning the door. "I'm not offended. It gives me some time to decompress."

"Be careful if you head out," Goodman cautioned, his voice dropping to a whisper. "There was a woman killed in the hotel."

"I was in that briefing, Brandon." Matti stopped walking just beyond the entrance. "Why are you reminding me?"

"I got more intelligence right before we landed." Goodman stepped closer to Matti. "They have a good picture of the guy from the surveillance cameras."

"And?" Matti's eyes scanned the lobby as if it would provide any clues.

"He's a beast." Goodman's eyes widened. He held up his phone, revealing a still frame of the surveillance video. "And even if it was a domestic, I wouldn't want to run into him."

Matti looked at the phone and then grabbed it from Goodman. She studied the image, not trusting what she saw.

The man on the screen, bald and thick-necked, looked remarkably like the unnamed man in Sir Spencer's NSA file. If it wasn't the same man, it was his twin.

"What?" Goodman reached for his phone. "What's wrong?"

"Uh...nothing." Matti cleared her throat and handed Goodman his phone. "He's...I mean...you're right. He's a beast."

"Like I said," he repeated, "be careful. You just never know."

"Thanks, Brandon." She smiled and grabbed her luggage. "I will. I'm gonna head to my room."

"I'll see you at dinner."

Matti got her key from the front desk and hurried to her room. She left her luggage by the door and pulled out her laptop, connecting to the provided Ethernet cable.

She initiated her safety protocols and opened her dummy email account. Before checking the updated, unsent message, she added to it.

> I need you to call me ASAP. Secure line. You have the number.

She saved the email and then reopened it to look at the additional information. She'd asked about Dr. Miguel Chapa, previous surveillance on Sir Spencer, and whether or not she was safe. The answers were concise and surprisingly blunt. The language was un-NSA-like.

> Chapa, as best we can tell, is the connection between your boss and Sir Spencer. The Jacksons needed to sell the medical practice or face losing millions. Chapa wanted to buy it but didn't have the cash. Sir Spencer came to the rescue in exchange for access. He got his claws into Jackson. End of story.
> Sir Spencer was on our radar for years. He is a political mercenary who has dark intentions. He also has friends who tie our hands. We've known about his connection to Jackson, the Russian mob, Iran, the Chinese, but can't do much. We gather information. Sometimes it gets passed along. Sometimes it gets buried. To that end, you are not safe. Be careful.

Matti read the message three times, trying to grasp it. The president of the United States was beholden to a known terrorist. There was evidence of it and nobody cared. Or better yet, nobody dared challenge it. Matti jumped in her chair when her phone rang.

She encrypted the call and answered it.

"Matti"—it was her former supervisor at the NSA—"I got your message."

"Something big is happening."

"It always is."

"You sent me a file about Sir Spencer and his known associates. One of them was an UNSUB, identified only by a photograph. Rome. A few years ago."

"I'm pulling it up," he said. "Go ahead."

"He's here in Barcelona."

"How do you know that?"

"I just saw a surveillance photo of him," she explained. "He's wanted for killing a woman in the hotel."

"What hotel?"

"Our hotel. The one attached to the World Trade Center."

"Where the G12 is happening?"

"Yes," Matti answered. "What if this is somehow connected to the Capitol? What if this guy, Sir Spencer, and the president are in on something together?"

"Matti—" he sighed "—those are dangerous questions. I've survived as long as I have in this business because I don't ask dangerous questions."

"You told me I'm already in danger," she countered. "And you're already helping me."

"Yes," he answered, "we think there could be something on the horizon. There's a threat."

"And you're not doing anything?"

"That's not my call, Matti. It's never been my call. Do you really believe our intelligence agencies are as inept as the 9/11 Commission had you believe? Do you really think we'd have put you to work in the Capitol conspiracy if we didn't already know the endgame?"

"So you let it happen?"

"I wouldn't go that far—"

"Apparently you don't ever go far enough," Matti snapped. "What's at stake here? Tell me what is about to happen. If nobody else is going to stop it, I will."

"No, you won't."

"What?"

"You got closer than any of us thought you would nine months ago."

"W-w-wait," Matti stuttered. "What are you saying?"

"Matti"—his voice softened, employing a hint of sympathy—"how clear do I need to be?"

"Crystal."

"We knew about Pearl Harbor. We knew about Kennedy. We knew about 9/11. We knew about the Capitol. We know about Barcelona. But nobody is going to stop it."

Matti's hand shook as it held the phone to her ear. Things she suspected, worried about, lost sleep over, were all true.

"I'm telling you this because you, more than anyone, deserve to know the truth about power," he said. "And frankly, it doesn't matter how much I reveal about that truth, because it's all publicly dismissed as conspiracy theory. Always has been, always will be."

"Why are you helping me, then?" Matti asked. "Why tell me any of this if it doesn't matter?"

"Because I like you. And deep down, I hope you can stop it in time. I really do."

"Then tell me what's about to happen," she said. "Give me a clue about what you know."

"Look, when I say we, I don't mean me. Don't go thinking I'm at the top of the food chain. I'm nowhere near it. I only know what I know because of what my people learn while they're eavesdropping. So I don't know exactly what's going to happen. I just know there's chatter that something will."

"That's not an excuse."

"An excuse for what?"

"You're complicit."

"Am I?

"You know about these plots, about people's lives being in danger, and you do nothing."

"I don't 'do nothing'," he snapped. "I do my job. I oversee the collection of intelligence. I make sure that intelligence is analyzed and passed along. I protect my country's interests."

"That's a cop-out." Matti flexed her left hand. It was trembling. Her pulse quickened and her breathing was shallow.

"I don't agree. I take orders just like any soldier. I don't question them. I'm no different than the drone pilot sitting in some dark office building in Texas who drops hellfire on unsuspecting villages. I'm no different than the special operations team that extracts a high-value target and kills everyone else around him. I do what I'm told."

"You're a patriot."

"Damn right, Harrold. Every bit as much as Washington and Adams. "

"Every bit as much as Felicia Jackson and Sir Spencer Thomas."

"Not fair. We do what we do to save lives to protect our way of life. And honestly, since the PATRIOT Act was gutted, we can't do as much protecting as we used to do."

"Then tell me why it's happening. Why the Capitol? Why here?"

"That's the million-dollar question, Matti Harrold. You're a puzzle solver. Figure it out."

Matti hung up more confused than ever. She'd learned the world was made of gray. There were no blacks and whites, no absolutes. Nobody was entirely benevolent, nobody wholly evil.

This was another level of haze and indistinction. The man she'd come to trust in the aftermath of the Capitol's destruction admitted he was a tiny cog in the vast machine that had brought down the nation's iconic symbol.

He knew something was coming, had always known something was coming, but was too much of a company man to see the immorality of what he was enabling. How many were there like him roaming the halls of government, doing their duty in the name of honor and sacrifice?

Matti was sweating. She walked to the thermostat and turned down the temperature. The fan kicked on and a cool breeze blew from a ceiling vent above her head. She couldn't stand still. She paced back and forth, flexing her hands. Finally, she reached into her bag and pulled out a blue pill. She walked the few steps to the bathroom and stuck her head under the faucet to down the medicine.

Without the pill, she wouldn't be able to focus. She needed to focus. And, she knew, she had to find the thick-necked bald man. He had something to do with what was coming. She was certain of it.

*

Fernando Barçes felt the pain before he fully awoke. When he opened his eyes, he had trouble focusing. His eyes fluttered as he tried to make sense of what he saw hovering above him.

"*És això un somni?*"

"It's not a dream, *viejo*," said the haloed shadow of a head above him.

"Estic morta?" His lips were tacky, sticking together from lack of moisture.

"You're not dead."

"Ets el diable?" Barçes could feel the evil surrounding him, burning inside his stomach.

"Ha!" The thick-necked man laughed, moving such that his angular profile was silhouetted against the bright light above him. "Perhaps I am the devil. But remember, *viejo*, the devil was once an angel, no?"

Barçes didn't like being called an old man, but he didn't have the strength to protest. His back ached, his throat was swollen, and his stomach was on fire.

"Qui és vostè?" he asked, his eyes still batting back the intense overhead light. He tried moving his arms and realized he couldn't. His legs were immobile too. He struggled against the restraints for an exhaustive moment before giving up. *"Per què ets aquí?"*

"I am Jon Custos," said the shadow, still speaking Spanish. "And I am here to deliver you."

There was an accent in the man's voice Barçes couldn't place. He knew the man wasn't a Spaniard.

"You are an important man, *viejo*," Custos said. "I have chosen you. It is a great honor."

Barçes knew the words had different meaning to the broad-shouldered giant than they did to him: Important. Chosen. Great honor.

"This world is fractured," counseled Custos. "There are those who are wealthy and those who are impoverished. Essentially none stand in the wide chasm between the two. You, Fernando Barçes, have worked hard your whole life, yes?"

The old man managed a faint nod, if only to appease the intruder. His eyes were adjusting to the light, and he kept them open.

"Here you are"—Custos spread his arms wide—"living in a clean but tiny flat. Your prized possession is a television. The walls here are thin. The rooms are small."

Barçes could see the man more clearly now. He was olive-skinned. His head was smooth and reflected the light above it. His lips were full. They were a sharp contrast to the tight, angular shape of his brow, cheeks, and jaw. Everything about the man exuded strength.

"You are poor," Custos observed. "While blocks away there are men and women of untold wealth. They don't work as hard as you. They don't sacrifice as you have."

"I am a happy man," explained Barçes. "I have no complaints."

"Of course." Custos laughed. "Why would you complain? What good what it do? None. It would do no good to complain. So you pretend you're happy with your tiny television and your rabbit paella."

Barçes tried to watch the man as he moved, but he couldn't turn his head far enough. The man's footsteps across the floor gave him a general idea of his position in the room. Barçes knew he was in his bedroom. He wasn't on the bed, he was on the floor. As the realization crystalized, his memory flashed what he'd thought was a dream. The pain in his gut confirmed otherwise.

"In the new world, there won't be poor," the man preached from the corner of the bedroom. "There won't be rich. There won't be nations or borders or war. The new world will provide order from the chaos that exists now. One world. One people. It's a marvelous thought, isn't it? And to think, it will begin with you, *viejo*."

Barçes assumed from the direction of the man's voice he was standing by the window. Then the voice grew louder, and Barçes heard the footsteps as the man moved toward him again.

"Do you want to know?" asked Custos, kneeling beside Barçes, his full lips close to the old man's ears. "Would you like me to tell you how you'll be the spark that lights the fire?" he whispered in Spanish.

Barçes winced against a wave of pain searing through his stomach and lower back. His muscles tensed involuntarily as the wave crashed. His shoulders spasmed.

"I'll give you something for the pain." Custos placed his hand on Barçes's forehead. "You're sweating. That's not good. I need you virile and strong."

Barçes would have laughed at the suggestion if he could. He knew he'd never be virile or strong again. Even for a man his age, whatever this beast did to him, he was weakened beyond repair.

"First, I'll give you a hint as to your role." Custos ran his hands through the old man's thinning hair, raking sweat through the tendrils. "Have you ever heard of the Red Terror? Of course you have. You're old enough, *viejo*. Maybe you lived through some of it."

Barçes knew about the Red Terror, the so-called Spanish Holocaust, and the endless acts of senseless violence committed during the Spanish Civil War. Tens of thousands died as leftist reformers rebelled against politicians, the wealthy, and the church. The Catholic Church beatified four hundred and ninety-eight of the victims in 2007.

"So many men and women died for their cause," said Custos. "They died so others could live. That is what you will do, *viejo*. That is your contribution and your destiny."

CHAPTER 34

HARRIS COUNTY SHERIFF'S OFFICE SUBSTATION
HOUSTON, TEXAS

"I've told you everything I know." Dillinger Holt rubbed his eyes and yawned. "I can't help you beyond what I've already volunteered."

"You've said that." The plainclothed investigator leaned forward on his elbows. He sat across from Holt in a room at the sheriff's satellite office. "And I believe you. Given what we're dealing with, however, I can't just let you walk out of here."

"Am I under arrest?" Holt had missed his deadline by two hours and ignored four calls from his editor. She'd texted him twice using all capital letters. Not good.

"No."

"Then you can let me walk out of here," Holt said. "You can't detain me."

"Actually, that's not true," said the investigator, rapping his fingers on the table. "You've watched too much *Law & Order*. I can hold you for a reasonable amount of time until I decide whether an arrest is warranted. Then you have to wait for the prosecutor to file charges. It can take a while."

"You're not charging me with anything, though."

"No. I don't have any reason to suspect you've done anything wrong."

"Then...?" Holt's eyebrows arched expectantly.

"Then nothing. I need to make sure I've been thorough here. I'm gonna need your phone."

"Why?"

"There's evidence on the phone. You showed it to me. We need to have our IT guys look at it, break down the data. It could help us."

"I need my phone."

"You can get another one."

"I don't get it."

"Then you're an idiot, Mr. Holt. Your girlfriend, or whatever she was, died from either strangulation or the multiple puncture wounds in her neck and chest. She was stuffed into a freezer drawer. It was a violent death. Don't you want to help catch whoever did it? Especially since, as you told me, you feel responsible?"

Holt slid his phone across the table. He held onto his guilt.

"Thank you." The investigator moved the phone to the side. "Now, you think she died because she helped you with information about the suicide of that rapper, Horus?"

"Yes."

"Why, again, would she die for that?"

"I'm not sure." Holt exhaled as he spoke. He'd already explained his theory twice. "I believe Horus's death was not a suicide. Using information Karen gave me, I publicly connected his death to a disgraced FBI special agent. Somebody didn't want that connection public. It's too coincidental."

"And who is this somebody again?"

"I don't know."

Holt wasn't about to raise his theory about a connection to Sir Spencer and maybe even the White House. He'd already made a mistake by trying to confirm Karen's identity at the crime scene. He knew it was stupid the moment he'd opened his mouth.

Now he was out two hours and his cell phone. Neither sacrifice would bring back Karen, and neither was likely to be enough to find the killer.

"All right." The investigator nodded. "You can go. I need some contact information so I can get in touch if I need anything. But don't report that stuff I told you about how your friend died. We don't want that getting out yet. Understood?"

"Got it. You know where the closest cell phone store is?"

*

Dillinger held his new phone away from his ear as his editor colorfully explained her disgust. Her bosses were angry, which made her angry. That anger, among other things, rolled downhill. She didn't care who died or why he'd lost his phone.

"I need the five hundred words," she demanded. "Do you have them?"

"No, but—"

"Not the right answer, Holt."

"I'll give you something in twenty minutes."

"Fifteen."

"Fine."

Holt sat in his rental car outside of the cell phone store. He slid his seat as far back as it would go and pulled his computer onto his lap. He checked the new phone. The voicemail was set up correctly with his old number. No messages. His White House source hadn't come through. He needed something good, something that would appease his editor and her angry uphill bosses.

Holt cracked his knuckles and started typing.

CONNECTING THE DOTS:
WHAT DOES THE WHITE HOUSE HAVE TO DO
WITH HORUS?
By Dillinger Holt, Senior Correspondent

What do a dead hip-hop star, a disgraced FBI special agent, a suspected terrorist, and the White House all have in common?

That's the question we're asking as we uncover more disturbing details involving each of the above players in what might be a grand conspiracy of unknown intent.

—EXCLUSIVE—

The death of hip-hop star Horus in his backstage dressing room in Houston, Texas, was the first dot in a picture we still can't quite decipher, but is slowly beginning to take form.

As we first reported, investigators have connected a DNA sample from Horus's death chamber to one analyzed at the alleged suicide of a disgraced FBI special agent years ago in suburban Washington, DC. That agent was Erik Majors. His death is dot number two.

We've uncovered that Majors, as a high school student, received a prestigious Grove Scholarship. The man who awarded Majors the scholarship? Sir Spencer Thomas. That Sir Spencer Thomas, the suspected terrorist accused of blowing up the United States Capitol.

The same Sir Spencer Thomas the White House contends was killed in an ambush this week, but who two sources now contend is, in fact, alive.

Sir Spencer is dot number three.

Why would the White House report the alleged terrorist's death if it were not true?

Why would an FBI agent with at least a tertiary connection to Sir Spencer die under murky circumstances?

Why would DNA found at his death match a sample found at the death of a famous musician?

Horus, known for his dark lyrics, often wrote of a "New World Order" and of a powerful, shadowy puppet master of an organization manipulating our collective consciousness.

Was he silenced for it? Was Erik Majors?

We cannot draw the lines between said dots just yet. But the longer the White House denies what sources are telling us is true, the easier it is to put crayon to paper.

Holt cut and pasted the post into his email and sent it to his editor. Then he called her.

"It's in your inbox. It's explosive. I'm not sure you should publish it."

"Give me a second," she said. "I'm opening it." She read the piece aloud and then turned off the speakerphone. "You're right. It's explosive. I love it."

"You're posting it?" Holt couldn't hide his surprise.

"Yes, I'm posting it. We're not *The New York Times*, Holt. Heck, *The New York Times* isn't *The New York Times* anymore. I'll run it by the lawyers. But everything you wrote is posed as a question. You're not accusing anyone of anything. Brilliant."

"I'm forgiven, then?"

"For what?" She laughed and hung up just as another call came into his line. The number was blocked. He figured it was the Sheriff's Office.

"This is Dillinger Holt."

"Dillinger?" It was a woman's voice. "My name is Matti Harrold. I'm the one who emailed you."

CHAPTER 35

WORLD TRADE CENTER
BARCELONA, SPAIN

"Are you there, Mr. Holt?" Matti cursed herself as her name slipped out. So much for being a good spy. In her drug-induced haze, she shrugged it off.

"I'm here," he said. "Are you the same Matti Harrold who testified before Congress?"

"That's me." She looked at her hand and flexed it. No tremors.

"And you're the one who's been sending me emails?" he asked. "You've seen Sir Spencer Thomas alive."

"Yes." She could hear tapping on the other end of the line. "You're taking notes already? I haven't really told you anything."

"You've told me enough already." The typing stopped. "Everything from here on out is a bonus."

Matti's mind flashed to nine months earlier and her conversations with the source who ratted out the Capitol conspiracy, Bill Davidson's prostitute girlfriend. She considered how the tables had turned. Now she was the rat.

"Ask me questions." Matti was standing in the hotel room bathroom, staring at herself in the wall-sized mirror. "I'll answer what I can. Then I'll ask you questions."

"Why?"

"Why what?" Matti leaned in as she spoke, studying the darkness under her eyes. It spread from either side of her nose to the outer edge of her lashes.

"Why are you talking to me?"

"Something bad is about to happen," she said. The whites of her eyes were webbed with red. Her pupils were blown. She leaned forward, trying to see through them. "I need help figuring out what it is before it happens."

"Are you drunk?"

"No."

"You sound drunk. You sound high."

"No."

"How do I know you are who you say you are?"

"You don't."

"I don't have time for games."

"Neither do I." Matti squinted and leaned closer to the glass, looking deeper into her own eyes than perhaps anyone ever had. "I'm in a hotel in Barcelona. The president is here. She's meeting with a small circle of advisors ahead of dinner tonight."

"Send me a picture with your phone."

"Your line isn't secure."

"So?" He laughed. "You've already told me your name and where you are. If I'm on the NSA's list, it's already too late."

"Good point." Matti held up her phone and snapped a selfie. It was similar to the countless mirrored, narcissistic snaps that cluttered social media and the Internet. Matti sent the photo and waited.

"Wow," Holt said. "That is you."

"I told you." Matti deleted the selfie.

"What is going to happen?" he asked against the snapping of computer keys. "Is it related to Sir Spencer?"

"Yes. I think so. He's planning another attack. It'll be at the summit, and I'm certain the president is involved."

"President Jackson?"

"Yes."

Matti detailed what she'd seen at Camp David and the president's subsequent denial and veiled threats. She told Holt about the hotel murder and the suspect's long connection to Sir Spencer. She spilled what she'd learned about Bohemian Grove and its membership. By the time she was finished, her phone's battery was close to empty. Matti moved from the bathroom to her bed and plugged in the phone.

She lay back on the bed and stared at the ceiling, focusing on the small waves of textured plaster coating the entirety of it. The waves were designed to hide the imperfections, the weaknesses in the ceiling. Matti admired how even the waves were, how they expertly masked the ugliness of cracks and bumps.

"Everything you're telling me," Holt said, "I understand it. I get how it fits together."

Holt reciprocated with everything he'd pieced together. He told Matti about the information and suppositions he couldn't include in his online postings. He suggested that Horus and FBI Special Agent Majors were killed to keep them quiet. He wondered aloud if President Blackmon was murdered too, despite not having any evidence to support his suspicion.

He believed the shadowy Brethren was behind all of it, a concern solidified by Matti's story of Bohemian Grove. There was something at hand. His finger pecked away at the keys. Matti could hear it on her end of the conversation.

"So what's coming?" Matti asked. "And what do they want?"

"You're right," Holt told her. The typing stopped. "The G12 summit is the perfect place to follow up the Capitol attack. And I know why. I can't believe it. It's been staring me in the face, and I'm just now seeing it. I know what they want. I know their endgame."

"You do?"

"Yes. I just don't know if we can do anything to stop them."

CHAPTER 36

CASA FUSTER HOTEL
BARCELONA, SPAIN

The assassin stepped from the car into the comfortable warmth of the Mediterranean air. She ran her fingers through the short brown pixie wig atop her head. Her Paris Hilton sunglasses slipped on her nose and she pushed them up as she slung her bag over her shoulder.

She waved off the valet at the curb and marched past him into the hotel. A rush of cool air replaced the heat, populating goose bumps along her arms and neck. She would have preferred to meet outside, along an avenue, sipping coffee or drinking a Spanish beer. Or even better, a park bench hidden amongst the shade of artwork and trees. That would have been best of all.

Instead, this was her instruction, to take a car to the highest point of Paseo de Gracia and to the Casa Fuster Hotel. She was to find a seat at the Café Vienés bar and wait. Her connection would find her. The instructions came as a surprise, an addendum to the job for which she was sent to Barcelona.

After having passed on killing the reporter, she was anxious to find her next mark, the political aide Matti Harrold. But duty called. She found a seat in the lounge and checked her phone. This was the right spot.

The space was an odd, garish collection of colors, shapes, and materials. The golden ceiling was arches and framed parallel rows of pink marble pillars. The floors were polished obsidian black granite.

The assassin was sitting on one end of a large curved salmon sofa. She sank into the plush, sunshine yellow pillow in the small of her back. Surrounding her were clusters of café tables and high-backed fabric chairs.

"May I help you?" a waiter appeared from seemingly nowhere. "You speak English, no?"

The assassin nodded. "Espresso."

The waiter scurried off. A minute later he was back with the cup and saucer. She took it black.

She sipped the coffee. Her lips pursed, her face sour as much from the bitterness of the drink as the offensive surroundings.

"You don't like it?" The voice came from behind her head. She swiveled quickly, sinking further into her seat as she did. "Your face betrays your distaste."

Standing behind her was a tall, large-framed man. He held his shoulders back, his chest forward, despite leaning on a cane. His hair was white more than gray, and his smile gave away that he was British.

"I know you," she said, turning her back to him to take another sip of coffee. "You're the terrorist. And my distaste is for this room. It tries to be too many things."

"So many of us try to be too many things, don't we?" Sir Spencer eased his way around the sofa to find a seat in a chair directly across from the assassin.

"Aren't you dead?"

"I am," he moaned, adjusting his girth in the chair.

She sipped the last drop of the coffee.

"You are the one they call Mariposa." Sir Spencer leaned his cane next to the chair, taking care to balance it so it wouldn't fall. His eyes moved from the cane to her legs. "I'm here to give you some intelligence that will help with your task. There are some new tidbits as well." He pulled an envelope from the interior breast pocket of his jacket and reached out to hand it to her.

"Who is they?" She snatched it before sinking back into the overstuffed sofa. She crossed her legs and rested her elbow on the sidearm.

"They is…they." Sir Spencer winked.

"I'm not interested in coyness," she hissed, slipping the envelope into the bag without opening it. "I'd prefer we get on with whatever business we have. Is the envelope all you have?"

"I'd heard you were direct, if not a bit rude." Sir Spencer waved off the waiter.

"I have a job to do." She leaned forward in the seat, struggling against its depth. "I'd like to do it."

"I've only met a handful of you." Sir Spencer's eyes swam across her body. "I've always been impressed. They do stellar work."

The assassin studied the terrorist's face. He wasn't joking, wasn't teasing her. He was serious.

"How many others?"

"Including the musicians, singers, and actors? Or are we focusing solely on the formerly downtrodden addicts and malevolents like you?"

A wave of heat coursed through the assassin. She rolled her hands into tight fists, digging her manicured, thickly shellacked fingernails into her palms, and bit the inside of her cheek. Now was not the time.

"Didn't like that characterization?" Sir Spencer licked his wormy lips and rubbed the white scruff on his chin.

"How many others?" She spoke through clenched teeth. Her knees were pressed together.

"I don't know, really." Sir Spencer flicked his tongue back and forth between his teeth. "Dozens at any given time. As some grow up or melt down, we add new ones. One Britney dies, and another Britney grows in social influence. Heath pops his clogs, and Zac sees a resurgence of opportunity. Those are the influencers, mind you. As for the malevolents…"

"You think you're funny." She looked at her watch. The time was right. To the second.

"There's no thinking about it, dear." Sir Spencer leaned on his knee and pointed at the assassin. "My sweet Mariposa, I am funny. You are malevolent. I am a commander and you are a soldier. I am atop the food chain, a veritable shark, and you border on chum. You are—"

The assassin lunged forward in an instant, her nails at Sir Spencer's throat. She gripped his larynx as a climber would a rope. His eyes bulged, his tongue wagged, and he grabbed his attacker as they fell backwards onto the floor. His head slammed against the obsidian, dazing him as she clawed his throat with one hand and gripped his manhood with the other.

"I might be malevolent," she growled into his ear before biting down on the lobe as if it were a raw piece of meat. "You are not funny."

Sir Spencer flailed, trying to use his brute strength against her wiry frame. The fight, in the middle of a hotel lounge, must have seemed surreal to those seeing it unfold.

One man tried to approach, briefly touching the assassin on the shoulder. She turned and bared her bloody teeth. The man backed away, pulling his hand from her. He tripped as he backed up and fell to the floor, so he scooted backward.

The feral assassin was like a cheetah on a wildebeest. His strength was no match for her tenacity. Straddling him, she dug her knees into his ribs. She knew from the color of his face and the gargle leaking from his open mouth he was losing his fight.

She looked around. The crowd was growing. They were yelling and screaming. She was running out of time. So she ended it.

Pulling her hand from his throat, she lowered her elbow into the same spot and used all of her weight to crush his windpipe.

He coughed up a mixture of fluids. His pounding fists weakened and his fingers relaxed and his body twitched before going limp.

Sir Spencer was dead.

The assassin grabbed his cell phone and wallet from his pockets and pushed herself to her feet using his face. She adjusted her skirt and grabbed her bag from the sofa before marching to the exit. A pair of security guards tried to stop her, blocking the doorway.

She pulled a small blade from the outer pocket of the bag and backhanded it into the first guard's chest before pounding it into the other's neck. She stepped over them to the street and merged into the pedestrian traffic. A dozen steps along the sidewalk, she pulled the wig from her head, tossing it into a trash can. A bus, the one described to her in the instructions, arrived just as she met the corner. She pulled herself up the steps and found a seat.

The assassin pulled her phone from the bag and sent a text.

It is done.

*

Sir Spencer's final moments were not how he imagined them. He'd long wished for a quiet death, perhaps in his sleep, after a good meal and a rich, nasal-clearing glass of scotch.

The knight was a man of incredible vision, among the few who could see the future as he wanted it to be and then mold it to his will. A combination of intelligence, brute force of intelligence, and sociopathic narcissism, his hands were printed on so many of the global events that shaped parts of two centuries.

He was at once deplorable and charming, a man as rare as the malted drinks he imbibed with passion. He died in an unforeseen, public way that so contradicted every aspect of his long life.

The girl, he thought, was beautiful. Her eyes were disarming, in fact. He didn't even notice the wig was askew atop her head, giving her the appearance of a woman who'd not finished styling it before leaving the house.

Her fingers were long and slender, the bright polish a compliment to her complexion. Her skin was bordering on flawless. She appeared made of porcelain in the odd lighting of the bar.

Sunken in the folds of the overstuffed couch as she was, he couldn't see her musculature, her wiry strength. The couch, as it were, served an unintentional camouflage.

He sat opposite her, confident the brief meeting would merely acquaint him with one of the few assets he'd not met. He'd heard of her, of course. Mariposa's reputation for lethality and discretion preceded her. It was that reputation that allowed Sir Spencer to relax in the small chair, to let go of his cane.

As he did with everyone over whom he felt superior, he spoke slowly. His eyes and lips revealed as much as his words. It was intentional. He wanted her to know he was in charge, he was delivering orders, he was doing her the favor of meeting her in person.

He wanted her to know she was one of many, a replaceable cog in a large, perpetually spinning wheel. And she played right into the conversation, as he predicted she would.

"How many others?" she asked.

Sir Spencer could see the disappointment in those eyes. She thought she was special. She thought herself an outlier. He'd wounded her with a single swipe of the blade.

"Including the musicians, singers, and actors? Or are we focusing solely on the formerly downtrodden addicts and malevolents like you?" He dug the knife a little deeper.

She didn't answer him. He saw her eyes transform from hurt to anger. They flashed as her pupils shrank to pinpricks. Her manicure disappeared as she clenched her fists into tight balls.

"Didn't like that characterization?" Sir Spencer licked his lips and awaited the verbal follow-up to her physical reaction. He smiled and scratched an itch on his chin. He needed a shave. He'd do that upon returning to his room. A nice hot shower and a heavily lathered shave. He could smell the menthol. After the shave, a good dinner. Some seafood would be good, maybe shellfish. Barcelona was known for its seafood. The closest he got to seafood in prison was something akin to fried catfish. They told him it was catfish. He doubted it.

"How many others?" she said through clenched teeth.

"I don't know, really." Sir Spencer flicked his tongue back and forth between his teeth, tasting the buttered prawns he planned to devour. They would go so well with a nice dry, crisp white wine. Even a rosé might do the trick. The shrimp and its buttery goodness would cut the acidity of the wine. He salivated at the Pavlovian thought of it.

"Dozens at any given time. As some grow up or melt down, we add new ones. One Britney dies, and another Britney grows in social influence. Heath pops his clogs, and Zac sees a resurgence of opportunity. Those are the influencers, mind you. As for the malevolents…"

Sir Spencer, for all of his discretion, was a name-dropper. He'd always let those dwelling on the seabed below him know he swam at the surface among the sharks.

"You think you're funny."

"There's no thinking about it, dear." Sir Spencer leaned on his knee, wondering if he was boring her. Did she have somewhere better to be? Of course not, she had to listen to him.

"My sweet Mariposa, I am funny." He pointed at her as he spoke, drawing her eyes to his. He wanted her full attention. "You are malevolent. I am a commander and you are a soldier. I am atop the food chain, a veritable shark, and you border on chum. You are—"

Sir Spencer couldn't react fast enough. The girl came at him so quickly, launched like a loaded spring from the sofa. He could see her long fingers coming at his face. He couldn't deflect her grip as those fingers and their sharpened nails dug into his throat.

He grasped at her head, but her weight forced them down. His head slammed against the floor and his vision blurred. He couldn't focus. He could feel the pressure against his neck, the pain of her nails digging in his skin, gripping his windpipe.

Sir Spencer would have pled for his life had he been able to speak. His tongue was thick in his mouth, lodged between his teeth as his body struggled for air. His body, already racked with pain and screaming for oxygen, flinched and throbbed when she gripped between his legs. He was powerless as she leaned into him. Her eyes, pupils large as dimes, were wild with rage.

"I'm malevolent," he heard through the heat of her breath. It was hard to know what she was saying; his mind blurred from the pain. He was fighting consciousness until a sting and throbbing pain pulsed against the side of his head. He couldn't hear what else she said. The world was darkening.

She was so strong, so powerful. She was the animal the Brethren bore.

In the dim haze, Sir Spencer saw a blur over the assassin's shoulder, which grew in size before shrinking from view and disappearing.

There was pressure against his ribs, pushing from his lungs the last droplets of air.

Sir Spencer's life didn't flash before him. There was no bright light toward which to walk.

It was pain, both acute and dull, and darkness. The yelling and screaming around him was his final symphony, the chorus of his final breath.

The darkness complete, there was a final push against his throat and he gagged. The pain subsided; the cacophony silenced.

Sir Spencer died unshaven and unfed.

*

"Excuse me for a moment," President Felicia Jackson interrupted her aide to check her phone. "I need to take this."

She stepped into a space adjacent to the conference room in which she and her team were discussing key elements of their SECURITY pitch.

The message told her the job was done. Sir Spencer was dead.

It wasn't something she'd planned. At least not so soon, especially after all of the trouble it took to free him. But his man, his asset, made a mistake with the hotel murder. It could compromise the mission.

If the mission failed, she risked being exposed. It was all the worse that reporters were printing stories about him being alive and that Matti Harrold saw him at Camp David.

He needed to die, regardless of the backlash from the Brethren. They would understand. If their plan succeeded and moved to the next phase, they'd forgive her indiscretion. If it didn't, she was likely out of favor anyhow.

He deserved it, regardless. He'd nearly killed her when the Capitol exploded. Had she not run as fast as her Jimmy Choos could carry her, she would have lain among the martyrs on the Mall.

Did he think she'd so easily forgive and forget? Was he naïve enough to believe that betrayal could go unpunished?

For years their relationship was built on a healthy, if not illegal, give and take. She would provide favorable legislation and the support to pass it in Congress. He would help with connections away from Capitol Hill. He would help her acquire true power, the invisible strength not seen on C-SPAN or the network news. Even when Dexter Foreman chose Blackmon over her for his vice presidential replacement, Sir Spencer assured her she was in the fold, that he wouldn't be confirmed.

"No worries," he told her. "You're poised to ascend. I promise."

It was fair trade, until it wasn't.

He'd cut her out of the loop in the days before President Foreman's death. He and his motley crew of idiots closed ranks. They left her out in the cold.

Even pleas to the Brethren yielded nothing. It was too dangerous to discuss, they'd told her. *See no evil, hear no evil, speak no evil,* or some philosophical crap like that.

She'd watched Blackmon stake his claim. She had to fight the urge to call him out on the floor of the rotunda when they first addressed the nation after Foreman's death. She wanted to expose the backroom deals, the president's murder, the secret plot underway, and the grand plan decades in the making.

But that would have exposed her as much as it would Blackmon or any of the so-called Daturan pawns. She'd have been done, her ascension cut short. So she'd kept quiet and fought for her rightful place on the throne.

She'd arrived in spite of Sir Spencer, not because of him. *She* was responsible for what she'd accomplished.

President Felicia Jackson took in a deep breath against the quickened pulse in her neck. She held her finger above the keyboard on the phone and paused before typing her encoded response.

```
Good. On to the next one.
A Deo et Rege.
```

The President smirked at the Latin turn of phrase. It was particularly appropriate given the untimely death of a man who called himself a knight.

CHAPTER 37

PASEO DE TAULAT
BARCELONA, SPAIN

Jon Custos sat forward in his chair, cycling through the channels on Barçes's prized television. He was growing concerned his indiscretion at the hotel would become the problem Sir Spencer feared.

There was, however, no news of the flight attendant's death on any of the channels. There was abundant coverage of the G12 summit and the arrival of the foreign dignitaries.

Custos stopped on one of the channels. A reporter was standing amongst the protestors outside the World Trade Center. The crowd was much larger than when he'd left hours earlier. He supposed it would grow bigger still, and that was good. He needed a large crowd.

He pressed what looked like a pause button on the remote, but the television didn't respond. He pushed it again. Push. Push. Push. The images on the screen wouldn't freeze.

Custos cursed in three languages and stood. Stomping into the bedroom, he yelled loud enough to wake up Fernando Barçes.

"You don't have a DVR?" he asked in Spanish. "You can't pause or rewind your television?"

Barçes, lying on the bed, shook his head. He smacked his lips and took a deep breath.

"You disappoint me, *viejo*." Custos slid to the edge of the bed and rested his hand on the man's chest. "I don't like disappointment."

Barçes blinked against the words. His muscles tensed.

"It's not your fault you are poor." Custos shrugged. He patted Barçes's chest. "I forgive you." The old man's body relaxed against his hand.

"It is the little things," Custos said as he stood, "that separate the poor from the wealthy. The little things, like a DVR or an automatic ice maker in the refrigerator." Custos walked toward the bedroom door and stopped. He turned around, his hands planted on his hips.

"You know that was a disappointment too," he said across the room. "I have to make my own ice. Get the plastic tray out of the icebox, pour water into the little, empty cubes, put it back into the icebox, and wait for it to freeze."

Barçes blinked back tears. Custos imagined the undulating, tidal ache in his stomach was returning.

"I'll get you some painkillers, *viejo*," he said. "I have to tell you, it's so inconvenient here. Think of how much television you miss because of the time it takes to make ice. And you have no DVR. Such a disappointment."

Custos ignored the faint, useless plea for mercy from Barçes, his unwilling martyr, as he hung in the doorway. His arms were extended above his head, his fingers gripping the molded frame. He looked as if he might try a pull-up. He whistled the first movement of *Carmina Burana to* drown out the soft cries, slowly swinging back and forth.

"Your mercy will come in the afterlife," he offered, stopping short of Orff's crescendo. "O Fortuna!" he said forcefully, the air rushing from his lungs as he spoke. He dropped his arms to his sides and turned back to the living area.

Again seated in front of the television, with the volume a touch louder, he watched a live report from the front of the World Trade Center. This reporter was much closer to the entrance, with no protestors visible in the scene behind her.

"*The president of the United States, Felicia Jackson, is now here,*" the narrow-waisted brunette explained in Spanish, turning her body to reference the entrance to the hotel. There was a cadre of security guards, uniformed and plainclothed, on either side of the large doors.

"*We also know the prime minister of the UK is here,*" she reported with credible enthusiasm. "*The Italian government is also on site and, sources tell me, is already meeting with representatives from the Spanish delegation.*"

Custos was paying more attention to the activity behind the reporter than to what she was saying. It appeared to him the front entrance was open to the public, despite an identification check and a security pat down. He could deal with that.

"There is a dinner tonight," the reporter droned as the camera moved past her shoulder and focused on the security checkpoint. *"We understand that representatives from all of the member countries will attend. The meal includes authentic Spanish dishes, including* salmorejo, pisto, salchichón, pulpo a la gallega, leche frita, *and both red and white sangria."*

Custos had one concern, looking at the checkpoint as another guest moved through and held up his room key: the bag check. He needed a way to smuggle the device past the manual search. An X-ray or metal detector would have been much better. He'd have to improvise.

The camera zoomed out and panned back to the reporter. *"Of course, the dinner is a prelude to the importance of these meetings. The United States is pushing a multilateral agreement that would force governments to share sweeping electronic surveillance of its citizens. President Jackson called it SECURITY for the future. Critics say it's something straight out of the George Orwell novel 1984."*

Custos laughed at the comparison and stood from the chair. He pointed the remote at the screen and powered it off, mimicking the sound of gunfire as he pushed the button.

"Painkillers, painkillers," he mumbled. He found a bottle in the cabinet above the sink. They weren't much, little more than migraine tablets. Custos read the back of the bottle, uncapped it, and shook out a few into his hand. He grabbed a glass, filled it with tap water, and whistled his way back to the bedroom.

He walked over to the bedside and offered the pills to Barçes, leaning over to cradle the back of the old man's head. When his fingers gripped Barçes's sweaty neck, his confidence evaporated.

Barçes was burning up. His skin was hot to the touch. His fever flushed his cheeks and forehead. The vacant pleas for help moments before were likely from febrile delirium.

Rather than helping his patient drink the water, he poured it across the man's forehead. He bolted to the kitchen and returned with a pair of ice-filled hand towels and placed one under each arm.

Barçes had an infection. He was dying. Custos had seen it before. If he couldn't keep the old man alive another twenty-four hours, the plot would fail. The new world was in jeopardy.

CHAPTER 38

HOUSTON, TEXAS

Dillinger Holt was at once brilliant and blind. He knew he'd figured out what was unfolding, yet he was disgusted with himself for not having seen it sooner.

"It's about the SECURITY Act," he said, the phone pressed against his face. "It has to be."

"How so?" Matti asked.

"The Act gives governments, namely the United States, unprecedented authority to engage in previously illegal electronic intelligence."

"We call it SIGINT," Matti said. "Signal intelligence. It's basically everything but human intelligence."

"SIGINT, then. Regardless, we're talking about the single biggest change in data collection since the PATRIOT Act. And this makes that look like a cracked kaleidoscope as far as what it allows the government to see and catalog."

"I know what it does," said Matti. "I'm part of the team selling it to Congress. I worked for the NSA."

"Then you know this goes far beyond AT&T helping the NSA wiretap all of the Internet communications at the United Nations for a decade, spying on billions of Americans' emails and more than a billion of their phone calls."

"I'm aware," Matti said. "That partnership was run through the agency's Special Source Operations. It handles eighty percent of the agency's SIGINT. What's your point?"

"My point is," Holt stressed, "the SECURITY Act is invasive enough as it is. When you throw in a treaty, a multilateral agreement for a collection of foreign governments to share this information amongst themselves, it's frightening. There's tremendous pushback from Congress, as you know, and from some of the other governments."

"What does that have to do with the plot here? Why would they kill—" The line fell silent.

"Matti? You there?"

"Yes." She sounded as if she'd been gut punched. "I get it now. Just as the Bush administration pushed through the PATRIOT Act in the wake of 9/11, President Jackson is using the Capitol bombing to do the same thing with the SECURITY Act."

"It wasn't enough," said Holt. "She, and whoever she's working with, didn't get enough of a sympathetic bounce. People aren't so willing to give up their privacy anymore. Not after what the PATRIOT Act did. Not after Edward Snowden."

"Snowden's a traitor," Matti snapped.

"Is he?" Holt posed. "Probably. Regardless, the stuff he dragged out into the light made people question what it is our government is really doing with this information and how far they'll go in the name of securing the homeland."

"So they need another attack," Matti suggested. "They need that final nudge to get everyone on board. What better place to do it than at the very place where the SECURITY agreement is being discussed?"

"Yes. That's what I think." Holt knew he was right. "The easiest way to take away people's liberty is when they ask you to do it."

"We need to stop it."

"We?"

"Yes. We."

"I'm in Houston," Holt explained. "What can I do?"

"You can write about it," Matti said. "I'll figure out what I need to do here, and then I'll get you information. You have a big voice. We can stop this."

"The attack or the legislation?"

"Both."

"How are you going to stop a terrorist attack? You don't know where to begin."

"I think I do," Matti said. "I'll email you when I have something new."

"Sounds good. I've got some calls to make."

CHAPTER 39

WORLD TRADE CENTER
BARCELONA, SPAIN

The last place Matti wanted to be was a formal dinner, but she needed to make an appearance. If she didn't show up, given the tension and mutual suspicion between herself and President Jackson, it would fly too many red flags.

She cranked on the shower and let the bathroom fill with steam before stepping underneath the powerful, pulsating stream of water. Matti closed her eyes and ran her hands through her hair, drenching it.

She knew Holt was right. Deep down, she'd known for a while the SECURITY Act was too far-reaching and impinged too much on the Fourth Amendment. Despite that, she'd tried to be a good soldier and rationalize the importance of SIGINT in the wake of the Capitol attacks.

It was a gray area, she convinced herself, and she'd gone along to get along. She'd put blinders on and marched back and forth to Capitol Hill, trying to sell the merits of legislation she knew was unconstitutional.

Now she was in hot water, mere hours away from failing again. If it weren't for Holt, she might never have opened her eyes. Now they had to work together, a continent apart, to prevent bloodshed and the foundation of what Matti understood would become the new order of things.

Her boss, Sir Spencer, and the Brethren all wanted a one world government. They wanted the global suppression of the people for the benefit of the enlightened few. There was nothing benevolent about that goal. It was dark without a hint of gray.

Matti found the bottle of shampoo and squeezed out a generous amount of the lemon-scented liquid. Rubbing it onto her scalp and through her hair, she wondered how she'd ended up here.

She never thought to ask herself that question before. She was so focused on where she'd been, or hadn't been, she couldn't look at where she was.

The lather spilled into her eyes, stinging them, and she turned around to rinse her face.

Her addiction was keeping her in the past. She knew it, her father knew it, even her coworkers knew it. She was chained to a past she could not change, from her mother's death to those at the Capitol.

Matti rinsed the shampoo from her hair and wiped her hand in a large arc across the condensation on the glass shower door. She looked through the glass to the mirror and stared at her reflection.

Beneath the ribbon of fog on the glass, she stood naked, her soul as bare as her body, and she lost herself in her own reflection. She hardly recognized herself, pale and waify. She had the appearance of someone who exercised too much and ate too little.

She embodied the worry and stress of an addict, a self-pitying narcissist who couldn't save herself, let alone the world. Matti swiped at the glass again, clearing the stubborn fog between her eyes and the mirror.

She'd told herself she could quit when she was ready. She'd promised herself the bennies she bought from C-Dunk were a temporary fix. Looking in the mirror at what she'd done to herself, she knew it was a lie. She needed real help.

However, now wasn't the time. She'd have to wash herself clean of the past, of the demons with which she currently struggled, and formulate a plan.

She couldn't dwell on where she'd been or how she'd gotten here. Matti knew her focus needed to be on what was to come and how she could stop it.

Her body clean, she turned off the water and grabbed a thick towel, burying her face in its commercial detergent smell and drying herself.

She'd go to the party, say hello to key people, shake a few hands. Then she'd get to work. She knew it would be a bomb and who would detonate it.

She just had to find him and his device before it was too late.

*

PASEO DE TAULAT
BARCELONA, SPAIN

Jon Custos slammed his fist into the wall, his knuckles leaving an impression in the thick drywall. He followed the punch with a kick that only managed to deliver a shooting pain into his foot.

"Antibiotics!" He grabbed his hair, leaning into the bedroom wall. "How could I forget the antibiotics?"

He'd remembered so many of the fatal mistakes he'd made the last time he operated on a mark. He was so careful with his preoperative procedure, the way in which he moved within Barçes's body before sewing him shut.

But as with his impulsive decision to kill the flight attendant, he'd not thought through the entirety of his actions. With his patient melting in front of him, Custos's mind whirled. He didn't need the man to live much longer, but he needed him conscious, coherent, and strong enough to stand upright.

Custos rifled through the old man's bathroom medicine cabinet, looking for anything that would suffice, any antibiotic or prescription anti-inflammatory that might provide temporary relief. There was nothing but a half-empty bottle of cholesterol medication. Custos gripped the bottle in his hand and squeezed. He was about to throw it across the room when he noticed the address for the prescribing pharmacy typed onto the label.

The pharmacy was next door. He'd seen it both times he'd come to the flat. Custos dropped the bottle into the sink and ran from the apartment, bounding down the steps and bursting out into the street.

He caught his breath and tucked in his shirt before walking into the pharmacy. He approached the back counter, smiling at the young woman pharmacist.

"Lupe?" he drew from her name tag. "How are you today?

"I'm fine," she replied in Catalan. "How may I help you? We're just a few minutes from closing."

"You look beautiful today," he said, noting the absence of a ring. "Your eyes…"

The woman looked away, blushing and working hard to hide a smile. She cleared her throat.

"I'm sorry," he said, lowering his voice and leaning across the counter that separated them. "Should I not compliment you?"

"It's very kind," she said, her eyelashes fluttering as she spoke. "I don't know you, sir."

"Yes, you do." Custos feigned offense. "We've met twice before. The last time, you were wearing that sundress. I'm Felipe, Fernando Barçes's nephew."

"Oh." Lupe paused, studying the stranger's face. She put her hand to her mouth. "I'm so sorry. I didn't recognize you. It's the…"

"It's the hair." Custos laughed, knowing she was lying. "I shaved it off. I think it's more masculine. What do you think?"

"It's nice," she said. "What can I do for you, Felipe?"

"My uncle isn't feeling well, and his doctor is on vacation," Custos said. "I think he's running a high fever. Maybe he has an infection or something. I don't know. He needs something strong."

"What about the hospital?"

"He's being stubborn," Custos said ruefully. "You know my uncle, Lupe, he won't listen to me. And he doesn't want to leave the house. Is there anything you can do? Anything you can prescribe?"

"Oh, now. I cannot prescribe anything. I'm not a doctor."

"Of course." Custos lowered his voice. "I wasn't suggesting you do anything illegal. I just thought…"

"Well—" Lupe pursed her lips and stared into Custos's eyes "—I could look to see if he has any open refills? If he does, I could give you that. Would that work?"

"Of course," Custos said, noticing Lupe eye the cut of his biceps peeking out from underneath his short-sleeved shirt. "Anything would be helpful."

Lupe clicked on a few keys, her eyes scanning the computer monitor in front of her. She clicked her teeth and she searched.

"I see he has a couple of refills for the cholesterol drug Repatha," she said, shaking her head. "I don't see anything else that's refillable. I'm so sorry. The hospital really would be your—"

"Is there anyone else I could ask?" Custos's flirtation soured. "A manager?"

"I am the manager." Lupe tilted her head for a moment. Custos wondered if she realized he wasn't who he claimed to be.

"So nobody else?"

"No." She shook her head. "I'm the only one here. And we're closing, so—"

Custos leapt over the counter and grabbed Lupe by her shoulders before she could react. He spun her around, wrapping one arm across her chest and the other hand over her mouth.

She struggled against him, her feet kicking and stomping, her teeth trying to find the meat of his palm. Her fight was brief.

Custos gripped his hand more tightly over her mouth, his enormous hand stretching from cheekbone to cheekbone, and he yanked Lupe's head to one side with a snap.

With a sickening cascade of cracks, her body instantly went limp, and Custos dropped her to the floor behind the counter in a heap. He jumped the counter again and went to the entry, locking the door and drawing the louvered blinds. Next to the door was a light switch for the neon pharmacy sign out front. He flipped it off and moved behind the counter again.

He moved amongst the rows of floor-to-ceiling shelves, searching for something that might work, something that would temporarily raise the old man from the dead. He found pills, lots of pills, and ointments, too many ointments.

Then he found a familiar-sounding drug: ceftriaxone. He picked up the white bottle with the flat blue cap and read the label. This was it. It was an injectable antibiotic he'd used years ago for a nasty case of gonorrhea. It was what his doctor called a "wide-spectrum antibiotic" that was great at fighting bacterial infections anywhere in the body.

He grabbed two bottles and a handful of syringes and dropped them into the paper prescription bag hanging on the end of the shelf. Then he searched for a steroid. Two shelves from the ceftriaxone he saw the generic methylprednisolone. It was perfect. He could inject it to help with any localized swelling or pain.

The combination of the two drugs should drastically help Barçes. Together, they'd give him a jolt strong enough to get him to the Trade Center.

He stuffed a couple of bottles of the steroid into the bag, tucked it under his arm, and made his way back out to the street. He locked the pharmacy door behind him and tossed the keys into a curbside gutter. Custos quickened his pace back to Barçes's flat.

CHAPTER 40

WORLD TRADE CENTER
BARCELONA, SPAIN

Brandon Goodman approached Matti as she walked into the ballroom. "You look nice and well rested." He smiled and gave her a friendly hug.

"I'm just clean." Matti laughed, returning the platonic affection with a kiss on his cheek. "It makes a difference."

The room was set with two dozen round tables, ten chairs each, adorned with elaborate floral displays featuring large red carnations, the official flower of Spain.

The room was filling up quickly with delegations from each of the invited nations. Matti noticed women admiring, or silently judging, the women around them as they sipped their sangria.

The men stood with their chests out, one hand in their pockets and the other gripped around their hard liquor of choice. Matti could tell the men were equally duplicitous in their conversations with other men, measuring each other as they name-dropped.

Formal dinners were just one aspect of the job to which Matti couldn't become accustomed. She wasn't much for small talk, dresses, or diplomatic protocol. Thankfully, in the wake of the Capitol explosion and the resulting economic downturn, the president was smart enough to limit the number of expensive bone-china soirees.

"Shall we find our seats?" Brandon led Matti toward a white linen table in the far corner of the room.

"Shouldn't you be near the front and center?" Matti looked over her shoulder toward the tables reserved for the heads of state. She caught a glimpse of President Jackson speaking with the prime minister of Japan.

"I should be," he admitted, walking a step ahead of her. "I asked to be in the back so I could better observe the room. Plus, I'm so focused on these negotiations, I'd rather not deal with the stress of putting on airs."

"I'm not much for it either," she said, finding a place card with her name embossed on it. The appetizer was already at her seat, along with glasses of iceless water and white sangria. There was also a white cloth napkin shaped into a swan.

"I have to be honest," she whispered to Brandon as he took his seat. "I'm not staying long." Matti paused and tried to gauge his reaction.

"How long?" He half-smiled. "Past…whatever it is that's on your plate now?" He referenced the salmorejo.

"It's a tomato and bread soup." Matti giggled. "Yes. I'll stay past the first couple of courses, but don't count me in for coffee and dessert."

"Gotcha," he said.

"So how was the meeting?"

"Long but constructive," Brandon said. "I think we're in a good position. The Spanish are still the stumbling block. The latest is that they don't think they can pass their version of the bill, so they're reluctant to sign anything."

"What are they afraid of?" Matti leaned on her chair, crossing her legs at her ankles; she wanted to appear relaxed.

"They don't necessarily like the idea of having to share their intelligence with us or any of the other parties," he explained. "They're wary of how foreign powers could use damaging intelligence against their citizens. It's about sovereignty."

"And the British?'

"They have security cameras on every corner in London." He laughed, shoving his hands into his pockets. "They're not concerned about privacy. Even the liberal parties there are okay with it. Plus, they know where their bread is buttered. They need to be in lockstep with us. The optics of defying the US don't play well."

"The others are on board? The French and the Italians?"

Brandon nodded. He rocked back and forth in his shoes. "We believe so. The French are getting some pressure from the Germans to defect. They're listening now, but we feel confident they'll come around."

Matti took a step closer to Brandon and looked over her shoulders in both directions before she spoke in a hushed tone.

"Why are we doing this?" she asked, searching his eyes for the truth. She wondered if he knew it or if he was as much a mushroom in the scenario as she was.

"How do you mean?"

"Why are we pushing this multilateral intelligence-sharing treaty? That's what it is. A treaty. Why would we share our information with other countries? Why would they want to share with us? What's this really about? Whose idea was it?"

"Matti—" Brandon smiled, cocking his head like a curious dog "—what are you getting at here? You know the answer to this. You've been part of the design team, the planning, the legislative negotiations."

Matti studied Brandon's expression as he spoke. He appeared befuddled by her questions. He was either in the dark like her or he was a good actor. She wanted to believe it was the former.

"I just…" Matti needed to drop another lure. She wanted to know what he might be hiding from her, if anything.

Brandon stood straight, pulling his hands from his pockets. "Madam President."

Matti spun to see President Felicia Jackson standing inches behind her. She adjusted her skirt and cleared her throat. Matti was not a good actor.

"Brandon." The president nodded and extended her hand to her chief of staff. "Matti, what am I missing over here? Is this the gossip corner? I love good gossip."

"Nothing you'd be interested in, Madam President," Matti said. "We were talking about lawyers and how much we hate them."

"Ha!" The president slapped Matti on the back and then gripped her shoulder. "Very good, Matti. You know how much I despise those snakes. If it weren't for the nest of lawyers slithering around DC, it might feel a little bit more like America."

"Very true." Matti nodded, sensing a bubble of tension about to pop.

"Any good lawyer jokes?" the president asked. "I could use a good joke right now. Prime Minister Hirimoto doesn't have much of a sense of humor. He doesn't like what we're doing."

"SECURITY?" asked Brandon.

"Exactly. He's worried we're creating an axis of power that excludes the rest of Western Europe and our allies in Asia. It's like we didn't send him a wedding invitation and all of his friends are going to attend."

"Why didn't we include Japan?" Matti asked.

"We?" the president mocked. "We picked the four nations with which we were the most comfortable. Switzerland and Luxembourg are the only other countries we considered. They may join later."

"I have a joke," Brandon said, changing the subject.

"Lawyers?" The president's glare lingered on Matti as she spoke.

"Unemployment."

President Jackson rolled her eyes. "My favorite subject."

"Actually I have a slew of good unemployment jokes," he said.

"Do you?"

"None of them work."

"Funny." The president didn't laugh, but she smiled and nodded her approval. "Well, it's six point nine percent funny."

"Six point nine?" Matti asked.

"The unemployment numbers were released yesterday," Brandon clarified. "We're up to six point nine."

"Matti," the president added, "you should better acquaint yourself with unemployment."

Matti bit her lip, resisting the temptation to lash out. She laughed lightly and excused herself. "I need to find the ladies' room."

"Of course." The president smiled flatly and stepped out of Matti's way.

Matti wove her way through the growing crowd, slipping between gowns and tuxedos, shuffling toward the ballroom exit. As she neared the doors, a slender woman in a black cocktail dress bumped into her.

Matti excused herself as she made brief eye contact with the woman. The woman, with a blonde pixie cut and a touch too much jasmine perfume, grabbed Matti's arm and apologized, then complimented Matti's dress.

Matti thanked her and reached the hallway, glancing back briefly to catch a glimpse of the woman as she disappeared into the crowd. She couldn't see the woman's face but did spot a butterfly tattoo on her shoulder. And from behind, her hair looked like a wig.

"Odd," Matti mumbled, then went in search of the restroom and a moment of Zen.

*

The assassin found a waiter carrying drinks and helped herself to a glass of white sangria. She took a sip and relished the mixture of sour and sweet. She felt the eyes of men as she worked the room, moving from table to table.

Some of them looked vaguely familiar. She couldn't remember where she'd seen them. Maybe on television, she guessed, maybe somewhere else. So many of her memories were clouded in a thick haze.

Another sip and she'd had enough of the drink. She set her half-full glass on a table near the front of the room, slipped her hand into the pocket of her chic dress, and felt two room keys. One was the key delivered in her instruction packet. It allowed her access to the hotel. The second belonged to Matti Harrold. She'd lifted it moments earlier with a quick dip into Harrold's open clutch. It was too easy, really. If she'd failed at securing the key, she'd have had to improvise. It would have taken time she couldn't be sure she'd have. It might have ended with more collateral damage. Now she was golden.

She plucked at her temporary blonde bangs as she slithered back to the rear of the ballroom and the exit. The dinner would last two hours, maybe less, and she'd need to be in and out of the room by then.

Once she reached the hallway, she picked up her pace, hurrying to the bank of elevators some fifty yards away. Out of the corner of her eye, she caught Matti Harrold exiting a restroom and returning to the dinner.

Plenty of time.

The assassin found Matti's room and used the key to enter. The lights were off. She slipped the key into a slot in the wall next to the door and flipped them on. The lights illuminated the space. It was at once modern and comfortable. The assassin walked to the bed and sat on its edge before laying back on the down-filled duvet.

She closed her eyes and breathed deeply through her nose. She allowed herself to imagine, if only for a moment, she was someone else.

She wasn't Mariposa the programmed assassin. Instead, she was a newlywed on a honeymoon. Her tall, young husband had surprised her with a Mediterranean holiday. She could feel his bronze skin on the tips of her fingers, his breathless whispers in her ear, laced with an intoxicating Turkish accent. He was strong and intelligent and protective.

They would have two children: a boy named for him and a girl named for his loving mother. Mariposa was a part of their family. She was loved and adored. She loved. She adored.

They'd live in the United States and summer every year in Europe. Their children would be multilingual. They would—

There was someone at the door. Someone trying unsuccessfully to get inside.

*

Matti rattled her hotel room door, hoping to will it open. It didn't work.

She'd left the dinner sooner than planned. A sip of the soup and a minute of conversation were enough. She told Brandon she felt sick and needed to go to her room.

"Are you okay?" he'd asked.

"I'll be fine. I just have a headache, and my stomach is a little upset."

"It could be jet lag," he'd suggested.

"I don't think it's that."

He'd helped her from her seat and she'd worked her way quickly to her room.

Matti couldn't focus on dinner or political conversation when she knew what lay ahead. She needed to quickly plot her design. The bald man responsible for killing the flight attendant was going to attack the G12 summit in some way. It could happen as early as day one of the meetings. Matti knew time was short and she had an impossible task ahead of her.

Thankful to have escaped, she reached her door and reached into her clutch, digging around for the key, and couldn't find it.

She turned the door handle and pushed and pulled the locked door back and forth. It was locked. She was keyless.

"Great," she huffed, and turned back to the elevator. "Just what I need."

Matti pressed the elevator call button. She pressed it again. And again. The elevator doors slid open and she banged the button for the first floor.

She checked her bag again, picking through the few items in her purse. No key. She exhaled again and trudged from the elevator to the front desk to ask for a replacement.

While she waited for the clerk to help her, she glanced up and noticed a camera staring back at her. She looked behind the counter to what looked like an office. There was a computer monitor with a grid of security feeds flashing from one angle to another.

She'd need to come back here once she was out of her evening wear. If she could get a look at the video stored on that computer's hard drive, she might have a better idea of where to look for the bald man.

With a new key, Matti rode back up the elevator to her floor and traipsed back down the hall to her door. She slid in the key and shouldered open the door to a rush of familiar jasmine in the air. Another key was in the power switch.

Somebody was in her room.

*

The assassin was running out of time. The attempted entry into the room had jarred her from her daydream and put her to work.

She moved quickly from the bed to the bathroom and flipped on the light.

On the counter next to the sink was a clear toiletry bag. It was zipped closed. The assassin opened it and picked through the deodorant and toothpaste. She didn't find what she needed, so she re-zipped the bag and placed it exactly as she'd found it.

She looked around the room and didn't see anywhere else she might find what she was searching for until she closed the bathroom door. Hanging on the inside of the door was a makeup bag. In the bag, along with an assortment of brushes, pencils, tubes, and compacts, was an opaque orange prescription bottle. The label indicated the pills inside were sumatriptan, a generic migraine medication. When she palmed open the top, the assassin knew the drugs inside were street. As a long-ago addict, she recognized the lack of craftsmanship and inconsistent labeling as familiar signs these were synthetic. She shook a couple into her hand. They were close enough to what she'd bought in Istanbul that she doubted Matti Harrold would notice at first. The pills were the same shape and virtually the same blue color.

She emptied the rest of the bottle into her hand and dumped the remaining seven pills into the toilet. She flushed it and then set the bottle on the counter, reaching into her pocket for the Turkish replacements.

The assassin emptied seven pills into her hand and then scooped them into the bottle, recapping it. She was turning to put the bottle back into the makeup bag when the door swung open, the corner hitting her in the side of the head.

She fell back against the toilet, dropping the bottle to the floor to catch herself before she hit the back of her head on the wall. In front of her, staring down at her, was her mark.

"Who are you?" Matti Harrold yelled. "What are you doing in—"

The assassin braced herself and swept her leg at Harrold's legs, causing her to lose her balance and fall against the door, banging it wide open against the bathroom wall. She grunted as she hit the tile, and the assassin pounced.

Matti Harrold was on her stomach, trying to press herself from the floor, when the assassin lunged at her back, grabbing onto her like a wrestler, tumbling against the open doorway.

The assassin tried getting her arm around the woman's neck, but she was wily, fighting as if her life depended on it.

"Who are you?" Harrold spat before biting down on the assassin's arm.

The pain was sudden and sharp, but she yanked her arm free and pressed down on the small of Matti Harrold's back just before Harrold launched the back of her skull into the bridge of the assassin's nose.

The crack preceded a searing pain across the assassin's face. Her eyes watered and blurred. Her sinuses swelled. She could taste blood at the back of her throat. She stayed on top, pinning the mark to the floor as she gasped for air through her mouth.

The assassin applied pressure with her weight and leveraged one arm to keep the woman on her stomach. She used the other to feel for her neck. She grabbed a fistful of hair and yanked backward as if starting a lawnmower, slamming the woman's head back to the floor. Her eyes closed, pressing back the tears, and her face throbbing, she gripped the woman's larynx and pressed her fingers against either side of it.

The woman was flailing like a flipped beetle, but she was weakening. She was slowing, losing air. She could sense the woman was giving up and giving in to the inevitable, so she loosened her hold just enough to give the woman another suck of air, planning to prolong this as much as she could.

She tried opening her eyes, but closed them instantly against the brightness of the bathroom light. Adjusting her grip, reapplying weight to the woman's back, she went in for the kill.

In the moment she took to breathe through her mouth, she sensed someone else in the room. She lifted up her head and was met with a concussive blow to the right side of her head.

*

Matti sensed the world darkening around her. She couldn't breathe. Her lungs were screaming for air that wasn't coming. She'd given it her best. It wasn't enough against whoever this killer was.

A warmth spread from her chest to her limbs and she relaxed. It was almost over. Then she heard, in the foggy distance, a thud, a crack, and felt the release of the pressure on her neck and back.

As she choked back to full consciousness, a voice powered through the haze and a hand touched her shoulder.

"Mahhhhttttiiiiii," it called. "Mahhhhttttiiiiii, ca-yun yeewww heeeaarr meeee? Arrre yeeewww oh-kayyyy?"

Matti's eyes blinked open, at first trying to focus on the bathroom floor. Then the hand helped her roll onto her back, and she squinted against the bright light directly above her.

"Matti?" It was the backlit shadow of a man. The voice was vaguely familiar. "Matti, are you okay? Can you hear me?"

Matti nodded but couldn't speak. She couldn't swallow. Her throat was raw, her neck bruised. She squinted to try to identify the man above her.

"Matti?" He leaned down, placing his hands on either side of her face. "It's Brandon. Are you okay?"

Matti tried to smile. She thought maybe she was smiling. She nodded again.

Brandon reached down to grab Matti's shoulders. "I'm going to move you into the bedroom."

Brandon lifted her, holding the back of her head as he would a baby, managing to position her in such a way that he carried her from the bathroom. Matti felt as if she was floating until she felt the soft down of the bed. Her body sank into it and she wondered if she'd ever have the strength or motivation to leave it. She breathed deeply, a hint of jasmine still in the air.

"She's dead," Brandon said, sitting next to her, "whoever she is. I hit her with the bottom of a lamp and caught her across the side of her head. It slammed her into the edge of the counter. She's dead."

Matti could hear Brandon talking, felt his hand on her thigh. She wasn't really processing what had happened. She heard a guttural moan and wondered if it came from her.

Was she attacked? Was there someone in her room? Why? Who? What?

"I followed you up here," he admitted. "I was worried about you. I heard a commotion, some yelling, and some banging around. Your key was still in the door, so…"

Matti used her returning strength to reach for Brandon's hand. She grabbed it and squeezed. It was a way to thank him.

"I need to call the Secret Service," he said. "They need to know about this."

Matti gripped his hand more tightly and shook her head. With clarity, Matti knew this was about the plot. She knew somebody, likely the president, had sent the woman to kill her.

"Don't call?" Brandon shook free of Matti's hand and stood from the bed. "Why? I don't understand."

Matti forced herself to swallow against the pain in her throat, but she couldn't speak. She pointed to the bedside table and the pad of paper on top of it.

Brandon helped her sit up in the bed and she scribbled a few words. He looked at the words and then into her eyes.

"Another plot? To do what?"

Matti wrote eight letters.

"SECURITY? A plot related to the SECURITY Act?"

Matti nodded.

Brandon started talking with his hands, something Matti hadn't seen him do before. "All of this is because of that? You're saying someone tried to kill you because of the SECURITY Act?"

Matti nodded, flipped the page, and scratched out a complete sentence.

Brandon read it and without saying anything disappeared into the bathroom. Matti closed her eyes and concentrated on trying to swallow. It was getting easier, if no less painful. She heard the water run in the bathroom sink for a moment, and Brandon returned with a glass of water.

"Try to drink this." He held the cup for her as he sat next to her and tipped it against her lips. "Just take a couple of sips."

Matti obliged and winced back two small sips of water. She took a deep breath through her nose and nodded again.

"She has no identification on her," Brandon said. "She has a couple of cell phones in one pocket. I'm guessing since I have your key, the one powering the lights is one she obtained somehow."

Matti motioned for the glass. Brandon handed it to her and she took another sip.

"Someone clearly sent her here," Brandon acknowledged. "But the idea that the president is involved, as you suggest"—he eyed the notepad on Matti's lap—"I don't know that I buy that. Why would she want you dead? She could just fire you."

"I know too much," Matti managed in a ragged whisper. "Sir Spencer is alive. I saw him at Camp David. She knows. I told her."

"What's the plot?" Brandon put his hand on her leg again. "And don't overdo it. If you have to write it down, write it down."

"Bottom line," Matti rasped, "is a new world order. SECURITY starts it. It's a tough sell. An attack gets support."

"An attack where?"

"Here."

"When?"

"Any minute now."

Brandon stood again and folded his arms across his chest. He bit his lower lip and paced back and forth. He looked into the bathroom again before wearing a path between the bed and the room's narrow entry hall. After several minutes, he stopped and buried his face in his hands.

"Do you believe me?" Matti asked, not sure if she was loud enough for Brandon to hear her. "Do you believe this is the Capitol all over again?"

Brandon pulled his hands from his face. "I have every reason to think you're crazy and overreaching. I just killed a person, a person sent to your hotel room to kill you. I believe you, Matti Harrold. I believe you."

"Good." Matti swallowed. "Then you need to help me stop it."

CHAPTER 41

HOUSTON, TEXAS

Dillinger Holt pulled an airplane-sized bottle of vodka from his bag and poured it into his empty coffee cup. He looked around at the café crowd. Nobody was watching him. He scanned his computer screen, reminding himself of his genius, and toasted his newest missive.

"They're gonna have to name the website after me," he half-joked, imagining for a split second how the masthead might appear with his name in large bold letters. It could wait. First, he had to cut and paste the new article and send it to his editor.

WHAT'S IN A NAME?
WOULD S.E.C.U.R.I.T.Y. BY ANY OTHER NAME
SMELL AS SWEET?
By Dillinger Holt, Senior Correspondent

If The SECURITY Act is meant to help protect us, why are so many against it? Congressional leaders from both parties express doubt in the legislation and in those pushing it at home and abroad.

—EXCLUSIVE—

President Felicia Jackson calls it "what the PATRIOT Act was meant to be". That may be more revealing than any of the language in the legislation's four-hundred-and-sixteen-page draft. The muddy, cloudy nature of the bill's text is raising flags among those who consider the document an overreach of authority and a threat to the Bill of Rights' Fourth Amendment.

"This is like Big Brother on steroids," said Florida Republican congressman Don Eaker. "I can't vote for something that gives such undeniable power

to our government. Throw in the fact that the president wants to share that intelligence with foreign powers? I think our founding fathers would roll over in their graves."

The SECURITY Act, an acronym for Surveillance of Electronic Correspondence Under Regulated Intelligence and Telecommunication, would grant unprecedented authority for local and federal law enforcement to eavesdrop and record conversations, emails, text messages, and social media postings, without warrants. They require only what the legislation calls "fair and reasonable cause". That ambiguous threshold has one high-ranking Democrat on the House Intelligence Committee crying foul.

"This is illegal," said New Hampshire Representative Steven Lawrence. "It's so far beyond what the Fourth Amendment would allow, I can't believe we're discussing it."

The measure does have its proponents.

"Is it going to take another terrorist attack before we take the threat seriously?" asked Democrat Senator Bentley Blakemore of Colorado. "How many more people have to die before we understand the threat?"

Senator Blakemore is a cosponsor of the upper chamber's version of the SECURITY Act. He has also been among the half dozen lawmakers to travel overseas in attempts to convince allies of its benefits. He made no apologies for the aggressive nature of those international trips.

"Yes, we pushed," he admitted. "We had to push. The terrorist threat is not exclusively domestic. If we are going to effectively cope with the growing global concern, our allies must share intelligence with us. We must share it with them. If it frays the edges of the Fourth Amendment, or the Magna Carta for that matter, so be it."

Blakemore believes he has the support to pass the legislation in the Senate, despite contrary reports, and his colleagues in the House already have the majority of votes secured for passage. He can't speak to the foreign, multilateral agreement pending at the G12 summit this week in Barcelona.

"This is unprecedented," concluded PLAUSIBLEDENIABILITY.INFO Security Analyst Bob Kurk. "Even if this passes both houses and there's an international agreement among three or four countries, the US Supreme Court could strike this down as unconstitutional."

Kurk served as Undersecretary of State during the Obama administration after fifteen years of service in the Central Intelligence Agency. Prior to that he served a decade in the US Marine Corps. He has a law degree from Harvard and is a graduate of the United States Naval Academy. He is currently a consultant for the security firm Wignock Homeland Intelligence Group.

"That said," he conceded, "under the right circumstances, the American people might acquiesce. If there were another attack, for example, that reawakened the fear we felt in the days after 9/11 or the Capitol attack, then I could see the justices concluding it has merit."

Congressman Lawrence reluctantly agreed with Kurk. "If there's another attack, another failure by the joint intelligence community, then there might be no stopping the momentum of this effort. It would pass. My constituents might demand it."

With suspected terrorist Sir Spencer Thomas apparently alive and on the loose, anything is possible.

Holt called the editor and held while she read through the article. She giggled as she mumbled through it on the other end of the line.

"You're killing it, Holt!" she squealed. "That last line? So inflammatory. I love it. Seriously. So good. All is forgiven. What's next?"

"Next?"

"You gotta give me more. This is gold and we're mining new territory here. Our unique visitor number is through the roof. Our retention is crazy. The shares on social media are enough to make me give you a raise."

"No rest for the weary?"

"None," she said. "Aren't you glad you're not in Barcelona? Maybe I should send you to Houston more often."

"Or not."

"You don't like the barbecue?"

"It's fine."

"So what's next?"

"I've got some sources in Barcelona at the summit," he said, but stopped himself from saying too much. "I think some big news is developing there. It's connected to Sir Spencer, connected to Horus, connected to SECURITY. It's big."

"When can you have it all sewn up?" she said, champing at the bit. "I'll need it lawyered, I'm sure."

"Twenty-four hours."

"Okay." She sighed. "I'll need a little teaser before then though. Anything you can give me."

"Fine."

Dillinger hung up and absently checked his text messages, hoping he'd find one from Karen. Then his memory caught up with him. He slapped the device facedown on the café table and raised his hand to catch the waiter's attention. He needed food. Coffee and vodka weren't cutting it. Not today.

CHAPTER 42

PASEO DE TAULAT
BARCELONA, SPAIN

The sweat-drenched Fernando Barçes lay in bed. It was a good sign, Jon Custos thought. It meant the drugs were working.

Custos wiped Barçes's forehead with a towel. He was sitting bedside, playing nursemaid to the patient he wanted to save long enough to kill.

Custos sat in the dark, only the dim ray from a hallway bulb casting a thin fan of light into the room. He knew this was the last night on Earth for both of them. They'd both die for the greater good in hours.

There were no seventy-two virgins at the other end of their martyrdom. Custos was more selfless than that. His sacrifice was for the betterment of man, for the new world.

He'd been taught that the United Nations and NATO weren't enough to amalgamate global power. Instead, they were as corrupt as any despotic government. They could not stop the United States from unlawfully invading Iraq. They could not prevent the genocide in Syria or the rise of ISIS in the fading days of al-Qaeda's influence.

Despite the best efforts of the Eurozone, western Europe was increasingly fractured by culture and religion. The Germans never wanted what the British sought. The French and Spanish couldn't agree what wine to serve with fish. The Greeks couldn't pay back a loan any more than they could keep graffiti from soiling the reconstructive architecture of Athens. And eastern Europe was so embroiled in civil conflict, its people longed for the security and stability of the Soviet Union.

The only way to solve the world's ills was unity: a single power, a single people. The citizens might resist at first, but in the end they would succumb to the notion that one world government was the way forward.

"*Extremis malis, extrema remedia,*" Sir Spencer had once explained. "Do you know what that means, Jon?"

Jon had recognized it as Latin, but hadn't understood it.

"It means extreme disease needs an extreme remedy," Sir Spencer had translated. "Guy Fawkes, the seventeenth-century inspiration who failed at his wonderfully deviant Gunpowder Plot, was rumored to have said it as he fought for his religious and political freedom."

"I've heard of him," said Custos. "The antiestablishment protestors always wear a Fawkes mask."

"Very good." Sir Spencer had nodded. "Yes. And loosely translated from that staid expression is the saying *'Desperate times call for desperate measures.'* These are desperate times, Jon. Very desperate."

Custos understood the desperation as he watched the world devolve into sectarian and racial violence on nearly every continent. He knew then, Sir Spencer was right.

Huxley and Orwell were right too, Custos believed after reading their novels, even if they didn't understand the benefit of their fantasies. Hidden in the sarcasm and political satire of their watershed fiction, they both saw what the world could be. They feared it perhaps, but they knew it was necessary and inevitable.

The Magna Carta was ancient. The Fourth Amendment was antiquated.

But one government, one financial structure, one umbrella under which all people would live and find shelter, was possible. It was prophesized in the Bible.

"Why do the nations rage and the peoples plot in vain?" Custos recited from the book of Psalms as he sopped up sweat from Barçes's neck and chest. *"The kings of the Earth set themselves, and the rulers take counsel together."*

Custos had not read the New Testament. He hadn't learned its parables or learned to live by the word. He'd only memorized the verses his teacher thought relevant.

He was unaware that the prophecy was for the end of the world and not a new beginning. He prayed there, in the relative darkness, mouthing counsel he didn't fully understand.

"Whoever is not with is against me," he recited from the book of Matthew. *"And whoever does not gather with me scatters."*

Custos, for all of his intelligence, guile, and brute strength, was a man who had been misled the entirety of his life. From the thieves who taught him how to fleece unsuspecting tourists to the knight who used him for his own selfish purposes.

He couldn't see that. He saw himself as a servant, a disciple.

Barçes moaned and Custos flinched.

"It's okay, *viejo*," he told the old man. "You are healing. You are improving. Soon you'll be strong enough." He flattened his palm against Barçes's forehead, which felt close to normal. The fever was definitely coming down.

Barçes's eyes fluttered open and he turned his head toward Custos. He inhaled through his nose and suppressed a cough, wincing until the urge subsided.

"You're a fighter," Custos said in Spanish, holding the man's gaze. "I knew you were the right choice. You were destined for this. I have no doubt. Together we will succeed."

Barçes closed his eyes and turned away. He mumbled something, a whisper Custos couldn't hear.

Custos held the old man's chin and turned his face back toward him. He lowered his ear to the patient's mouth and asked him to repeat himself. The old man tried to shake free of Custos's grip but couldn't.

"Tell me again," Custos insisted, tightening his hold. "I want to know what you said to me, *viejo*."

"L'infern t'espera, diable," Barçes said. "Hell awaits you, devil."

Custos smiled at the old man before he pressed his lips to his sweaty forehead. *"Tal vez te veré allí, viejo."*

"Perhaps, I'll see you there."

CHAPTER 43

WORLD TRADE CENTER
BARCELONA, SPAIN

The assassin was heavier than she looked. It took both Matti and Brandon to move her from the floor into the shower. Matti retched a couple of times.

"You've never seen a dead body before?" Brandon flipped on the faucet and unwrapped a bar of soap. He looked at her reflection in the mirror.

Matti shook her head and closed the glass shower door. She wiped her lower eyelids with the tips of her index fingers. Her mascara was running and it stung.

"My mother's funeral was closed casket," she admitted, sniffing. "I wouldn't have wanted to see her anyway. I guess you've seen plenty?"

"I have." Brandon wrung his hands free of soap and held them under the running tap. "Afghanistan. Iraq. Syria. Ours and theirs."

"Do you ever get used to it?"

"No," he said. "Faces stay with me. I probably have hundreds of them floating around in my head. This one will join the rotation."

"Have you ever..." Matti looked at her feet. She couldn't finish the question.

"Yes." Brandon dried his hands with a towel and turned to wrap his arms around Matti. She buried her face in his chest and shuddered. Her arms slipped around his back and she squeezed.

They held each other for what felt to her longer than it probably was. She squeezed again and let go of him, pulling away from his hold.

"We have work to do." She sniffled. "I can't wallow."

"So we leave her here? I'm the White House chief of staff. I killed someone. Shouldn't we report this?"

"We don't have time. By the time we deal with this, it could be too late."

"Okay." He exhaled, planting his hands on his hips. "We'll figure this out. I'll deal with it."

"Good."

"What's first, then?"

"We find the guy who's about to light the fuse."

"Where do we start?"

"I think he's the guy who killed the flight attendant." Matti led Brandon out of the bathroom. "I know they've got him on surveillance. We need to figure out where else in the building he's been."

"Good."

"Turn around," Matti said, twirling her finger. "I need to change."

Brandon obliged. Five minutes later they were in the manager's office, making an argument to view the security video.

"There's way too much footage for you to review," he suggested. "I don't know about showing you what I have, regardless. Who did you say you are?"

"Let's go about this another way," Matti suggested. She was standing across from the manager, leaning on his desk while he sat behind it. "Have you had any alarms in the last seventy hours? Any alerts for doors that shouldn't be accessed or that automatically trigger notifications?"

The manager looked at Matti and then at Brandon. He pursed his lips and turned to the computer monitor on his desk. He pecked at the keys and then clicked the mouse.

"We've had three alerts. One was a rear service entrance. One was an emergency exit. One was a basement storage closet ceiling tile."

"A ceiling tile?" Matti asked. "You have cameras in ceiling tiles?"

"Not a camera," the manager corrected. "It's a sensor. Some of our ceiling tiles have sensors if they provide access to our infrastructure—plumbing, security, electrical."

"That's odd, isn't it?"

"Not necessarily," he said. "Rodents can trigger them. That's what happens most often."

"Can you check the alert?" asked Brandon. "Is there a camera nearby? Maybe we could narrow our video search that way."

"Possibly," the manager huffed. "This is highly irregular. You're not police."

"No," said Brandon. "But we do work for the president of the United States." He flashed his White House badge again. "I know this isn't a badge. But we wouldn't be asking if this weren't critically important."

The manager studied them again. He clucked his tongue against his teeth before picking up his phone to call security.

"I need someone to walk me through video access," he said, cradling the phone in his neck and banging the keyboard again. "I'm looking for a basement storage closet feed. It would coincide with the alert code I'm emailing you."

Matti hoped this would work. If it didn't, she was out of luck. She didn't know where to start if this stalled.

"Thank you," said the manager. "I'll need five minutes on either end of the alert."

Brandon sat down in the empty chair next to Matti and motioned for her to sit too. Matti reluctantly plopped into the chair and waited.

"Stop," Brandon whispered, touching her arm.

"Stop what?"

"I can tell you're chewing on the inside of your cheek," he said. "Being stressed out isn't going to help our cause. You need to stay calm and in control, Matti."

Matti ran her tongue along the inside of her ragged cheek. She hadn't even noticed she was doing it. She stopped, folding her arms across her chest and looking away from Brandon without saying anything.

"I've got something," said the manager. "I can't give you a copy of this, but you can look at it." He spun his monitor around to face Matti and Brandon.

On the screen, in muted color, was a high overhead camera aimed at an empty hallway. After twenty seconds, a man appeared in the frame from the top of the screen and approached the door. He looked in both directions and then inserted a key into the door. He opened the door and disappeared.

"Could you play it one more time and freeze it when he turns toward the camera?" Matti asked. She leaned forward in her seat, already knowing she'd struck gold.

The manager complied and froze the video at the right moment. He pressed a couple of keys, which expanded the image, despite making it grainier.

"That's him." Matti pointed at the muscular, bald man on the screen. "That's definitely him. Why does he have keys?" She glared at the manager.

"I can't answer that," the manager said, tugging his collar. "I don't know. He's not an employee. He looks like the man who killed the flight attendant."

"That's exactly who it is." Matti stood from her chair, leaning in toward the manager. "Whose keys are those?"

"I don't know."

"Do you have any employees who haven't been to work in a few days?" asked Brandon. "Anyone who would have access to storage closets?"

"Let me ask the head of our maintenance team." He raised a finger and then dialed an extension on his phone. Speaking in Spanish, he asked about missing employees. He cradled the phone again as he wrote down a name. He hung up and slid the paper to Matti.

"This man hasn't been to work for the last few days," he said, swallowing the words as he spoke. "His name is Fernando Barçes. He hasn't called in sick and he hasn't returned any phone calls."

"Do you have an address?" Matti barked. "We need an address."

"I...don't...I'm not—"

"Give us the address," Brandon ordered. "I don't think you want us talking to the security teams from every head of state visiting your establishment as to why nobody reported a missing employee on the eve of an international summit."

"It's not as though we are the Casa Fuster Hotel," the manager reasoned.

"What does that mean?" asked Matti.

"A man was killed in their bar today. A woman attacked him and strangled him right there on the floor. Then she walked out and disappeared."

"I'm not sure I'd make that comparison," suggested Brandon. "Give us the address."

The manager nodded vacantly and began typing again. He kept mishitting keys as he searched for the man's address. His eyes were wide, his complexion decidedly more sallow than when Matti and Brandon first entered his office.

He touched his screen and ran a finger across it, mumbling as he scratched the address onto another piece of paper. He slid it across the desk and Matti snatched it.

"Thank you," she said without a hint of appreciation, her focus three steps ahead. She turned to Brandon. "We need to go now."

"By the way," Brandon said to the manager on the way out of the office. "Please stop maid service to both of our rooms."

*

President Felicia Jackson yawned. It was late and she was fighting jet lag.

"I'm sorry to bore you," said the British prime minister. "Usually I'm far more engaging."

"I'm sorry." The president sat forward in her seat and reached out to touch the prime minister's hand. "I don't intend to be rude. It's been a long day."

"I can imagine," he said. "Making that dreadful flight across the Atlantic. I remember the last time…"

The president checked her watch and tuned out the prime minister. Another half hour and she could leave without causing an international incident. She reached for the cup of coffee next to the large porcelain charger sitting empty at her seat.

She'd eaten only bites of her dinner and eagerly handed the waiter her plate. She'd take Italian or French food over Spanish any day of the week. Paella was next to lawyers on her list of least favorite things.

She took a sip of the coffee and winced at its tepid bitterness. It had been sitting too long and was stronger than she expected. Glancing around the room, she noticed a near-empty table at the back of the room.

"Excuse me," she said to the prime minister, interrupting his story about a midflight leg massage. "I need to check on one of my staffers."

"Of course." He pushed back his chair and stood as the president left the table.

She thanked him and wove her way to the back of the room, occasionally stopping to say hello to other guests as she passed their tables. She reached the back table and noticed two empty seats. Matti was gone, as was Brandon.

"Has anyone seen the man who was sitting here?" she asked the others at the table. She placed both of her hands on the chair back and patted it as she searched the unfamiliar faces staring back at her.

A few of them shook their heads and returned to their conversations, apparently unimpressed by the president of the United States. A couple more told her they hadn't seen anyone at that seat all night.

"He left a while ago," offered a woman with a French accent. "The woman who was here left first. Then perhaps a half hour later, he left too."

"Interesting." Felicia Jackson rapped her fingers on the chair. "Thank you all." She quickly moved to her table and pulled her phone from her purse. The president, unlike most of her predecessors, didn't rely on an aide to carry her personal belongings.

She scrolled through her contacts to find Brandon Goodman's number and called it. It rang twice before he answered.

"Brandon," the president started without waiting for a response, "you left without telling me. Where are you?"

"I'm in the hotel," he answered, breathing heavily. He sounded as if he was running or walking. President Jackson listened for ambient sound to place him. There were no clues.

"Where in the hotel?"

"The lobby."

"Wait for me," the president ordered. "I'm coming to talk to you."

"Right now?"

"Right now." She caught the eye of a Secret Service agent and motioned him to follow, then marched from the room into the large, wide hallway outside of the banquet room.

Flanked by her security team, Felicia Jackson hurriedly walked to the main lobby. She brushed past an elderly couple moving too slowly, leaving a member of her team to apologize, and pushed her way through the large doors leading to the front entryway of the hotel.

Brandon was standing, phone in hand, waiting for her. He waved awkwardly as she approached, waiting for her to speak first. Jackson eyed him and then glanced past him. She looked toward the grouping of chairs near the reception desk and then beyond the desk to the spiral staircase.

"Where's Matti?" the president barked as she approached.

"What do you mean?" Brandon shoved his hands into his pockets. "I haven't seen her since she left the dinner. Is everything okay?"

"Brandon," the president scolded with one eyebrow raised, "don't play dumb. Where is she?"

"I'm not playing anything, Madam President. I know you've had issues with her lately, as have I, quite frankly, but I don't know where she is."

"The only members of my delegation who aren't at that dinner are me, my guys here, you, and Matti. And I'm here because you are."

"What are you—?"

"What are you doing with Matti?"

"Listen, Madam President," Brandon said, widening his stance and setting his jaw, "with all due respect, I don't get what you're insinuating. Matti is sick. She's an addict. Why you still employ her is beyond me. But you do. And so, as your chief, I maintain relationships with everyone in your inner circle. Matti is in that circle until you pull the trigger and remove her."

President Jackson was surprised, but pleased, to see the former Army Ranger show some backbone. "Brandon, I—"

He held up his hand. "Wait a minute, please. Let me finish. Whatever your paranoia is regarding Matti, you need to let me know. I can't help you if I'm out of the loop."

The president studied Brandon's eyes, searching for a twitch. He held her gaze until it was uncomfortable, and she looked down at her feet, considering how to respond. She was concerned that she'd not heard from the assassin that the job was done. However, if there was, in fact, a problem, Brandon would be lying in a bloody, breathless heap next to Matti Harrold.

Nonetheless, Felicia Jackson wasn't sure she believed Brandon Goodman. She hadn't hired him because she knew him well. She made him chief because he was an outsider. He'd do her bidding as any good soldier would. Until tonight, she was sure she'd been right about him. He'd done as he was told, carrying out every mission with military precision. He led the West Wing troops with the ease of a natural leader. His experience in the State Department was an asset. His knowledge of the White House in the Foreman administration was invaluable.

"Maybe," she said, drawing out her words to give her time to think, "I was…a touch brusque. Call it jet lag."

Brandon nodded, the tension visibly leaving his body. He ran a hand through his hair.

"This is Matti's last trip with us," the president revealed. "She's proving unreliable. Her demons are too strong. I'd so hoped that she would be the trusted sidekick I needed when I stepped into this role."

"Are you sending her home now?" Brandon asked. "Or are you letting her know when the talks are over?"

"I warned her before the trip." President Jackson stepped into Brandon's space, her voice lilting. "I told her to shape up. But leaving dinner tonight? That's it for me."

"She wasn't feeling good."

"Don't be an idiot, Brandon. She needed her fix."

"Perhaps," Brandon conceded. "Weren't you counting on her to secure Congress? Don't you need her to be part of what's going on here so that she can effectively communicate the urgency of the legislation?"

"No." Jackson bit her lower lip. "I'm afraid not. I wanted that. It's too risky. We can't leave such an important job to her. I need you to keep your distance from her. I need you by my side these next couple of days. Then I'll send you to the Hill. It'll be more conciliatory to have you do the pitching, anyhow. Matti's good looks only get her so far."

"She's pretty sharp, Madam President."

"She was." Felicia Jackson stepped away from Brandon, pivoting to make her way back to the dinner. "You've seen it, soldier. The same moment that brought out the greatness in someone was the same moment that led to his ultimate undoing."

The president spun and called out to Goodman as she strode away from him, "Get some sleep. I need you sharp in the morning. I'll tell Matti she's not needed. We'll send her home commercial."

*

Matti sat in the back of a taxicab, listening to the driver talk on his cell phone. She'd hopped in his cab at the end of the long drive leading to the World Trade Center, insisting she wasn't one of the dozens of protestors crowding the edges of the boulevard.

She looked at the empty seat next to her and wondered what she'd do when she arrived at the janitor's apartment. She was alone in a foreign city. What good could she do against a murderous would-be terrorist?

When Brandon's phone rang, their plans had changed. He'd told her to run, not walk, from the lobby and find her way to the janitor's place. He'd be right behind her, he promised.

She'd walked briskly from the lobby, pulled off her heels once she'd passed security at the entry, and ran to find a cab. The driver was at a red light, not expecting a fare when she'd slipped into the back of the black Prius with the bright yellow doors.

Matti checked her phone, wishing for a text from Brandon. None came. As they neared the address she'd given the driver, he slowed.

"I don't think I can take you any farther," he said in broken, Spanish-accented English. "The road is blocked."

Matti looked up from her phone and squinted against the flashing lights fifty yards ahead of them. She leaned forward and looked through the windshield.

"What happened?" she asked. "Is it an accident?"

"I don't know. It's blocked. You have to get out here."

Matti passed the driver twenty euro and slid out of the Prius. She walked toward the flashing lights. The closer she got, the more she understood the scene unfolding in front of her.

This wasn't an accident scene; it was a crime scene.

Sitting on the curb was a young man bathed in alternating light and darkness, his head in his hands. An older man sat next to him, his arms draped over the young man in consolation. There was organized chaos swarming around them.

Matti counted four police cars and an ambulance. There were another three unmarked cars she assumed belonged to investigators. There was a cadre of black-clad, beret-wearing police officers clustered near the front of a building. Above them was a neon green cross, the emblem for a pharmacy.

Groups of men walked in and out of the business, talking and gesticulating. Matti moved closer to the yellow plastic tape separating the scene from the crowd gathering outside of it.

She checked her phone. Nothing yet.

"What happened?" she asked a sweater-cloaked elderly woman standing amongst the onlookers.

The woman looked up at Matti, her hand over her mouth, and shook her head.

"A woman was murdered," said a man standing behind the elderly lady. "Somebody killed her. Her brother found her. He's the one sitting over there."

"Murdered?" Matti stepped closer to the man. "How?"

"I don't know," he said, rubbing the scruff on his chin. "She was a nice lady. Always helpful."

Matti thanked him and looked past the activity on the other side of the tape to the pharmacy building. Next door was an oddly colored high-rise. It almost looked purple and orange in the dark and strobing emergency lights.

Matti opened the Internet browser on her phone and punched in the janitor's address. She tapped the link for a Street View image. The photograph on the screen matched the building next to the pharmacy.

She moved through the crowd, pushing her way more closely to the apartment building. She got within twenty feet or so of the entrance before she was certain it was behind the tape.

Her phone buzzed. It was Brandon.

I am on my way. U ok?

Matti saw the man on the curb, the victim's brother, talking to someone she assumed was a detective. The brother was shaking his fists. The detective had his hand on the brother's shoulder. She looked back to her phone and replied to Brandon.

I'm good. Have cab stop on the corner. I'll meet you there.

Matti hit send and started walking away from the scene. By the time she reached the corner, Brandon was stepping from his cab.

"What's going on?" He nodded past Matti's shoulder toward the flashing emergency lights. "Are you okay?"

"I'm fine. A woman was murdered in a pharmacy down there. It's next door to the janitor's apartment building."

"That's weird." Brandon took a step closer to Matti.

"It is. It's got to be connected somehow. Regardless, we can't get into the apartment building right now."

"So what do you want to do?" Brandon put his hand on Matti's shoulder. "We can't wait around the rest of the night."

"We could."

"I've got a few hours, I guess," Brandon said after checking the clock on his phone. "The president wants me with her first thing tomorrow."

Matti turned back to look Brandon in his eyes. "Yeah, what was that about? Why did she need to see you?"

"She thought I was with you," Brandon said, slipping his phone back into his pocket. "I assured her I wasn't."

"And she bought it?"

"I guess." Brandon shrugged. "If not, I probably wouldn't be here."

"You know she thinks I'm dead or soon will be."

"Yeah. That's why she told me she was sending you home. She said she's handling it personally. You're to be on a commercial flight in the morning."

"So you believe me when I tell you President Jackson tried to have me killed?"

Brandon nodded without saying anything. His hands were on his hips. He looked down at the sidewalk and kicked his toe into the brick.

"Let's wait for the scene to clear," Matti said. "You've got until sunrise, right?"

"Probably. The first meetings are at seven. What's the plan?"

"I don't know." Matti shrugged. "We'll wing it. You have a lamp with you?"

Matti had no idea where she'd found humor. Her life was in danger, she'd discovered the president was a mafia boss, and there was an imminent terrorist attack she was trying to stop. Maybe it was a coping mechanism.

"Not funny." Brandon frowned. "Not funny at all."

*

Jon Custos peeked through the thin opening between two blue curtains framing the bedroom window, looking down on the anthill madness beneath him. This wasn't good. He'd not anticipated anyone finding the pharmacist's body so quickly.

Another unforgivable mistake!

His eyes darted from the grieving man on the sidewalk to the crowd huddled on the other side of the street. Several of them crossed themselves, and he followed their line of sight to see the gurney emerge from the pharmacy. The woman's body was strapped underneath a blue sheet.

The griever dropped to his knees and slapped the brick sidewalk repeatedly. Uniformed police officers tried to comfort him. He shook free from their hold and curled into a ball, wailing as the gurney clunked into the back of an ambulance.

Custos turned from the window and checked the bedside clock. He had a couple of hours until he wanted to be on his way back to the World Trade Center.

As long as the crowd and the police cleared out before then, there'd be no problems. He didn't want to consider what would happen if there was still activity buzzing around the street.

His patient was resting comfortably. The fever gone, his breathing was syncopated, if a little rapid. His color was closer to normal. Custos quietly padded out of the room. He wanted Barçes as rested as possible.

The living room was bathed in the flashing blue and red hues from the emergency vehicles below. A short siren blast told him the ambulance was leaving the scene. He plopped into the easy chair opposite the television, hopeful that meant the rest of the responders and gawkers would disperse.

Jon Custos set an alarm on his cell phone and rested his head on the back of the chair. He closed his eyes, trying to remember the last time he'd slept.

After running on adrenaline and purpose for days, his body was revolting. His knees ached, his lower back hurt, his eyes burned. He closed his eyes, pressing tears that rolled to his ears. This would be his final respite, the last time he would dream.

He drifted off thinking about the task ahead, playing it over and over again in his mind. He could see the explosion and the ensuing panic outside the World Trade Center. It would give him time to return to the basement and cut the power.

Then he'd deliver the final blow, sacrificing himself for mankind. He wondered how that last instant would be. Would the searing heat consume him first? Would the explosion instantaneously obliterate him? Would there be pain? If so, for how long?

It was inconsequential. It would be whatever it would be.

At least he knew what was coming. Fernando Barçes did not. Not really.

By the time he figured it out, it wouldn't matter. He'd be in a billion unrecognizable pieces, splattered from one side of the street to the other, blended with the hundred others unfortunate enough to be unwitting martyrs for a cause they didn't know existed.

But what a cause it was! The transformation of the Western world into a homogenous protectorate. It would start with only a few countries, but would spread quickly east. Before long, it would truly be one world. And it would begin with him.

"*A Deo et Rege,*" echoed in his mind as he fell asleep. "*A Deo et Rege.*"

CHAPTER 44

HOUSTON, TEXAS

It was getting dark outside and the barista shot Dillinger Holt a nasty look. She'd gone from welcoming, to pleasant, to tolerant during the course of the day he'd spent occupying a table in the café. Now Dillinger was convinced she hated him.

"Could I get another espresso? I'll tip you three times the cost of the coffee."

The barista huffed and wiped her hands on her apron. Rolling her eyes, she stepped to the espresso machine, cranking it to life.

Holt checked his email again. Nothing. It was in the middle of the night in Europe, but he was impatient. He needed a quick something to satiate his editor's appetite.

He scrolled through his recent calls, found the right one, and called it. It rang twice before Matti Harrold answered the phone.

"What do you have for me?" he asked without saying hello.

"Seriously?"

"You promised me new information. I haven't heard from you. I've got to post something soon. I can't wait to write about the fireworks after the smoke has cleared. I need something ahead of the explosion."

"Poor choice of words."

"Sorry. Newsroom humor."

"I've been kinda busy, Dillinger."

"Look, you called me, Matti. You offered me reportable information. Give me something."

She sounded out of breath, as if she were running or walking quickly. "I've been busy. I haven't forgotten about you."

"Good to hear." Holt took the cup and saucer from the barista and handed her a ten-dollar bill. She took the bill and smirked. She was cute, Holt thought. With her hair pulled back, she looked a little like Karen.

"I really don't have time right now," Matti insisted.

"Give me a nugget," he pressed. "Give me something I can verify on my own. I'll do the legwork."

"Hang on," Matti relented. She was talking to someone, her voice muffled. Holt couldn't decipher the conversation, but the other person was a man.

"Thank you," Holt called out to the barista, toasting her with the coffee cup. "I appreciate it." She saluted him sarcastically. He imagined she'd reached her executive potential with an attitude like that and was forever destined to wear a name tag with her name written in Sharpie.

"Here's something," Matti said. "There was a murder in the same hotel playing host to the G12 and it's been buried. Barcelona police worked it. The victim was a Canadian flight attendant. The suspect is missing and may also be responsible for the disappearance of a hotel employee."

"Do you have names?" Holt typed on his laptop, playing catch-up with the information Matti was quickly unloading.

"No."

"Is the suspect identified?"

"There's video of him."

"Do they know his name?"

"I don't know what they know," Matti said coyly, and Holt knew she was holding back.

"Do *you* know his name?"

"Jon Custos," she said with hesitation. "That's on background and not reportable unless someone tells you on the record he's suspected of being involved."

"How do you know his name?" He clicked the keys as he spoke. His questions were as much for information as they were a stalling tactic to give him time to finish his notes before she spoke again.

"I just do."

"C'mon, Matti," he whined. "How do you—"

"I gotta go. I'll get back to you. You've got enough for now."

"Yeah, but it's the middle of the night there. I can't confirm anything."

Matti didn't answer.

"Matti? Matti, can you hear me?" He pulled the phone from his ear to look at the screen. She'd hung up.

"Fu—" Holt stopped himself, remembering he was in public. He swigged his coffee with one hand and rubbed his neck with the other. Matti Harrold had given him a goldmine then took the pickaxe with her.

"Think." He thumped at his forehead with the side of his fist. "Think, Dillinger."

Who could he call who might have information? Who might know something about a murder in Spain? Who would be working late enough to answer their phone at eight o'clock at night?

Maybe it was the jolt of caffeine or the genius of exhaustion that struck. Perhaps it was just the dumb luck of an experienced reporter. But Holt had an idea.

He scrolled through his contacts, found the one he was looking for, and pressed send. The person on the other end answered after a single ring.

"Department of Homeland Security," answered a pleasant voice, "this is Redden."

"Rick, it's Dillinger Holt."

"Dillinger Holt," repeated Rick Redden. "My favorite reporter named after a gangster."

"Do we need to go there?"

"What was your middle name again?" Redden went there.

"You know my middle name."

"I just like hearing you say it," said Redden. "Your dad had the best or worst sense of humor in the history of baby naming."

"Not cool."

"I'm just kidding." Redden laughed at himself. "What do you need? It's been a while."

"Yeah, it has been. My fault. No excuses. I owe you dinner."

"Old Ebbitt's?"

"Sure thing. I need some information."

"Do I need to go secure?"

"Yes."

"Hang on. Let me call you right back." The line went dead. Twenty seconds later Holt's phone buzzed in his hand.

"So what's the information?" Redden asked.

Holt knew if it was possible to get any confirmation out of Spain, Rick Redden was the man to make it happen. The two had been college roommates. One went to the dark side, digging for dirt, spreading information that was sometimes only mostly true, and worked hard to climb the rungs of power and influence. The other had gone into politics. Despite taking two different paths, they'd remained friends.

"I got a tip there was a murder in the hotel hosting the G12. The suspect is a man named Jon Custos. Barcelona Police have video of him. He may also be responsible for the disappearance of a hotel employee."

"How do you spell Custos?"

"C-U-S-T-O-S."

"Do you have a nationality? Any other identifiers?"

"No."

"Who did he kill?"

"A Canadian flight attendant."

"Are you working the crime beat now?"

"No."

"Sorry." Redden laughed. "Didn't mean to demote you. The intel is for a story?"

"Yes."

"Usual ground rules apply?"

"Yes. You're a second source. On background. No name, no agency. I'll qualify it with something like 'a source familiar with the investigation but not directly involved'. That work?"

"Yep. Give me thirty minutes. I've got some people who may know. If Secret Service is aware, I should be able to get you something."

"Thanks. Old Ebbitt Grill is on me."

"Of course it is," Redden agreed. "Remember, I'm on a government salary."

CHAPTER 45

PASEO DE TAULAT
BARCELONA, SPAIN

"Should you have given him so much information?" Brandon asked Matti as the last of the police cruisers rolled away from the crime scene.

"We've got nothing to hide," Matti said. "We'll need him to tell our story if we survive this."

"Our story?" Brandon bristled. "I hadn't thought of it that way."

"Brandon," Matti said earnestly, "you killed a woman the president sent to kill me. You're standing here now trying to stop a terror attack designed to change the course of our country. I'd say it's our story now."

Matti took his hand and squeezed it before stepping into his body and wrapping her arms around him. He hesitated before he put his hands on her shoulders and slid them down to the small of her back.

"We're in this together," she said. "Like it or not, you're stuck with me." She buried her face in his chest. His heart thumped with excitement. His fingers slid from her back to the curve of her hips.

"We—we should get going." Brandon cleared his throat and gently pushed himself away, leaving his hands on her hips. "I'm running out of time, and now might be our only chance to check the apartment."

Matti wondered if she'd misread his signals. She searched his eyes for the answer but couldn't find it. He looked away, his eyes dancing in every direction but hers. Matti blinked back her disappointment and immediately refocused on the job.

"Yes," she said, brushing her top for no apparent reason. "Of course. Let's go."

Together they walked across the street and down a block to the oddly hued apartment building next to the pharmacy. Matti stepped up the concrete stoop and tried the glass door, tugging on it.

"It's locked," she said. "What do we do?"

Brandon climbed the steps, cupped his hands at his temples, and pressed them to the glass door. He stood there for a moment before backing away.

"What?" Matti asked. "Did you see something?"

"No," he said. "Well, maybe."

Matti turned to the door and repeated Brandon's efforts. She didn't notice whatever it was he'd seen.

"What?" she asked.

"There's a wooden door on the opposite end of the hallway. It's past the stairs. Looks like it might be another entrance. Maybe it's unlocked."

"Should we try it?"

"I think so. We won't lose anything. Standing here outside of a locked door gets us nothing."

They walked around the edge of the building, sidestepping their way through a narrow, dank alleyway between the apartment building and another stuccoed high-rise next to it. Matti sidestepped the puddles dotting the alley, visible only by the light reflecting from them.

She turned the corner behind Brandon and found herself at the back side of the building alongside large gray, brown, and blue trash containers. The odor was nauseatingly sweet and she covered her nose with her forearm as Brandon led her to the wooden door he'd seen from the other side of the building.

"It's open," Brandon said, turning to Matti, his hand on the doorknob.

"That's good, right?"

"I don't know."

*

Helping Fernando Barçes down the steps was more difficult than Custos had anticipated. So much of this mission was, in reality, more difficult than he'd anticipated.

"Venga, viejo." Custos willed the man as he guided him down the stairs like a wounded soldier, holding Barçes's arm around his neck. "Our destiny awaits us."

Custos was wearing a wig and large black-framed eyeglasses. Though it wasn't a foolproof disguise, it was enough for his purposes. A duffel bag was strapped to his back like a messenger bag. In the bag was the magical Russian device that matched the one inside Fernando Barçes, white electrical tape, a black magic marker, and plastic tie wraps.

It was less than an hour before their final sunrise. When the crowd and police finally cleared the street, Custos decided it was time to move. While they slowly navigated their way toward the first floor, Custos heard a banging at the front door.

He stopped, helped Barçes to sit on the landing between the second and first floor, and peeked over the railing toward the glass front door. A man and then a woman were peering through the glass. They must not have been residents, because they didn't have keys to open the door.

Custos waited for them to disappear, and then he quickly pulled Barçes to his feet and to the first floor's rear service entrance. It was the door through which residents emptied their trash into the city's color-coded receptacles.

He pushed through the door and, without bothering to shut it behind him, moved as quickly as he could to the corner. Barçes did a remarkable job of keeping up as they limped around the corner and hailed a cab.

"*Un buen trabajo, viejo,*" Custos said as he settled into his seat. "You did a good job. I'm impressed."

The old man's chest was heaving and his face was etched with the pain of labored breathing. He tried breathing through his nose, but Custos could tell it wasn't providing enough air.

"Only a few minutes," Custos said, "and we'll be there. Just hang in there for a few minutes more."

As they approached the beach and turned parallel to the coast, the sky took on a more purple hue. The sun was just below the horizon of the Mediterranean. Custos looked past Barçes through the rear driver's side window. The sting of tears welled in his eyes and he knuckled them away. He bit down hard on the inside of his cheek.

Focus.

The cab rolled within two blocks of the World Trade Center and Custos told the driver to let them out. The driver barked he needed more of a warning but stopped nonetheless, and he gratefully took fifty euro without further complaint.

Custos plunked Barçes onto a stone bench on the side of the road and leaned him against the back. Barçes mumbled something unintelligible and tugged his sweaty shirt. It was sticking to his chest.

Custos knelt in front of the bench and unzipped his duffle bag. He fished around, plucking out his supplies.

"Sit still," Custos instructed as he laced tie wraps around the old man's ankles and then connected them with a third looped plastic tie. He left enough slack to allow Barçes to shuffle, but not enough to do much more than that. He took Barçes's wrists and repeated the process. Then he took a long piece of electrical tape, ripped it from the roll, and stuck it to the edge of the bench. He took the black marker and wrote on the tape G12 POLITICAL PRISONER. He pulled the tape from the bench and affixed it to Barçes's face, covering his mouth.

"This will keep you from saying something you shouldn't." Custos slapped the old man's leg and spun on the bench to him. He looked across the boulevard to the beach and beyond. The sun was minutes from crowning at the horizon. It was worth sitting in quiet for a few minutes more. He pushed the glasses up on his nose and whistled.

It was the overture to Mozart's *The Magic Flute*, one of Sir Spencer's favorite classical pieces. A two-part opera, it was unique because it consisted of both sung and spoken word. He stopped whistling and whispered the opening lines from the "chosen one", Prince Tamino.

"Help me! Oh, help me or I am lost, condemned as sacrifice to the cunning serpent," he said, his eyes vacant as he stared at the rising sun. *"Merciful gods! It's coming closer! Ah! save me, ah! Defend me!"*

*

Matti followed Brandon up the steps, holding onto the iron rails as she navigated the dark stairwell from the first floor. The smell of late dinners lingered in the heavy, warm air as she climbed, feeling the remnants of peeling paint slide along her palm as she moved upward.

They reached the janitor's floor and quietly moved along the hallway toward his apartment. The only ambient light came from windows at either end of the hall.

"I think this is it." Brandon stopped at a door and slid his hand along the jamb. "Somebody's broken in here or used a lot of force to gain entry."

"Why do you say that?"

Brandon gripped the door handle and turned. It cranked open with ease, and the door hung funny in the open frame.

"It's off kilter," he said, holding his hand up to stop Matti in the hall. "Wait here."

Matti ignored him and was a step behind him as they entered the apartment. What hit her first was the odor. It smelled like a locker room, but worse. There was a hint of antiseptic, like a hospital or a nursing home. It wasn't enough to mask the strong suggestion of decay.

They walked into an open living room. A single lamp was on, glowing yellow in the corner of the room. A television was turned on, its volume off.

Matti was unarmed. She didn't see anything that could serve as a weapon should she need it. This was reckless. They were trespassing. A homicidal nutcase might be just feet away.

Nonetheless, she stepped to the kitchen. Water dripped from the faucet, tapping the sink every couple of seconds. A half dozen prescription bottles littered the counter near the sink.

She walked back to the living room, noticing a broken piece of wood lodged into the handles of two large glass doors. To the right, the large room was empty, the flickering of the television casting a horror-movie-like glow onto the wall.

The room was otherwise empty. Brandon wasn't there, and Matti's heart rate accelerated. She moved from the living room to a hallway close to the entry door.

To the right was a bathroom. A nightlight flickered above the sink. She reached into the room and flicked the light switch.

There was a reddish brown streak across the lip of the bathtub that dripped over the edge to the floor. It looked like dried blood. Matti moved closer and knelt down.

"Nobody's here," Brandon called from behind her, startling her, causing her to nearly fall over. She caught herself on the tub, avoiding the blood.

"You checked the rest of the apartment?

"There are only two bedrooms," Brandon said, reaching to help Matti to her feet. "Nobody's home. Something weird happened here. Without question, the janitor is not okay.

"What do you mean?" Matti stood and adjusted her shirt.

"There's a dried bloodstain on the floor of one bedroom," he said. "There's more in the bed, which is a mess. There's also something yellow, like pus, staining the sheets. It almost looks like someone had surgery."

"And the other room?"

"Nothing there. It's clean, like nobody's been in it for a while. The blinds are pulled. Spare bedroom, I guess. What did you find in the kitchen?"

"Nothing really. Just a bunch of prescription bottles," she said. "The back doors are barricaded."

"Really?" Brandon walked back to the living room. Matti followed. "Huh. Clearly the janitor was trying to keep someone out."

"Or someone was trying to keep him in," Matti countered.

Brandon shrugged and walked to the kitchen, where he picked up a couple of the bottles. He tossed one of them to Matti.

She looked at the bottle. Nothing stood out. "It's a steroid. Methylprednisolone."

"There's no name on it," he said. "It's the kind of bottle a pharmacy would stock behind the counter. This one"—he held up the other bottle—"ceftriaxone? It doesn't have a name on it either."

"He did kill the woman at the pharmacy," Matti said, rolling the bottle over in her hand. "I knew it."

"It's probably a safe assumption the janitor is dead," reasoned Brandon, setting the bottle back on the counter.

"Or he's part of the plan. We know he killed the flight attendant and left her body in the room. He did everything he could to prolong someone finding her."

"Okay." Brandon stepped closer to Matti, lowering his voice, "so he learned his lesson and took the body with him."

"I don't think so." Matti rubbed her chin, unaware of the tremble in her hand. "Whatever this guy did to the janitor, he did it in the bathtub or on the floor of the bedroom. And then he moved the janitor to the bed."

"Why do you say that?" Brandon's eyes moved toward the hallway and the two bedrooms. He planted his hands on his hips.

"You said it yourself, Brandon," Matti replied. "It looks like someone performed surgery. And if there's blood and pus on the top sheet of the bed, that means it was covering a wound. The janitor was in bed. It just makes sense. Despite the smell of cleanser, the killer didn't really care to hide anything this time. This place is a mess. Plus it was unlocked."

"So that means he took the janitor with him." Brandon pulled his hands to his hair and tugged it with his fists. "We're too late."

"No, we're not," Matti said. "Not if we get back to the Trade Center right now. He's headed for that closet in the basement."

Brandon checked his phone and cursed. "I'm late. I'm supposed to have breakfast with the president in forty-five minutes. Then the meetings start a half hour later."

"We can make it," Matti said, moving to the door. "But we need to go now."

CHAPTER 46

WORLD TRADE CENTER
BARCELONA, SPAIN

President Jackson clenched her jaw and gripped her personal cell phone as if it were a stress ball. For five hours she'd been trying unsuccessfully to contact the assassin.

It was not unusual for the assassin to go radio silent for days. However, given the stakes and the proximity to the impending events, Jackson had assumed she would be more communicative.

Felicia Jackson dropped the phone onto the dresser in her suite and tucked in her blouse. She was wearing a cream-colored silk shell underneath a fire engine red suit. After she slipped on the jacket, she affixed an American flag pin to the left lapel.

She considered ordering the Secret Service to Matti's room, but she worried that might create problems if Matti were already dead.

Her phone buzzed atop the dresser, vibrating against the wood. She grabbed at it, almost dropping it to the floor, and flipped it over. She rolled her eyes when she saw who was calling.

"Yes?" she answered in a tone that intentionally conveyed her irritation.

"I was just calling to wish you luck today," her husband squeaked. "I know you've got a lot at stake."

"Is that a sincere wish or a sarcastic one?" She adjusted the pin so it sat just so on the lapel.

"It's sincere, Felicia," he bemoaned, mourning the loss of even the smallest kindness in their marriage. "Why would I call you and be an ass?"

"You just would," she snapped. "If it's sincere, thank you. We can use all of the good wishes, kismet, karma, serendipity, and whatever else we can get."

"Do you have a thesaurus in front of you?"

"Is that supposed to be sincere or sarcastic?"

"If I'm considered an ass regardless," he said, "I might as well enjoy the spoils, the riches, benefits, rewards, and whatever."

"I'm hanging up," she told him, but held the phone to her ear for an extra moment.

"The truth is, I'll always love you, Felicia," he said, his voice hushed. "Despite what you—we've become, I'll always love you."

She pulled the phone from her ear, ended the call, and dialed another number.

"Hello?" It was the young Western European policy analyst. "Who is this?"

"It's your president," she said.

"I didn't—I mean—this—I didn't recognize the number," he fumbled. "I'm very sorry, Madam President."

"Not a problem. I'm on my personal line. It's encrypted. We're free to talk."

"Okay," he said. "What can I do for you?"

"Tell me again about the meeting schedules this morning and who is with whom."

"First thing after breakfast, you're meeting the delegations from the UK, Italy, Canada, Sweden, and Japan. There's another simultaneous meeting that includes the French, Spanish, German, Australians, Belgian, and Swiss delegations."

"Good. And the topics? Refresh my memory."

"SECURITY is on the table in both meetings," he answered. "Even the countries that are not a part of the initial treaty are included in the discussions. They want their voices heard. We've been sure to include a healthy mixture of proponents and naysayers in both conference groups."

"What else?"

"SECURITY should take up most of the time," he said, "but there's also a discussion about Greece and its position with the EU, given their repeated financial shortcomings."

"How does the EU feel about our discussing this?"

"They don't like it."

"Good."

"Then lunch?"

"Yes."

"Excellent," she said. "I'll want you sitting near me. You seem to have a level head about all of this. I need someone who doesn't succumb to emotion."

"Yes, Madam President," he said. Felicia could almost hear him snap to attention over the phone.

"I'll see you downstairs for breakfast in fifteen minutes," she said. "Understood?"

"Yes, Madam President."

"You're not a lawyer, are you?" she asked, pouting her lips in the mirror affixed to the dresser.

"No," he said. "I have a PhD in International Development from Southern Miss. My thesis was about Western Euro—"

"Nevermind," she said. "See you in fifteen." She ended the call.

Felicia slinked over to her window. She'd wanted an ocean view, but the Secret Service suggested it would be easier to protect her with a room facing the concrete peninsula that stretched from the World Trade Center to the Plaça de les Drassanes. She pulled back one of the linen sheers and peered out the window.

In the distance she could see rows of satellite trucks parked along a narrow parking strip along the right side of the peninsula. The sun, rising over the Mediterranean, reflected the new day on the large white metal trucks.

Beyond the trucks to the southwest and closer to the plaza was a large group of protestors. They were too far away for her to make out individuals, but she could see some of them were shaking large signs, their fists pumping in unison. She could only imagine what they were shouting. She didn't have to imagine how they smelled: a putrid mix of sweat, hemp, and patchouli oil. It was eau de dissent, she supposed. She let go of the sheer and checked the Patek Philippe on her wrist. It was time to go downstairs.

CHAPTER 47

PLAÇA DE LES DRESSANES
BARCELONA, SPAIN

Custos guessed there were two, maybe three hundred protestors gathered at the plaza across the World Trade Center peninsula. They were pushed against the police barricades, chanting and screaming at the line of black-clad police standing at attention fifty feet from them. The police were in riot gear, armed with billy clubs and tear gas cannons.

The crowd was swollen past the containment of the plaza. It was spilling onto the street, adding the cacophony of frustrated car horns to their protest.

Unshaven and weary, Custos blended seamlessly with the nonconformists, tugging a bleary-eyed Fernando Barçes behind him. The old man didn't struggle. He followed as would a well-heeled dog, shuffling to keep up with his master.

Custos looked back at his chosen martyr, his human delivery system, and saw a recognizable look in the man's eyes. He'd seen it in other people in the moments before they died. There was resignation, a recognition that no matter what he did, the end was near.

Some mistook it for peacefulness, a serenity that only came as the pain slipped away and the dying ascended to heaven. Custos knew better. He'd looked deep into the eyes of too many people in their waning seconds of life to believe there was peace.

He turned back to navigate the dissenters, trudging toward what he could best reason was the center of the amorphous mass of anarchists. Once there, he found a post, something like a traffic barrier to prevent cars from running onto the curb. He pulled a pair of large zip ties from his pocket and linked them together. He attached one of them to Barçes's ankle and the other around the post. Nobody seemed to notice, their eyes up and across the street. They apparently were too focused on screaming obscenities at the police, who could hear them, and the world leaders, who could not.

Custos wrapped his hand around Barçes's neck. The heat of a returning fever warmed his touch. He pulled the zombie's ear to his mouth and told him what was about to happen. He explained that he would die regardless. A remote trigger would kill him, and if he started to move or struggle, it would only hasten the inevitable.

"Eres todo muertos," he whispered. "You're all dead."

Custos kissed Barçes on the cheek and slipped away into the crowd. He distanced himself from the mob and walked nonchalantly toward the peninsula. He adjusted his wig and straightened his glasses.

It was time.

*

Matti jumped from the cab four blocks from their destination. Traffic was gridlocked in both directions. They weren't moving.

Brandon stuffed ten euro into the driver's hand and slid out of Matti's open door, jogging to catch up with her. She was moving with purpose as she passed the intersection of Passeig d'Isabel II and Via Laietana, running south toward the World Trade Center.

Up ahead she could see the Mirador de Colom, the famous statue of Columbus. She knew once she reached the statue she was only a block from the entrance to the Trade Center peninsula. As she ran, she inhaled the salt air, thick and ripe with the distinct smell of a barnacled port.

She caught a rhythm, breathing in and out, in and out.

"Matti," Brandon called to her.

Matti didn't turn around. She sensed something was about to happen. She couldn't turn around.

Breathe. In and out. In and out.

Her mind flashed to Washington, DC, nine months earlier, when she'd frantically raced to stop the Capitol plot. She remembered the acrid black smoke billowing from the Hanover Institute when a remote trigger blew up the political think tank in Georgetown. She'd known at that moment Bill Davidson was dead.

Breathe. In and out. In and out.

Minutes later, her world changed. The Capitol had exploded and collapsed in on itself.

Wait!

Matti stopped and whirled around to face Brandon.

"What is it?" His face was contorted with confusion.

"There are going to be two explosions," she said. "Two attacks."

"How do you know that?"

"That's their MO. The janitor is the decoy, just like Bill Davidson was."

"Decoy?"

She rolled her eyes. "For an Army Ranger you're a little slow on the uptake. The first explosion won't be the big one. He did something to that janitor. I'm telling you."

"So where will the first explosion be? If the second one is the Trade Center…"

"I don't—" Matti never finished the sentence. From the corner of her eye she saw a bright flash of light. Almost immediately, her knees buckled as the earth shook from a percussive blast. She collapsed into Brandon. He tumbled backward and she landed on him. Matti, though dazed, knew what had happened.

From the ground, she turned her head to look south. A familiar plume crawled its way into the sky, framing the statue of Columbus in black. Car alarms were wailing in the distance.

"Are you okay?" Brandon asked, his hand rubbing his neck.

"No," Matti said. "I'm not."

*

Jon Custos was standing far enough away from what he believed to be the blast radius. He braced himself against a concrete wall at the southern edge of the peninsula, just outside of the police barricade. He looked over his shoulder toward the security at the entrance to the hotel some fifty yards away.

Though the entrance was heavily guarded, people were moving in and out of the hotel. He pushed the glasses up on his nose and brushed the thick bangs of the wig from his forehead.

He noticed a police officer on the edge of the riot line glance at him twice. Custos wouldn't wait for a third.

He took out his phone and held it horizontally, pretending to take a photograph of the protestors. But as he opened the screen, he autodialed a preprogrammed number and closed his eyes.

*

Dirty bombs were always a fear in the Western world, an urban legend that grew in the days after the Cold War and were amplified post 9/11.

Equally as mythical was the undetectable explosive. Terrorists bragged they were close to formulating the perfect weapon, one that could pass through security checkpoints without question.

Combining the two into one singular device? Not even the most radical ordinance expert thought it possible. The Russians had done it.

Hidden in a laptop computer, the thermite components registered as part of the device in any standard airport machine.

Glycerin was hidden inside an e-cigarette vaporizer, and the nuclear bomb was inert until it wasn't.

Once through a checkpoint the carrier could easily reassemble them into a palm-sized plastic-resin container rendered on a commercial-grade 3D printer.

None of those components, none of the threat or the glory of the undetectable thermite dirty bomb were a reality until Jon Custos sent the signal. Only then did the world see what was possible.

Fernando Barçes was the hypocenter of the attack, and he never knew the bomb was triggered.

When activated, a magnesium ribbon was sparked. Its heat initiated the reaction. Iron oxide and aluminum burned white hot. That, in turn, ignited glycerin, which caught fire. Those flames detonated the dirty bomb. The chain reaction took less than a half second.

It was the nuclear material that vaporized Barçes, those within twenty feet of him, and killed scores more. Much of the explosion's energy was an intense burst of heat. Traveling at the speed of light, it burned its way through most of the protestors. Those who didn't die immediately would succumb to flash burns or shrapnel wounds. Unlike a conventional, aerial nuclear detonation, wide-scale radiation was not a concern. A dirty bomb, or a radiological dispersal device, was far more a psychological weapon than a physical one.

Custos knew when torturing a prisoner the threat of pain was often far more effective than the infliction of it. Such was the case with the dirty bomb. Smoking five packs of cigarettes a day or fake-baking in a tanning bed were more of a mortal threat to the general population. But like the fear of being eaten alive by a great white shark, people could be irrational. Their minds would run wild with the threat of pain.

That was why this attack had to be a dirty bomb. That was why it had to be public. That was why there had to be two of them: one blowing up people without protection, the other blowing up world leaders under the tightest of security. Americans would beg to give up their freedom for their security. The Spanish and French would too. The Italians would ask for it. The British would clamor for it.

A new world order was wafting into the air with the smoke clouding out the newly risen sun. Custos inhaled the acrid air and steadied himself. The job wasn't finished.

He turned his attention from the charred, bleeding aftermath in front of him and started toward the entrance to the hotel. As he suspected would happen, the men guarding the door abandoned their posts, running toward the carnage. He looked at the ground as he lugged his bag and swam against the tide of first responders. Nobody gave him a second look as he shouldered his way through the door and disappeared down an emergency stairwell along the edge of the lobby near the elevators.

He hustled down the first flight, his heavy steps echoing against the concrete walls of the stairwell before stopping at the first landing. He leaned back against the wall, its cold seeping through his shirt. It wasn't until he stopped that he noticed the half dozen shards of wood protruding from his thigh like porcupine quills. His pants were soaked with blood that pooled on the floor. Custos looked behind him and saw droplets leading their way back up the stairs.

He dropped the duffel to the ground and picked at one of the thick splinters. It was embedded deeply in his leg, as he imagined the others were, so he left it. But the longer he stood there, the more acute the pain became, the more aware he was of the damage to his leg.

A throbbing burn clouded his mind. He clenched his teeth, inhaled deeply, and pressed himself from the wall, using the handrail to lower himself another flight of stairs step by step.

*

"There has been an incident."

The words from the head of the security group for the High Command of the Spanish Royal Guard echoed against the silence of everyone in the room. The delegations were using headsets and translators to negotiate the finer points of SECURITY and its affiliated bills.

"Somebody detonated a bomb outside the hotel. We are secure here and urge you to stay in this room."

President Jackson gauged the reactions from her British counterpart. He didn't react, but shot her a knowing glance. The Italian and Canadian delegations were abuzz. The Swedish prime minister stood from his seat and yelled something to his team of Säkertpolisen, the Swedish Security Service. Through the translator, Felicia could hear him dispute the intelligence of staying put.

"I want to leave," he said. "I want my men to get me out of here."

"The area outside of the hotel is not secure," repeated the Spanish guard.

"I don't care." The Swede, with the help of his trio of Dolph Lundgren look-alikes, pushed his way out of the room.

The Japanese prime minister sat quietly. President Jackson noticed him taking in the scene, absorbing the reactions of others. He whispered into the ear of his aide and then leaned into the microphone at his seat.

"I agree we should stay here." His voice was calm and even, almost without inflection. "It is not secure outside. It is secure in here."

The Canadians and Italians voiced their agreement. President Jackson and the British prime minister followed.

"We'll need a situation report ASAP," ordered the president. "As much information as you have. The other working group, are they holding as well?"

"Yes," the Spanish guard replied after waiting for the translation. "All of the delegations are in the room. They've agreed to stay in the secured room. We've assigned additional guards to that post."

"Remind me again," said President Jackson. "The French, Germans, Aussies, Swiss, Belgians, and, of course, your own delegation are all there. Correct?"

"Correct," replied the guard.

Felicia Jackson would have done a happy dance if she could. Everything was falling into place. She, a woman, was about to preside over the single biggest shift in power since the fall of the Roman Empire. Too consumed by her own narcissism, it was lost on her that the fall of Rome brought about the Dark Ages.

She caught her reflection in a large mirror on the wall opposite her. She managed to pry her eyes from herself and waved over her press secretary, who was sitting quietly in a chair along the wall behind her. He shot up and gave her his ear, bending at the waist so she could speak to him.

"Three things," she said, gripping his shoulder to draw him closer. "Where the hell is Goodman? I haven't seen him since last night."

The press secretary shrugged. "I haven't seen him either."

"Then get someone to find him," she said. "He was supposed to meet me for breakfast."

"I'm on it," he said. "What's the second thing?"

"Issue a statement," she said. "I'll give you unilateral discretion on this. Just make sure it says something like, 'I join the American people in grieving the loss of innocent lives in this senseless, preventable terrorist attack in Barcelona. We stand shoulder to shoulder with our partner nations to bring the perpetrators to justice. These cowardly acts, designed to weaken our resolve and test our strength as one global people, must stop. We must do everything in our power to stop them.' Blah, blah, blah."

"Got it."

"It doesn't have to be exactly those words," she said, "but do include 'preventable' and 'one global people'. Understood?"

"Yes."

"Good." She released her grip. "Now go sit down and make it happen. Then find Goodman."

"What about the third thing?" he asked. "You said there were three things."

She handed him her phone. "Deal with this."

The press secretary scanned the information on the screen. It displayed the newest post at the salacious PlausibleDeniability.info site. Dillinger Holt was reporting about a murder in the Eurostars Grand Marina Hotel and its possible connection to a security breach and missing Trade Center employee. It contended the White House knew about the two and kept them quiet. He was citing multiple highly placed sources. It then drew a veiled connection to Sir Spencer and the death of Horus and read like a federal indictment.

"How do you want me to deal with this?"

"The people of the United States pay you one hundred and seventy-two thousand dollars a year to deal with it. Make it disappear."

*

Matti gagged, bent over at her waist, and retched. She felt Brandon's hand on her back.

"We need to keep moving," he said. "If he is where you think he is, we don't have much time."

Matti wiped her nose with the back of her hand and looked at the scorched earth in front of her. There was char mixed with a slurry of blood and entrails. Men and women were wailing or bleating like sheep. She saw a man mumbling to himself, dragging himself on the ground toward the lower half of one of his legs. Matti's vision blurred and she bent over and retched again.

Brandon grabbed her elbow and pulled her with him. His pace now faster than hers, he maneuvered their way past ground zero, around the police trying to secure the scene while trying to triage the wounded survivors. Matti closed her eyes, relying on Brandon to drag her past her newest failure.

A shot of cool air blasted her as they burst into the hotel lobby, and she opened her eyes. Brandon was holding her hand now, gently guiding her toward the stairwell.

"What about the elevator?" Matti asked. "Would that be faster?"

"Look at the floor," he told her, pointing to their feet. "There's a blood trail. It's him. I'm sure of it. Anyone else hurt in that blast wouldn't be here."

Matti took a deep breath and flexed her hands. Both of them were shaking. She needed a pill. She needed C-Dunk. Maybe she could go to her room for just a minute and…

"Matti!" Brandon snapped her from her daze.

"Okay." She shook her head. "Okay." She refocused and pushed through the heavy metal door separating the stairwell from the lobby. The bright red droplets guided them down the first flight of stairs. At the landing there was a thin pool of blood stamped with a footprint.

"He must have hurt himself in the blast," Brandon observed. "It's gotta be him."

Matti and Brandon sidestepped the blood on the landing and trotted down the next flight. Their hurried footsteps echoed loudly in the vertical tomb of a stairwell.

They reached the basement level at the same time. Matti nodded at Brandon and she pulled on the door, feeling the cool whoosh of air-conditioning hit as she stepped into the hallway.

Then something else hit her. Her world went black.

*

Custos heard voices and pounding feet echoing in the stairwell above. He thought there was a man and a woman, but through the flames of pain shooting up and down his leg, he couldn't be sure.

He was certain, however, whoever it was intended to stop him. Why else would someone bound down the obscure stairwell on the heels of an explosion?

He quietly opened the basement door and slipped through it. Next to the door was a combination ashtray/trashcan. He grabbed the brass ashtray insert and gripped it in his left hand. He stood flat against the wall, dropped his bag to the floor next to the door, and waited.

The footsteps got louder until he knew they were at the basement landing. Custos used the back of his arm to wipe the sweat beading along his brow. He blinked away the drops that stung his eyes, holding his breath when he saw the handle crank and shifting his weight to his uninjured leg.

When the door opened, he waited a half breath and swatted the ashtray against the side of the intruder's head. It slammed her into the wall and she slumped to the floor, blocking the other person from moving through the door.

Ashtray still vibrating in his hand, Custos swung open the door and stepped over the heap. He charged the man still in the stairwell and tackled him against the cement wall.

A surge of air left the man's lungs as he sandwiched him with leverage. But the man was strong, and despite having the wind knocked out of him, he managed a thick punch to the side of Custos's head.

Dazed already from blood loss, Custos staggered backward and offered a wild swing with the ashtray. It caught the man on the nose and dropped him to the ground.

Custos made the decision to bolt. With one of the intruders unconscious and the other struggling to breathe, he limped back into the hallway and grabbed his bag, hobbling as quickly as he could to the supply closet.

He wasn't certain he was headed in the right direction. His path to the closet was indirect at best. He stumbled against the wall and fell down twice before he reached the door.

Custos was nearly blind with sweat, incapacitated from his injuries, and out of breath from his waning burst of adrenaline. He fumbled around in the bag, looking for the access key. His hands were trembling, his mind was foggy, and he questioned whether or not this was, in fact, a dream.

He couldn't fail. Failure was not his destiny.

*

"Mmmaaadddeee," the voice called to her through the darkness. "Mmmaaadddeee, caaannn youuuu hearrrrr meeee?"

Matti fought her way back to consciousness, unaware of what had happened. The last she remembered, she had her hand on the door handle to the basement entrance. Then nothing.

She sucked in a deep breath and open her eyes to see Brandon's face above hers, a large, swollen purple knot on the left side of his nose. His hands were on her shoulders.

"Matti? Can you hear me? Are you okay?"

His nose was bleeding.

Matti tried to nod her throbbing head. The left side of her face and her neck ached. Her left ear was ringing; sounds were muffled.

With Brandon's help, she pushed herself onto her elbows and then sat up. She looked around and looked back to Brandon, her eyes asking him for help.

"We're in the basement. The terrorist was waiting for us. Now he's ahead of us again. Can you walk?"

Matti grabbed Brandon's shoulder and pulled herself to her feet. The room spun around her for a moment. She steadied herself and started walking toward the supply closet.

With Brandon following, their pace increased until the trail of blood stopped at the closet door, disappearing underneath it. The door was shut. They had no way inside.

Brandon looked at Matti, his eyes sad with defeat. Matti dug into her pockets and pulled out her cell phone. She scrolled through the screen, typed in some information, scrolled some more, and then punched a number. She nodded at Brandon and placed the phone to her ear.

"I need the manager now." She waited a moment, impatiently flexing her free hand. She winced against a wave of pain and braced herself against the wall. The overhead lights flickered, and for a moment, Matti thought she was about to pass out. Then the manager came to the phone.

"We were in your office earlier. We're with the White House. I need you to remotely unlock the supply closet in the Trade Center basement." She paused. "Do it now!"

The door hummed and clicked open, and Matti shoved her phone back into her pocket. Brandon yanked it open as the lights went out. They had access to the supply closet. But they were completely in the dark.

CHAPTER 48

WORLD TRADE CENTER
BARCELONA, SPAIN

All of President Felicia Jackson's concerns about a mission failure disappeared when the power failed. She knew they were moments from a successful completion and braced herself against the desk for what was coming.

The multilingual murmurs in the room crescendoed when the lights failed. There were shrieks from some of the young women translators before the assurance from the king's guard that all was safe and they should not panic.

Jackson knew from lengthy discussions with the group of planners that, after the distraction attack outside of the hotel and Trade Center, power failure was next. Both were intended to induce confusion and to spread thin those responsible for immediate response.

Initially, the idea was to leave the second explosion inside the accessible area above the supply closet and detonate it remotely. But that proposed too many risks, too many opportunities for failure.

So the decision was made the bomb should be delivered by hand. The carrier, a Sir Spencer protégé, was the logical choice. He'd always performed well.

After his release, Sir Spencer was told he'd be the one to deliver the news to the protégé. That, as far as President Jackson knew, had happened. That was where the plan revealed its weaknesses.

The protégé recklessly, without forethought, killed a woman in the very hotel where the plot was to unfold. Then Matti Harrold spotted Sir Spencer alive, corroborating a tabloid report about his prematurely reported demise.

The president had to improvise. She had to task her asset with cleaning up leaks both foreign and domestic. From the loudmouthed rapper, Horus, to the whore of a medical examiner and that disappointing addict Harrold, all of whom threatened to unravel what she'd worked so hard to attain, Felicia Jackson resorted to the one tool so many world leaders had authorized long before she ascended to the Oval Office: assassination.

Each of the murders was tricky. Each posed its own risks. However, those risks were far outweighed by their rewards. And here, in the darkness of a G12 summit, Felicia Jackson's heart raced with the knowledge she'd succeeded.

She, alone, had managed to pull together the most extravagant of revolutions. She'd stitched its seams as they threatened to tear. She'd resuscitated it as its life support failed. She could almost feel the rumble of the explosion before it happened. She envisioned the nameless, faceless Sir Spencer protégé clinging to the infrastructure, his body pressed against the floor underneath the room in which French, Spanish, German, Australian, Belgian, and Swiss would die together. She chuckled to herself, imagining a real-life melting pot.

She adjusted her grip on the edge of the table, prepared for what was about to come.

The new order was at hand.

*

Custos was nestled amongst the pipes and wires that ran along the underside of the basement's true ceiling. He'd managed to find his way into the closet and close the door behind him. He slung the bag onto a low workbench and fished out what he needed for the coup de grâce before strapping the explosive to his chest.

He clumsily climbed the shelving unit, refusing to put any weight on his injured leg. The low light in the closet was enough for him to find his way to the ceiling tiles. His chest burned from the effort to get that far. Sitting awkwardly on the top shelf, he tugged his drenched shirt collar with his free hand, wiped his hand dry on the back of his pants, and then punched his way into the space between the tiles and true ceiling. Now, secured in that space aboard a wide iron support beam, he took a wire cutter and snipped through a series of wires labeled "*primer a través d'un tercer pis elèctrica*". The lights below him flickered.

He found his phone and fumbled with it, finding the flashlight app. He flipped it on and aimed it above his head. He couldn't afford to be in the dark. With the help of the light, he cut through another trio of wires, and the light below him died.

With the lights out, now he needed to move twenty yards along the beam, about halfway to an insulated firewall. That would place him underneath the center of the targeted conference room. From that position, with the bomb pressed against the floor, the explosion would inflict maximum damage. He slid a couple of yards in that direction and lost his balance, almost falling from the iron beam. He took his phone and stuffed it into his mouth, trying to aim the light straight ahead of him on the beam. He shuffled on his knees another five yards, the pain in his thigh blindingly intense. He stopped to weather the burn, biting down on his phone to ease the intensity of it. When he tried to move again, he couldn't. Something was wrapped around his ankle, stopping him. He turned around, the light flashing on a hand gripping his ankle. Then he saw the arm and the man at the other end. He was balanced on the beam behind him, trying to yank himself forward.

Custos tried to mule kick the man, grunting and growling to free himself, but he didn't have the strength. The man was too strong. Or he was too weak. Either way, he was stuck.

His vision blurred again. It was going in and out like a television with poor reception. He knew he wasn't near the center of the room. Maybe he was at the edge of it. He couldn't be sure. When the man tugged on his ankle and yelled at him, Jon Custos concluded now was as good a time as any.

He needed to detonate the charge.

*

Matti followed Brandon into the darkness, where a pinprick of light was dancing in a space above their heads. It looked to Matti as if it was above the ceiling.

Brandon turned on his flashlight app on his phone and scanned the room. It cast a pale, narrow glow on shelves, cleaning supplies, a workbench.

"Go back," Matti said, placing her hand on Brandon's arm. "On the shelves."

Blood painted the shelves. Brandon guided the light skyward and saw the hole in the ceiling. Two of the large square tiles were missing.

"He's up there," Brandon whispered. "What do we do?"

"We go get him." Matti started climbing the shelves. She'd pulled herself halfway up when Brandon stopped her.

"I'll go."

"What are you going to do?" Her voice was barely above a whisper, her feet planted on the third shelf from the floor. "How are you going to stop him?"

"I don't know. How were you going to stop him?"

"I don't know." Matti shrugged and motioned for Brandon to lead her toward the ceiling.

Brandon pulled himself up to the top shelf, a couple of feet from the ceiling, and poked his hand into the opening, waving it around. He glanced back down to Matti, who was holding onto the top shelf, her arms wrapped around one of the vertical framing rails.

"Better to lose a hand than a head," he whispered and then hoisted himself into the opening, latching onto a large iron beam before sliding past the opening.

Matti followed him up into the darkness. She squinted into the distance, and about fifteen or twenty feet ahead she could see the bounce of a small light. As her eyes adjusted, she could make out the outline of the bald man up ahead. She tugged along the beam, inches behind Brandon's feet, trying to keep her focus on the man up ahead.

She slid inch by inch until Brandon's foot caught her in the shoulder. Matti backed up and lifted her head again. She could see the man clearly, despite the ache stretching from her temple to her jaw. Brandon was holding onto his leg. The man tried kicking him and grunted loudly.

"Help me!" Brandon called to Matti. "I'm losing my balance."

Matti, her head thumping with pain, wrapped her legs around the beam and grabbed onto Brandon's calves. Brandon was struggling with the bomber. Matti held onto his legs as she would have a bucking bronco. Twice, his heels knocked her in the forehead.

"He's wearing the bomb!" Brandon yelled. "It's strapped to his chest!"

Without thinking, Matti let go of Brandon's calves and pulled herself on top of him. She pressed her body against his, sliding along his back. When her face reached the back of Brandon's head, she swung herself upside down. Matti was clutching the beam from its underside, her body in the tight space between the beam and ceiling tiles. She stuck her heels into the groove between the top and bottom of the beam, gripped the bottom of the beam, and slid herself directly underneath the bomber. She could hear him cursing as he fumbled with something above her.

Matti reached around with her right arm and grabbed at his side. She clutched his leg and yanked downward as hard as she could.

The man howled, losing his cell phone as it banged against the beam and tumbled below. It landed on the tile beneath Matti, the light shining upward toward the bomber.

Against the light, she caught a flash of the device. It was strapped to his chest. He was struggling to activate it, but being facedown on the beam and unable to turn enough to gain any leverage, he couldn't reach whatever was needed to detonate himself. Matti didn't know he needed the phone to spark the bomb.

Matti reached up again, her arms and legs burning with weakness, and ripped at the man's leg. He screamed and instinctively jerked to grab at her hand. When he did, he lost his balance, tumbling over the side of the beam. He fell headfirst, his momentum taking Brandon with him.

The bomber crashed through the ceiling tiles with a gasp, hitting the floor some twenty feet below with a sickening slap. His cell phone tumbled with him, landing on the floor next to his face. It shone on his eyes, wide and fixed. A bright white bone protruded from the side of his neck. He was dead.

The threat was eliminated.

Matti managed to swing herself back on top of the beam and found Brandon's fingers gripping the bottom of the beam. She braced herself and reached down to grab his arm above his elbow. Both of them grunting and groaning against fatigue and pain, they managed to pull Brandon back onto the beam.

Matti laid her head on the beam, its cold iron soothing the throbbing pain. She closed her eyes and started laughing. It was an uncontrollable laugh from her belly that forced her to wrap her legs tightly around the beam so she wouldn't fall.

"You're laughing?" Brandon was breathless, the weight of his exhaustion sinking into his arms and legs. "What's so funny?"

"Nothing." Matti chuckled, trying to contain herself. "Nothing at all." Matti didn't know why the laughter overtook her. Maybe it was relief. Maybe it was nerves. Perhaps a combination of the two.

"We need to get down from here," Brandon said. "And call the Secret Service."

"I agree with the first idea," Matti said, sliding along the beam toward Brandon, "but not the second."

"Why?"

"I don't trust our government," she said. "Our second call needs to be to the Barcelona police."

"And our first?"

"The hotel manager," Matti said. "We need the surveillance video from the hallway and the stairwell and the lobby. Without it, our dear president might try to pin this on us."

"Us?" Brandon grunted as he wormed his way closer to the hole above the supply closet. "Why me?"

"You were with me," she said. "You helped me."

"You're right," he wheezed, finding the hole and lowering himself back into the supply closet. He waited for Matti on the top shelf and helped her down.

They reached the floor and embraced. Matti placed her hands on either side of Brandon's face and pulled his lips to hers. His lips were salty with sweat, as she imagined hers were, but she didn't care. She held him against her, not wanting to let go.

They stayed there in the dark for minutes after their kiss ended, with their arms wrapped around each other. For the first time in a long time, Matti was whole. She was protected. She was safe.

CHAPTER 49

WORLD TRADE CENTER
BARCELONA, SPAIN

President Felicia Jackson checked her phone. Too much time had passed. Something was wrong. She swallowed hard, clenching her jaw. Her grip on the table tightened and she dragged her nail across the glass.

"What's the latest?" she called out to the royal guard. He stood by the door, his face awash in the glow of his cell phone. "Is the threat contained?"

"I've not heard." The guard looked up from the screen and shook his head. "They've not given me an update."

"Well, then get one." President Jackson stood from her seat and marched to the door. "I'm not sitting in here forever."

The guard murmured softly into the microphone at his wrist. He waited, his eyes avoiding contact with the president, and then spoke again. His eyebrows twitched and he asked what sounded like a question. President Jackson could hear the overmodulated voice speaking to him in his earpiece.

"What is it?" President Jackson demanded. "What are they saying?"

"They've found the bomber," said the guard. "He's dead. He had another bomb. They also have the people who stopped him."

Felicia Jackson was having trouble understanding what the guard was telling her. It didn't make sense. She stepped back from the guard.

"W-w-what people?" she asked. "Who's dead?"

"The bomber is dead," the guard repeated. "The people who stopped him, they are talking with Barcelona police."

"Who is?" she demanded, her fists balled so tightly her nails dug into the soft flesh of her palms. She was on the verge of a tantrum. "Who is talking to the police?"

The guard held up a finger and then murmured again into the mic. The answer came quickly.

"They're your people," he said. "Chief of Staff Brandon Goodman and Special Assistant Matti Harrold."

The names echoed in Felicia Jackson's ears, snaking into her brain like a venomous eel. She wanted to scream. Instead, she thanked the guard and turned to walk back to her seat. Her press secretary met her halfway.

"What?" she snapped.

"I talked with Dillinger Holt," he said. "He's got a lot of questions I can't answer. He seems to think there's a conspiracy of some kind. He's about to publish what he calls another, more damning post that connects the SECURITY Act to today's bombing. He says he thinks there's a connection to the Capitol plot too, though he admits he's still got work to do on that angle."

"Call his editor," Felicia said through her teeth. "Put pressure on them. Threaten to revoke their White House credentials."

"Well, Madam President," the press secretary said, inching closer to her ear, "we don't control the passes; the White House Correspondents' Association is in charge of that. Plus, why would we do that? He can't prove any connection to anything."

The president took a deep breath and looked down at her shoes. "I don't know what he can prove."

"So what do you want me to do?"

"Nothing," she said. "I'll deal with it."

Felicia Jackson pulled out her chair and sank into it. Dazed and disillusioned, she tried not to consider the repercussions of her failure. There was still an outside chance the initial attack was enough to sway some of the undecided. SECURITY could still pass domestically, and she could cobble together enough support to at least initiate some international cooperation.

But with Matti alive and Goodman helping her, there were complications. With the idiot of a bomber identifiable, given he hadn't blown himself into countless pieces, there were complications. With a reporter asking questions and already having too many answers, there were complications.

Her superiors, the men to whom she answered, would not be pleased. She pulled her finger into her mouth and chewed on the cuticle. She didn't see the British prime minister approaching her from behind.

"They'll be very disappointed," he said, the words barbed with derision. "I warned them you weren't up to the task. I told them

Secretary Blackmon would have been the better option. They were convinced you'd rise to the challenge, as it were. It seems, unfortunately, I was right."

Felicia Jackson said nothing. She didn't even turn around to face him. She knew he was right. No matter what happened with SECURITY, she hadn't delivered. She'd left loose ends. And because she'd already killed Sir Spencer, there was nobody else upon whom they could lay blame. She was done.

Matti Harrold had won.

EPILOGUE
PHOENIX

"We are not going to achieve a new world order without paying for it in blood as well as in words and money."
—Arthur Scheslinger Jr., Historian

Matti Harrold adjusted the towel beneath her on the chaise and pulled the water bottle to her lips. The sun was dipping below the horizon and the Pacific Ocean was an artist's canvas of blue, orange, and gold. For the last four months, this was a daily ritual: the towel, the chaise, the water, and the sunset. It centered her. It made her grateful for the day she'd lived and hopeful for the one to come.

A woman in a pale blue cotton uniform approached her from the north. She smiled in advance of reaching Matti and waved meekly.

Matti smiled and toasted the woman with her water bottle. She recognized the nurse as a woman named Dottie. She was pleasant enough. She always introduced herself as "Dottie with an i-e on the end."

Matti slid her sunglasses onto her forehead and recapped the bottle, setting it on the arm of the chaise. She anticipated the pear-shaped nurse was retrieving her, about to summon her back to the main house on campus.

"Matti, you have some visitors." Dottie planted her feet in the sand, her toes buried, and she stood with her hands on her wide hips. "Would you like them to come here, or would you like to go to them?"

"I have a choice?" Matti was incredulous, her tanned arms folded across her chest.

"You always have a choice, dear."

"Who are the visitors?"

Matti had only seen two people from the outside since she'd entered rehab sixteen weeks, five days, three hours, six minutes, and thirty-four seconds earlier. Brandon Goodman was a regular every Thursday. Her father was every Saturday. This was Tuesday.

"Mr. Goodman"—Dottie counted on her fingers—"a man named Holt, and some other gentleman whose name escapes me. He looks official."

Matti's heart fluttered hearing Brandon's name. Holt, she knew, was the reporter who'd been writing a series of scathing web posts about SECURITY. President Jackson had blamed Holt publicly for the legislation's failure in both houses. She claimed he was reckless and corrupt. That assertion had only fueled his popularity. Brandon had told Matti that Holt was working on a book.

Matti wondered who the third man was but didn't ask.

"I'll come to them." She slid forward on the chaise and stood. She caught a last glimpse of the dipping sun and turned to follow Dottie to the main house. The security guard assigned to Matti followed five paces behind them. Brandon was paying for twenty-four-hour protection. He didn't trust anyone.

The trio trudged across the beach to a white wooden gate and then climbed the limestone steps up the grassy dune toward the main house. They reached the top of the dune and followed a crushed granite path lined with lit tiki torches to a circular seating area. The plush chairs and loveseats surrounded a limestone fire pit. The pit's black lava glowed hot and a small flame licked into the breeze pushing from the shore. Dottie kept moving along the path toward the main house, leaving Matti to her guests.

Matti saw Brandon first, the soft glow of the fire making him all the more attractive. Matti couldn't contain her smile. She was so focused on Brandon, she didn't notice Holt or the man sitting next to him.

Brandon reached out and hugged Matti. His broken ribs were healing, his nose was fixed, he was in good shape. He'd left the White House, taking what was officially a "medical leave," and was hotel-hopping across southern California. He never spent more than one night in the same place. His guard was awaiting him in the facility's lobby at the front of the main house.

"You know Dillinger Holt," he said, motioning to the reporter on the couch.

"Nice to meet you in person." Holt stood to shake Matti's hand. His grip was firm, his knuckles oversized. He had the musculature of a boxer. "It's about time."

"Yes." Matti returned the firm grip. She'd gained strength from daily yoga classes and was as fit as she'd ever been. "It is about time. I hear you're writing a book."

Holt looked at his feet and let go of her hand. "I've had a couple of offers," he nodded sheepishly. "I'll keep working at the website. It's too much fun. By the way"—he reached into his pocket—"I brought you this."

"Thanks." Matti took the thumb drive from him and held it up.

"It's the newest Horus release," he said. "There are maybe ten songs he recorded before his death. It's pretty good."

"Matti," Brandon interrupted the exchange, "I'd also like you to meet Holt's friend. He's the reason we're here tonight."

Matti turned to face the man. She knew immediately he was all business. His haircut was high and tight. His neck was thick and his shoulders broad. The deep creases along his brow and those that defined his cheeks told her he was an experienced man who spent more time deep in thought than smiling.

"Bob Kurk." The man snapped his arm straight and offered a salute of a handshake. "I work for a private security firm called Wignock Homeland Intelligence Group."

Matti shook his hand, her eyes dancing between Brandon and Holt. "I have an offer for you," he said, his staccato a bit unnerving. "I want you to come work for us."

"I'm in rehab," she said, laughing uncomfortably.

"You're out in two months," said Brandon. "That's no time."

"Of course," chirped Kurk, "we'd wait to officially extend the offer until you completed your rehabilitation. We'd need assurance you were fit for the tasks we'd assign you."

Matti's eyes narrowed.

"You're a brilliant woman, Ms. Harrold," said Kurk. "You have incredible potential."

"Thank you," Matti replied. "I guess."

"We think a relationship with you could be mutually beneficial."

"How so?"

"You won the battle when you stopped the second bomb in Barcelona, but you didn't win the war. " Kurk glanced at Brandon then turned his attention back to Matti. "There are forces at work, as there have been for hundreds of years, whose goals contradict free will and democracy. You hit the pause button on their plans. However, rest assured, they will redouble their efforts once they've regrouped."

"I don't understand." Matti shook her head. "Where's the mutual benefit?"

"You and Brandon have already faced the dragon and won." Kurk crossed one leg over the other and adjusted his tie as he leaned back in the chair. "We believe you could do it again. And again."

Matti stiffened. "I don't—"

"Listen, Matti," Brandon interrupted her, his hand on her knee. "Let him finish."

"You're not safe, Matilda Harrold," Kurk said. "Flat out. Not safe. Neither is Brandon here, despite his tactical military skill. You're both targets. You can't expect to live long lives, even with the help of these rent-a-cops."

The security guard scowled at the characterization but said nothing. He cleared his throat and cracked his neck sideways.

"We can provide you with new identities," Kurk offered. "Both of you. You'd start new lives working for us, working for the benefit of a free world. You and Brandon might go two or three years without hearing from us. Then, when the right job comes along, we'll put you in play."

"So we say goodbye to our old lives?" she asked, the flames from the pit reflecting in the tears welling in her eyes. "That's it. No more Matti? No more Brandon?"

"Correct."

"What about my father?"

"We'd afford you an opportunity to say goodbye."

"Brandon?" Matti reached for his hand and squeezed it.

"I'm in only if you are," he said, rubbing her knee. "If you say no, I say no."

Matti bit her lower lip, considering the lose-lose scenario. Either way, her life wasn't hers anymore. She looked over at Holt. He appeared unfazed by the revelation of this secret global security force and the idea that a dark, ancient institution was bent on world dominance.

"What about you?" she asked Holt. "Why are you here?"

"I'm here because I already work for Kurk," he said. "I'm one of his new operatives."

"Really?" Matti chuckled. "I'm a certified genius who can break codes. Brandon is ex-Special Forces with ridiculous diplomatic experience. What do you bring to the table other than sarcasm and a salacious appetite for women?"

Holt laughed, without a hint of offense.

"Dillinger Holt," Kurk offered, "is a world-class survivor with a penchant for gathering human intelligence. It takes all types to save the world, Ms. Harrold."

Matti's smirk disappeared. "I'm sorry. I shouldn't have—"

"It's fine," Holt cut in, "you didn't say anything I wasn't thinking when Kurk approached me."

"I'll give you some time to think about it," Kurk said, standing. "I know it's a difficult decision."

"I don't need any time," Matti said. "The decision is black and white. I'm in."

THE END

EXCERPT FROM ALLEGIANCE: A JACKSON QUICK
ADVENTURE

The sniper never missed. Never.

The job was always simple: target, breathe, pull, kill.

No emotion. No second thoughts.

This target, this place, this job, though, were different.

The mark was not some nameless insurgent or foreign ally turned enemy. He was one of the wealthiest men in the world.

The location wasn't a frozen mountain perch on the Afghani-Pakistani border or the humid, tangled jungles of Central America. This was on US soil.

There was no payment on the other end of the bullet. This was a favor, a freebie the sniper didn't typically grant.

All of it was irregular.

The sniper lay belly down on the roof of the George R. Brown Convention Center in downtown Houston, Texas. The crowd on the grassy area below was small. The sky was clear. The wind was slight and from the south.

It was the loud rush of traffic on Highway 59 from behind that was distracting. The sniper slipped in a pair of earbuds and pressed play on a black iPod.

AC/DC always helped clear the sniper's mind and focus on the task ahead.

The sniper thumbed the volume up a click and took a deep breath. Eyes closed, the sniper didn't see the figure to the left approaching with purpose.

A large man, his muscular frame was hidden by the gray ghillie suit used to disguise his presence on the convention center's roof. His dark, polarized sunglasses hid his eyes, and his muscles flexed as he crouched low, moving to the shooter.

The sniper spun as the man approached.

"Where have you been?" whispered the shooter, pulling out the earbuds.

"Checking the escape route." The man was the sniper's spotter. He was the senior, more experienced member of the team. "You want coffee?" He nodded at a large stainless canister to the sniper's left.

"Thanks."

"You set?" The spotter inched onto his belly next to the sniper. "Crowd's beginning to fill in."

The sniper took a sip of the coffee without making a sound.

"That road noise sucks." The spotter nodded his head back toward the highway behind and below them.

"That's why I'm amping up with music. Helps me focus."

"This I know." The spotter smiled. The pair had been through a lot in their time together: Parachinar, Al Fashir, Benque Ceiba, Tampico. They were always in and out. They always hit their mark. They knew each other as well as they knew themselves. Hours, or days, in a snowdrift or mud hole had accelerated their personal learning curves.

"'Shoot To Thrill'? AC/DC?"

"You know it," the sniper said, feeling the wind shift.

"Trite." The spotter adjusted his elbows.

Another silent sip from the cup.

The spotter rolled his eyes, reached into a gray sack, and pulled out a scope. "Okay, time to get serious. I see the car approaching."

"Roger that." The sniper set the coffee to the side and scanned the crowd, which now numbered at least two hundred people.

High above the target, the sniper team quietly pressed forward with their pre-shot routine, despite using a new weapon given to them for this assignment.

The M110 rifle was longer and heavier than the sniper's weapon of choice, the thirty-six-inch, nine-pound CSASS. Still, it would do. There was, after all, no such thing as a single best sniper rifle. Any rifle in the hand of a sniper was equally effective.

The spotter put his eye to his adjustable power scope. He zoomed in to 45x and spun it back to 20x, giving him a wide field of view and the ability to trace the bullet once fired. Scanning left, he saw the target getting out of a vehicle.

"Target spotted," he whispered above the swoosh of the traffic. "Dark suit, near intersection three. Waving hands. Smiling."

"Roger," answered the shooter. "Got him." The sniper moved the rifle from right to left, following the target. "Now approaching intersection one."

The target shook hands with a handful of men and women lining the path to the hurriedly assembled stage. He looked at the skyline to his right and extended his arms as if to embrace the city. He turned to the crowd, clapped his hands, and bounded up the steps to the lectern. Every move was choreographed.

The spotter checked his range finder. He lifted his head and looked, without aid, at the scene below them. "That intersection is 350 meters. I laze him at 351 meters. Come up to six plus four."

"Roger that." The sniper adjusted again. "Elevation six plus four."

"We have right-to-left wind now. Come right 1.3 MOA." The spotter looked at the flags blowing to either side of the target. The gusts were slight, but they'd switched from south to north.

"Roger that." The sniper made the adjustment. "Right 1.3 MOA."

The crowd below them was cheering. They were waving signs. The target was relatively still. He was in a single spot, not working the crowd as he normally did.

Through their scopes, the team saw the target remove his dark suit jacket and tug his tie. He was wearing a white shirt, making the mark increasingly visible against the reflective glass and steel of the downtown buildings behind him.

The spotter and sniper exchanged knowing looks. The two were telepathic, almost. They were ready.

"Spotter up." The spotter shifted on his elbows. He'd done this countless times before. With each one, the moment before the shot, he felt the adrenaline course through his body. He was anxious, ready to pull the trigger himself and see the extraordinary result of his godforsaken skill. He was the eyes, not the muscle. He looked to his right at his partner's hand on the trigger and returned to the scope.

The target had his finger to his lips, quieting the chanting crowd.

The shooter exhaled and settled in for the pull. Everything around the target blurred. Concentration was critical. One last breath before the shot.

"Aaaahhhhh," the sniper exhaled audibly, signaling the spotter.

"Send it." The data was good. The target was there.

At that moment, the sniper pulled the trigger, which, in turn, engaged the sear. Instantly, the sear released the firing pin, which struck the back of the bullet primer. A small, internal explosion propelled the 7.62 x 51 millimeter bullet down the barrel and into the air toward the mark.

Traveling at 2600 feet per second, the bullet tore through the flesh, muscle, and bone of the target before the sniper released the pressure on the trigger.

"One o'clock, three inches," the sniper said softly.

"Roger that." The spotter confirmed with the scope. "Target hit."

The sniper chambered another round as the spotter scanned the field one last time. Both were motionless until the spotter, out of habit, picked up the brass casing to his right and dropped it into his bag. It was still hot.

By the time the target's blood began pooling around him on the stage, the sniper and the spotter were off the roof. Within minutes they'd easily merged into the whirring traffic on Highway 59.

The M110 was in a dumpster on the rear loading dock of the convention center. It was wiped clean and dropped onto a stack of corrugated cardboard, the team making no effort to hide it.

ACKNOWLEDGMENTS

My never-ending thank yous begin with my wife, Courtney, and our children, Samantha and Luke. They are a daily source of inspiration and encouragement. They make me laugh. They make me proud. They make me a better writer with every effort.

Felicia A. Sullivan, editor-in-chief, you're invaluable. Thanks for another killer job.

Pauline Nolet, thanks for catching the things most everyone else would miss. You're a pro.

Hristo Kovatliev, again you've mastered the cover art. I'm honored to work with you.

Gina Graff, Tim Heller, Mike Harnage, Steven Konkoly, and Curt Sullivant, I appreciate your critical eyes and willingness to be brutally honest. Additional thanks to Curt for his aviation expertise and to Mike for his knowledge of weaponry. Thanks also to a source within the US Marshal's Office for your help and to defense attorney Guy Womack for your insight into the criminal justice system.

To my parents, Sanders and Jeanne Abrahams; my sister, Penny Rogers; brother, Steven Abrahams; my in-laws, Don and Linda Eaker; thanks for your support and belief in my work.

Finally, thanks to the readers who share with me their love of the characters I create and without whom these stories wouldn't find life.